# YOU *NEVER* STOOD A CHANCE

# YOU *NEVER* STOOD A CHANCE

A Novel By:

## I.V. Monroe

ISBN: 979-8-9951286-0-1 (paperback)

Cover design by Antonio Fagiolino

First Edition

Published by Monroe House Publishing

Published in the United States of America

*For the dream I refused to abandon*

# Control 36
## The Illusion of Control

The taste of copper was the first thing she noticed. It filled her mouth as if she had bitten through her own tongue. The ceiling tilted above her, and for a moment she couldn't understand why she was on the floor. She tried to breathe, but the air barely reached her lungs. Each breath came shallow, like trying to breathe through water. Her fingers dragged across the polished hardwood, slipping uselessly. She tried to push herself up, but her arms trembled and gave out beneath her.

Footsteps approached, and then his voice broke through the haze. "Victoria."

Relief surged through her as Davis knelt beside her. His sleeves were rolled to his forearms, as if the evening had been ordinary, as if nothing about this moment required urgency. He brushed damp hair from her temple, his touch careful, almost tender.

"Hey," he said softly.

Her throat burned. She tried to answer, but only a broken rasp escaped. Panic flared. Something was wrong. Something was very wrong. "D… Davis…" The name barely formed.

He watched her steadily. No panic. No rush. No reaching for his phone. Why wasn't he moving? Her hand weakly caught his wrist. She needed him to help her.

"Easy," he murmured. "You're okay."

She wasn't okay.

The light above him blurred into a pale halo. A tremor ran through her body, and the metallic taste grew stronger.

He exhaled slowly. "I stayed," he said quietly. "I never left you."

The words didn't make sense. Her heart hammered unevenly, pounding in her ears. "Davis…" she managed again.

His expression softened, almost sad. His thumb traced her cheek. "You should've trusted me," he whispered.

Her vision tunneled, darkness closing in. Her grip on his shirt loosened.

He leaned closer, voice barely sound. "Shh. It's alright now." A gentle kiss touched her forehead, familiar and warm. "I'll take care of it," he said softly. "Like I always do."

Her body went weightless. Then darkness.

✷ ✷ ✷ ✷

Morning sunlight filtered through the sheer bedroom curtains, stretching softly across the bed, and signaling the start of a new day.

She rolled onto her side, her gaze landing on her husband, Davis, who lay beside her in peaceful slumber. Her lips curled into a smile as she propped her chin in the palm of her hand, taking in the sight of the man who made her life so easy.

Normally, by this time, he would already be up, his disciplined routine pulling him from the comfort of the bed long before she even opened her eyes. But today was his day off, a rare moment of reprieve from his obligations, and he was using it to get some much needed rest after spending the last few days visiting his sick mother in Louisiana.

The sharp chime of her phone pulled her back to reality. The relentless pings of notifications from her assistant were a jarring reminder that her day was already in motion whether she was ready or not.

With a reluctant sigh, she slipped out of bed and dressed quickly, pulling on a fitted pencil skirt and silk blouse before heading into the kitchen. She settled on a granola bar and a bottle of orange juice, more out of necessity than actual desire.

Just as she twisted the cap off the juice and took a sip, she felt his presence before she saw him. She turned around, and there he was, her six-foot-two husband, leaning casually against the wall, watching her with intensity.

His gaze was gentle, almost amused, like he already knew her mood before she said a word. Davis had always been like that. Attentive in ways that required no effort from her.

For a moment she wished she could stay, forget the schedule waiting for her and the decisions she kept putting off. Reality didn't pause for comfort, and neither did she. The sharp chime of her phone sounded again from inside her purse. She reached for it, but as she lifted the bag, something small and black slid against the lining.

Her breath caught. The *burner* phone.

For a split second she froze. Davis was only a few feet behind her, pouring himself coffee. She angled her body toward the counter, blocking his view, and slipped her hand inside the purse. Her fingers closed around the smaller device, and she quickly shoved it deeper beneath her makeup pouch.

"You okay?" Davis asked, his voice casual.

"Yeah," she answered immediately, a little too quickly. "Just looking for my lip gloss."

He stepped closer, his warmth settling at her back as he set his mug down beside her. "You're jumpy this morning."

She forced a small laugh and zipped the purse shut, resting her hand on top of it as if to steady herself. "Just a lot on my mind," she said.

He studied her for a moment, then brushed his thumb gently across her cheek. "Don't carry it all alone."

Guilt flickered sharp and sudden in her chest.

"I won't," she said softly, though her hand remained on the purse.

He pulled her into his embrace, pressing a soft, lingering kiss to her lips before murmuring, "Seems like you're in a hurry."

"You know how Mondays are."

He ran a hand down her back, stopping at the curve of her waist. "Mmm. You work too much," he murmured, his lips brushing her forehead before he flashed her that heart stopping smile. "Have a good day, baby. I love you."

She swallowed past the lump in her throat, forcing the guilt away as she whispered back, "I love you too."

She stepped away before she could hesitate, grabbed her bag, and slipped into her heels. Outside, the morning air was cool and quiet as she pulled out of the driveway. At the first stop sign, she exhaled and opened her purse. Was this the day she finally changed? The day she left her past behind? She blamed her father for this. For instilling in her the belief that control was the only thing that mattered, but in the end... she was the culprit. She made the decisions and lived with them.

The burner phone was still there. She stared at it for a moment... then closed the bag and drove on.

# Control 35
## Her Life, Curated

Victoria pulled up to her office and took a deep breath before stepping out. The Atlanta sun was relentless, pressing against her skin as she made her way toward the entrance of the sleek, modern building that housed her business. Just as she pushed through the glass doors, she heard the sharp, high-pitched voice of her assistant.

"You're ten minutes late for our prepping session," Tabitha exclaimed, her heels clicking rapidly as she practically chased Victoria down. "And I have so much to go over with you."

Victoria barely turned her head as she flashed her a pointed look, the kind that, over time, Tabitha had come to understand that the look meant to watch yourself. Tabitha immediately backtracked and softened her approach.

"I mean… I was just reminding you that today is insanely busy, and I know you'll want to be as prepared as possible," Tabitha added quickly, flashing a big, nervous smile.

Victoria smirked. "You know, Tab, sometimes I wonder…" She lifted an eyebrow. "Who's really the boss here, you or me?"

Tabitha grinned, but didn't answer, as she immediately dived into a breakdown of Victoria's first meeting of the day. Victoria listened as she settled into her chair, already shifting into work mode, slipping seamlessly into the role of CEO, the woman who built this business from the ground up, the woman in control.

Victoria worked as a social media marketing consultant, specializing in brand expansion and digital strategy. What started as a solo venture, Victoria sitting at a coffee shop, hustling for clients, quickly evolved into a thriving business. Now, she leads a team of over thirty staff members, all dedicated to transforming the online presence of businesses, taking them from obscurity to viral success.

Victoria's clients ranged from small businesses to major corporations. She would meet with them, dissect their current digital footprint, and show them how she could improve their brand, increase their revenue, and create a social media presence that made them unforgettable, but her work didn't stop at consulting. She developed training materials, hosted seminars, and led community-based programs, teaching entrepreneurs and businesses the true power of social media.

Victoria maintained a powerful *business* presence on social media, but always with precision. She controlled every image, every post, every glimpse the world was allowed to see. Just as she curated her clients' brands, she curated herself, methodical and untouchable. People knew her name, but her private life remained locked away, exactly as she intended.

By the time Victoria finished her last meeting for the day, the clock read 3:00 p.m., and she exhaled deeply, finally allowing herself a moment to breathe. She pulled out her phone and called Davis. He answered on the first ring, his voice filled with warmth.

"Hey, baby," he said, his deep voice immediately wrapping around her like a hug. "I've been waiting on your call all day. You must've been hella busy."

"Hey, honey, you have no idea. It's been one of those days."

"I figured," he chuckled. "That's why I didn't bother you, but damn, you sound drained."

"I am drained," she admitted.

Victoria glanced at the clock: 3:25 p.m., she needed to get moving. "What time are you starting dinner tonight?" she asked, already imagining a hot meal waiting for her when she got home.

"I figured you'd be pulling an all-nighter," he said knowingly.

"I won't work too late tonight," Victoria assured him. "I should be home by 9:00 p.m."

"Good. I'm making one of your favorites, lasagna and asparagus."

Her stomach tightened in anticipation. Davis knew how much she loved his cooking, especially when he made that. They chatted for a few more minutes, his voice a comforting hum in her ear, and for a fleeting moment, she allowed herself to be there, to just be present with her husband. By the time she hung up, the exhaustion was still there, but a part of her felt lighter. She checked the clock one last time, 3:30 p.m.

She gathered her things, lifted her purse, and felt the weight inside it.

The burner phone.

Her hand lingered on the bag for just a second before she picked it up and headed toward the exit doors.

Next stop: The W Hotel downtown.

✳ ✳ ✳ ✳

The elevator doors opened with a soft chime, revealing the hushed, dimly lit corridor of the executive floor. Stepping out, she let the cool, perfumed air of the W Downtown's Presidential Suite wing wash over her. The quiet luxury of the space was intoxicating; this was a world tailored for indulgence and people like her who lived by their own rules and played by no one else's.

Her heels barely made a sound on the plush, imported carpet as she moved toward her suite: the Townsend Presidential Suite, a space reserved for those who knew how to wield power behind closed doors. This wasn't her first time here. The staff knew her. They knew that she was a businesswoman and that when she was there, it was for business.

As Victoria approached the suite, a discreet concierge waited by the door, standing with practiced stillness, his posture immaculate. His black uniform was pressed to perfection, a small gold nameplate pinned to his lapel, subtly indicating his high rank within the hotel's elite guest services.

"Ms. Sheena," he greeted smoothly.

Not Victoria, but Sheena, the woman she would become the moment that door closed behind her. The woman who checked in alone and left no paper trail of who, if anyone, ever joined her inside.

"Your suite has been prepared exactly to your specifications. A selection of wines, fresh fruit, and Belgian chocolates have been arranged in the sitting area, along with a bottle of your preferred champagne chilling by the fireplace."

Victoria nodded approvingly, slipping a neatly folded bill between her fingers and passing it to him. "Thank you. I won't need anything else for the evening."

He accepted the tip without reaction, his professionalism unwavering. "As always, your privacy is our highest priority. Should you require anything, simply dial zero. Enjoy your stay, Ms. Sheena." With a graceful dip of his head, he stepped aside, allowing her to pass.

The moment the door closed behind her, the silence settled. Victoria exhaled slowly, letting her eyes roam over the sheer decadence of the suite. Every detail was designed to seduce; from the sleek, velvet furniture to the low hum of jazz playing faintly through the surround sound system. The air carried the faintest hint of white jasmine and amber that lingered on the skin long after the night was over. This wasn't a hotel room. This was a carefully curated experience, and she knew exactly how the night would unfold.

Victoria set her bag down on the polished mahogany table, as she moved toward the suite's private bar. A crystal decanter of aged whiskey sat beside a tray of hand selected cigars, an indulgence for men who fancied themselves in control. She smirked, pouring herself a glass of red wine instead. She liked to savor things and take her time.

As she sipped, her gaze drifted to the clock on the fireplace mantle: 4:17 p.m., right on schedule. Anticipation curled through her, slow and delicious. Thomas would be here soon. Victoria had chosen him specifically, watched him from afar and tested him in ways he would never fully understand. He was tall, broad shouldered, and dangerously confident, the kind of man who walked into a room and commanded attention without a word. But what intrigued her most wasn't his appearance, it was the way he carried himself. He had restraint. Discipline. But she wanted to see how long it would take before she unraveled that carefully contained control. That was always the best part.

Victoria stepped into the master bathroom, catching a glimpse of herself. Her reflection stared back at her, poised and collected, but beneath the surface, she felt it, the slow burn of desire, the hunger she only allowed herself to indulge in with moments like these.

Every detail of her appearance was intentional, from the deep crimson polish on her nails, to the way her perfume clung to her pulse points. There was a power in knowing how to make a man ache before he even laid a hand on you, and she wielded that power effortlessly.

Another glance at the clock: 4:25 p.m. A knock at the door. Right on time. A slow smile curved her lips as she stepped toward the entrance. Victoria opened the door and there he was.

Thomas stood in the threshold, tall, powerful, intoxicatingly male, dressed in tailored slacks and a fitted black button-down that emphasized every hard line of his physique. His cologne drifted toward her, wrapping around her senses. His gaze raked over her, darkening with unfiltered hunger. She leaned against the doorframe, letting him take in the sight of her.

"Hello, Sheena," he murmured, his voice thick with unspoken promises. "I hope I've impressed you by being on time."

Victoria smirked. "Being on time means you're late, but for you, I'll make an exception." She stepped aside, motioning for him to enter. He obeyed without hesitation. The door closed. The world outside ceased to exist, and the night began.

Victoria stared at Thomas's muscular body as he walked by and noticed how tall and toned he was through his skintight shirt. He turned around, leaned against the conference table and said, "I received your message earlier about the time constraint placed on us. I had hoped our meeting would have lasted longer tonight, but since we're pressed for time, we should start with no time to waste."

He pushed himself off the table and grabbed her hips as he pulled her body toward his. Victoria could smell the powerful scent of his cologne wrapping around her as he caressed her body. He kissed her passionately as he rubbed his hands through her hair. As he kissed her, his hands roamed over the sexy, sheer, red lace negligee she had on. His eyes lit up with passion as he grabbed her from behind, sliding his grip to her thighs, picking her up, and wrapping her legs around him.

Victoria looked into his eyes, dark, filled with unspoken hunger, and a smirk played at the corner of his lips. He carried her to the conference table and cupped her breasts as he took them, one at a time, into his mouth. She leaned her head back, basking in the pain, which quickly turned into pleasure.

He pulled back and stepped away from the table, while she carefully watched as he stripped completely naked. He stood there with his sexy, tall frame glistening in the light. His six-pack abs and his perfectly chiseled body were awaiting to give her all the pleasure and passion she craved. He pulled out a magnum condom, and with one fast motion, he slid it on.

He came back to the table and pulled off her lingerie. He spread her legs as he kissed the inside of her thighs, and she could feel her body reacting to his touch. Victoria placed her hand on his head as he made his way down her body. He rolled his tongue in a slow and deliberate motion, making her moan as her body arched toward him.

He didn't just eat her, he devoured her like he owned her. His hands locked around her thighs, holding her open so wide that she couldn't even think about closing them. His tongue lashed over her clit, hard and merciless, then he buried his face deeper.

"You taste so damn good," he growled. "Ride my face, Sheena. Use me."

She gasped, trembling, but he didn't wait for her to move, he yanked her down, forcing her to grind over him while his tongue plunged inside her, raw and relentless. She could feel his nose crushing against her clit, circling, rubbing, destroying her in the filthiest way imaginable.

"Oh my God," Victoria managed to gasp.

"Come for me," he snarled. "Right now. I want to drown in you."

Her orgasm slammed into her so brutally she couldn't stop the scream that tore from her throat. She clutched his hair, riding his face, soaking him while he groaned against her, licking her raw, filthy and greedy like a man addicted.

But he didn't stop. Even when she was shaking, even when her legs tried to close, he shoved her knees wider and held her there, licking her overstimulated core until she sobbed. He owned every savage stroke of his tongue, dragging it from her soaked folds like he was claiming her. When he finally lifted his head, his mouth glistened, and he licked his lips slowly, hungry, unashamed, savoring her. His gaze locked on hers, feral and starving, and a crooked grin cut across his face.

"I could eat you all night," Thomas smirked.

Victoria looked at him with lust blazing in her eyes. "You've only felt the tip of the iceberg," she barked.

He didn't need a second invitation. He grabbed her, his hands rough and possessive, dragging her off the table. They stumbled into the parlor room, every step charged with the kind of hunger that burned and clawed like fire, until she shoved him down onto the sofa hard enough to make him grunt.

Victoria climbed onto him, straddling his lap, and stared into his sexy eyes. She gripped his shaft in her hand, teasing just long enough to make him twitch and curse under his breath, then slid down on him in one filthy, relentless motion. He filled her to the hilt, stretching her so good she couldn't stop the scream that ripped out of her throat.

"Yes," she moaned, nails raking down his chest as she started riding him, hips snapping down with brutal rhythm.

He gripped her backside so hard it bordered on painful, dragging her down onto him with each thrust until it was nothing but wet, raw sounds and gasps. "Goddamn, Sheena. You feel so fucking tight," he groaned, his voice breaking, his head tipping back like she had him worshipping her.

Her pace was merciless, bouncing on him, slamming down so hard she could feel every inch of him grind deep inside her. He caught her breasts, rough palms cupping them, squeezing them like he owned every inch of her body. He shoved them together and buried his mouth between them, licking and sucking until he caught her nipples, biting down just enough to make her yelp.

"Shit," she panted.

He groaned again. "Slow down, damn Sheena, I'm gonna come—"

"Don't," she snarled, slamming herself down harder, her wetness coating him, every thrust obscene and loud. She didn't let up.

He lost it. His orgasm hit like an explosion, his hips bucking, his shaft pulsing deep inside her as he emptied himself, moaning her name like a man unraveling. His hands clawed, holding her in place, dragging her down to take every drop.

But Victoria didn't stop. She rolled her hips in tight, filthy circles, milking him until his head fell back, shuddering from the overstimulation. Her climax hit her just as hard, ripping through her so fast and deep that she screamed, clutching his shoulders, her body convulsing as she came all over the condom.

She collapsed against his chest, breathless, sweat-slick, and grinning with the kind of satisfaction that could ruin a person. He licked his lips, tasting her, tasting everything filthy about what just happened, as he was already hungry for another round.

He carried her toward the oversized chaise lounge by the window. He pressed her forward over the chaise, his palms sliding down the length of her spine before seizing her shoulders with a firm, possessive grip.

A tremor ripped through her as he positioned himself behind her, his breath searing against her neck, the tension in his body coiled and unrestrained. And then, without warning, he slammed into her, burying himself deep, his thrusts raw and unforgiving, each one pulling a sharp cry from her throat. Her fingers clawed into the fabric beneath her, her hips meeting him with a desperate, hungry rhythm.

He drove into her with ruthless control, his pace merciless. Victoria's eyes squeezed shut, he stroked every aching, tender place inside her until she could barely breathe. She let herself drown in it. For this moment, she was not Victoria Hart. She was Sheena Wells; Untouched. Unclaimed. Unapologetic.

When it was over, when the air between them was thick and heavy with the scent of sex and their ragged breaths began to slow, she did what she always did best. Victoria stood and slipped her clothes back on. Her movements were quiet and calculated, but the silence between them was almost oppressive. When she looked up, she caught Thomas watching her, his gaze locked on hers, something dark and unreadable flickering behind it.

"That was…" he began.

"What it was," Victoria finished for him.

He studied her for a long moment, then nodded, standing to retrieve his clothes. "Will I see you again?"

Victoria didn't hesitate. "No."

His lips pressed into a thin line, but he didn't argue.

She opened the door, signaling the end of their time together. "Have a good night, Thomas."

He lingered only for a moment before he stepped past her, disappearing down the hallway without another word. She called to the security desk to have her guest escorted out, as their meeting for the evening was complete.

Victoria exhaled, letting the remnants of Sheena Wells slip away, because this is how it always was. One night. One experience. One man who would never know her beyond this moment, and that was exactly how she wanted it. Because to hold power, to stay in control, to never become prey, she had to remain untouchable, and she intended to stay that way.

✳ ✳ ✳ ✳

The drive home felt longer than usual, though the streets were nearly empty at this hour. The faint hum of the tires rolling over the pavement blended with the low music playing in the background would have soothed her on any other night, but tonight, her mind was elsewhere: still lingering in the Townsend Suite, still lost in the ghost of Thomas's touch.

She felt an unfamiliar ache, something lingering and unsatisfied, something that made her skin feel too tight and her thoughts too loud. She never thought about them after. That was the rule. Once the door closed, once the night ended, they were gone. Her flings became nothing more than an experience, a name she would forget by morning. But Thomas… Thomas had left a mark.

Victoria could still feel the imprint of his hands on her hips, the way he had gripped her like he owned her, like he knew exactly how to unravel her piece by piece. A sharp exhale left her lips as she pulled onto her street, pushing the thought away. He was a one-night indulgence, nothing more. She repeated the words in her head like a mantra, forcing her heartbeat to slow.

By the time she reached the driveway, she had buried the remnants of Sheena Wells deep inside her, locking her away for another night, another man, another escape. Now, she was Victoria Hart. The devoted wife. The woman who had everything.

She stepped into the house, immediately enveloped by the warm, familiar aroma of garlic and basil. A soft flicker of candlelight glowed from the dining room. The faint sound of Miles Davis played from the living room speakers, wrapping the space in smooth, intimate energy. It was a scene straight out of a romance novel. A scene she should have wanted.

"You're home." His voice came from the kitchen.

Victoria turned to see Davis standing at the stove, stirring a pot with careful concentration, a kitchen towel slung over his shoulder. He looked good, exactly the kind of man any woman would be lucky to have, but as she watched him, she felt nothing.

He wiped his hands on the towel and made his way toward her, his eyes filled with something pure and unwavering. Love. Real love. And it made her feel hollow.

"I missed you today." He wrapped his arms around her, his embrace familiar and steady. He kissed her forehead, letting his lips linger there for a beat too long before pulling back to search her face. "I'm so glad you're here."

Victoria forced a smile. "Me too." The words felt thin.

"I made your favorite, just like I promised I would." He motioned toward the dining room. "Lasagna, asparagus, the works. I even got your favorite wine."

His words should have moved her. His effort should have meant something. Instead, all she could think about was Thomas's hands on her body. The way he pushed her to the edge until she was trembling and gasping for more.

Victoria forced a smile, pushing the thought away. "That's really sweet, Davis."

They ate in relative peace, engaging in small talk about his day, about work, and the house repairs he was considering. She nodded, responding when necessary, but she was barely present.

Just as she thought the night was winding down, Davis stood and took her hand, pulling her gently from her chair. "Wait," she said, laughing softly. "Where are we going?"

He smirked, backing her against the wall, his hands pressing lightly at her waist. "You didn't think dinner was the only surprise, did you?" He leaned in, his lips warm against her neck. Victoria knew where this was going. She knew the routine and yet, as his lips moved lower, as he lifted her into his arms and carried her toward the bedroom, she felt nothing but dread.

The bedroom was draped in soft lighting, rose petals scattered across the bed. He had put so much effort into this, but she couldn't bring herself to care.

Davis undressed her with slow reverence, his lips trailing over her skin in a way that was meant to be sensual, but all she felt was the weight of obligation. He moved lower, parting her legs, his mouth exploring her in ways that should have made her moan, but instead, she lay there, waiting for it to be over.

Victoria pretended. She moaned at the right moments. She clutched the sheets, arched her back, did everything she was supposed to do, and yet, her mind was somewhere else. When Davis finally finished, he collapsed beside her, a satisfied smile on his face.

"That was amazing," he murmured.

Victoria forced a smile, biting back the exhaustion, the frustration, the disappointment. "Yeah," she lied, "it really was."

He grinned, pressing another kiss to her forehead before rolling onto his back, staring at the ceiling like he had just conquered the world.

Meanwhile, she slipped out of bed, the weight of the night pressed down on her. She stepped into the bathroom, closing the door behind her, exhaling sharply. The hot spray of the shower cascaded over her skin, washing away the night, the lie, the dull, lifeless intimacy that left her feeling emptier than before, and as she stood there, water streaming down her back, one thought consumed her. What would it take to get Davis to play out her fantasies? Could he? Would he ever be enough, or was she too far gone? Because if Davis couldn't give her what she craved, she would find someone who would.

# <u>Lestie</u>
## (12 Years Earlier)

Atlanta, Georgia—her birthplace, her home, her foundation. No matter how far she traveled, no matter what heights she reached, this city would always have her heart. It was woven into the fabric of who she was, a constant reminder of where she came from, and in some ways, where she could never truly escape.

Celeste Victoria Taylor or as her family called her, Lestie, a name she had always felt was too soft for someone like her. There was something about it that felt powerless, like a child's name, meant for someone who needed protecting. She never liked it, and outside of her family, she never allowed anyone to use it.

She grew up in a traditional two-parent household, the picture-perfect image of stability, or at least that's how it looked from the outside. Her parents, Sabrina and Martin Taylor, were well respected. Their family was well off, not wealthy, but comfortable; quiet luxury before it had a name. She had everything she needed and most of what she wanted, as she was her parents' only child.

From the outside looking in, her childhood was ideal. A home filled with love, tradition, and warmth. But beneath the surface? There were lessons being taught that no child should ever learn, and she learned them well.

# Control 34
## The Woman I Get to Be

Victoria's life was a masterpiece of carefully crafted control and indulgence, a delicate balance that only she could maintain. On the surface, she was Victoria Hart: polished, accomplished, untouchable. A woman of power and discipline. But beneath that? Sheena Wells lived.

Sheena was untamed. Free. Indulgent. She explored the depths of pleasure without hesitation, ventured into spaces Victoria could never be seen, and surrendered only to her own carefully constructed rules. Her two lives could never intersect. That was the key to keeping them both alive.

Sheena never went to the same place twice. If she found a fantasy partner at the gym, she would never return to that gym again. If she met someone in a bar, a café or a high-end lounge, she erased that location from her future visits.

Atlanta made it easy. A city sprawling with opportunity, filled with thousands of places and potential lovers who could fill the space for one night and then disappear like ghosts. That was the thrill. The absolute power of knowing that a man could have only one taste of her, to experience something unforgettable.

Once Sheena chose a fantasy partner, Victoria stepped in. She took control of the narrative, handled every logistical detail, and ensured that the encounter unfolded exactly as planned. No deviations. No lingering. No loose ends, and yet somehow, Thomas had broken through. She had done everything right. She had taken her pleasure, left him behind, and never looked back. But her body and mind had other ideas.

Thomas had touched her. It was the way his body had pressed against hers with such authority, how he held her in a way that made her feel powerless, yet in complete control all at once. Victoria hated it. She craved it. She wanted to erase him from her thoughts, but the more she tried, the more he sank into her. That was what led her to the gym that day.

# Jamie

The gym was crowded, too crowded. The moment she pulled into the parking lot, she felt the urge to leave. Victoria thrived in privacy, in controlled environments where her body was hers alone to command, and yet, something kept her there. She lingered in the car debating whether or not to go inside.

Then—a text.

**Davis:** *Hey babe, working a little overtime. Gonna be home late.*

Of course. Ever the devoted husband who prioritized responsibility over desire, routine over spontaneity, commitment over indulgence. A good wife would have been relieved, would have gone home and played the part, but she wasn't in the mood to be a good wife.

Victoria typed a quick response.

**Victoria:** *Okay, see you when you get home.*

The moment she entered the gym, she fell into her routine. Victoria slid her earbuds in and let the pounding bass of hip-hop music drown out the world. Her feet struck the belt in steady strides. Her breathing synced with the rhythm of the music. She pushed herself harder. Faster. Every step was meant to erase the thoughts of Thomas.

But then, he appeared. Not in front of her or in the gym, but in her mind. Like a shadow slipping through the cracks of her carefully constructed focus. A slow, pulsing heat built between her thighs. A sharp ache settled deep in her core. Her fingers gripped the treadmill's rails for balance; her legs faltered beneath her as the surge of arousal hit her like a freight train. And then, she lost control. Her foot slipped and her body tilted forward.

The treadmill's moving belt yanked her down mercilessly, sending her crashing to the ground. A collective gasp erupted around her. For a brief moment, the world faded to black.

She came to, seconds later, her mind scrambling to catch up with reality. The moment she realized what had happened, a slow, creeping horror crawled over her skin. She had fallen. In the middle of a crowded gym, surrounded by strangers, with no control over her body or desires.

She was never clumsy, reckless or vulnerable, and yet, here she was, humiliated, breathless, and soaked from an orgasm she had not even meant to have. The gym staff rushed over, concern etched across their faces. She forced a smile, masking the storm raging inside her.

"I'm fine. Just… pushed myself too hard. Probably dehydrated."

They handed her a bottle of water, instructing her to take it easy, to rest. She nodded, but her mind was in a war zone. Victoria grabbed her towel and made a beeline for the bathroom.

When Victoria finally walked back out into the gym, she felt the lingering echoes of the humiliation she had just suffered. She forced herself into composure and ignored the brief glance in her direction. Victoria sat down on the bench, exhaling as she grabbed her water bottle, taking several long sips, forcing herself to regain her center. Victoria straightened her spine, preparing to rise, as she knocked her water bottle over. But before she could reach down to grab it, a hand beat her to it.

Victoria looked up and her breath caught. He was gorgeous. The kind of gorgeous that made you pause. He had perfectly straight, white teeth and a smile that could undo a woman with a single glance. But it was the dimple that trapped her attention.

For a moment, she didn't hear a single word that left his mouth. She was too busy imagining how those lips would feel against her skin. Too busy picturing the way that dimple might deepen when his mouth was against her thighs, his tongue tracing slow, teasing paths over her body.

His grin widened. "You good?"

"Yeah," she exhaled, reaching for the bottle. "Thanks."

Jamie was his name. The moment he said it, she knew that Sheena had chosen her next fantasy partner. It was instinct, the way her body automatically decided who was worthy of the experience she had to offer. Jamie was perfect. He was confident and dripping with the kind of cocky charm that she loved to break down, and just like that, Thomas was gone, and she had a new distraction. A new game to play. A new fantasy to create.

✳ ✳ ✳ ✳

The suite was quiet. Jamie sat across from her on the edge of the bed, his eyes dark with intent. His gaze never left hers, the intensity between them building with an unspoken promise. Victoria should have been eager for this moment. For the way his hands had already traced her arm, her waist, coaxing her closer. This was what she wanted. Victoria needed this night to be the one that finally erased Thomas from her mind, from her body, from the spaces where his memory still burned. She needed Jamie to make her forget.

He leaned in, his lips grazing hers. She let herself sink into it, let her hands slide over his strong shoulders, feeling the strength beneath his skin. His kiss deepened, tilting her head just so, giving him better access to claim her mouth. She focused on the warmth of his body pressing against hers, the way his hands moved with practiced ease. She should have felt the fire, but all she felt was the phantom touch of someone else. Thomas.

Jamie's hands slid lower, his fingers tracing over her thighs, his mouth drifting to her neck, leaving a trail of fire in its wake. And then, she betrayed herself. A name slipped from her lips: quiet, unbidden, a confession that was never meant to be spoken aloud.

"Thomas."

The second it escaped, the entire room changed. Jamie's lips froze against her skin. His hands stilled on her body, and when he pulled back, his face was unreadable; a mixture of disbelief, irritation, and something colder. His eyes met hers, and for a moment, neither of them spoke. Then, slowly, as if he was giving her a chance to correct what he already knew he had heard, he said it back to her. "Thomas?"

Victoria scrambled for an explanation, for a way to undo what had just shattered the atmosphere between them. "I-I'm so sorry," she stammered, her heartbeat pounding in her ears. She shook her head, trying to reset, but the damage was already done.

Jamie exhaled, his expression shifting into something distant and guarded. His grip on her waist loosened, his warmth fading from her skin as he pulled away. "Wow," he said as he shook his head.

The words hit her harder than they should have. She opened her mouth to say anything, to fix this, but she already knew there was no fixing it. Jamie was no fool. Jamie wasn't the kind of man to be second best to anyone.

Despite the weight of her mistake pressing between them, Jamie made the choice to continue. Maybe out of ego. Maybe because he wanted to prove to himself that he could make her forget whatever ghost still lingered inside her mind.

The pace of their union became measured, their breaths synchronized in a subdued rhythm rather than the heated rush of earlier moments. Victoria tried to lose herself in the physicality of it all, but with every passing minute, the stark reality pressed in: Jamie was fulfilling his part as another fantasy; a prey in her meticulously organized list, never meant to break through the walls she had built.

When the climax came, it was clinical and prompt. The afterglow was punctuated by a long palpable gap where passion should have been. Jamie disentangled himself with a quiet sigh as he gathered his clothes. "I should get going," he said softly.

Victoria laid there for a moment, feeling a hollow regret settle in. His departure underscored the truth she had been trying to outrun. The magnetic pull of Thomas was rewriting her rules, even as she clung desperately to the familiar structure of her predator-prey routine.

As the door clicked shut behind him, she was left with a bitter aftertaste. In the quiet afterglow, she couldn't help but wonder if she would ever be able to reclaim the passion she so desperately sought, or if every encounter would continue to echo this disheartening emptiness. The silence mocked her certainty, leaving her to wonder: Would she remain faithful to her rules, or would the lure of Thomas eventually shatter the fragile equilibrium of her double life?

# Control 33
## Davis Hart

Davis pulled into the driveway just before the last of the evening sun dipped below the horizon. The house before him was a testament to his discipline, his patience, his order. A two-story contemporary home, strong and steady, just like him. His father had always told him, "A man don't just walk into his house. He enters it knowing he's its foundation. If that foundation's weak, the whole thing crumbles." He never forgot that. Davis had always been the foundation. The unwavering presence that held everything together.

Davis moved with the ease of a man who had nothing to prove. His body was a machine, carved from years of discipline, training and pushing himself beyond his limits. The military had taught him that, but Louisiana had made him.

His roots ran deep in Lafayette. His father's blood was in the bayou, in the marshes, in the very land that raised him, and his mother? She had shaped him. Molded him into a man who knew how to listen, how to wait. She had been the first and most important teacher of his life. "You watch people like you watch a pot of gumbo," she would say as she stirred, her dark eyes glimmering with unspoken wisdom. "They tell you what they are if you let 'em sit long enough." She meant more than food. Davis learned early that people showed themselves in the quiet moments, in the spaces between words. He had spent his life listening, observing, and knowing. Not everything needed a reaction, not immediately. Davis never acted without thinking. Never moved without intention, but when he did, it was always final.

Davis had built his life with precision. He believed in structure, in discipline, in a home that reflected control and care. Everything in its place. A house was supposed to be a sanctuary, and he had made sure theirs was just that. Victoria never had to lift a finger. He took care of everything. Victoria worked hard, but at home, he ensured she had nothing to worry about. That is what a man did.

In the kitchen, cooking wasn't just a chore for him, it was a ritual. A way of showing love, of bringing pieces of his Louisiana upbringing into their home. His mother had taught him that food was more than sustenance; it was a means of control, of comfort, of understanding people. A man who knew how to cook knew how to take his time, how to blend flavors, how to be patient. Davis was nothing if not patient.

He had been an aircraft mechanic for years now, his hands trained to be steady, precise and methodical. A man who could fix a failing aircraft with nothing but a wrench and sheer willpower; he was a man who could handle anything, including his wife.

Davis had always been the kind of man people trusted. Unshakable in his values. He didn't demand attention when he walked into a room, but he didn't have to, his presence alone commanded it. There was a quiet power in him, something steady and immovable, something that made people feel safe. Victoria had fallen in love with that about him. She had always told him how much she admired his discipline, and how secure he made her feel. When they first met, she had been drawn to his confidence, his steadiness.

He wasn't the type to be reckless with his affections. Eight years in the military had shaped him into someone structured, deliberate, and unfailingly loyal; not just to his country, but to the people in his life, and Victoria had been one of those people.

They had met shortly after she finished her master's program, at a networking event for young professionals in Atlanta. He had been freshly out of the service, adjusting to civilian life, looking to establish himself in the business world. And Victoria had been ambitious, driven, more focused on her career than settling down, but Davis had been patient. That was part of why she married him. He made sense, and so did his family.

Victoria's parents had always been cordial with the Harts. While they lived separate lives in different states, there had always been a quiet respect between them.

Davis's mother had always been quite fond of Victoria's parents, specifically Martin. She never failed to bring him up whenever Davis and Victoria visited Louisiana, her sharp eyes lingering a little too long, or when Victoria would sometimes speak to her over the phone, her questions always careful, always curious. Victoria felt like there was something more behind it, though she could never quite put her finger on what. It always stuck with her as odd, how intently she would listen whenever Victoria spoke about her dad, her expression unreadable, but Victoria brushed it off. She figured that's just how older people were, always interested in the past, always weaving stories between generations. Besides, Davis adored his mother. He called her every night, no matter how late it was or how busy his day had been, and she adored him back. He was raised to believe that love was a responsibility, not just a feeling.

# Girls' Night Out

It had been nearly two months since Victoria's encounter with Thomas, and by all outward appearances, she had been sticking to her regular terms. She woke up refreshed, ready to get another long day at the office over and done with because tonight was girls' night out with Tabitha. She had been raving about some new love interest and Victoria was interested to know who the new guy was this time around.

The city shimmered under the glow of streetlights; the skyline stretched against the dark canvas of night as Victoria and Tabitha's cars pulled up to the valet stand. Victoria stepped out, adjusting the hem of her fitted dress as she took in the scene. The restaurant's sleek, asymmetrical design gleamed under the city lights, its long glass windows reflecting the vibrancy of Atlanta's nightlife. Tabitha followed, her energy infectious as she looped her arm through Victoria's. "I don't care what happens tonight," Tabitha grinned, "we're drinking, we're talking, and we're going to indulge, at least for a little while."

Victoria smirked as she shook her head at her best friend getting caught up in her own fantasy world. Tabitha's spontaneity was a quality that had been at the heart of their friendship since high school. They were polar opposites from the very beginning. Victoria was quiet, reserved, methodical, and always calculating her next move, while Tab was a vibrant social butterfly who never met a stranger.

Victoria remembered their freshman year in gym class. While Victoria lingered at the edges, barely interacting with anyone, Tabitha, driven by an insatiable curiosity and a fierce desire to know everyone, noticed Victoria immediately. With a persistence only she could muster, Tabitha broke through Victoria's shell that day, and from that moment on, they became inseparable. In a world where Victoria often felt isolated by her careful planning, Tabitha became the one person who truly understood her, a kindred spirit who brought color and chaos into her otherwise controlled life.

After high school graduation, they vowed never to part ways. Tabitha went off to Georgia State University, while Victoria attended Georgia Tech. Despite their different paths, they still spent countless hours together.

Over the years, Tabitha's wild nature led her down a string of fleeting romances. She would meet a guy, fall head over heels, only to see it all unravel when things went wrong. She never could quite hold down a steady job either. Time and time again, she was either fired or quit because the nine-to-five life never suited her untamed spirit.

After Victoria started her company, however, Tabitha became her rock, her support person, the backbone of everything she built. Even though her chaotic energy sometimes got on Victoria's last nerve, she couldn't imagine navigating her days without Tabitha. Victoria treated Tabitha like the sister she never had, even though Victoria kept Tabitha in the dark regarding her secret alternate life as Sheena, a world Victoria had kept to herself because it grounded her and fueled everything she was. Their shared history, filled with both their triumphs and their beautifully messy moments, remained the foundation of their unbreakable bond.

As soon as they settled in, Tabitha let out a satisfied sigh. "Now, this is exactly what I needed. It's been a hell of a week."

Victoria raised a perfectly arched brow. "Oh? What happened? Some clueless intern drive you crazy?"

Tabitha leaned back against the plush leather, a sly smile playing on her lips. "Not work-related this time. More like... my man."

Victoria smirked. "Oh God, here we go. Already?"

Tabitha held up a hand. "Before you roll your eyes, hear me out. This one is different."

Victoria tilted her head, feigning intrigue. "Different how? He has a job? He has a car in his own name? Or wait, he actually calls you back?"

Tabitha gasped dramatically. "Rude! But yes, actually. He's a real man. Like, the kind you read about in novels. And Victoria, I think I finally found the one."

Victoria chuckled. "Tab, you say that every time."

"No, this time, I mean it." Tabitha's tone shifted. "I've never been with a man like this. He's gentle, thoughtful, but still knows how to take control. He just gets me in a way no one else ever has."

Victoria's fingers stilled against the menu. There was something in Tabitha's voice, a kind of reverence that she rarely used when talking about men. Normally, her 'flavors of the month' were fun distractions, men she played with before discarding them, but this time, she sounded real.

"Okay," Victoria said slowly, setting down the menu. "Tell me about him."

Tabitha's smile softened. "He's not my usual type, which is probably why this feels different. He's stable. Grounded. Romantic. And God, V, he actually listens, and the sex is out of this world!"

Victoria laughed, shaking her head. "Of course, you already slept with him."

Tabitha shrugged. "Listen, when it's right, it's right."

Victoria sighed. "Tab, I just think you need to slow down. I mean, you barely know this guy and now, you're already fucking him."

Tabitha scoffed. "And people barely know the person they marry sometimes. Sometimes you just know, V."

Tabitha had a point. It was pure hypocrisy for Victoria to preach caution when she had built an entire secret life around one-night stands and disposable lovers. Because even as she sat there, giving Tabitha half-hearted advice, her mind drifted to Thomas. She wanted more of him. The craving had become unbearable, like an itch that burrowed deeper the longer she tried to ignore it. The worst part was that it wasn't just about sex anymore.

She had tried to tell herself that it was just physical, but it wasn't just that. It was the way he saw through every front she had ever constructed. Like he knew she was playing a game, and he wasn't afraid to challenge her at it. No one had ever dared to do that before. No one had ever made her feel like she was the one being hunted instead of the hunter.

Victoria swallowed hard, her fingers tightening around the stem of her glass as she forced herself to listen to Tab again. She needed to be present. She needed to push Thomas out of her mind, even if it felt impossible. She needed to focus on Davis, on the life she had built, on the life that, on paper, was perfect.

Tab finished her thought; her cheeks flushed with happiness. Victoria forced a smile and reached across the table, squeezing her friend's hand. "I'm really happy for you, Tab," she said. "I hope this guy is everything you think he is. I hope he makes you happy because you deserve that and more."

As the words left her mouth, Victoria realized how much she meant them. Tabitha deserved happiness. A love that was real, not built on secrets and deception. And in that moment, Victoria found herself wondering if she would ever be able to say the same for herself. Neither of them knew the truth, only one of them would survive it.

# Control 32
## Chasing Ghosts in His Skin

Victoria clenched the steering wheel tighter as she made the drive home from her night out with Tabitha. As Victoria pulled into the garage, her mind was already made up before she even reached the door; she would take Davis tonight. She would use him to quiet the restless ache that Thomas had left behind. Maybe if she lost herself in the feel of her husband, she could reclaim some part of the woman she was before this insatiable hunger took over.

The moment Victoria stepped inside, she found him in the living room, lounging on the couch. He barely had time to register her presence before she lunged forward, grabbing the front of his shirt and yanking him up. His eyes widened in surprise, but he didn't resist.

Victoria kissed him hard, lips crashing together in a desperate collision of need. Her hands were already working to rid herself of her clothes, pulling them off with an almost frantic determination. Victoria barely noticed when he tried to steady her, when his hands came up to cradle her arms as if to slow her down.

"Victoria—" he started, his voice laced with confusion.

She cut him off with another searing kiss. "I don't want to talk," she murmured against his lips. "I want you to fuck me. Right now."

Davis hesitated, just for a moment. This wasn't her. This wasn't how she usually was with him. Their intimacy had always been softer, more controlled, but tonight, she wasn't looking for tenderness.

Victoria grabbed his dick, forcing him to feel just how badly she needed this. "I said fuck me," she repeated.

His breath hitched slightly, his body responding even as his mind still reeled from the sudden shift. He let out a quiet exhale before nodding, his hands moving to grip her hips as she hopped up onto the cool marble of the kitchen island. Victoria spread her legs, hooking them around his waist, guiding him into place.

His lips found hers again, as if trying to reclaim some control, but she didn't allow it. She bit his lower lip, her nails digging into his shoulders as she pushed her hips toward him, demanding more. His grip tightened on her thighs as he finally gave in, sliding his hard shaft inside her with a sharp, deliberate thrust.

Victoria moaned loudly, throwing her head back as pleasure shot through her like a lightning strike. "Yes, just like that," she panted, rocking her hips against him, urging him deeper. "Harder, Davis. Fuck me harder."

He obeyed, his pace increasing, his hands gripping her waist with bruising force. She felt him throbbing inside her, felt his body tense with every powerful thrust. Victoria closed her eyes, willing herself to get lost in the sensation, but there it was. A whisper of a memory. A phantom touch. Thomas.

Her nails raked down Davis's back as her mind betrayed her. She wasn't here with Davis. She was back in that suite under Thomas's commanding touch. And suddenly, Davis felt like a placeholder, a poor substitute for the fire she truly craved.

Victoria forced her focus back to the present, back to Davis's ragged breathing, to the tension building between them. He was close, she could feel it. His pace grew erratic, his grip tightening as he buried himself deeper, chasing his release.

"I'm about to come," he groaned.

She unhooked her legs from around his waist, pushing him back slightly. "Come in my mouth," she demanded.

His eyes flickered with hesitation, but he did as she asked, pulling out just as she sank to her knees. Victoria took him between her lips, her tongue circling his swollen tip as she sucked him greedily. His moans filled the air, his fingers tangling in her hair as she took him deeper, hollowing her cheeks around him.

It didn't take long before he tensed, his body shuddering as he came with a strangled moan. She swallowed every drop, licking her lips as she pulled back, staring up at him with a satisfied smirk.

Davis exhaled heavily, running a hand over his head as he stared down at her, still trying to catch his breath. "Damn," he muttered, shaking his head in disbelief.

Victoria stood, brushing her hair back as she leaned in close, her lips grazing his ear. "You should fuck me like that more often," she whispered before pulling away, leaving him standing there; bewildered, breathless, and completely at her mercy.

After their wild encounter, Victoria retreated upstairs to shower away the remnants of the night and to prepare for bed. Under the warm cascade of water, her mind churned with a mix of satisfaction and longing. In that intimate heat, she found herself reflecting on Davis, proud that he had yielded to her commands, yet painfully aware of the boundaries he never crossed.

Victoria couldn't help but think: Davis is reliable and gentle, always following her explicit instructions to the letter, but he holds back when it comes to spontaneity. Every time she pushed for something raw and unfiltered, she had to guide him, instruct him in excruciating detail. He does what he's told, but he never ventures into that wild territory that she so desperately craved.

After their showers, they crawled into bed. Davis laid there, still reeling from the intensity of their makeshift kitchen encounter, his mind swirling with questions and uncertainties. But before any answers could emerge, Victoria drifted off into a deep sleep, leaving him to wonder about the unspoken desires that had erupted so suddenly tonight.

✳ ✳ ✳ ✳

Victoria laid still beneath the covers. She inhaled deeply, closing her eyes against the morning light. Her body was still sore in places from the way she had thrown herself at Davis last night. The air in the bedroom seemed to shift, growing warmer, heavier, like an invisible force had crept in and settled against her skin. She let her breathing slow, let her thoughts wander, and then, as if answering the silent call of her deepest desires, the world around her blurred, and suddenly, he was there.

The door creaked open, and Victoria looked up.

Thomas.

He stood in the doorway, his powerful frame silhouetted by the morning sun, his skin glistening with a fine sheen of sweat, as if he had just finished an intense workout. His muscles were tight, rippling beneath his deep, caramel skin. The slight gap in his front teeth, something that only made his smile that much sexier. Victoria couldn't move. Couldn't breathe. She could only watch as he stepped into the room.

"Did you miss me?" His voice was a low, teasing rumble.

Victoria tried to respond, but her throat was dry. Her body was already on fire.

He peeled off his shirt in one smooth motion, revealing the deep ridges of his abs. She felt the sheets slip from her fingers as he closed the distance between them. His fingers trailed along her thigh, sending a ripple of goosebumps across her skin. And then, without hesitation, he gripped her legs and pulled her toward him hard, and so fast that a gasp escaped her lips.

"You've been thinking about me, haven't you?" he murmured. "You've been lying next to a man at night, wishing it was me touching you instead."

Victoria shuddered. His lips trailed down her neck, over her collarbone, down between her breasts. She arched against him, aching for more. Thomas chuckled against her as he pinned her down. "That's what I thought," and with a wicked grin, he spread her legs apart.

The world outside ceased to exist. All that mattered was him. The first flick of his tongue against her throbbing clit sent a violent shudder rolling through her. He worked his way lower, his mouth claiming her with an expertise that had her hands flying to his head. He took his time, moving in slow, taunting circles before lapping deeper, his tongue pressing into her with a pressure so perfect, she couldn't stop the moan that tore from her throat.

"Fuck, Thomas," Victoria gasped. "Don't stop."

He devoured her, owning her in ways no one else ever had. Her thighs trembled as the pleasure built higher, and then, it hit her. A violent, uncontrollable climax surged through her, her body convulsing as she gushed into his waiting mouth, soaking his chin and the sheets beneath them. The intensity of it was overwhelming, leaving her breathless and trembling. Victoria fell against the bed, her skin blazing from the force of her release.

And then, she blinked.

The room was silent. Her body was still shaking. Fuck. She was alone.

Her hands were clenched in the damp sheets beneath her, the lingering remnants of her orgasm still pulsing throughout her. Her body ached from the intensity of the fantasy she had just lost herself in. She squeezed her eyes shut, trying to steady herself, but the truth was undeniable. She wanted Thomas. Again. And again. And again.

Without another thought, Victoria threw off the covers and climbed out of bed. She stumbled toward her closet, her fingers fumbling as she yanked open her work bag digging deep inside until she found it, her burner phone.

A rush of adrenaline coursed through her as the screen flickered to life. Her fingers hovered over the keyboard for only a second before she typed a single message.

**Sheena:** *Hey you.*

Realizing what she had just done, Victoria threw the burner phone on the floor. She stood frozen, her breath shallow as she tried to process what she had just done.

Her own fucking rule shattered in a single reckless moment. Victoria clenched her jaw and tore her gaze away from the phone, pacing the massive expanse of her master closet.

*Why did I do that?*

*What the fuck is wrong with me?*

Victoria tried to rationalize it. That she was still riding the high from her girls' night out with Tab, that she wasn't thinking clearly, but deep down, she knew better. This wasn't an accident. This was a choice. She could pretend it never happened, but as she stared down at the device, the screen suddenly illuminated.

*1 new message.*

A jolt of electricity shot through her, her stomach twisted violently. Her hands trembled as she reached for the phone, her fingers hovering over it, hesitating.

**Thomas:** *Well, my my my. Sheena? I've been waiting.*

Her breath caught in her throat. The room suddenly felt too small. He had been waiting. For *her.*

A slow, involuntary shudder rolled down her spine, and Victoria gripped the phone tighter as if it might anchor her. She thought to herself, *I should end this now, before it gets out of hand,* but her fingers moved before her mind could stop them.

**Sheena:** *Waiting? For what?*

Seconds stretched into eternity. Then, the dots appeared.

*Typing…*

**Thomas:** *For you to finally stop fighting what we both already know.*

He wasn't wrong. She had been fighting it from the moment she left him that night. Victoria exhaled shakily. This was it. This was the moment where she either regained control or let it slip completely from her grasp. She took another breath and typed her response.

**Sheena:** *Funny. I don't recall ever fighting anything.*

Victoria hit send, then she turned off the phone. She needed time. And for the first time in a long time, she wasn't sure if she wanted to fight it. She was in the midst of a reckoning with the very essence of who she was, and who she might become.

# Lestie
## (12 Years Earlier)

Where did she even begin with Martin Taylor? The man who made her, not just biologically, but in the way that truly mattered. Her father. The first man she ever loved. The first man she ever hated. The man who, in so many ways, shaped the person she is today.

Martin Taylor was an accountant by trade, but he was more than that. He owned his own private firm, a small but successful storefront where he handled financials, taxes, and investments for small business owners and individuals looking for expertise. He was brilliant with numbers, a man who could calculate equations in his head before most people even had the chance to reach for a calculator. But more than that? He was brilliant with people. He knew how to read a room, how to charm, how to manipulate without anyone ever realizing they were being manipulated. It was a skill, one he wore like a tailored suit, always sharp, always effortless, always dangerous. If there was one thing her father loved more than his business, more than his family, more than anything in this world, it was himself.

Martin Taylor was a beautiful man, and he knew it. Growing up, she watched him command attention without saying a word. Women stared. They always stared. And her father? He soaked it in.

He bathed in their admiration, in their longing gazes, in the way they whispered about him when they thought no one was listening, but Victoria was always listening. She would watch him in public, taking mental notes as he laughed a little too hard at a woman's joke, as he subtly adjusted his tie when he caught someone's eye. Victoria saw the way he fed off the attention, the way it made him stand taller, smirk wider, and exuded even more confidence. She saw the way he used it to his advantage.

And she learned. She learned that power is not always about strength. Sometimes, it's about presence. Sometimes, it's about knowing that you can have anyone and anything, if you moved the right way. Her father always told her that he had missed his calling. That he should have been a male model instead of an accountant. That he was too good looking to be behind a desk, too handsome to be buried in paperwork. It was a joke, one he made often, but Victoria knew the truth. It wasn't really a joke. It was his reality. A reality her mother ignored. She sat beside him for years, listening to his self-indulgent monologues, smiling at his arrogance, playing the role of the grateful wife who had somehow won the grand prize of his love, but Victoria knew better. She knew that Martin Taylor was no prize. He was a lesson. A warning.

And yet, as much as she despised the way he moved, the way he thought, the way he saw the world, Victoria was just like him, even when she didn't want to be. Even when she tried to suppress it. Even when she fought to unlearn what he had ingrained in her since childhood. Because the truth? The truth was that Victoria wasn't her mother. She would never be her mother. She wasn't the one sitting at the table, waiting for someone to come home to her. She was the one choosing where she wanted to be. The one who held the power. The one who understood that, in this world, you were either the prey… or the predator. And Victoria? She had learned from the best.

# Control 31
## Breaking the Rules

The meeting was scheduled for 5:00 p.m. sharp. Victoria had spent the entire afternoon preparing, ensuring that every detail was in place. Everything had to be flawless.

A knock at the door snapped her eyes wide open. 5:00 p.m. on the dot. She paused for just a moment, fingers hovering over the handle. Deep breath. "You've got this," she whispered to herself.

Thomas. He stood in the doorway with that knowing smirk, the one that made her thighs clench involuntarily. This time, it was real. This was no wet dream fantasy, like the one she had in her bedroom.

"Sheena." The way he said it destroyed her.

Her body betrayed her instantly. "Thomas." Her voice came out breathless.

Before another word could be spoken, he stepped inside, his presence commanding the space as he closed the door behind him in one smooth motion. And then suddenly, his hands were on her. Victoria didn't hesitate, she crashed against him, their lips colliding in an explosive reunion.

Thomas wasted no time. He devoured her, lips trailing down her neck, his tongue flicking against her pulse point as he whispered, "I've missed this."

Her head lolled back, a moan slipping from her lips as he unbuttoned the top of her dress and peeled it down, revealing the bare skin he had been aching to touch again. He kissed her everywhere.

"Thomas," she gasped.

His hands wandered lower, fingers grazing her thighs, parting them as he moved down. And then, he reached the spot that had been throbbing for him since the moment she saw him. Victoria let out a sharp cry. "Shit," she panted, gripping the couch as he worked her over, burying his tongue deep inside her very wet core.

Thomas took his time. His tongue moved in slow, deliberate strokes before picking up speed, swirling around her swollen clit before pulling it into his mouth, sucking just the right way that made her feel like she was going to break.

She trembled, surrendering completely. "Oh my God, Thomas," she whimpered. I've never felt this way before. You feel so good."

He groaned against her, the vibration sending a shockwave through her, but then, he pulled away.

Before Victoria could protest, he flipped her over, pressing her stomach against the couch until his tongue found her ass. Thomas parted her cheeks gently, spreading her wider as his tongue teased and explored.

"Fuuuck, Thomas," she whimpered, clutching the cushions. He delved deeper, tongue fucking her in slow, rhythmic strokes. She didn't know what was happening. She had never felt this before, never been touched like this before. It was pure, unfiltered pleasure.

She had barely caught her breath when Thomas flipped her over yet again, gripping her thighs as he positioned himself between them. "You ready for me?" His voice was dark and teasing; Victoria bit her lip and nodded. "Then take me," he murmured, as he buried himself deep.

A strangled moan ripped from her throat as she felt every inch of him. He started slow and then he snapped. He slammed into her, setting a brutal rhythm that had her screaming.

They made love for hours, shifting between slow, torturous passion and frenzied, reckless fucking. By the time it was over, they laid tangled in the sheets, bodies slick with sweat, completely spent. Victoria stared at the ceiling, chest heaving and mind spinning in a whirlwind. She had just destroyed every rule she had ever made, but as she laid there in Thomas's arms, she knew one thing for certain. This was only the beginning.

Victoria laid soundly in Thomas' strong arms; their bodies tangled in the warmth of an afterglow. Unable to resist, she scooted closer to him, pressing her lips softly against his cheek, then his lips; an attempt to rouse him from his slumber. He stirred slightly, but didn't open his eyes, a lazy smirk forming on his lips. "My Sheena, my Sheena," he murmured. Victoria smiled against his skin.

His arms wrapped around her, pulling her flush against him. With his eyes still closed, he murmured, "You better watch yourself, girl, before you get something else started. We'll be having round twenty if you keep this up."

She giggled, but before she could respond, her gaze flickered to the clock on the bedside table: 10:45 p.m. Her stomach dropped. Her eyes widened in sudden panic. "Oh my God… it's 10:45," she gasped, sitting up abruptly. "It's 10:45!"

Thomas blinked, sluggishly sitting up as he rubbed his eyes. "What's the rush?" he asked.

"I have to go!" she blurted out, slipping on her panties and reaching for her dress. "I'm going to be late for… um… for work. I'm a flight attendant and I have a briefing for my flight."

Thomas tilted his head, studying her. "A briefing?"

"Yes," she said quickly, fastening the clasp of her bra. "The briefing is at 4:00 a.m. I have to get back home and freshen up."

"So, you have five hours until that time and you're running out of here like Cinderella at midnight?" He reached for her wrist, pulling her gently toward him.

"What's really going on, Sheena?"

"I promise I'll call you tomorrow," she said softly, placing her hands on his chest, feeling the steady thump of his heart beneath her palms. "I'll be back the day after tomorrow."

Thomas searched her face. "So, will it be four months this time before I hear from you again?" His voice was teasing, but there was something deeper beneath it. "Because I never stopped thinking about you, Sheena. I don't want to wait forever again."

She looked away briefly, swallowing hard, then met his gaze again. "I'll never make you wait that long again," she whispered. "I promise."

He exhaled then finally nodded. "I'm going to hold you to that."

She smiled, and before she could say anything else, he pulled her back onto the bed, his strong arms lifting her effortlessly. "Thomas, I have to—"

"Shhh," he silenced her with his lips, capturing her in a kiss so deep it stole whatever excuse she was about to make. He laid her back against the mattress, his body pressing into hers, his need for her palpable.

"Just one more time," he murmured against her lips, his hands already stripping her bare again. "Let me please you before you go."

"Thomas…" she breathed, trying to fight it, but the second his mouth traveled between her legs, all her resolve crumbled. He worked her up so quickly she had no choice but to surrender. Her orgasm hit fast and violently, her body quaking beneath him as she came undone on his tongue. And then, before she could recover, he reached for the last condom from the nightstand, rolled it on, and plunged into her, fucking her hard and deep, chasing one last moment of reckless pleasure before she had to slip back into the illusion of her real life.

When he finally released inside of her, he kissed her deeply, lingering for just a moment before whispering, "Don't make me wait too long, Sheena."

The mission was clear inside of her head as she thought: *I need to plan our next meeting.* The anticipation of seeing him again was the only thing that made her current reality bearable.

* * * *

The house was silent as Victoria sat in her home office. She had woken up earlier than usual, restless with anticipation, her mind already plotting. Davis would be up soon for his Saturday morning jog, giving her just enough time to craft the perfect plan. He was normally out of the door by 5 am on Saturday mornings, but he slept in a little later due to their late-night quickie session that she was trying to forget about.

She tapped a manicured finger against her temple, running through scenarios in her head. *What could I say to justify being gone an entire night?* She discarded several ideas as quickly as they came. The last thing she needed was Davis asking too many questions.

And then, *click.* The perfect excuse crystallized in her mind. A work-related conference. It was flawless. Completely in character, impossible to disprove, and, most importantly, justifiable. The best lies were always laced with a little truth.

Just then, she heard the faint creak of the bedroom door upstairs. *Right on time.* Davis was awake, moving about in his morning routine before his jog. She knew he would come looking for her. He always did.

She quickly grabbed her AirPods, popped them in her ears, and pulled up her call screen, making it seem as if she was in the middle of a conversation. As she heard his footsteps coming down the stairs, she switched on the performance.

Davis appeared at the doorway, his brow furrowed in curiosity. She turned her head toward him and flashed him a look of frustration, widening her eyes as if to say, *Can you believe this?* Davis mouthed, *What's going on?* Victoria held up one finger, signaling *one second,* before continuing.

*"Felecia, I don't have anything prepared. I can't just throw something together last minute. You know I don't operate like that. Why are you doing this to me?"* Her voice was laced with exasperation, with just the right amount of hesitation to make it believable. Davis stepped farther into the room, crossing his arms as he listened closely.

She ended the call with a dramatic sigh, shaking her head before glancing up at Davis, who was now perched against the doorway, arms folded.

"Okay, spill it," he said.

Victoria sighed again. "Ok, long story short, a business colleague of mine, Felecia, is hosting a conference in Tennessee. She reached out to me because one of her keynote speakers canceled last minute due to a family emergency, so she called me to see if I could fill in and speak about social media influence and business branding."

Davis nodded, still listening.

"But babe, it's *so* last minute. She wants me to drive up tomorrow, get settled, and spend Monday speaking at the conference, maybe even Tuesday. I'd have to rearrange my whole schedule, and put together a full presentation overnight. It's just too much."

Davis tilted his head. "But you already have presentations done, don't you? You've done these talks a million times. You could pull this off in your sleep."

She frowned, pretending to hesitate. "I mean, yeah, but—"

"Babe, you should do it," he interrupted. "This could be great for business. It's exposure, networking, more clients, and it's helping out a friend."

Victoria pretended to be conflicted. "I don't know. I was really just going to call her back and say no."

"You should absolutely say yes," Davis said. "You'd be amazing at it."

Victoria smiled, keeping her excitement internal. "Thank you, baby. Since I have your blessing, I guess I'll do it. I'll call her back and finalize everything." She leaned in, pressing a kiss to his lips. "See, this is why I love you so much."

Davis returned the kiss before grabbing his running shoes. "Love you too. Alright, I'm heading out for my jog. You go get ready for your big conference," he said with a teasing wink.

As soon as he was gone, she practically collapsed into her office chair, spinning in circles like a giddy teenager. *This worked out perfectly.*

She reached for her burner phone and immediately pulled up her messages.

**Sheena:** *Operation Thomas is a go. I'm all yours tomorrow.*

She hit send with a slow, devious smile spreading across her lips. The lie had already been planted with Davis and perfectly executed. But now, she had to make sure Social Brilliance was squared away. She grabbed her phone and hovered over Tabitha's name before she tapped it.

"Good morning, stranger!" Tab chirped. "Calling me this early on a Saturday? What's up?"

Victoria forced a sigh, playing into the exhaustion she wanted Tab to pick up on. "Girl, I need a favor."

"Of course you do," Tab teased. "Hit me."

"Can you clear my schedule for the week? Cancel any meetings that need me to be physically present, and if there are any trainings scheduled, can you take over?"

Tabitha hesitated for a second. "Uh, I can handle everything, but what's going on? Everything okay?"

Victoria expected the question. She had already crafted the perfect response. "Yeah, everything's fine. Davis and I are going to Louisiana to handle some personal matters with his mom."

"Ok. Yeah, of course. Is everything okay with her?"

Victoria smiled softly, guilt briefly tightening in her chest. Tab's concern was genuine, and yet, Tab had no idea that her best friend was weaving an intricate web of deceit right before her eyes.

There was a small pause before Tab sighed contentedly. "His mom is such a sweet woman. The way she cares for Davis, and the way he cares for her. I just love that about them."

# Control 30
## Time Reserved for Sin

The moment Victoria had been waiting for had finally arrived. Today was the day. She pulled out of her driveway and headed to what felt like her second home, the W Hotel. The W wasn't just a hotel, it was a sanctuary. A place where Sheena Wells existed in full form, untouched by the reality of Victoria Hart's perfect suburban life.

She had built a flawless reputation here, spending thousands of dollars on penthouse suites, high-profile business meetings, and luxury accommodations. Money talked and Victoria had a lot of it. Her influence gave her unparalleled privacy and discretion. She wasn't just a guest; she was a priority. The staff knew her by Victoria Hart, but she had informed them that for security reasons, she conducted business under an alias: Sheena Wells. They never questioned it, and she loved that.

Victoria pulled up to the private VIP entrance, where a dedicated valet took her car. She made her way to the exclusive elevator that led directly to the penthouse. Thomas arrived right on time, as always. The moment she opened the door for him, she couldn't help but laugh. There he was, standing in the hallway, holding the biggest bouquet of flowers she had ever seen, so large that it completely covered his face. Then, from behind the massive arrangement, his deep, playful voice rang out. "Special delivery!"

She giggled, her stomach flipping like a teenage girl with a crush. He peeked out from the side of the bouquet, flashing his signature grin. Victoria felt her entire body react. Thomas had that effect on her. He made her feel alive.

She shook her head at his ridiculousness. "You're so silly."

He stepped inside, handing her the bouquet. "Beautiful flowers for the most gorgeous girl in the world."

He always knew exactly what to say. She buried her face into the flowers, inhaling deeply. "I love them," she murmured. She wasn't used to men thinking about her like this. It made her feel special and that was dangerous.

Thomas moved behind her, his presence instantly sending a shiver down her spine. He wrapped his strong arms around her waist, pulling her against him. "I missed you, baby," he murmured, his lips grazing the sensitive skin of her neck.

She turned in his arms, staring up at him. "I missed you too."

Their eyes locked. For a moment, there were no words. Just heat and desire. Then, suddenly, his lips were on hers. She felt herself melting into him, surrendering without even realizing it. But just as he began to kiss his way lower, she gently pushed him back.

"Lunch first," she whispered. "I want us to actually talk today," she said. "Get to know each other."

Victoria led Thomas into the dining area and his eyes scanned the impressive spread. His lips curled into a slow, appreciative smile. "Damn, girl, you sure do know how to take care of your man in more ways than one."

Victoria smirked. "Oh, so you're my man now?"

He chuckled, pulling her chair out and then sitting down across from her. "I mean, I ain't fighting it. But really,

I should be catering to you. How much did all this cost? I'll reimburse you."

She rolled her eyes, waving off his offer. "Don't be silly. It's my treat. I wanted us to actually sit down and talk for once."

He tilted his head, amused. "Oh? You mean you actually wanna know who I am, not just what I can do to you?"

She laughed, cutting into her steak. "Something like that."

As they started eating, she took the opportunity to really study him. There was something about the way he carried himself, confident but not arrogant, playful yet grounded.

"So, tell me," she said. "Who exactly is Thomas?"

"Well," he started, "I've always been good with my hands."

Victoria raised an eyebrow, smirking. "I've noticed."

He chuckled. "Nah, I mean really good with them. I build things. Fix things. Take something that's falling apart and make it better than before."

She watched him, intrigued. "Like what?"

"Real estate," he said simply. "I buy properties, flip them and sell them for a profit. I started out as a self-taught contractor. I did that for a while and honed my craft. Then I got my real estate license and sold a home or two, but being an agent wasn't for me. I didn't want to just sell houses, I wanted to make them better."

Victoria's interest piqued. "So, you went from selling to flipping?"

He nodded. "Yep. I started buying run-down properties, did most of the work myself, and flipped them. Took a while to get the hang of it, but once I did, I never looked back."

She could hear the pride in his voice. The way his eyes lit up when he talked about it. "That's actually really impressive."

He shrugged. "It's just something I love. I don't like things that don't have purpose." He looked her in the eyes. "I like to create. To build."

She felt it. That quiet intensity behind his words. He wasn't just talking about real estate. He was talking about life. And for the first time, Victoria realized this man was more than just a fleeting distraction.

She cleared her throat, trying to regain control of the moment. "It's crazy," she said, cutting into her food. "I'm almost embarrassed to ask this but, are you married?"

Thomas smirked, wiping his mouth with a napkin. "Nope. Never been."

Victoria exhaled slightly, relieved. "Good, because I don't do married men."

Thomas raised an eyebrow. "That so?"

She nodded. "Never. That's a line I don't cross." And yet, as she said it, she felt the hypocrisy burn in her throat. Here she was, married, sitting across from a man she was sleeping with, a man she was starting to crave more than she should, but Thomas didn't know that, and he never would.

"Well lucky for you, I'm happily single. Until the right woman comes along, that is," he said.

Victoria quickly changed the subject. "And do you have kids?"

He shook his head. "Nah, none. Hopefully one day. But for now, I'm just enjoying life. Bouncing from woman to woman, breaking hearts every night," he said with a straight face.

Victoria's eyes widened, nearly choking on her drink. "What?"

Thomas let out a deep laugh, shaking his head. "I'm kidding, I'm kidding. Damn, I knew you'd give me that reaction."

She threw a napkin at him. "Not funny."

"It was kind of funny."

She narrowed her eyes at him, but she was smiling because he was funny as hell and that was dangerous because the more she laughed with him, the harder it would be to keep him in the category of temporary.

"You seem like a man who has been through some things," she mused. "What's your story?"

Thomas sighed softly, running a hand over his jaw. "Well, I barely knew my mom and my dad was just a sperm donor. I was in the foster care system most of my life."

Victoria's smile dropped slightly.

He continued, "I was an only child, bounced around a lot. Never really had a place to call home."

"Damn," she murmured. "That must've been hard."

He nodded but didn't dwell on it. "When I turned eighteen, I aged out of the system. I had no idea what to do with myself, so I joined the Navy for a few years."

"What made you leave the Navy?" she asked.

Thomas smirked. "It wasn't for me. I don't like people telling me what to do."

She chuckled. "Yeah, I can see that."

He nodded. "After I got out, I moved to Atlanta and I've been here ever since."

She let the weight of his story settle over her. A man who had built himself from nothing. A man who had no family, no roots, no attachments. He was everything Davis wasn't. And maybe that's why she couldn't seem to let him go.

Thomas sighed, flashing her with a small smile. "That's pretty much my story."

And for the first time since she met him, she realized she wanted to be part of his story.

Thomas leaned back in his chair, "Alright," he said, smirking. "Now tell me all about Sheena."

Victoria arched a brow. She met his gaze, composed and effortless.

"Sheena Wells," she said smoothly.

He smirked. "So, tell me, Sheena Wells, what's your story? Let me guess…" He leaned in, eyes dancing with mischief. "You're some married woman, unhappy in her marriage, your parents left you with a boatload of money, and you have nothing better to do than to bring men here to this fancy-ass hotel, seduce them, and then, I don't know, murder them after a while?"

Victoria's eyes widened as she burst into laughter. "Oh my God, you are crazy!" she choked out.

Thomas grinned. "I mean, it's possible." He gave her a slow once-over. "You're sexy, mysterious, always in control… sounds like a serial killer to me."

Victoria laughed hysterically. "You definitely need to quit real estate and start a career in stand-up comedy."

He leaned in, smirking. "I'd rather be your next victim."

She shook her head, still laughing, before letting out a soft, exaggerated sigh.

"Fine. You got me. I'll tell you all my secrets," she teased.

He lifted his wine glass. "I'm listening."

She tilted her head slightly. "I'm a flight attendant," she began, setting the lie into motion with expert precision. "I travel all the time, always on the go, barely home."

Thomas nodded, intrigued. "Makes sense. That's why you're always busy."

"Exactly," she said, offering him the truth within the lie.

"And where do you live when you're not in the sky?" he asked, pressing her lightly.

She smiled. "I have two roommates, both flight attendants, too. We all share an apartment."

Thomas let out a low whistle. "So, no stability, huh?"

She shrugged, giving him the illusion of a carefree woman. "I love it. It keeps life exciting."

"Hmmm," he mused. "That's a lot of time in hotel rooms. Must get lonely."

"Not tonight."

A slow, satisfied smirk spread across his face.

She cleared her throat. "So yeah, it's just me. No family. No kids."

Thomas nodded slowly. "That's wild. You're really out here just living life, huh?"

She flashed him the perfect smile. "Something like that."

They continued talking, laughing, sharing little stories and trading playful remarks. And with every moment, Victoria felt herself falling deeper. She was captivated and wanted to know more. She was charting new territory and had no idea where it would lead. So, she did the only thing she could do. She ignored the warning signs and let the wave take her.

# <u>Lestie</u>
## (12 Years Earlier)

Martin was a serious businessman, the kind of man who carried himself with the air of someone who never made mistakes, never left things to chance. Everything about him was calculated, from the way he structured his day, to the meticulous way he handled his clients. He was thorough, succinct, diligent; a man who thrived on control.

In his profession, he was respected and admired. His financial acumen was unmatched, his attention to detail flawless, his ability to navigate complex tax codes and financial loopholes was nothing short of genius. But beneath the polished surface, beneath the tailored suits and the firm handshake, there was another side to Martin Taylor. A side that was just as meticulous, just as detailed, just as ruthlessly efficient, but in a way her mother refused to acknowledge.

He was a man of structure, habit and careful planning; and one of the most important rules in his carefully curated world? No one ever showed up at his office unannounced. He made that clear from the time she was a child.

Her mother, as expected, understood and obeyed without question. She accepted his explanation: business meetings, private client calls, and highly sensitive financial files as gospel, never once considering the possibility of another truth, but Victoria knew better. She knew that "busy with clients" was just code for fuck sessions, both impromptu and scheduled. Victoria knew that the same precision he used in handling tax documents was applied to his affairs: strategic, careful and leaving no trail. She knew because she watched. She paid attention to the way he operated, the seamless way he divided his life into separate, compartmentalized worlds.

Victoria watched the way women flocked to him, the way they melted under his charm, the way they wanted him, not just for a night, but for the experience. The *Martin Taylor Experience.* That's what Victoria called it, because that's exactly what it was. He wasn't just a man. He was a fantasy, a dream wrapped in a crisp suit, an unattainable legend that women whispered about in private.

And her father? He played the role perfectly. She had always known what he was. A businessman, a provider, a sinner. But October 10, 2012? That was the day she realized he was something more. That was the day everything changed. That was the day Celeste Victoria Taylor was reborn.

* * * *

It began like any other Saturday. The scent of breakfast wafted through the house: buttery biscuits, crispy bacon, and eggs whipped into soft, fluffy perfection. Her mother was already in the kitchen, moving through her routine with the ease of someone who had done this for decades.

Saturday mornings were sacred in their house. The entire week was structured: Dad worked Monday through Friday, 8:00 a.m. to 5:00 p.m. sharp.

Saturdays? Those were reserved for his private business matters. He always left by 9:00 a.m., claiming he needed to catch up on work, and meet with clients who couldn't make it during the week. He never wavered from this schedule, never gave a reason for her mother to doubt him.

And her mother? She accepted it blindly. After breakfast, as always, Sabrina retreated to her sewing room, precisely crafting costumes for dance studios and private clients, humming softly as she worked.

Victoria was a freshman at Georgia Tech, still adjusting to the fast pace of college life, still trying to balance her academic ambitions with the rest of the world. Normally, Saturdays were for studying. For getting ahead. For ensuring her grades remained flawless, untouched, superior. Because that was who she was. An overachiever. A woman who never did anything halfway.

But today? Today was different. Today, something in her gut pulled her in another direction. Something inside of her whispered that today would be a day she would never forget. Victoria didn't know why. She didn't know what it meant, but she knew one thing: she wasn't going to spend the day studying, because today wasn't going to be a normal Saturday.

Her gut was telling her to do something she had never done before, which was to follow her instincts, and to see for herself what her father did on Saturdays. Victoria didn't know what she would find, but something deep inside of her whispered that whatever it was, it would change everything.

Victoria told her mother she was heading to the library, and Sabrina didn't think twice about it. It was a part of Victoria's normal Saturday routine, her usual excuse to get out of the house for hours at a time. Sabrina kissed Victoria on the cheek, told her not to work too hard, and went right back to sewing, unaware that Victoria was on a mission. A mission to confirm what she had always known in her gut; that her father, Martin Taylor, the respectable businessman, the devoted husband, the "upstanding" man of their household, wasn't who he claimed to be. Or maybe... just maybe... she was wrong.

That thought gnawed at the edges of her certainty, making her question herself. What if he had changed? What if she was just looking for something that wasn't there? No, she knew him too well.

Victoria had spent her whole life watching him, observing the way he moved, how he spoke, how he operated with such seamless duality. A devoted family man at home, but a charming, elusive enigma outside of it. She needed to see it for herself. Not rumors. Not suspicions. Proof.

Pulling into the shopping center, Victoria parked far enough away from his office that he wouldn't notice her car, but close enough that she had a clear view of his front door. His office was tucked at the far end of the building, connected to the row of businesses, yet separate, as if he had intentionally designed it that way. The mirrored windows reflected the bright afternoon sun, offering no glimpse inside. A large promotional poster covered the lower half of the glass door, blocking the view completely. He thought of everything.

Victoria tapped her fingers against the steering wheel, debating her next move. If she wanted to get closer, she would have to be careful. But just as she was contemplating her approach, the office door swung open. A man and woman stepped out. Her breath caught. Victoria leaned forward slightly, keeping her face shielded just in case. They weren't just clients; she could tell by the way they lingered, the way the man leaned against the door, holding it open in a way that felt... casual. Comfortable. Familiar.

The woman smiled, her body turned slightly toward her father. The man stood close to her, their postures relaxed, their energy too synchronized for them to be strangers. A couple, maybe, or at least something close to it.

Victoria rolled her window down slightly, straining to listen. Their voices carried just enough for her to catch bits and pieces. Her father's voice, smooth and charismatic, thanked them for their business, adding something about being hungry and needing to finish up before heading home in an hour. She frowned. That was it? No lingering flirtation, no signs of something inappropriate. They said their good-byes, and the couple walked off toward the parking lot while her father stepped back inside.

Victoria let out a slow breath. Had she really just projected her assumptions onto something innocent? Had she been so convinced of her father's sins that she was seeing things that weren't there? She sank lower in her seat, feeling ashamed. Maybe her father really was working. Maybe, after all these years, he had changed. Maybe he wasn't the monster she had made him out to be. For the first time, doubt crept in. She felt guilty.

As if on cue, a thought surfaced. He said he was hungry, so maybe this was an opportunity to do something good. She could surprise him with lunch, make up for doubting him, and show him that she appreciated him. She proceeded across the street to his favorite bistro to grab sandwiches for the two of them. It wasn't much, but maybe it would ease the guilt clawing at her chest. Victoria glanced at the time. If he was planning to leave in an hour, she needed to move quickly.

* * * *

Victoria inhaled deeply, bracing herself, then reached for the bag of food. Her fingers trembled slightly as she grabbed the handle and stepped out of the car and onto the pavement. The familiarity of the office should have been comforting; she had been there before, but something about today felt off.

Victoria stopped at the door, staring at the large promotional poster plastered across the glass, blocking most of the view inside. A small sliver of space remained at the edge, just enough to see through if she angled herself the right way. She leaned in, pressing her palm lightly against the cool glass as she peeked through the gap. Nothing.

His desk was empty. The chair pushed back just slightly, as if he had just gotten up. Victoria glanced back at the parking lot; her father's car was still parked in its usual space. He was there. She knocked lightly. Nothing. She knocked again, this time a little louder. Still nothing.

Victoria chewed her bottom lip, as a flicker of unease curled through her stomach. He was always so punctual, so aware of his surroundings. Why wasn't he answering? She reached into her pocket, pulling out her phone. Her fingers hesitated over the screen before she finally tapped his number. She held her breath as it rang once. Twice. Three times. Then his voicemail picked up. *"Hey, this is Martin Taylor. Please leave a message."* The line went dead. She pulled the phone away from her ear, staring down at the screen as a knot tightened in her stomach. Something wasn't right.

Victoria looked back at the door, her fingers brushing against the familiar shape in her purse, the spare key. It was a key she had never used. A key her father had given her once with an explicit warning: This is only for emergencies, Lestie. Was this an emergency? No. But the nagging feeling in her gut told her it might be.

The weight of the key felt heavier than it should have, as if it carried the burden of whatever truth lay behind that door. Victoria slid the key into the lock. Her fingers hesitated at the last moment, hovering over the handle. This was the last chance to turn around, but she didn't. With a sharp inhale, she twisted the knob and pushed the door open.

# Control 29
## A Morning Like No Other

It was Monday morning, and Victoria stirred lazily beneath the soft sheets, as the lingering sensation of last night's passion pulsed through her. For once, her mind was clear. No racing thoughts, no planning, no worrying about what came next. Just a blissful stillness wrapped around her like a warm embrace.

She stretched her arms above her head, feeling the delicious ache between her thighs, a reminder of the man who had spent hours worshipping every inch of her body. A slow, satisfied smile stretched across her face. This wasn't just some fantasy. This was real.

Reaching across the bed, she expected to feel the warmth of Thomas's body, maybe even the teasing stroke of his hand pulling her in for another round before breakfast. But all she found was empty space. Her eyes fluttered open. She frowned, patting the sheets beside her. Gone.

The faint aroma of something warm and buttery teased her nose, mingling with the rich, smoky scent of bacon. Her stomach fluttered with excitement, but for a fleeting second, she felt a strange disorientation. The smell of breakfast. A kitchen in the distance. A man cooking. Her mind flashed back to Davis. For a moment, she almost expected to hear him humming an old blues song, the way he always did when he made breakfast in the morning.

She slipped out of bed and made her way out of the room. The moment she stepped into the kitchen, her breath hitched. There he was. Completely naked. Thomas stood at the stove, a spatula in one hand, flipping thick slices of golden-brown French toast in a pan. The muscles in his back flexed with each movement. Victoria had never seen anything sexier in her life. Davis would never cook naked. Hell, Davis would probably look at her crazy if she even suggested it. But here was Thomas, standing completely bare, cooking breakfast as if it were the most casual thing in the world.

She leaned against the doorframe, biting her lip as she admired him. Thomas must have felt her presence because he turned his head slightly, flashing her that devastating crooked smile.

Her eyes scanned the massive spread of food on the island. "Wait a minute. You cooked all this?"

"Yep. Ya boy can throw down when it comes to breakfast."

Her eyes widened at the feast before her. French toast, crispy bacon, sizzling sausage, fluffy scrambled eggs, buttery breakfast potatoes, and corned beef hash. Her mouth watered.

He turned toward her, his eyes locked on hers. "After what you did for me yesterday, the least I could do is make sure my woman enjoys a delicious home cooked meal from her man."

Her heart skipped. She stared at him. He said it so casually. *His woman.* The words sat heavy in her chest. She forced herself to brush past it. Instead, she asked, "How did you manage to get all of this food here to cook."

He chuckled, pulling out a chair for her at the dining table. "Instacart, baby. Had the groceries brought straight up to the hotel. Concierge dropped it off. I figured since you were still snoring and slobbering like a newborn baby, I had plenty of time to get everything prepped."

Victoria gasped, picking up a rolled napkin and tossing it at him. "I wasn't snoring, and I definitely don't slobber."

Thomas let out a deep laugh, shaking his head. "Girl, you were over there sounding like a damn grizzly bear."

She squinted at him. "Wow. That's how you do me?"

He put a hand to his chest in fake sincerity. "I mean it in the most endearing way possible."

She fought back a smile. There it was again. That warmth. That ease. That undeniable pull toward him that had nothing to do with sex and everything to do with who he was.

Before sitting down to eat, Thomas disappeared into the bedroom for a moment, returning in a pair of sweatpants.

Victoria pouted playfully. "You didn't have to put on any clothes. I was enjoying the view of your anatomy."

He smirked, sitting beside her. "Well, you were enjoying a whole lot more last night."

She chuckled, shaking her head as she picked up her fork. Thomas loaded her plate, making sure she had everything before digging into his own food.

She cut into the French toast, watching him as she took the first bite. Her eyes widened.

"Oh my God, Thomas."

He raised a brow. "Good?"

"Good?" she repeated. "This is insane. Like, ridiculously good. Where'd you learn to cook like this?"

He shrugged, cutting into his own food. "Breakfast is my thing. If we were at my place, you'd really see me in my element. I got my spices and seasonings galore; this is just basic."

"Basic? If this is basic, then I need to come over for the five-star version."

He gave her a sly grin. "Oh, so now you're trying to come to my place?"

"Maybe."

He studied her for a second, something unreadable flickering in his eyes. Then he looked down at his plate, shaking his head with a soft chuckle.

She tilted her head. "What?"

He glanced at her, smiling. "Nothing. I just—" He exhaled, looking around. "This feels kinda… normal, you know?"

Victoria's stomach clenched. She quickly took another bite, avoiding his gaze. "Yeah, it does."

They continued eating, the conversation flowing effortlessly, filled with laughter, teasing, and stolen glances. Victoria knew she should pull back, remind herself of the rules she had put in place. But with each passing moment, she felt herself slipping further and further into this dangerous, intoxicating pull toward him. And deep down, she knew it was already too late to stop.

Thomas studied her for a moment, something playful yet deliberate in his gaze. "I want to take you out today."

Victoria's hand froze midair, her fork hovering just above her plate. She blinked, forcing her expression to remain neutral, but inside, her heart slammed against her ribs. "Take me out?" she repeated slowly. "Today?"

"Yeah. Is that a problem?"

Victoria hesitated, searching for the right words, something to buy her time to think. "No, I just thought we'd chill here," she said.

Thomas shrugged. "Well, don't get me wrong, I love spending time here with you, but I'm starting to get a little cabin fever. It feels weird being cooped up in this suite all day. I thought maybe we could step out for a bit, get some fresh air."

Victoria internally panicked. Her mind spun with excuses, scenarios, possible escape routes, but on the outside, she remained calm, her expression unreadable. She didn't do public. Not with Thomas. Not with anyone she had ever entertained in her secret world. The thought of being out in the open with him made her pulse spike. Atlanta was big, but it was also small in the worst ways. Tabitha was always everywhere, moving through the city like she owned it. And Davis, her loving, unsuspecting husband, could be anywhere at any time. She'd never risk that. That's why she always traveled far, far away when she went on the hunt for new prey. But how could she say no without making it obvious?

She leaned forward, reaching for his hand. "I hear you, babe. I can see how being in this suite all day might feel a little stifling."

Thomas gave a slight nod, waiting for her to continue.

She exhaled, pretending to think. "But you know me… I'm always on the go, traveling from state to state and always working. It's rare that I get time to just relax and enjoy the moment. And I just want to enjoy you right now." She let her fingers trail up his arm. His shoulders relaxed slightly.

Still, she could see he wasn't entirely convinced, and she pivoted. "But I'll tell you what," she said, "why don't we go out to dinner? Maybe somewhere away from the city. Take a drive, enjoy the night air, and have some great food. What do you think?"

Thomas tilted his head, considering. "Hmm. I like the sound of that."

She smiled, relieved.

"Where were you thinking?" he asked.

Victoria tapped her chin, pretending to think it over, when in reality, she had already mapped out her safest option. "There's this amazing steakhouse in Suwanee. It's got this chill vibe and a live band that plays soft jazz. It's the kind of place where you can just lose yourself in the moment."

"That sounds like my kind of place."

"So, it's a date then, Mr. Carter?"

He reached out, pulling her chair closer to him, his lips brushing against her ear as he whispered, "It's a date, Miss Wells."

Victoria exhaled slowly, forcing her nerves to settle. She successfully dodged that disaster for now. But deep down, she knew it was only a matter of time before her worlds started to collide.

* * * *

As they pulled onto the highway, heading toward Suwanee, they settled into a comfortable rhythm. The drive was smooth in Thomas's luxury Land Rover. Victoria rested her head against the seat, allowing herself to relax as the city lights blurred past them. Thomas had the perfect playlist. Smooth R&B, D'Angelo, Maxwell, Jill Scott; a little bit of old-school and new school, but all of it set the perfect tone.

The conversation flowed effortlessly. Thomas was easy to talk to and laugh with. Victoria found herself studying him more and more, realizing just how much she liked the way he balanced masculinity with ease. He was strong and commanding, but he also had this soft, playful side, a charm that was completely disarming.

The restaurant had the perfect ambiance. Thomas leaned back in his seat, taking it all in. His sharp black attire complemented the sleek interior, his confidence radiating effortlessly.

"Damn, this place is nice," he murmured, his gaze scanning the room before settling on her. "You really know how to pick a spot. This place is a whole vibe."

Victoria smiled, pleased with his approval. "Told you it was nice. It's one of my favorite hidden gems outside the city."

"Hidden gem, huh?" he teased. "Do you bring all your men to your little secret spots?"

She matched his smirk. "Only the special ones."

His eyes darkened slightly. "That so?"

Before she could respond, her phone vibrated inside of her bamboo handbag.

She had intentionally left her phone locked away these past couple of days, wanting to be completely detached from her reality. But tonight, she made an exception. If something happened at work, she needed to be reachable, even though she hadn't expected anything to happen.

Victoria's stomach dropped. Tabitha was calling. Victoria's pulse spiked, heat rushing to her face as her mind immediately went into overdrive. What the hell. Why was she calling?

Her mind started racing. Something must have happened at work. Something urgent. Her stomach twisted. If this was an emergency, she would have to cut her night short and leave Thomas. A wave of frustration rolled through her. *I trusted Tab to handle one job*, she thought to herself. She inhaled deeply, forcing herself to stay calm. Maybe it was an accident. Maybe Tab just hit call by mistake. Victoria let the call go to voicemail. She hesitated before reaching for her phone, keeping her movements casual.

Thomas noticed immediately. "You know," Thomas said, watching her carefully, "this is the first time I've seen you with a phone since we've been together. Most people have theirs glued to them, but not you. Makes me think you've got something to hide."

Victoria's pulse spiked, but she kept her expression neutral. Their eyes met, and for a second, she wondered if he knew. If he could sense it.

Then, he laughed. "Relax, baby. I'm just messing with you."

She let out a breath, matching his energy with a playful chuckle. "You got jokes, huh?"

"Always," he responded.

She tried to slip her phone back into her bag, but then her screen lit up with a text.

**Tabitha:** *Hey girl. There was a piece of mail addressed to you and Davis at the office today and it looked important. I'm on my way to your house to just drop it in the mailbox. You don't have to call me* *back. I was just letting you know. Hope y'all are having a good time. Love ya, babes!*

Victoria stared at the message for a moment, her brain shifting into damage control mode. She thought to herself: *No, no, no. Tab cannot go to the house.* Tab was supposed to be in Tennessee at the conference with Victoria. If Davis saw Tab, it would blow up everything. Every single carefully constructed lie. Every detail Victoria had meticulously designed would fall apart. This wasn't just inconvenient, it was catastrophic.

Victoria clenched her jaw, trying to breathe through the rising panic in her chest. Everything had been perfect. Her getaway with Thomas. Her lies, airtight. Her tracks, covered. And now Tab, clueless fucking Tab, was seconds away from setting a match to it all. Victoria felt like she was losing it, and she had to think quickly on her feet and keep her composure. Victoria swiftly texted back.

**Victoria:** *Hey Tab. Don't trouble yourself. You can just put it on my desk at work in my mail divider and I'll grab it whenever I get back. Thank you for thinking of me. And yes, everything is going well. We're having a good time.*

Victoria hit send and set the phone down, forcing herself to stay present and trying to calm herself down from the disaster that could derail everything.

Thomas raised a brow. "Everything good?"

Victoria nodded, playing it off effortlessly. "Yeah, it's my roommate. She gets a little emotional when she drinks. Starts randomly texting. I was just letting her know I'm out and I'll check in later."

Thomas chuckled. "That sounds like a lot."

"You have no idea," she lied.

Thomas turned his attention back to the live jazz band, bobbing his head slightly to the music. Victoria reached for her wine glass, trying to steady her nerves with a slow sip, but just as she brought it to her lips, her screen lit up again.

**Tabitha:** *Hey babes. I'm approaching your neighborhood, so it's no worries at all. I'm just gonna pop it in the mailbox and scoot.*

Victoria's hand slammed the wine glass back onto the table. Thomas looked at her with a perplexed expression. Victoria grabbed her phone, her pulse thundering in her ears. *This girl is really about to blow up my entire life.* Victoria immediately texted her back.

**Victoria:** *No.*

"Excuse me," Victoria said suddenly, rising from the table and forcing a calm smile. "My roommate seems a little off, I just need to check on her. I'll be right back."

Thomas gave a small nod, his gaze lingering on her as she made her way toward the restroom with measured urgency.

Before she even stepped into the restroom, she was calling Tab. Victoria's entire demeanor shifted. The façade cracked wide open. She was livid.

Tab answered on the first ring. "Hey babes, what's up, girl?

Victoria didn't even wait. "Hey, you don't have to worry yourself with that mail. Whatever it is, I'll get it when I get back. It's really not that important for you to drive to my house." Her voice was tight.

"V, I wasn't just driving to the house because of the mail," Tabitha said. "I stopped at my Mediterranean spot to eat, and since I was already nearby, I figured I'd just drop it off."

Victoria clenched her jaw. *Nearby?* Of course she would be nearby. *Of all days!* "That's nice and all, but I'm good. You don't have to go to my house."

Tab wasn't taking the hint. "V, I'm literally in your neighborhood, so I'm just going to put it in the mailbox."

"What?" Victoria snapped. "Why are you in my neighborhood?" Her voice came out harsher than she intended, but she couldn't stop now. The panic was rising like a tidal wave.

"Girl, relax," Tab said, confused. "You act like I'm about to burst through your door. It's just the mailbox."

Victoria closed her eyes, gripping the edge of the marble sink as she struggled to stay composed. She took a deep breath and softened her voice, just barely. "Tab, you really do the most," she said. "I don't like people just coming by and dropping stuff off. I have nosy neighbors, and I don't feel like dealing with them. So can you just leave and put the mail on my desk at work?"

"Wow. Okay. I hear you loud and clear. I see I'm not welcome over here," Tab said softly.

"Tab, you are welcomed. It's just… my neighbors are very observant, and I don't need them thinking you're doing something you have no business doing. They really have me on edge. I'm sorry, you know I love you."

Tab's voice was abrupt. "I understand. I'll just bring it back to the office and put it on your desk." She paused. "Sorry I bothered you."

Before Victoria could respond, the line went dead. She stared at her phone, heart still racing. *Dammit, Tab.* She leaned over the sink, gripping the porcelain like it might anchor her. She couldn't afford any slip-ups. Not after everything she'd done to keep this under control.

Victoria made her way back to the table. The weight of the confrontation with Tab still clung to her skin, but she had no choice now but to slip back into character, smooth and confident.

She offered a soft smile as she reached the table. "Sorry about that."

"Do we need to leave?" he asked. "Go check on her?"

Victoria slipped into her seat, forcing herself to appear composed. "No, no," she said gently, laying a reassuring hand over his. "It's not that serious. I managed to get it all handled. Hopefully."

Her fingers curled slightly around his, grounding herself. Thomas nodded slowly, though the concern didn't fully leave his face. His thumb grazed hers once, a subtle gesture, warm and steady. She inhaled deeply and blinked away the storm brewing behind her eyes. Because the truth was, no matter how perfectly crafted her world had once seemed, no matter how secure she thought she was with Davis, things were shifting. And Thomas was the only thing that felt real anymore.

And for now, she pushed Tabitha, Davis, the lies, and the crumbling truth away from her mind. But even as she laughed and flirted, her mind remained tangled in a web of deception. The lies kept coming, one after another, and soon, she would have to find a way to keep them from unraveling.

✱ ✱ ✱ ✱

Back at the suite, the energy of their two-day escape was beginning to settle, the reality of time was slipping through Victoria's fingers like sand in an hourglass. The moment she had been avoiding was now staring her in the face. Tomorrow, she had to go back to Davis. The thought of it sat heavy in the pit of her gut.

Thomas made himself comfortable on the couch, lounging in nothing but a pair of loose sweatpants. Victoria climbed onto the couch beside him, her body instinctively gravitating toward his warmth, resting her head in his lap.

"What's wrong, baby?" he asked.

"I don't want this to end," she admitted. "I've been enjoying every moment of this. It's not fair that we have to go back to our normal lives tomorrow."

Thomas exhaled. "Baby," he murmured, "just because we leave here tomorrow doesn't mean we won't see each other again. You know that, right?"

Victoria's heart clenched. Did she know that?

"I promised you I'd make you dinner," he continued, "and I want you to come to my place so I can show you where I live. Maybe, when you're comfortable, I can come to your place."

Victoria's entire body stiffened. She had been so lost in the passion and the thrill of sneaking around and indulging in something she had convinced herself was temporary. But now, Thomas was making plans. Plans that didn't just exist within the walls of a penthouse suite.

She scrambled for a response. "Oh, um… That might not be the best idea. My roommates, you know… it's just a crazy situation."

Thomas wrinkled his brows slightly, his head tilting in curiosity. "Your roommates?"

"Yeah," Victoria nodded. "They're kind of all over the place. My apartment wouldn't be very ideal."

Thomas didn't seem convinced. "I don't mind. I'm there for you, not them."

Victoria felt her chest tighten. He was pressing. "We'll figure it out," she said, hoping that would be enough to move the conversation along. But Thomas wasn't done.

"Or maybe you won't have to worry about getting your own place. Maybe you can move in with me."

The words knocked the air from her lungs. She blinked at him, stunned.

"I'm starting to fall hard for you, Sheena. I can see us together, happy, in a real, healthy relationship."

Victoria felt like the room had started spinning. This isn't what she envisioned. What happened to men just being glad to get laid and having a woman to screw with no strings attached? Since when did side lovers start making plans for a future? Her thoughts were running wild, but she had to get in front of this. She couldn't afford for him to be this invested, not yet, not this fast.

"Thomas," she said carefully, "I want this to work out too, but we have to take it slow. I've been hurt too many times before, and even though I know you're not like those other men, I still have to protect my heart. I just need to proceed cautiously." She let out a small sigh. "All I ask is that you understand that I just want us to take our time."

Thomas studied her for a long moment, the warmth in his eyes never fading. "Baby, I won't hurt you. Just give me the chance to show you what it means to be loved by a real man."

Her heart skipped.

"I'll protect your heart with all that's within me." His words seeped into her skin, wrapping around her like a drug, intoxicating and weakening her. "There's something about you, Sheena. Something that drives me wild, that I've never felt before. It's crazy, and I can't describe it." His fingers trailed down her arm, sending chills over her skin. "You're the woman I never knew I needed. The woman I never knew even existed."

Victoria felt herself slipping. But before she could stop herself, she lunged forward, capturing his mouth with hers in a desperate, searing kiss. The weight of Thomas's words had sent Victoria spiraling.

Without a word, she climbed onto his lap. "Let me take care of you, Thomas," she whispered, her lips grazing his ear, sending a shiver down his spine. She slid off his lap and onto her knees, her hands gripping the waistband of his sweats and pulling them down in one swift motion. His cock sprang free—thick, hard, and pulsing in anticipation. A wicked smile spread across her face as she reached for a flavored condom and rolled it onto his hardened length with expert precision. Then, without hesitation, she took him into her mouth. Thomas groaned, his head falling back against the couch as her warm, wet mouth engulfed him. She didn't start slowly. She went straight for the kill. Deep. Hard. Intense.

She moaned around his cock, sending vibrations through his shaft, making his whole-body shudder. She hollowed her cheeks, sucking harder, taking him even deeper until her nose was buried against his pelvis. His hips bucked involuntarily, chasing the intoxicating pleasure she was drowning him in. He was losing control.

"Sheena... fuck, I'm about to—"

She didn't stop. Didn't slow down.

He let out a loud, raw moan and came, his entire body shuddering. He sucked in heavy, ragged breaths, trying to catch himself from the overwhelming waves of pleasure. But Victoria wasn't done. She barely gave him a moment to recover before he suddenly sat up, grabbing her by the waist.

"You're mine," he growled, his hands roaming her body.

Their mouths crashed together in a hungry, desperate kiss, his lips traveling down her neck, biting, sucking, marking her. Her back hit the wall, and before she could process what was happening, he was inside her. A sharp gasp escaped her lips as he filled her in one deep thrust.

"Thomas—"

He didn't wait. He gripped her thighs, pinning her against the wall as he drove into her with unrelenting force. "You like that, baby?" he growled against her ear.

"Oh my god, yes!"

"I want you to come for me, baby," he commanded. And just like that, her body obeyed.

✳ ✳ ✳ ✳

Victoria lay still, her body humming from the aftershocks of their wild, unrelenting night. The scent of sex and heat lingered in the air like an unspoken promise.

Thomas shifted beside her. His touch was gentle, affectionate, and possessive. Then, in a low, husky voice, he murmured, "I don't ever want another man to have you. You're mine, Sheena."

Victoria stiffened. The room, which had once felt like their secluded paradise, suddenly felt small. Mine? The word echoed in her head. She turned her head slightly to look at him. Thomas laid there, his face softened with post-orgasm exhaustion as he drifted toward sleep. His expression was peaceful, almost vulnerable, so different from the demanding, dominant lover who had just had her pinned against the wall, claiming every inch of her body like it belonged to him.

Victoria's throat tightened. She tapped him lightly. "Thomas, are you okay?"

He barely responded, only offering a sleepy grunt before his breathing evened out. He was out cold. Her stomach twisted again, unease creeping up her spine like a slow, suffocating fog. What did he mean, she was his? She wasn't his. She belonged to her husband, Davis. This felt dangerous.

She turned onto her back, staring up at the ceiling, her mind racing. Had she misread him? Had she been too caught up in the high of their passion to notice the shift in his energy? She replayed their time together, the way he had looked at her, how he had touched her, the way he studied her every move like he was memorizing her. Had she underestimated him?

A lump formed in her throat. Thomas wasn't just some casual fling anymore. He was deeply attached. Her fingers curled around the edge of the sheets, gripping them tightly as her mind spiraled further. What if Thomas wouldn't let go? What if he wouldn't accept that this was supposed to be temporary? She tried to steady her breathing, telling herself she was overthinking it.

Victoria inhaled deeply, letting the breath settle in her lungs. Tomorrow, she would talk to him. She would get inside his head, figure out exactly where his mind was, and set some boundaries if necessary. She needed to make sure he wasn't thinking long-term. Because if he was, if he truly believed he owned her, she might have just stepped into a dangerous game. One that she wasn't sure she could win.

# Control 28
## Leaving the Fire, Returning to Frost

Tuesday morning arrived, but Victoria had barely gotten any rest. She had spent the night tossing and turning, her mind trapped in an endless loop of replaying Thomas's words from the night before. The intensity of it lingered in her mind like a haunting melody she couldn't shake.

As she slowly blinked awake, she turned over and noticed, once again, Thomas wasn't in bed. Moments later, Thomas appeared in the doorway, completely naked, carrying a tray of food like some kind of domesticated god. The way his muscular frame caught the morning light would have made any other woman melt, but for Victoria, the unease from last night still clung to her like a second skin.

"Good morning, my sunshine!" he said cheerily. "I hope you slept well last night, because I slept like a damn baby. You turned me on something fierce, girl."

Victoria forced a half-smile, trying to ignore the gnawing feeling in her gut. She glanced at the breakfast: toast, bacon, and scrambled eggs mixed with peppers and cheese. He had gotten creative with what was left from the groceries that he had delivered yesterday.

"I figured I'd make you something light," Thomas continued, "just a little something to get your morning started right."

She swallowed down her discomfort and murmured, "Thanks." But her voice lacked its usual enthusiasm.

Thomas frowned, his playful expression flickering into something more serious as he sat down beside her. "Baby, is everything alright? You seem different."

Victoria inhaled deeply, debating how to approach this. "Thomas, what was that last night?"

"What was what?" he asked, genuinely looking confused. "You didn't enjoy last night?" His brows creased as he studied her. "I mean, I know I was a little rough, but damn, you had me so turned on, I couldn't control myself. Did I hurt you? Are you feeling sore?"

"No, Thomas. I'm not talking about the sex. I'm talking about what you said. You said to me, 'You're mine, I don't ever want another man to have you.'"

Finally, a flicker of recognition passed over his face, but he shrugged, brushing it off like it was nothing. "Baby," he chuckled, reaching for her hand, "I honestly don't even remember saying any of that."

Victoria didn't move.

"You know how it is when you're caught up in the moment. You say shit when the sex is good. It's just dirty talk, Sheena. That's all." He laughed. "Come on, you really think I'd say some shit like that and mean it?" He smirked.

Victoria studied him, searching his face for any signs that he was lying. His body language was relaxed, his expression easy, unreadable. But something in her gut told her otherwise.

"You know I respect you," he said. "I'd never do anything to hurt you. You know that."

The way he spoke was so convincing, so certain, that for a brief moment, Victoria questioned if she was overreacting.

"This has been the best two days ever," Thomas murmured, his lips brushing against her temple. "I know you want to take things slow, and I'm willing to take it as slow as you need."

The words were exactly what she needed to hear. And yet, her stomach twisted. Victoria inhaled deeply, keeping her expression neutral as she laid against his chest. Whatever this was, however far he thought this would go, she had to ensure that she could get back in front of it. She had to be several steps ahead of Thomas.

# <u>Lestie</u>
## (12 Years Earlier)

A familiar, crisp scent of cedarwood and expensive cologne enveloped her as she stepped inside. The air was still, thick with the unmistakable warmth of an occupied space, the kind that settled after long hours of work.

The first thing she noticed was the shift in decor. She hadn't been inside her father's office in a while, and though the bones of the space were still the same, he had rearranged things, infused the place with new energy, new life.

The Keurig coffee station sat against the far wall, an assortment of gourmet coffee pods and herbal teas lined up in perfect rows beside it. A polished ceramic mug, still half full, rested beside the machine. Martin never let a cup of coffee go cold. Strange.

She took another step inside. Her gaze drifted toward his desk, and there it was, the signature chaos of a man always working, always thinking, always moving. The stillness of the room pressed down on her like a weight, thick and suffocating.

A part of her wanted to believe that the nagging sensation in her gut was simply paranoia, an overactive mind spinning stories from whispers of suspicion. But the deeper she moved into the office, the more those whispers grew into screams.

Victoria shook it off, gripping the bag of food in her hand a little tighter as she finally made her way toward the relaxation room. She could hear something now: soft, muffled sounds just beneath the hum of the air conditioning. Her pulse quickened. Victoria hesitated at the door, fingers hovering just over the handle. This was ridiculous. She was being ridiculous. He was probably just taking a nap or listening to one of his old school records.

Victoria exhaled sharply, shaking off the ridiculous weight pressing against her chest.

It's just Dad, there's nothing to be nervous about. But as her fingers twisted the knob, as she slowly pushed the door open… that illusion shattered. Because at that moment, Victoria saw, and once she saw it, there was no unseeing it. There was no going back. There was only the truth, and it was uglier than she had ever imagined.

Victoria's breath caught in her throat, her lungs seizing as her mind struggled to process what was unfolding before her. She couldn't move. The scene before her was like something from a movie, except this wasn't fiction. This was real, and it was him.

Her father stood behind a woman, his powerful frame looming over her as he gripped her hips with both hands, pulling her back into him with each brutal thrust. The woman, young, supple, and moaning like she had lost all sense of herself, arched against the force of his movements, her spine bowing like a worshipper at the altar of his touch. The wet slap of skin meeting skin echoed in the room: a steady, obscene rhythm that only grew louder as he picked up his pace. Each movement was deliberate, punishing and owning.

Victoria felt her stomach clench, nausea creeping up her throat, but she couldn't look away. She was drowning in the moment. Every flicker of motion, every broken cry, every bead of sweat rolling down her father's spine as he claimed this woman as though she belonged to him, it all seared itself into her memory, branding her with a horror she would never be able to scrub away.

Martin's grip in the woman's hair tightened, his fist twisting at the roots as he yanked her head back, forcing her to arch for him. A sharp cry slipped past her lips, part pain, part pleasure, but she didn't resist. If anything, she melted under his control, letting him manipulate her body however he wanted.

Victoria had never seen her father like this. This wasn't the man who sat at the head of the dinner table, who preached discipline and self-control, who carried himself with the poise of a man who always had the upper hand. No, this man was something else entirely. Something darker, primal and terrifyingly free.

He slapped the woman's ass hard, making her cry out, her hands scrambling against the armrest of the couch to steady herself. Victoria flinched at the sound, at the raw dominance in the way he took pleasure in her suffering.

"Say my name," he growled.

The woman gasped, her body trembling. "Martin—"

"Louder," he told her.

Her voice rose, quivering with desperation. "Martin, oh God."

Victoria's entire body felt detached, like she was floating outside of herself, watching a nightmare unfold that she had no power to stop. She wanted to scream. She wanted to run. She wanted to undo whatever cruel twist of fate had led her to this moment, but she was frozen. How could this be the same man she had looked up to her entire life? How could this monster be her father?

The walls of the office seemed to close in around her, suffocating, pressing down on her until she thought she might explode from the sheer weight of it all. And then, her grip on her phone slipped. The device tumbled from her hands, hitting the floor with a loud, unforgiving thud. The noise cut through the room like a gunshot.

Martin's body went rigid, his head snapping around so fast it was almost unnatural, and then, their eyes met. His eyes widened in shock, his face draining of color, his mouth parting in stunned silence. For the first time in her life, Victoria saw something in her father she had never seen before: Fear.

The woman gasped, scrambling to cover herself, but Victoria didn't see her anymore. She only saw her father. A man she no longer recognized, and in that moment, something inside her broke.

The moment her father turned around and their eyes met, the world as she knew it shattered. Martin's usual confident stance faltered as he scrambled to cover himself. He looked as though he had seen a ghost. No, worse than that, he looked as though he had been caught, and he had.

The woman beside him, Mia, she would later learn, let out a sharp gasp, her body jerking upright as she frantically searched for her discarded clothes. Her face was flushed, her chest heaving from the exertion of what they had been doing, her hands trembling as she struggled to pull her dress back over her head. Victoria's body betrayed her, the shock locking her limbs in place. She couldn't move. She couldn't breathe. She was frozen in time, stuck in a moment that didn't feel real.

Her father saw it. He saw the way Victoria was unraveling, how her body was reacting to the trauma of everything. He was moving toward her now, his expression torn between panic and forced composure. She took a step back, lifting a trembling hand in protest. "Don't touch me." Her voice was barely above a whisper, but the command was clear.

His lover stood frozen near the doorway, her arms wrapped around herself, her eyes darting between the two of them. Her father turned to his lover and motioned for her to leave. She hesitated for a split second before scurrying out the door. The moment she was gone, Martin turned his attention back to Victoria. He pulled a chair close and sat down, his face still flushed with embarrassment.

Martin exhaled, shaking his head before finally speaking. "What are you doing here in my office unannounced?"

Victoria blinked. For a moment, she thought she had misheard him. That was the first thing he had to say? Not an apology. Not remorse. Not regret.

A bitter laugh bubbled up from her throat, but it was drowned out by the overwhelming rage swelling in her chest. "Are you serious?" Victoria's voice came out sharper than she intended. "I walk in here, catch you screwing some random woman, and that's your first response? Not 'I'm sorry' or 'let me explain.'"

Martin leaned back in his chair, his expression unreadable now. He was not panicked anymore. If anything, he seemed to be regaining his footing, settling into the version of himself that had always unnerved her, the version of him that was calculated.

"I called you before I showed up," she continued, her voice trembling, but firm. "You didn't answer. I knocked on the door before I came in. I wanted to surprise you with lunch." Victoria gestured toward the untouched bag of food that she had dropped onto the desk. "But I see I'm the one who got surprised."

Martin exhaled again, this time slower. "Lestie—"

"No." She cut him off before he could even attempt to spin this in his favor. "How could you do this? To Mom? To me?"

He didn't flinch. He didn't shrink beneath her accusations. Instead, he leaned forward, clasping his hands together, his expression composed. "I see you have a lot to learn," he murmured. "I'm about to give you some valuable life lessons," he said. "Lessons that you can choose to listen to or not. It's your choice what you do with them. I'm not doing anything your mother doesn't know about."

The words sliced through her like a blade.

"She knew from day one that I would never be a one-woman man." His voice was calm, steady, as though he were explaining a simple fact. "I live life from my own script. I make the rules, and whatever I decide gives me pleasure, I go after it. Your mother knows she could never be enough for me."

Victoria shook her head, refusing to believe what she was hearing. "That's not true."

Her father tilted his head. "Isn't it?"

Her stomach twisted violently.

He kept going. "I get bored easily. I'm always seeking the next high, the next pleasure-filled moment. I don't hold onto relationships outside of my marriage. I don't have a secret family. I don't have some mistress I see regularly. I hook up with women at my discretion, at my call, and when I'm finished, I leave it right there."

Victoria wanted to vomit.

"They know what it is," he continued. "I make sure of that."

Victoria shook her head again, standing abruptly. "Stop."

He ignored her. "Mia? She's someone I've known for a while. She knows my stance. She knew what today was: a hit-it-and-quit-it type of deal." He shrugged. "She'll be fine."

Victoria pressed her palms against her temples, trying to stop her head from spinning.

"You're disgusting."

He smirked. "I'm a man who knows what he wants."

Victoria inhaled sharply. She had come there expecting to surprise her father with lunch. Instead, she had walked into a horror she would never be able to erase.

"I always knew that I'd have to marry the type of woman like your mother." His voice was calm and deliberate. "A woman who's submissive. Who does what I say, when I say it, and asks no questions."

Victoria stared at him, her pulse hammering in her ears. His words felt like acid, burning away the last remnants of the father she thought she knew.

"Now, I love your mother very much," he continued, leaning back in his chair as if this were some casual conversation; as if she wasn't sitting here barely holding herself together. "And I'll always take care of her and give her everything she needs and wants, but she alone will never be enough to fill the void inside me."

Victoria sucked in a sharp breath, recoiling from the words, from the audacity of what he was saying. What kind of person thinks like this? What kind of man knowingly marries a woman with the full intention of betraying her over and over again?

"How can you look me in the eye and say that?" Victoria asked.

He sighed, shaking his head like she was being naïve. Victoria hated that. She hated the way he looked at her, like she was just some clueless girl who didn't understand the real world.

"Lestie, every man wants stability at home. Every man wants a woman they know will hold it down. Men desire just as much as women to have children, to create their picture-perfect model family unit."

Victoria let out a bitter laugh. A model family unit? This was his version of a model family? Victoria lifted her gaze, locking eyes with him, and for the first time in her life, she saw her father for what he really was. Not the strong, admirable head of their household. Not the man she had once respected, but a selfish, egotistical liar.

"What did Mom ever see in you?" Victoria said, her voice laced with venom. "A man who has zero respect for his own wife?"

His jaw tensed slightly, but he didn't look away. "You don't get it," he said simply.

"No," she shot back. "You don't get it. I've always looked to you to be the head of our family. To guide and love us. To be the example of a man I could be proud of, but instead, you're nothing but a selfish, disgusting, despicable excuse for a man."

His eyes darkened. "Watch your damn mouth," he snapped.

Victoria flinched slightly, her body stiffening as his entire demeanor shifted.

"I understand that you're hurt," he went on, his voice firmer. "But I'm still your father, and you will respect me."

"Respect?" She let out a hollow laugh. "You think you deserve respect?"

"Lestie." His voice was sharp. "Look at me when I'm talking to you."

Victoria hesitated, but eventually met his gaze, as she was still burning with rage.

"What I'm about to tell you is valuable information. Information that I pray you live by."

Victoria stared at him, her stomach twisting.

"Listen to me good because I'm about to change the whole trajectory of your life."

A chill ran down her spine.

"There are two types of people in this world. Those that get preyed upon… and those that do the preying."

Victoria swallowed hard.

"Who are you meant to be, Lestie?" His eyes bore into hers, unblinking. "The prey or the predator?"

She clenched her jaw, but she didn't respond.

"I made up my mind a long time ago," he said, his voice growing darker, heavier. "I would never allow anyone to prey on me. Ever."

Victoria sat frozen, every fiber of her being screaming at her to get up, to walk away, to leave this moment behind, but she couldn't, because the truth was, his words weren't entirely foreign to her. They stirred something inside her that she wasn't ready to face.

"I create the paths in my life," he went on. "I choose my own destiny, and when I look at you, I see myself."

"No. I'm nothing like you."

He smirked, tilting his head slightly. "You may not want to believe it, but it's the truth."

Her fingers curled into fists again, her nails biting into her skin.

"You're a Taylor," he said, his voice thick with certainty. "The true definition of a born leader of domination."

She wanted to argue, but a part of her knew he wasn't entirely lying.

"Now," he continued, "you can choose to work in it or choose the opposite path. The decision is yours. But I know deep down, you'll choose the path that was created for you."

Silence stretched between them. Victoria couldn't stand to be in this room a second longer. She turned away and headed straight for the door. She didn't say another word to him. She walked out of that office with her father's voice still ringing in her ears. She didn't remember driving. She didn't even remember pulling into the park. All she knew was that when she finally came back to herself, she was sitting on a bench, staring out at the lake, her father's words looping in her mind like a twisted mantra. There are two types of people in this world. The prey and the predator.

Is this really what life was supposed to be like? Or was her father just full of shit? The more she thought about it, the more it started to make sense. Victoria had always taken after her dad in so many ways. The realization sat heavy on her, like an unshakable weight. Victoria was a natural born leader. She took charge in every aspect of her life. She moved with confidence, calculated every step, and made sure she was always in control. Victoria was good with numbers, sharp in business, and had an instinct for strategy that never had to be taught. It existed in her, like an innate skill woven into her DNA, but most of all, she despised her mother's meek and mild way of life.

Sabrina lived in the shadows of Martin; her mother's entire existence centered around pleasing a man who barely acknowledged her effort. Victoria swore she would never be that woman. That she'd never allow anyone to dominate her the way her father dominated her mother.

But then, a thought slithered into her mind, uninvited. Did she feel this way because she saw the way her father treated her mother, and it repelled her, or was it because deep down, Victoria was just like him. That she was bound to follow the same path, destined to make the same choices, no matter how much she pretended otherwise. Only time would tell.

# Control 27
## Back to Business, Not Back to Normal

Victoria settled into her office chair; she was not in the mood for work just yet. Her mind was elsewhere. Her calendar was empty. That was strange. Tab always scheduled everything down to the last detail. Victoria figured maybe she had just cleared it since she didn't know exactly when she'd be back. Still, something felt off.

Victoria glanced out the glass window of her office, scanning the workspace. Everything looked normal. The employees were buzzing about, getting things done. Several cheerful "welcome backs" had greeted her the moment she walked in. Her team respected her, and she made sure she always took care of them as an amazing boss does. But something, or rather someone, was missing.

Her eyes landed on Tab. She was seated at her desk, flipping through some paperwork, her face unreadable and yet, she hadn't so much as glanced in Victoria's direction. No eager smile or dramatic sighs about how exhausted she was from doing "all the work" while Victoria was away. Tab always lived for a moment to gloat about how much she had done.

Victoria narrowed her eyes. What the hell was up with her? She leaned back in her chair, watching Tab for a moment longer. She was starting to get the feeling that this wasn't just exhaustion. Something wasn't right. Tab was never this quiet. She wasn't avoiding Victoria's office because she was tired, she was avoiding Victoria.

Victoria pursed her lips and thought back to their text exchange from a couple of days prior. *Was she seriously still mad about that?* She hadn't thought it was a big deal, but Tab was obviously upset about something.

Victoria walked over to Tab's office and leaned against the doorframe, arms crossed, waiting for Tab to look up. Tab didn't. She kept writing, her pen scratching against the notepad, deliberately ignoring Victoria's presence. This was new. This wasn't the Tab she knew.

Victoria cleared her throat, expecting to snap Tab out of whatever trance she was in. Finally, Tab looked up, but instead of her usual bright, enthusiastic grin, she gave Victoria a half-hearted forced smile. Then, just as quickly, she looked back down and continued writing.

"Tab…?" Victoria's voice was cautious, laced with growing irritation.

Without looking up, Tab mumbled, "You're back, huh? Welcome back."

Victoria blinked. "Um… yeah. Obviously. What's up with you?" she asked, trying to keep her voice steady.

Tab finally looked up again. "Nothing," she said flatly. "Just trying to get things done, and get through the week, is all."

Trying to get through the week? Victoria's eyes subtly darted around the office, scanning for any signs that the staff might be catching on to the strange energy. Everyone seemed immersed in their own work, completely unaware of the tension brewing between the two women.

Victoria turned back to Tab, her jaw tightening. Okay. This is bullshit. "Hey, Tab, when you're finished writing whatever you're writing, can I see you for a moment in my office?"

Tab held her gaze for a moment before shrugging. "Sure. I'll be there in just a moment."

Victoria nodded slowly and walked away, but inside, she was boiling.

Tab's demeanor was beyond unprofessional, it was disrespectful, and Victoria wasn't the kind of boss who tolerated blatant disrespect. She prided herself on being a fair, lenient leader. She wasn't a micromanaging tyrant or one of those insufferable, nagging CEOs who barked orders for the sake of power.

Tab strolled across the office, her face completely emotionless, void of the usual playfulness and warmth. Victoria inhaled deeply, bracing herself. The second Tab stepped inside, Victoria gestured toward the door. "Close it."

Tab wordlessly obliged, pushing the door shut behind her before gingerly sitting down in the chair across from Victoria's desk. And then, for the first time since Victoria walked into the office this morning, Tab locked eyes with her.

Victoria sat back in her chair and inhaled deeply, keeping her tone light and conversational. "Tab, listen. I was actually excited to come back and see my best friend in the whole wide world. And yet, I walk in here and you're acting funny with me. I don't know what's going on, but we're not about to sit here and play these little silent war games. That's not us, Tab. We tell each other everything."

The second those words left Victoria's lips, Tab laughed a dry, bitter, almost mocking laugh. Victoria's confusion deepened, but she pushed forward, refusing to let this go.

"Tab, what's going on with you? If there's something wrong, let's squash it now."

Victoria was trying to sound like the same best friend Tabitha had always known. But the moment was slipping away, and Victoria could feel it, because Tabitha didn't look at her like a friend anymore. She looked at her like a stranger.

Tab finally spoke, "You're right. We shouldn't have weird energy here at work. So, tell me about your trip. How was Lafayette? That's where you went, right?"

A slow, creeping nausea coiled in Victoria's stomach, but she didn't flinch. Instead, she forced a casual smile and played it cool. "Lafayette was good," she said evenly. "It went quick. Davis handled his business with his mom, and all is well."

Tab nodded slowly. "I see. And when did you guys get back?"

The question hit like a slap. Victoria tilted her head as if the question was oddly specific, as if she couldn't understand why Tab would even care.

"We got back Tuesday afternoon," Victoria said smoothly.

Tab nodded again. "Both you and Davis got back Tuesday?" she asked.

"Yes. We both went together and we both came back together."

Tab leaned back in her chair. "Ah," she said softly.

And just like that, Victoria knew. She fucking knew. And for the first time in a long time, Victoria felt something she never allowed herself to feel. Panic. But she was Victoria Hart, and Victoria didn't panic. So, she swallowed it down.

Without breaking eye contact, Tab said, "Well, glad to hear all is well. Are we done here, because I have a lot of things to get to today."

Victoria saw red. She knew what Tab was doing. She was taunting her. Testing how far she could push. Victoria's lips curled into a smirk, but her blood was boiling.

"No, actually, we're not done. You're still acting off, and I'm so serious when I say I can't have this attitude in the office, so cut the bullshit, Tab. Stop this little facade."

Tab's jaw tightened. "Oh, I'm the one bullshitting? Are you kidding me?"

Victoria's pulse spiked.

"Victoria, are you really sitting here, with a straight face, telling me that I'm the one putting up a facade?"

Victoria didn't move.

Tab let the silence sit between them for a moment. "You are unbelievable."

And at that moment, Victoria felt it. The ground beneath her was crumbling. She had lost control. The energy between them was thick, about to ignite.

"Let's just lay this shit out, Tab. Because obviously, you have something to say, and you need to say it."

Tab let out a long breath before she finally looked Victoria in the eyes. "V, I've been nothing but a good friend to you. I would never do anything to hurt you. I love you. But you? You lied to me."

Victoria blinked, her expression unreadable.

"I trusted you, V. I've told you every deep, dark secret. And for you to look me in the face and lie to me?" Tab shook her head, tears filling her eyes. "It hurts."

Victoria stayed still.

Tabitha inhaled sharply. "Do you even see me as your friend? Or do you just see me as some dumb bitch who can't hold down a relationship and is beneath you?"

The words stung. Victoria swallowed, shifting slightly in place. "Tab…"

"Victoria, I know you weren't in Lafayette. Why would you lie to me?"

Victoria forced herself to stay composed, but she could feel the blood draining from her face. What did Tab know? How much did she know? "What are you talking about, Tab?"

"Don't do that. Don't sit there and pretend like you don't know what I'm talking about. Are we seriously doing this, Victoria? Are you seriously gonna sit there and lie to my face?"

Victoria's mind raced. She had to stay in control. Keep her story straight.

"After our conversation ended, you know, the one where you yelled at me to leave your neighborhood, I was parked at the edge of the street and I turned down your street to leave out; just as you instructed me to do, and that's when I saw food being delivered to your home. And Davis answered the door," Tab said with deep conviction.

Victoria's vision blurred. She was caught. Her carefully crafted double life was cracking.

Tab's voice softened just slightly, but her eyes burned with betrayal. "And when you called me, I could hear background noise. It sounded like you were maybe in a bathroom, but I could hear faint music playing."

Victoria could barely breathe.

"Victoria, I know that you weren't at home with Davis."

Victoria's entire body locked up. Her pulse roared in her ears. Tabitha stared her down, waiting. Begging for an answer.

"Please, Victoria. Tell me what's going on."

Victoria's lips parted, "I'm sorry." That was all she could say.

Tab's face twisted in pain. "That's all you have to say to me?"

Victoria could barely think. The walls were closing in. Victoria grabbed her purse, her hands shaking. "I… I have to go."

Tab snapped. She stepped in front of Victoria, blocking the door. "So that's it? You're just gonna leave and not say a damn thing?"

Victoria looked at the friend she had betrayed and lied to. And she couldn't do it. She couldn't tell another lie. "I love you, Tab," she whispered. "And I'm sorry."

Then she pushed past her. And she ran out of the office, away from the truth. But she knew that this was far from over.

＊ ＊ ＊ ＊

Victoria burst through the doors of the office building, the sudden rush of warm air colliding against her skin barely registering as her mind raced wildly. The moment she reached her car, she yanked open the door and hurled her bag onto the passenger seat with such force it nearly toppled onto the floor.

She didn't know where she was going; she simply needed to escape from the walls closing in around her. She had crafted an empire built on lies, perfectly balanced deceptions that allowed her to be everything to everyone: a loyal wife, an unstoppable executive, a seductive lover. But the delicate threads binding it all together were unraveling faster than she could mend them.

The pressure to maintain the illusion had become unbearable, suffocating. The conversation with Tab had stripped away the disguise, exposing the fractures she had so carefully hidden. Every carefully rehearsed lie, every calculated risk, was collapsing inward, threatening to bury her beneath the wreckage of her own making.

Victoria's vision blurred, the road before her becoming indistinct as her eyes filled with unshed tears. She swerved sharply onto an empty side street, jerking the car to an abrupt halt. *Get it together, Victoria,* she whispered, her voice hoarse and unsteady. But the command fell flat, powerless against the tidal wave of emotions engulfing her.

With trembling hands, she reached for her phone, her thumb hovering uncertainly over Tab's contact. Her stomach twisted with dread and guilt, shame coursing through her veins.

Victoria's thumb finally pressed CALL, each ring echoing ominously until Tab's concerned voice broke through the unbearable silence.

"Victoria, is everything alright?"

"Tab…I'm sorry," Victoria choked out, her voice barely above a whisper.

Tab hesitated briefly, her tone softening even further. "Victoria, where are you? Please talk to me. Tell me what's going on. I've never seen you like this."

Victoria clutched the phone like a lifeline. "Are you on your way home?"

"Yes, I'm heading home now," Tab replied gently. "Are you okay to drive?"

Victoria hesitated. "Yeah, I just need to talk. I need to come over."

"Okay, babes, come over. Take your time," Tab said soothingly. "I love you, V."

Victoria's heart clenched at the sincerity in Tab's words. "I love you too," she whispered softly, ending the call with a shaky breath. She stared numbly ahead, the weight of her lies pressing heavily upon her shoulders. The mask she had worn for so long was revealing the frightened woman beneath.

# Control 26
## Spilling Secrets, Losing Control

Victoria pulled up to Tab's condo. Before she could raise her hand to knock, the door swung open. Tab stood there, and without a word, she opened her arms, and Victoria collapsed into them. Tab led her to the couch, never letting go. Even as they sat, she kept her arms wrapped around her.

"I'm here, V," Tabitha whispered. "Whenever you're ready to talk. Take your time."

Victoria closed her eyes and drew a deep breath and slowly exhaled. "Tab, there's so much going on, I don't even know where to start."

Tab reached for her hand, giving it a reassuring squeeze. "Start from the beginning."

Victoria exhaled shakily. "I'm unhappy, Tab."

Tab didn't flinch. She just waited, her grip steady.

"I love Davis. I really do. I need you to know that first. He's a good man. A great husband. He provides for me, takes care of me and supports me. Davis is predictable and for years, I thought that's what I needed. He's safe, but something's missing, and somewhere along the way, it stopped being enough."

Tab's brows drew together slightly. "Not enough in what way?"

Victoria continued, "I've been living my life on auto-pilot, running my business, playing the role of the perfect wife, trying to hold it all together. But inside, I feel empty. And then, I met Thomas."

Tab's entire body stiffened. "Who the hell is Thomas?"

Victoria hesitated, swallowing hard. "He's someone I met a while back. It started out as innocent, you know. Just a conversation. But there was this energy between us, something I haven't felt in years. And I chased it. He's everything. He's magnetic, charming, and sexy. He makes me feel alive again. Like I'm actually seen. And the sex…" She gave a bitter laugh. "It's unreal. It's consuming. I can't stop, and I don't want to."

Tabitha's gaze locked onto Victoria's as if she were seeing her for the first time.

Victoria continued. "He's everything Davis isn't—passionate, spontaneous, and dominant. He takes control in a way that makes me feel like I can finally let go. I don't have to be strong with him. I don't have to have all the answers. I can just… be."

Tabitha's voice finally broke through the silence. "So, when you told me you were with Davis in Lafayette, you were actually with Thomas?"

Victoria hesitated for a moment before nodding. "Yes."

Tabitha leaned forward. "Where?"

Victoria swallowed hard. "At a hotel. Downtown."

"Okay," Tabitha said slowly, exhaling through her nose. "So, where did you tell Davis you were?"

Victoria looked away. "I told him I was at a work conference in Tennessee with you."

Tabitha leaned back slightly as if trying to process the weight of what Victoria had just admitted. "You put me in your lie?" she asked.

"I panicked, Tab. He was asking me questions, and I just thought it would make the most sense. You're my business partner. If I was on a work trip, it would be with you."

Tabitha's head tilted slightly, disbelief clouding her features. "You didn't just lie to him. You made me a part of it. Jesus, V, what the hell?"

"Tab, I never wanted it to be like this. But Thomas…" Victoria's voice softened. "Thomas makes me feel seen and desired in a way I didn't even realize I was missing. With him, I can be vulnerable. I don't have to be perfect. I can just be his woman."

Tab shook her head. "V, this isn't just some reckless mistake. This is a full-blown affair."

Victoria nodded slowly. "I know."

Tabitha's tone remained serious. "What happens if Davis finds out and all of this falls apart? You're playing with fire, V."

"I know," Victoria whispered. "But what if I don't want to stop?"

Tabitha's voice was firm now. "Then you need to figure out what the hell you really want. Because one way or another, this is going to explode."

And Victoria knew, with every fiber of her being, that she was right.

Tabitha stared at Victoria, her mind racing, struggling to grasp what she had just heard. Of all the things she thought Victoria might confess, this was the furthest thing from what she had imagined. Her best friend, the woman who always had her life perfectly together, was living a double life.

Tabitha rubbed her temples, exhaling sharply. "So, who is this Thomas guy? Where's he from? What does he do for work? Is he married? Does he have kids? Where does he live? I have so many questions."

Victoria sighed. "I met him a few months ago, totally by chance. I had just left the gym and stopped off at a nearby café, and that's where I met him; he had struck up a conversation with me at the café. It was so effortless. He wasn't trying too hard, he wasn't being corny, he was just himself. He had this confidence that drew me in immediately."

Tabitha folded her arms, watching Victoria closely. "Okay, but that doesn't tell me who he is, Victoria. You're talking like a woman smitten, and it's scaring the hell out of me. Give me the basics. Who is he?"

Victoria sighed. "He's from Miami, originally, but he's been here in Atlanta for a while now. He's an entrepreneur. He's into investments, real estate stuff, that kind of thing."

Tabitha raised an eyebrow, suspicion gnawing at her insides. "So, basically, he does whatever the hell he wants and makes his own schedule?"

A tiny, ironic smile tugged at the corners of Victoria's lips. "Pretty much."

Tabitha scoffed. "So, he's charming, makes money, has game, and probably has access to women throwing themselves at him left and right."

Victoria tensed slightly but nodded. "Yes, but it's different with me, Tab."

Tabitha narrowed her eyes, feeling her chest tighten with a mix of protectiveness and anger. "Is it? Because it sounds like he's the type that can have any woman he wants. And that means he's used to having women. Is he married, Victoria?"

Victoria shook her head immediately. "No. No wife. No kids."

Tab studied her, her concern deepening by the second. "And you believe that?"

"Yes," Victoria said firmly. "He's not married, Tab."

"Okay, fine. But how long has this been going on?"

"Our first hookup was a couple of months ago, and I've seen him a few times since then."

Tab's mouth fell open slightly. "A couple of months?"

Victoria nodded, bracing for the reaction she knew was coming.

"Jesus, V. I thought this was some fling. A spur-of-the-moment mistake. But you've been carrying this on for months?"

"It wasn't supposed to be like this, Tab."

Tabitha shook her head. "How the hell are you keeping this from Davis? You run a whole business. You have a husband who adores you. When the hell do you even have time to be with him?"

"That's the crazy part. Somehow, I've managed to balance it. I've been careful. Davis doesn't suspect a thing," Victoria said.

Tabitha gave her a skeptical look. "Are you sure about that?"

Victoria flashed a confused look. "I was sure… until now."

Tab sighed. "Victoria, I have to ask, and don't get mad at me, but are you safe?"

Victoria's brows wrinkled in confusion. "Safe? What do you mean?"

"I mean… you don't really know this guy, V. Yeah, you know what he's told you, but do you really know him? What if he's lying to you? What if he's dangerous? What if he has a whole other life somewhere? What if he's watching your every move?"

Victoria shook her head vehemently. "Tab, Thomas isn't like that."

"You don't know that."

"Tab, listen to me. I know what I'm doing. Thomas isn't some creep, he isn't some scam artist, and he damn sure isn't a psycho."

Tab exhaled slowly. "You're falling for him, aren't you?"

Victoria's lips parted slightly. She didn't answer right away, but the look on her face was telling enough. "I—"

Tab cut her off. "Don't try to deny it, V. I can see it all over you. You're glowing when you talk about him. You're defending him, and willing to risk your marriage for him."

"Tab, it's not that simple."

"Then make it simple, Victoria. Because right now, this is a disaster waiting to happen. You can't juggle all of this forever. Something is going to break. And when it does, are you ready for what comes next?"

The question hung in the air like a final blow, stripping away whatever half-truths or justifications Victoria might have clung to. She knew this was unsustainable. Yet the thrill, the hunger for Thomas, it all outweighed the looming consequences, at least for the moment.

"I don't know," Victoria whispered. "I really don't."

"Well, you better figure it out, V. Because this… you… everything you've built… it's all on the line."

Tabitha let out a long, frustrated sigh. "Victoria, this is dangerous. Davis doesn't deserve this, you know that, right?"

"God, I know, Tab. Do you think I'm proud of this? I didn't want this, it just happened."

The admission hung between them, betraying the storm of emotions swirling beneath her calm facade.

"Oversleeping just happens. Stubbing your toe just happens. But an ongoing affair? No, Victoria. That doesn't *just happen*, that's intentional."

Her tone carried both incredulity and sorrow, the kind that comes from seeing a friend hurt herself through choices made not by fate, but by deliberate action.

"V, you know I'm only looking out for you. I don't know Thomas. He could be an amazing guy. Or he could be a piece of shit, I don't know. But I do know that you're playing with fire, and I just want to make sure you're protecting yourself."

Tabitha paused, then leveled a serious look at Victoria. "Do you use protection?"

Victoria's eyes flickered with something unreadable before she answered, "Yes. He always makes sure he practices safe sex."

Tab closed her eyes briefly, her lips pressing into a thin line as though she was relieved to hear her answer.

Victoria continued. "Thomas always thinks ahead."

Tabitha saw the glow on Victoria's face and it infuriated her. "V, do you even hear yourself right now? Because I feel like I'm talking to someone I don't even know."

Victoria's smile faded. "Tab—"

Her attempt to interject was soft, almost pleading, but it was quickly silenced by the rising tide of Tabitha's insistence.

"No, listen to me!" Tab snapped. "I don't know shit about being married, but I do know that you took vows. And correct me if I'm wrong, but shouldn't you be doing everything in your power to make your marriage work?"

Victoria let out a dry laugh and rolled her eyes. "Tab, come on. You act like I haven't tried. But Davis is so boring and predictable now. He acts like life is just perfect, like everything is fine when it's not. And I don't know, maybe I need more. Maybe I deserve more." Her tone was a blend of defiance and despair.

Tab sat forward, her eyes dark with anger. "You deserve more? Davis deserves better than this bullshit you're feeding him. That man would throw himself in front of a bus for you. If he's not pleasing you, did you even try to communicate that to him? Have you thought about a sex therapist? Or even telling him what you need?" The question was laden with the weight of all the unspoken frustrations Tabitha had harbored for far too long.

Victoria snorted. "A sex therapist. Are you kidding me? No therapist in the world can magically make a man better at fucking, Tab. It's more than that. Davis is just… Davis. Safe, predictable and complacent."

Tab bit her lip so hard she almost tasted blood. Spoiled. That's what Victoria was. Completely spoiled by a good man who worshipped the ground she walked on, and she didn't even realize it. "Victoria," she said carefully, "if you're that unhappy, why don't you just leave and divorce him? Let him find someone who will actually love him the way he deserves to be loved."

Victoria's head snapped up, and her face twisted in anger. "First of all, I do love him. He's my husband, and I love him. He's my best friend." Her retort was fierce, a mix of indignation and hurt.

Tab's face was unreadable. "Best friends don't do this to each other."

Victoria exhaled sharply. "You don't understand because you've never been married, Tab." Her voice carried a note of wounded pride, an attempt to justify the pain and complexity of her choices by drawing a line between experience and naivety.

"And thank God for that!" Tab shot back. "Because if this is what marriage is, I don't want any part of it."

The room was heavy with silence. Victoria's hands trembled as she gripped the armrest of the couch.

Tab sighed and leaned back. "Look, I get it. I get that you want excitement and passion. But what happens when you and Thomas get bored with each other?"

Victoria's throat tightened. "That's not going to happen." The denial was immediate and reflexive.

Tab laughed bitterly. "You sure about that? Because even the best player at this game can get sloppy, start to slip and get caught up in the lies."

Victoria's chest rose and fell rapidly. "I've got it under control."

Tab shook her head. "No, you don't."

Silence stretched between them. And then Tab asked the one question Victoria wasn't ready to hear. "Does Thomas even know you're married?"

Victoria's stomach twisted into knots. The silence that ensued was pregnant with dread, each heartbeat a reminder of the fragile web of lies she had spun.

Tab leaned forward. "Does he?"

"No." Her voice was quiet, almost inaudible.

"You're telling me this man has no idea you're someone's wife?"

Victoria shook her head slowly.

"Wow. Okay. So, what does he know about you? Because from where I'm sitting, it doesn't sound like much."

Victoria hesitated. "I told him I was a flight attendant." Regret edged her voice.

"A flight attendant? You told him you were a damn flight attendant, Victoria?!" The shock in her tone was unmistakable; a mixture of disbelief and frustration at the lengths to which Victoria had gone to fabricate a life that wasn't her own.

"I had to say something," Victoria snapped. "I wasn't going to tell him the truth. I needed something believable, something that explained why I could only see him sometimes."

"Oh my God, Victoria, so you've been feeding this man a whole damn fantasy? Do you even know his last name? His real story?"

Victoria glared at her. "Of course I do. I know plenty about him." Her retort was sharp.

"But does he know plenty about you?" Tab shot back. "Because this is a two-way street, and it sounds like you've built an entire fake persona for this man. You don't even truly trust him. Jesus Christ, V. You're not just cheating. You're lying to everybody—Davis, Thomas, and me." The exclamation was raw and unfiltered, a moment of brutal honesty that left no room for excuses or justifications.

Victoria's stomach knotted up. "I did what I had to do."

Tab's face twisted in disgust. "No, you did what you wanted to do. And you keep telling yourself that you have it all under control, but guess what, babes? The lies are piling up, and one day, they're gonna come crashing down. And when they do?" She shook her head. "You'll have no one to blame but yourself."

Victoria felt her breathing grow shallow. "Tab…" The word was barely a whisper.

Tab held up a hand. "Don't. Just… don't." Her plea was firm, almost pleading, as if she were trying to stop a runaway train hurtling toward inevitable destruction.

Then Tab whispered, "Who even are you anymore?"

Victoria couldn't answer. Because for the first time, she didn't know either.

In that moment of desolation, the mirror of her life reflected back not the confident woman she once was, but a stranger, a mosaic of secrets and half-truths, questioning the very essence of who she had become.

# Control 25
## In His World Now

Victoria lay motionless in bed, her eyes tracing shadows across the ceiling as if they could untangle the chaos of the past twenty-four hours. She exhaled sharply and rolled onto her side. The other side of the bed lay empty, a reminder of the distance between her façade and her private despair. Davis had kissed her forehead that morning before heading to work, a tender act she barely acknowledged as she pretended to sleep. Today she couldn't muster the energy to play the doting wife. The pretense felt too heavy.

Her phone vibrated insistently on the nightstand. With a reluctant sigh, she reached for it and saw Tab's name flash across the screen.

**Tabitha:** *Not much for you to do at the office today. With everything weighing on you, just take the rest of the week off and do some self-care. I got things covered here. Just take care of yourself.*

A gentle warmth spread through Victoria at the sight of Tab's message, a reminder that even in the midst of her self-inflicted turmoil, someone cared enough to worry.

**Victoria:** *Ok, thanks for holding everything down. Call me if you need me.*

She jumped up and went to retrieve her burner phone, her fingers closing around the small, inconspicuous object.

For a moment, she hesitated, then pressed the power button, watching as the screen flickered. She hovered over Thomas' name, as Tab's earlier admonishing words crept into her thoughts like an unwanted whisper: *You don't even know where he lives, V. That's dangerous. What if he's married? What if he's feeding you the same lies you're feeding him?*

Victoria bit her lip, could Thomas be another illusion? She told herself no, but the doubt gnawed anyway.

The phone barely rang before his deep voice washed over her. "Well, hello, Ms. Sheena."

A warm rush flooded through her. She smiled, twirling a strand of hair. "Hi, Thomas. How are you?"

"I'm well, baby girl. How about yourself?"

She hesitated. "I've seen better days, but I'm making it."

His tone shifted subtly, laced with concern. "Oh? What's wrong?"

"Just life," she replied vaguely. "I can tell you more about it later. I was wondering if you were home and maybe wanted some company because I miss you and need to take a load off."

He chuckled under his breath. "Umm, yeah, sure. I'm not home right now. I'm out handling some business, but I can wrap it up and head home." There was a charged pause before he added, "Or I can just come to you?"

A sudden, tight knot formed in her stomach as Tab's earlier warning echoed in her mind: You don't even know where he lives. The irony of it all was not lost on her. "Nah, driving actually helps me relax. I don't mind coming to you."

"Okay then," he said smoothly. "Let me finish up here, and I'll drop the location."

"Okay, see you soon then," she replied, her voice light with an excitement that belied the storm inside.

"Can't wait," he murmured, leaving a trail of anticipation in his wake.

She ended the call and reclined against the pillows, her mind a swirling canvas of conflicting emotions. Her phone vibrated with the location info from Thomas. Victoria quickly copied the address and pasted it into Google Maps. Her eyes lit up with admiration as she zoomed in on the neighborhood. Brookhaven—affluent, quiet, nothing like a run-down bachelor pad. Not that she expected anything less. She smirked to herself as she dressed to head over to his place.

✳ ✳ ✳ ✳

The loft building was modern and sleek, with exposed brick and large industrial-style windows that made it feel quietly luxurious. She parked, heart pounding, not from nerves but anticipation. She was stepping into his world, more real than any hotel room.

"Hey, beautiful," Thomas said, leaning casually against the door frame.

She smiled. "Hey you."

"Come in," he said, stepping aside to invite her into his space.

Victoria took a deep breath as she walked in. The loft opened before her—brick walls, tall windows, modern furniture, sleek counters. Vinyl, books, and photos gave it life.

Victoria turned to him, her eyes wide with genuine admiration. "Wow, Thomas. Your place is really nice. Is this one of your properties, or do you reside here permanently?"

He chuckled as he shook his head. "Nah, this is all mine.

"So, this is where you bring all your women?" she teased.

He laughed. "Yeah, pretty much."

She smacked his arm playfully. "You better be joking."

He pulled her close, eyes dark. "I'm single… until the right woman locks me down."

Her breath caught. His voice sent a shiver through her. She pressed against him. "I missed you," she whispered.

His hands slid down her waist. "Yeah?"

She nodded, then kissed him, slow and deep.

He groaned against her lips. "Damn. Straight to it, huh? You don't fuck around."

"I'm just happy to see you."

His eyes darkened with desire as he kissed her again. "Come on, have a seat and make yourself comfortable. Can I get you anything to drink?"

"No, I'm good."

He vanished into the kitchen, then came back grinning with his hands behind his back.

"What are you doing?" she asked.

"Well, earlier you said you were feeling down, and I wanted to cheer you up. So, I got something for you."

She was intrigued. "What is it?"

"Close your eyes," he instructed softly.

She hesitated for a moment. "Oh my God, Thomas. If this is some kind of prank, I swear—"

He laughed. "Just trust me."

With a dramatic sigh, she closed her eyes. "Alright."

"Okay," he said, placing something in her lap. "Open."

She opened her eyes. "A helmet?" She turned it over in her hands. "Uh, thank you?"

"Girl, you are so funny. Put it on. We're going for a ride on my motorcycle."

"A ride?"

"Yup. Your man is taking you on his bike. And I got something special lined up for you."

"I've never ridden a motorcycle before," she admitted, nervously.

He tilted her chin. "You're safe with me. Do you trust me?"

"Yes. One hundred percent."

He kissed her softly. "Good. Now let's go."

Victoria exhaled a deep, excited breath as she carefully slid the helmet over her head. She had no idea what Thomas had planned, but one thing was clear. Today, she was his. And she couldn't wait to see where this ride would take her.

The motorcycle rumbled beneath them as Victoria tightened her arms around his waist, pressing herself against his back. The wind whipped through her hair, and for the first time in what felt like forever, she allowed herself to truly let go.

Thomas's careful presence made every second more precious. As she clung to him, he reached down with one steady hand, gently rubbing her fingers. His touch sent little sparks of warmth racing up her arms, and she felt an overwhelming rush of tenderness mixed with desire.

Thomas slowed the bike at a secluded park, a calm hidden gem. He parked near a grassy clearing and smiled back at her.

"Hold on, baby girl, let me help you," he said.

"I could've gotten down myself, you know," she said.

"I know. But I like having my hands on you."

"That was the best bike experience. I've never felt so alive. I want to go again." She laughed.

Thomas squeezed her hand. "That was just part one. I brought you here for a reason."

Curiosity lit in her expression. "Oh yeah? And what's that?"

"A picnic," he said, tone mischievous.

She frowned, scanning the scene. "Correct me if I'm wrong, but don't you need food and a blanket for that?"

Thomas gasped theatrically. "Wow, genius."

She rolled her eyes, nudging his arm. "I'm serious. Where's the picnic?"

At that moment, a sleek black sedan pulled up to the curb. A man stepped out, opened the trunk, and unloaded picnic essentials: a burgundy blanket, matching pillows, a cooler, and a wicker basket stuffed with treats. Thomas's eyes sparkled with satisfaction as he accepted the delivery.

Victoria watched as he carried it to the clearing, smoothing the blanket and arranging everything with care. Victoria's eyes drank in every detail, stunned by the thoughtfulness of it all.

While they ate, laughter and soft conversation filled the space as they exchanged stories about bad dates, childhood pranks, and even played a silly game where they fed each other bites of food with their eyes closed, trying to guess the flavors. Every shared laugh deepened the connection between them, and Victoria felt herself drifting into a rare state of contentment.

Thomas reached out and gently wiped a crumb from Victoria's lip. "You're so beautiful, Sheena."

"You're just saying that," she whispered.

"Nah," he replied firmly. "I mean it."

Their faces came closer, until the space between them was scarcely more than a breath.

"This is the best day I've had in a long time," she whispered.

"Me too, baby."

In that quiet spot, she let herself sink into him, seeing freedom in his eyes, his smile, his touch.

✳ ✳ ✳ ✳

Back at the loft, Victoria stepped inside and was immediately welcomed by the lingering traces of their previous encounter.

"Get comfortable, baby," he murmured against her neck, his lips teasing her skin with a promise of more intimacy yet to come.

"I am comfortable."

Thomas tilted his head. "I mean really comfortable"

She shivered as his hands grazed her waist, his fingers slipping under her top.

He kissed her collarbone, murmuring, "I can't wait to taste you all night."

Each word set her on fire.

His fingers trailed lower, moving deliberately against the fabric of her clothes, right where he knew she ached for him the most. A soft moan escaped her lips, betraying the control she was desperately trying to maintain. And then reality pressed in. As much as every fiber of her being screamed for more, she knew she couldn't stay in this cocoon of passion forever. Davis was waiting and she couldn't risk it. Not tonight.

With a regretful sigh, she took his hands and gently pulled them away. "Thomas, I have to go."

He blinked, momentarily caught off guard by the sudden shift. "What?"

"I have to get back home."

"Why? I thought you were staying longer."

"I wish I could, but—"

"You don't wish hard enough," he snapped. "I want you tonight and I've been longing for you. You're really gonna leave me hanging?"

She hated when he looked at her like that, like she was betraying him by leaving, as if she owed him more time than she could ever give. She pivoted quickly. "I took on another flight and I have to get ready."

"Another flight?" he echoed, the disbelief evident in his tone.

"I have bills, baby. I have to work."

"You'd never have to work if you were mine."

Victoria's stomach flipped at the sound of his words, the way he said it, with such conviction. She forced a smile, trying to play it cool despite the ache it caused. "I appreciate that. But I like to earn what I get. I like making my own money."

"I get that, but I'd take care of you."

"I know," she said softly.

After a pause, Victoria continued softly, "I love flying. It's fun." Her voice held a mix of honesty as she reached for his hands, squeezing them. "But I'll be back."

Thomas exhaled, shaking his head with a bittersweet smile. "I bet you will."

"I want to ride again."

He raised a brow and smirked. "The bike or me?"

Victoria looked at him with an evil grin and said, "both."

Thomas wrapped his arms around her waist, pulling her flush against him in one last, lingering embrace. "You know I got you, baby girl. I'll take you riding whenever you want."

Thomas brushed his thumb over her cheek. "Be safe driving back home," he said.

"I will."

As she walked to the door, she could still feel his eyes on her. She felt the weight of the lie she had told, a small but searing fracture in the perfect moment they had shared. She left the loft with her heart pounding and her body aching for him. But she had no choice. She had to go back to the life she had built, to the reality she could no longer ignore.

# Control 24
## I Don't Know Her, But I Want Her

The next morning, Thomas woke up restless. Sheena had left with a kiss and a smile, and silence that lingered. Every glance, every laugh, every whisper of his name felt electric. But beneath it was all discomfort. She was beautiful, magnetic, but also ghostlike.

And Thomas wasn't stupid. He knew when something didn't sit right. Sheena glowed, but nothing felt solid. She hid behind excuses—flights, assignments—and only came around when she felt like it.

*Who the hell are you, Sheena Wells?* He searched Instagram, TikTok, X, and Facebook; nothing. No photos, no tags, no posts. For someone who supposedly lived a glamorous life, she had no online presence. It didn't add up.

Frustrated, he dropped the phone onto the bed and stared at the ceiling. He needed help; someone with connections. One name came to mind: Ryan Johnson. Ryan served in the Air Force, but they were good friends that went way back. Ryan retired from the Air Force a while ago, and currently works as a Safety Inspector with the FAA, with reach into the airline industry. If anyone could quietly pull up information on a flight attendant, it was him.

He found Ryan's contact and hit dial.

"Well, I'll be damned. Is that the ghost of Petty Officer Thomas Carter?" Ryan's voice rang out. "Calling me before nine in the morning? Bro, did hell freeze over?"

Thomas chuckled. "Shut up, man. You act like I don't check in on you."

"You don't," Ryan fired back. "The last time you called me was when your drunk ass locked yourself outta your apartment at three a.m. in boxers and a damn hoodie."

"I wasn't drunk," Thomas grumbled.

"You were slurring, bro. You said the doorknob was 'judging you.'"

Thomas laughed despite himself. "Alright, alright. I deserve that."

"So, what's up? You in jail? Got a secret love child? They got you locked down in the psych ward at the VA?"

"None of that," Thomas said. "I just… need a favor."

"Oh boy," Ryan said. "You got that tone. Who is she?"

Thomas hesitated.

"I fuckin' knew it," Ryan barked. "Alright, lay it on me. What's her name? What did she do? Break your heart or steal your credit cards?"

"Sheena Wells," Thomas said quietly. "I think she's playing me man. I think she might be lying about who she is."

Ryan whistled. "Damn. Already? She at least fine enough to lie to you?"

"She's beyond fine. She's… different. Feels real when I'm with her. But I can't shake the feeling something's off."

"Go on."

"She said she's a flight attendant. Flies all over the place. But I never get a straight answer about her schedule. No social media, no tags, nothing. And she only hits me up when it works for her. Never the other way around."

"That's suspect," Ryan agreed. "So, you want me to do a little digging."

"Yeah. See if she even works for Delta."

"Alright," Ryan said. "What do you have on her? I'm gonna need more than a name, Romeo."

"Name and birthday. That's all I got," Thomas said hesitantly.

"You serious?"

"Dead serious."

"You falling for a woman you don't even know the address of?" Ryan laughed. "Damn, bro, I thought Navy boys were smarter than that."

"Just shut up and help me," Thomas growled.

Ryan chuckled. "Alright. What's her birthday?"

"September 1, 1994."

"Oh no," Ryan said, dragging out the words. "Not a Virgo."

"What's wrong with Virgos?"

Ryan let out a bitter, theatrical sigh. "Man, my first wife was a Virgo. Calculated. Cold with it. Cheated with surgical precision. She was methodical, bro. Planned her shit out like she was leading a covert op. She'd cheat, cover her tracks, smile in your face, and still pack your lunch for work like she was Betty fuckin' Crocker."

Thomas burst out laughing. "You gotta let that go."

"I will never let it go," Ryan said firmly. "That woman had me in therapy for two years and still had the nerve to ask if we could be friends. Hell no. Virgos are sneaky good liars, bro. Stealth level: Navy SEAL."

Thomas laughed. "You're really holding a whole zodiac grudge?"

"You damn right I am. Star signs, red flags, shoe size, I don't care. I got trauma."

"Alright, alright. I'll tread carefully."

"You better," Ryan muttered. "Alright. What does she look like?"

"Brown skin, about five-six, curvy, silky, curly hair. Eyes that make you forget your damn name. And a smile that'll have you pulling out your wallet and your social security number."

"You down bad," Ryan teased.

"Yeah," Thomas admitted. "I might be."

"Okay, well… best-case scenario, she's just private as hell. Worst case? She's married. Or on the run. Or in witness protection."

"Why are those your default options?"

"Experience," Ryan said grimly. "You meet enough women in airport lounges, you get a feel for the red flags."

"I don't know, man. She got me feeling things I haven't felt in a long-ass time."

Ryan sighed. "And that's why you're in trouble. That's how it starts. Next thing you know, she's got your passwords, your credit cards, and your cousin's Netflix login."

"Not the Netflix," Thomas joked.

"I'm telling you, it's a slippery slope," Ryan laughed. "Alright, so all I've got is name and DOB. Anything else at all? A coworker's name? Her crew number?"

"Nope. Just stories about layovers, reroutes, and last-minute assignments. And she always dodges when I ask questions. Gets vague real fast."

Ryan hummed. "That's a big red flag, my guy. If she was really flying that often, her schedule would be chaotic, yeah, but she wouldn't be allergic to conversation. Flight attendants talk. It's part of the job."

"You think she's lying?"

"I think," Ryan said carefully, "you're either dating a very private woman... or a damn CIA operative."

"I'd actually feel better if she was CIA," Thomas joked.

"Yeah, because at least then the lies would be government approved."

They both laughed, but the tension hung in the air.

Ryan was quiet for a beat. "Alright. Gimme a couple days. I'll put in a few calls. Might poke around the Delta roster, see if she's in their system. If she's real, I'll find her."

"Thanks, man."

"And Thomas?"

"Yeah?"

"If this chick turns out to be a real one, and you end up married with kids and a dog and a white picket fence, just remember to name your first kid Ryan. That's all I ask."

Thomas grinned. "Only if it's a girl."

"I'll take it."

After hanging up, Thomas sat staring at the ceiling, gut twisted with anticipation. He gripped his phone. Sheena Wells wasn't who she said she was. The thought settled bitter in his chest. *I have to know who you really are, Sheena.* The vow burned in him. He would uncover the truth, no matter what.

Thomas opened his text message thread with Sheena. Every "hey baby," and "thinking of you" replayed in his head. She knew how to keep him dangling. And now he realized he wasn't the only one at the table.

He needed her. After that picnic, after the way her arms tightened around him on the bike… how the hell was he supposed to just go back to life as usual. But every time he reached for her, she slipped away with missed calls, unanswered texts, and excuses. His patience was thinning.

He stared down at his phone before finally calling Sheena. The phone rang once. Twice. Three times. Voicemail. He didn't even wait to hear her message before ending the call and tossing the phone. His jaw clenched tight. "Don't start this shit, Sheena," he muttered. He picked up the phone again and typed a text.

**Thomas:** *Hey, baby, call me. I'm missing you.*

He hit send and stared. Waited. Watched. Nothing. Not the little dots. Not the read receipt. Not even the illusion of her typing something back. Just silence.

Thomas wasn't built to wait. Navy taught him strategy and control. Right now, she held all the control. His gut was screaming. He smirked bitterly. *You think you can outplay me?* Once he had answers, there would be no more hiding.

# Control 23
## Fucked and Found Out

Victoria smiled faintly as Davis hummed by the dresser, sliding into a polo and adjusting his collar with practiced precision. She admired his steadiness. Rolling onto her stomach, she teased, "You're in a good mood."

Davis smirked. "That makes two of us. You were glowing last night. Whatever happened at work must've been damn good."

She bit her lip, feigning a shrug, though her body still thrummed with the memory of Thomas.

Davis sat on the bed and kissed her forehead. "I was thinking. We should get away; it's been a while since we've done a getaway. How about a weekend in Savannah? Just the two of us."

"Savannah?" she echoed.

"Yeah. We'll drive down tomorrow and stay until Monday. We can take a stroll through the Riverfront, eat some good food, and visit that jazz bar you love. Just us."

Victoria's mind spun. A weekend away meant no Thomas, but it also kept Davis close and unsuspecting. She smiled, looping her arms around his neck. "That sounds perfect."

"Good. I'll book the hotel today."

"Sounds great, baby."

"I love you," he whispered.

She met his gaze, steady. "Love you more."

Davis gathered his things and left, the garage door rumbling shut behind him. Victoria laid back against the pillows, her earlier smile fading. Savannah would be the perfect cover; a trip that kept Davis content and unwary. But her thoughts drifted to Thomas. That hunger for him still pulsed, impossible to quiet. As long as no one found out, she had nothing to fear.

With Davis gone, Victoria had the day to herself. Like most days with down time, she started with cardio and exercise at her home gym. She threw on her playlist and cleared her mind as she passed the time with a rigorous workout routine.

After cooling down, she blended a smoothie and checked her phone. Nothing. Then she picked up the burner phone and saw some missed calls and a text message that read:

**Thomas:** *Hey, baby, call me. I'm missing you.*

Her lips curved into a smirk. He thought she was out of town, just like she had told him. But she wasn't. She was right here, and she didn't want to rest. She wanted him. Her fingers barely hovered over his name as she hit call. The phone barely rang twice.

"Sheena, baby girl," Thomas drawled.

"Hey, you."

Thomas exhaled. "Damn, I miss you. Where are you?"

"Atlanta," she lied smoothly. "My flight got canceled because of a mechanical issue."

There was a beat of silence on the line. "Oh yeah?" he asked.

"Yeah. I was stuck at the airport for hours before they finally called it."

Thomas raised a brow where he sat. "What kind of mechanical issue?"

Victoria blinked. The question caught her off guard. "Huh?"

"The mechanical issue. What was wrong with the plane?"

Shit. "Oh, um…" she stammered, buying time. "I wasn't really paying attention."

"You weren't paying attention?" Thomas echoed, amusement creeping into his voice. "Isn't that your job? Knowing what's going on with the plane? Communicating that to the crew, passengers… or at least being briefed?"

Victoria's stomach twisted. "Oh, well, I do know what happened. I just don't really feel like going into all that. It was one of those 'better safe than sorry' things. They grounded it. Now I have the day off, so I'm trying to enjoy it."

Thomas didn't answer right away. She was slipping. He let out a low chuckle, shaking his head. "Well, that's good news for me. Since you're in town, I'll come by your place. Spend the day with you."

Victoria's heart stopped. *Absolutely not.* She couldn't let that happen. "Oh, um—" she rushed, "I'm actually already out."

Thomas smirked. Of course she was. "Out where?" he asked.

"Just doing some light shopping," she lied quickly.

Another beat of silence.

"Light shopping?" he repeated, his disbelief barely hidden.

"Yeah," she said, forcing a light laugh. "Just treating myself."

"Uh-huh. Right."

Her pulse thudded in her ears. He knows. He's doubting me. She had to redirect. "So, should I just come to you instead?"

*There it is*, Thomas thought. "Yeah. I'll be waiting."

"See you soon," she murmured.

As soon as the call ended, Victoria rushed into action. She texted Davis a quick excuse about working late, grabbed her purse and burner phone, and headed for the garage, heart thundering.

At the loft, Thomas leaned back with a sly grin, murmuring to himself, *Sheena, you're fine as hell, but I'm about to catch you in your own game.*

By the time Victoria pulled up, she was already lost in anticipation. Thomas was her escape, her secret refuge. She rang the doorbell, and he opened the door bare-chested in a robe.

She barely had time to register the heat in his eyes before he yanked her inside, slamming the door shut behind her. "I see you have—" she started, but before she could finish, Thomas grabbed her waist, spun her, and pressed her up against the door, his lips crashing into hers with unrestrained hunger.

His tongue plunged deep into her mouth, consuming her. His hands roamed down her body, his grip firm and unrelenting. He yanked at the hem of her dress, sliding it up her thighs before pulling it over her head.

"Baby, slow down," she managed to whisper between breaths.

But Thomas wasn't listening. His lips found her neck, sucking hard. His fingers reached behind her, expertly unhooking her bra and sliding it off. He didn't pause, he never hesitated. His hunger was insatiable, his movements rough and urgent. He tugged down her panties and let them drop to the floor, leaving her bare, exposed and trembling.

Victoria gasped as he lifted her effortlessly, wrapping her legs around his waist. He carried her to the oversized sectional, laying her down with a controlled force that sent a rush of heat through her veins.

His mouth was everywhere. His teeth scraped against her sensitive skin, the pain mixed with pleasure in a way that made her toes curl. "Thomas," she moaned.

But he was lost in her. His kisses trailed lower. She squirmed beneath him, anticipating his next move. He spread her thighs wide and his mouth hovered just above where she needed him the most. A trembling ache spread between her thighs in anticipation of his tongue. He rolled his nose and tongue around her outer and inner walls, and then he devoured her. His tongue plunged into her depths with a savage intensity.

Victoria cried out, her back arching off the sofa, her hands clutching at the cushions for some kind of grounding, but there was none. He had full control and she was his to consume.

"Thomas! Thomas, wait!" she gasped.

But he ignored her. He gripped her thighs tighter, holding her down, refusing to let her move away from his mouth, until she was begging, until her body couldn't take it anymore.

Her orgasm hit her like a tidal wave, her body shaking. Before she could even catch her breath, he moved up her body again. "Turn over," he commanded.

She hesitated for a fraction of a second, the intensity in his eyes sending a shiver down her spine. But then she obeyed, rolling onto her stomach, her body still pulsing from the orgasm he just ripped from her. His hands roamed over her ass as he spread her cheeks apart and without hesitation, his tongue found her tight entrance.

"Thomas!" she gasped, her body jolting forward.

He licked her there until she was moaning his name, pressing herself back against his face, wanting, no, needing more. She had never let a man do this before... until she met Thomas. He had her unraveling, breaking every rule she had ever set for herself, and she loved it.

He pulled back just long enough to reach for the condom tucked inside his robe pocket. She barely had time to breathe before he was back, positioning himself at her wet entrance. Victoria cried out, gripping the cushions as he claimed her. His thrusts were slow at first, then grew deeper. He wasn't just fucking her, he was branding her, making her his in a way that left no room for doubt.

The sounds of their bodies colliding filled the loft. Moans and grunts, skin slapping against skin, created a symphony of pure, carnal pleasure. "You're mine," he whispered. "Tell me you're mine."

"I'm yours," she gasped.

That was all it took. With one final thrust, he buried himself deep inside her, groaning as his release hit him, his entire body stiffening before he collapsed on top of her. For a moment, neither of them moved; their bodies tangled together.

Victoria laid beneath him, her mind hazy, her body completely wrecked. She had just given herself to him in every possible way. But as she laid there, Thomas's arms wrapped possessively around her, she couldn't shake the unsettling feeling creeping up her spine. Because as much as she had let him have all of her today, she knew, deep down, that he wanted more, and he wouldn't stop until he had it.

Thomas and Victoria laid side by side in the soft afterglow, silence stretching between them like a fragile thread. "You're so gorgeous," he murmured.

Her stomach flipped. The echo of his earlier words, *you're mine, tell me you're mine,* still throbbed in her head. In the rush of passion, it had thrilled her. Now, in the stillness, it pressed like a weight.

Thomas sat up and stretched. "Damn. I worked up an appetite and I sure could eat."

"Something delicious, I hope," she teased, grateful for the distraction.

They scrolled through food options together, trading jokes until they settled on a particular restaurant. For a moment, it felt almost too domestic and dangerously close to something more than either of them had promised. Shaking it off, Victoria stood and smoothed her hair. "I need to clean up. I'll try to make it quick."

Thomas kissed her lightly and leaned back, hiding the unease flickering just beneath his calm. He sat rigid, the shower hissing in the background like a ticking clock. He thought he could ignore the inconsistencies, but now, after today, her flimsy canceled flight story, the way she fumbled when he pressed, his gut screamed otherwise.

His gaze drifted toward the counter where her car key fob sat. He thought it was odd that she never brought in a bag, but only a single key fob. He stood, the hush of the shower drumming like a countdown. Without letting himself hesitate further, Thomas grabbed the fob and headed for the loft door. He had minutes before she emerged, which was enough time to find something that might confirm or deny his suspicions once and for all.

He pressed the unlock button, waiting for a flash of headlights. A sleek black sedan blinked twice: sleek lines, spotless exterior, precisely the kind of car he imagined for someone as polished as Sheena. He climbed into the driver's seat, his heart thrumming in his chest like a war drum. The interior was pristine, no sign of the usual commuter's chaos; no crumpled receipts, half-empty coffee cups, or random wires.

He tried the glove compartment first: nothing. Center console: empty. Door pockets: zilch. Thomas clenched his jaw, leaning back in the seat. Maybe he was overreacting. Maybe she was just meticulous. But that sense of unreality nagged at him, feeding the suspicion that this car wasn't used by a constant traveler. It was more like a prop. A show.

His breath caught as he felt beneath the driver's seat, and his fingers brushed against something soft and leather. He tugged it out slowly, dread and adrenaline mixing in his veins. A wallet.

A wave of guilt washed over him, but he swallowed hard and flipped it open. The first thing he saw was her photograph on an ID. But the name... Victoria Hart.

He blinked, mind hitching as if it had slammed into a wall. He scanned the text, reading it again. Same face. Different name. This was no small secret. This was her entire identity. Another wave of anger pulsed through him as he took in the address, the plain text spelling out a life he knew nothing about.

He pulled out his phone, snapping a single photo of the license. Then he hunched over the device, staring at the image in silence. Victoria Hart. The betrayal cut deep, sharper than anything he had felt before. She had stood in front of him, made him believe he was special, given him wild, unforgettable nights, and she was lying through her teeth about the most basic piece of who she was. Sheena Wells… didn't exist.

He forced himself to place the wallet back exactly as he found it, taking a moment to quell the trembling in his hands. How far did this go? Why had she chosen him? Was she a criminal? Married? Running from something?

With a shaky breath, he locked the car and returned to the loft, his mind spinning in a hundred directions. He pictured the license, replaying the name and address over and over. Victoria. Not Sheena. Victoria. Everything took on a different light. Every excuse, missed call, every half-baked story about canceled flights. Did she even work for Delta?

Inside, the shower still roared. She would be out soon, flushed-faced and unsuspecting, certain he would be exactly where she left him. His hands flexed as he tossed the key fob back on the counter. He tried to steady his breathing, fighting to keep the rage from spiraling out of control.

Ryan might come back with news in a day or two, but Thomas no longer needed his friend's confirmation to know something was deeply wrong. He had seen it with his own eyes: Victoria Hart.

The hiss of the shower cut off. Thomas's gaze flickered to the bathroom door. He pictured her stepping out, water droplets clinging to her bare skin, lips parted in an inviting grin. That was how she would approach him, like she had the upper hand. But she didn't, not anymore.

A part of him wanted to confront her right now, to demand answers, to see her face when she realized her lie was exposed. Yet an equal part of him insisted he play it cool. Let her think everything was normal. Let her tie her own rope a little tighter and keep spinning stories until she was caught so deep, she couldn't escape.

He inhaled slowly, shaking off the sense of betrayal enough to compose himself. That was how the Navy taught him to handle emergencies. You didn't panic; you assess. This wasn't war, but it felt just as explosive.

# Control 22
## Beneath the Illusion

Early the next morning, Victoria and Davis loaded the SUV and headed to Savannah for their weekend getaway. R&B music filled the car, and they sang along to old favorites, their voices blending until the miles seemed to pass unnoticed.

When they reached the JW Marriott on the Savannah Riverfront, Victoria felt a wave of calm settle over her. The hotel rose in gleaming glass and marble, sunlight catching on its façade, while the river churned gently beyond. Bellhops moved briskly at the entrance, and the hum of conversation floated from inside.

Victoria turned to Davis. "Baby, you really outdid yourself. This place is exquisite."

"I know what you like," he said.

Check-in went quickly, and soon they were escorted to their suite. After settling in, they changed into comfortable clothes and took a slow, romantic stroll along River Street. The cobblestones bustled with saxophonists, dancers, and laughter spilling from the open bars. At River Street Sweets, Victoria bought pralines and moaned at the first bite. "This is heavenly."

Davis chuckled as she fed him a piece, teasing. "You and your sweet tooth."

"Don't act like you're not enjoying it."

They wandered further, snapping pictures of the bridge, the jazz trio, and steamboats drifting down the river. Victoria noticed that Davis was unusually active with the camera and taking many pictures, selfies and scenic shots. She joked with him and said, "You're quite the photographer today. You hardly ever take pictures. Usually, I'm the one snapping all the photos."

He shrugged. "Well, it's time I start living a little, you know?"

By evening, they returned to their suite, arms heavy with souvenirs and spirits lightened by the day. Victoria slipped off her shoes and sighed with contentment. "This day was so great. I needed this."

"Me too," Davis said.

She climbed into his lap, wrapping her arms around his neck. "We need to do this more often."

"We will," he promised.

She nodded, letting the calm seep into her. For once, everything felt right, and for a while the strain of her double life slipped away.

# Control 21
## The Woman Who Didn't Exist

Thomas woke up on Saturday morning, eyes gritty from a restless night, his mind still tangled from the past day. Sleep had been impossible. Between last-minute Airbnb repairs and the whirlpool of thoughts about who she really was, he barely slept at all.

The possibility that the woman he had been falling for might not even be real, gnawed at him like a hungry beast. He needed answers. He deserved them.

The impulse to uncover the truth was like an itch he couldn't ignore. But before he could start searching, he grabbed his phone. Thomas scrolled to his text thread with Ryan and fired off a quick message:

**Thomas:** *Yo, any updates?*

The nerves in his stomach twisted. He needed to hear what Ryan had found, but he also dreaded that confirmation.

His phone buzzed almost immediately. Instead of a text, Ryan was calling.

"Yo," Thomas answered, trying to keep his voice steady.

"T, what's good, man?" Ryan's tone sounded light, almost playful.

"I can't call it. Stressing out over what you might've dug up."

Ryan let out a quick whistle. "Oh, straight to business, huh? Fine, fine. Let's get into it. Don't want you poppin' a blood vessel."

Thomas felt his chest tighten as he switched the phone to his other ear. "Spit it out already," he demanded.

"Alright, man. Here's what I got. I called a couple of people at Delta and asked if they had anything on a Sheena Wells."

Thomas closed his eyes, bracing himself.

"And guess what I found?" Ryan paused like he was building suspense on purpose.

"Ryan, you better talk."

"A whole lot of nothing."

Those words sank like a rock in Thomas's gut. He didn't speak, only felt his pulse hammering in his ears.

Ryan sighed, filling the silence. "There's no record of her with any airline, T. Not as a flight attendant, not in baggage claim, not behind a desk, nothing. She's not in any system at all."

Thomas's head swam. He had suspected it, but having it confirmed was like a punch to the stomach. He gripped the phone tighter, anger prickling along his nerves.

Ryan continued. "So, then you hit me with the name Victoria Hart. I ran that one too, same search. Same result."

Silence.

Thomas ground his molars as a blaze of betrayal surged through him. He had been falling for a ghost.

"Look," Ryan said, "this girl is playing you. No other way to slice it."

Thomas tried to speak, but only managed a low grunt as fury and heartbreak collided in his chest.

Ryan's tone softened, like he was worried about his friend. "You still there?"

"Yeah. I'm here."

Ryan blew out a breath. "Damn, man. I'm sorry. I know how much you were feelin' her."

"Yeah, well… guess I'm an idiot."

"Nah, not an idiot," Ryan argued gently. "Just a good dude who got hustled by some chick running a con. Could be anything; maybe she's catfishing you for kicks, or maybe she's on the run from the law, or I don't know, maybe she's a damn spy. Point is, she's not who she said she was."

Thomas stayed silent, images of Sheena—no, Victoria—playing in his head, the warmth of her smile seeming so genuine. Suddenly it all felt like one giant game.

Ryan forced a little chuckle, trying to break the tension. "Could be she's a serial killer, dude. You ever watch those true crime documentaries? They be forging whole identities and hooking unsuspecting guys. You gotta watch out."

Thomas shook his head, though Ryan couldn't see him. "She's not a killer."

Ryan scoffed. "I'm just saying, you don't actually know. She's covering up her entire life. That's not normal."

A throbbing ache pounded in Thomas's temple. His friend was right. He had let a complete stranger into his bed, into his heart, only to discover she might be a total fabrication.

"What are you gonna do?" Ryan asked gently after a moment.

"No clue," Thomas admitted. "I just… I need to find out the truth."

Ryan gave a supportive grunt. "Alright, man. You know I got you. Just don't do anything crazy. Keep your head on straight."

"Yeah. I will. Thanks."

"Sure thing. Hit me if you need me, T."

"Later," Thomas said, ending the call.

He sat there on the edge of the bed. The confirmation stung, even though he had expected it. Sheena Wells, Victoria Hart was a fraud.

Anger ignited in his gut, mingled with a deep ache of heartbreak. He had given her so much of himself, and she had played him like a fool. He thought of her lying in his bed, moaning his name, letting him believe she was some flight attendant with a busy schedule. She never told him anything real. She always dodged. She was a ghost, slipping out of his grasp just when he reached for her truths.

Thomas sat at the dining room table, staring at the screen of his laptop. The picture of Victoria's driver's license glowed back at him. Anger pulsed through his veins, so intense it made him tremble.

He typed her name, Victoria Hart; fingers moving with a cold, controlled fury. The first search result hit him like a punch: a LinkedIn profile. Thomas narrowed his eyes, clicking the link, and there she was, smiling in a professional headshot, Victoria Hart, CEO.

His lips parted in shock as he scrolled. CEO of a successful social media marketing company. Nationally recognized businesswoman. Keynote speaker. Several high-ranking industry awards. His chest rose and fell quickly as he absorbed the scale of her success.

He clicked away from LinkedIn, searching her social media profile. Everything was corporate, polished, and curated. *She was hiding something*, he told himself.

His gaze flicked back to the address on her driver's license. He copied it and opened a property records search. The results popped up, making his heart skip a beat. Victoria Hart. Then a second name appeared: Davis Hart.

Thomas's stomach twisted. Who the fuck is Davis? Another man's name tied to her address. Another presence in her life that she never mentioned, no, that she intentionally hid. He forced himself to search: Davis Hart, Georgia. The first few results were unhelpful. He tried social media: nothing on TikTok, nothing on Instagram. Finally, he clicked on Facebook and a profile loaded.

He froze. A photo album opened and there she was. Her smile bright, pressed against Davis, arm tight around her waist. The caption read: Me and my beautiful wife.

Thomas's lungs forgot how to function. She was already claimed. Married.

He slapped the laptop shut so violently that the table rattled. A water glass shattered on the floor. His breathing came in ragged bursts, his body shaking. She had a husband. Every kiss. Every touch. Every whispered promise. All of it was fake. Thomas thought about how she had gone to bed with him and then returned to another man's arms.

He stood abruptly, the chair screeching against the floor. Rage blurred his vision red. She told him she was his, that her body belonged to him, but she was married the entire time. SHE LIED. He slammed his fists onto the table and the laptop wobbled. That photo burned in his mind: Davis with his arm around her, the word *wife* branded across her.

Sweat gathered at his temples. He squeezed his eyes shut, but the images burned brighter. She had built a perfect lie. She had stolen his trust, and he despised her for making him love her and fall so hard. His rage swelled until he thought he would explode. But slowly, he forced himself to breathe. The truth was a blade, leaving him raw, furious, and hungry for retribution.

She thought she could walk away. She thought she could lie and return to her husband's arms like nothing happened. She had no idea who she was dealing with because Sheena—Victoria—was his. And now, she would feel the weight of that truth.

# Control 20
## Love vs Rage

Thomas was unraveling, falling into rage, betrayal, and obsession. The loft laid in near darkness, air thick with liquor and a lingering musk from his most recent, meaningless sexual encounter. He had hoped it would take the edge off, that some random body would quell the fury churning inside him, but it hadn't worked. The moment he finished, an emptiness swallowed him whole.

On the sofa, he stared at his phone until his eyes burned, scrolling her LinkedIn, every conference photo, every article, polished lies. He swore under his breath and took a long swig of brandy. He needed to know where she was and who she was with.

He opened Facebook again and navigated to Davis Hart's profile. He expected the same photos as before or maybe no update at all. But when he refreshed, his pulse pounded at the sight of a newly posted album: Savannah, Georgia.

Thomas's pulse pounded as images bloomed. Victoria poolside in a skimpy black bikini, radiant and carefree. Victoria in a red dress that fit like sin. He swiped again, and there she was, feeding Davis a piece of praline candy. They looked playful, in love, and wrapped in intimacy. In every shot she shone with happiness he had believed belonged only to him.

Then, the final image drove the rage home. A photo of Victoria and Davis standing forehead to forehead, arms looped around each other, locked in a romantic embrace that screamed devotion. Thomas's vision blurred; the rage in his chest boiling over into something uncontrollable.

He rasped out a furious whisper, "Does he really think he can keep what's mine?"

A violent tremor ran through his body. In a burst of frustration, he hurled the brandy bottle, liquor splattering the wall. "She's MINE, Davis," he snarled. "You mother-fucker."

He slammed a hand onto the table as a hoarse cry ripping free. The fantasy that had fed him now strangled him. This wouldn't be the end of their story, not by a long shot. He glared at the phone again, half-tempted to smash it too, but he needed it to track her, to watch her moves, to plan. The sense of wanting control overwhelmed him. He needed to reclaim what was rightfully his.

He stood, unsteady from alcohol and fury, shards of the broken bottle crunching underfoot. Pain was irrelevant. She was in Savannah playing the devoted wife, but soon she would see what happens when you steal a man's heart and trample it under false promises. Thomas exhaled a ragged breath, questions spiraling into resolve. He would show her and him.

# Control 19
## Unveiled

Victoria returned to work feeling like she was on top of the world. The Savannah getaway with Davis had felt like a second honeymoon. By the time they drove home, her heart felt lighter, as though she had left her troubles behind.

The workday began with her usual morning routine. As she scanned her calendar, she saw it: a private, twenty-minute slot labeled simply "Boss' Office." She had scheduled it herself, intended for just her and Tab.

Tabitha strolled into Victoria's office, shutting the door behind her, a joking smirk on her lips. "Alright, V, you got me here. So, what's this special meeting about? Is something wrong? Did I mess up an account last week or something?"

Victoria let the pause stretch, then laughed. "Girl, no. Relax. I just wanted to tell you about me and Davis's getaway."

Tabitha rolled her eyes with an over-the-top sigh of relief. "Don't do that to me! I thought I was about to get my ass handed to me. Alright, dish, tell me everything."

Victoria lit up, recounting the resort, the private dinner under lights, pralines, live music, and for a moment Tab was swept up, almost envious, but quickly shut the feeling down.

"Must have been some weekend," Tabitha teased. "You're shining like a diamond." Then Tab's tone shifted. "So, tell me, V, did it feel good being with Davis, or was your mind on Thomas the entire time?"

Victoria's grin vanished. "Tab…"

"This is what it's supposed to be like, V. The way Davis treats you. Tell me you dropped Thomas."

Silence pressed in. "V," Tabitha said firmly. "You dropped him, right?"

Victoria sighed. "I'm working on it."

"You're *working on it?* You told me you were done."

"Soon, okay? I can't just get rid of him like that. It's a process."

"A process? Tabitha scoffed. "I didn't know side dudes needed a fucking divorce proceeding."

Victoria's jaw tightened. "Things are complicated."

"How complicated can it be? Stop picking up his calls. Stop meeting him for sex. Stop lying to Davis. It's not rocket science."

"It's not that simple. Thomas isn't some fling. Look, I just need another week."

"A week for what? So he can keep fucking you while you lie to your husband?" Tab stood, shaking her head. "Let me know when you finally do something about it. I need lunch before I lose my appetite. Are we done here? May I be excused?"

Victoria sank back as the door clicked shut, guilt swirling.

Alone again, Victoria opened the bottom desk drawer and took out her burner phone. A single missed call. Her heart raced seeing Thomas's name. She hesitated, then redialed.

Thomas picked up after the first ring, his voice gravelly.

"Hey, baby," she purred. "You sound awful. What have you been up to?"

Thomas paused for a beat, then played it off smoothly. "Yelling at the game," he said.

"Men and their sports," she teased. "Anyway, when can I come see you?"

He chuckled. "I thought you'd never ask."

"You have no idea how much I need you right now."

"That's perfect," he said, a dark smirk creeping in. "Because I have a surprise for you."

"A surprise? For me?"

"Yes, baby. And it's to DIE for."

She giggled. "You spoil me."

"That's because you're mine, baby. And this one's gonna blow you away. Quite literally."

Her stomach flipped. "All of your surprises are out of this world."

"Come over a little early on Wednesday. I'm making dinner for you. We're going to celebrate."

"I can't wait."

"Me too," he said. "Can't wait to see the look on your face."

They hung up. Thomas tapped the counter, hiding his fury under charm. Keep her close. Let her walk into it. Because when Wednesday came, he intended to show her exactly what it meant to be under his control. He wanted the reveal, the confrontation, to hit her like a tidal wave.

✳ ✳ ✳ ✳

Wednesday arrived before Victoria realized it. By noon, she knew she wouldn't last the entire day pretending to be fully engaged in business matters. She powered down her laptop a few minutes before three o'clock, telling Tab she had to leave early for a doctor's appointment. She arrived at the loft in a tight dress and high heels, her nerves humming. She pressed the doorbell and held her breath.

The door swung open moments later, revealing Thomas, looking better than usual. "Wow, baby. You look amazing," he said.

"You're not so bad yourself," she said, catching the scent of steak, garlic, and butter.

When she walked in, she noticed the lights were low, and gentle music hummed in the background. She glanced over toward the dining area and saw the table set up nicely with plates and wine glasses; he had gone all out it seemed. "What's the occasion?"

"You," he said. "I'm celebrating you."

He laid it on thick. "My amazing flight attendant, always working distant cities every night…"

The emphasis was odd, but she soaked up the praises and his kiss.

"Are you hungry?" he asked. "I made everything you love. The steaks smell good, right?"

"Oh my God, yes. I'm starving."

He led her to the dining table, pulling out a chair for her like a perfect gentleman. Victoria felt a rush of gratitude and excitement. She thought, *Tonight is going to be amazing. He's in such a mood, we'll probably end up having the best sex of our lives.* Her anticipation grew.

They ate, traded jokes, and sipped red wine. His gaze kept turning intense; she read it as lust, not the anger underneath.

"I have a gift for you," he said. "I'll bring it out later, but first, tell me all about your trip this past weekend. You said you were assigned a flight to Hawaii, right?" He was holding on to the last shred of self-control.

She had no idea that everything was about to erupt. "Hawaii? Um, it was cool. I just sat by the pool and read a book."

"So, the flight there… was it rough, lots of turbulence?"

She took a long gulp of wine. "No, I connected through California and then to Hawaii and both flights were fine."

"I thought you said it was a direct flight."

She froze for a second, then tried to wave it off. "Oh, right. That. They switched my assignment at the last minute." Victoria took another swig of wine, as if that might stop her heart from galloping out of her chest.

"Yeah, I'm sure Delta does that all the time. Speaking of Delta, I ran into an old buddy of mine named Ryan. He served in the Air Force when I was in the Navy. He's retired now, doing something fancy with the FAA."

Victoria's heart hammered. "Oh?"

Thomas kept his eyes on her. "Yeah, we got to talking about you. I told him how you're a flight attendant; my baby, working in the skies. He said he's always in the Atlanta airport and knows a lot of the flight crews, but he said he hadn't met you yet and that Sheena Wells didn't ring a bell."

"I keep a low profile." She could feel the back of her neck dampening with anxiety.

"Sure," Thomas murmured, "but I recall you mentioning something about a special aviation committee you were on, I figured that would let you meet plenty of folks."

Victoria felt the walls closing in. "Actually, it's been so hectic that I stepped back from the committee."

He kept testing her. "I was telling Ryan about how I miss you when you're away. He started tossing around all this flight attendant lingo; stuff about the 35-7 rule? I don't remember the exact numbers, but I figured you'd know it."

Victoria's eyes widened. A dryness clogged her throat. She'd never heard of any 35-7 rule, or that it even existed, she didn't know what it meant. Her entire body felt ready to burst with panic. "You know, um, I might've heard of it, but it's not something I deal with much."

Thomas was ready to press further, but before he could, Victoria stood up slightly and twisted her body, pretending that she was in pain.

"Ouch, ow, ow," she gasped, clutching her side.

"You okay? Did you pull something?"

She hunched, breathing heavily. "It feels like my side twisted. Can you help me to the couch?"

"Sure," he said. *She's faking this shit.* The cornered animal, spinning lies to escape.

"I think I just moved too fast, but I'm okay."

"Let me get you some water."

She forced a wide grin. "Thank you. And thanks for dinner. Everything was delicious. I can't believe how well you can cook, especially after that breakfast at the hotel. This was on another level."

"I aim to please."

Her eyes darted around, searching for a change of subject. She decided to seduce him. She beckoned him closer, whispering that she had missed him. But Thomas recognized her attempt for what it was. She straddled him, trying to create a spark of lust that would shut him up. "I missed these lips," she breathed.

He felt the press of her body, but as turned on as he might normally be, all he felt now was disgust at the ease with which she lied. "Slow down, baby," he murmured. "What's the rush?"

"I just want you. I've been thinking about you since the last time we were together." She tried to slide her fingers along his chest, but he caught her wrists gently, pushing them aside.

He snarled. *She's so diabolical.* He put on a calm smile. "Don't worry, we'll get there. But first, your gift. You remember, I said I had something for you."

"Oh, right, I almost forgot. You're too good to me."

He inwardly sneered, *Isn't that the fucking truth.* He stood and picked up a medium-sized box from a table. It was wrapped neatly in patterned paper, complete with a fancy bow. The sight made her eyes glow with excitement.

"Thomas, wow, this box is beautiful."

"Open it," he urged. "I can't wait to see your face."

She carefully removed the bow, peeling back the wrapping. She lifted the top, finding a large white envelope. Her lips twisted in confusion. "What's this?" She opened the envelope and pulled out a stack of photographs. Her entire body froze.

She stared at the pictures from her past weekend in Savannah. Evidence, pure and blatant, of her real life. The life she had hidden from Thomas.

Her chest felt ready to cave in. She couldn't breathe. The room spun around her.

She looked up at Thomas, tears already forming in her eyes. Her lips trembled. "Th-Thomas," she stammered, "I— I can explain—"

He cut her off with a dark, humorless laugh. "What, you don't like your gift, baby?" he said, his voice dripping with sarcasm. "Funny, I thought you'd appreciate the reminder of your... *vacation*. Or maybe I should say, *second honeymoon*."

She stared, wide-eyed, her mind screaming for a way to fix this, to talk her way out. But the words wouldn't come.

"Imagine how I felt, **Victoria**, when I found out the love of my life wasn't who I thought she was."

"Thomas, please, just let me—"

"Explain WHAT? How you're not a flight attendant at all? How you're the fucking CEO of some big social media company? How you lied to me about every single thing I thought was real?" His voice rose, unsteady with fury. "How you're another man's FUCKING WIFE?"

She flinched at the force of his words, tears now spilling down her cheeks. "I wanted to tell you... I just... I couldn't—"

"You let me believe you were falling for me. You let me pour my soul into you. You made me think I was your whole world, when you had some other guy at home, a ring on your finger that you hid every time you saw me." He slammed a fist onto a nearby table, rattling glasses.

Victoria trembled. "I swear, it wasn't supposed to—"

"SHUT UP," he snarled. "You told me I was the only man you wanted. Told me your body belonged to me. And all the while, you were crawling back to your husband like nothing happened."

She broke down in sobs, struggling to speak. "Thomas, I'm sorry. I never meant to—"

He grabbed the pictures from her lap, waving them in her face. "You see these? This is who you really are. Victoria Hart, *wife*. Not Sheena Wells, flight attendant. You took me for a fucking idiot."

"Let me explain," she pleaded.

"Explain what, exactly? That you're a goddamn liar? That everything we had was built on bullshit?" His chest heaved, fists balled at his sides.

She reached for him, but he jerked away.

"Don't fucking touch me," he spat.

They faced each other across the loft, each breath thick with tension. She'd never seen him like this, so full of rage.

"Get the fuck out of my house," he said. "Before I do something I'll regret."

She moved to step closer. "Thomas, please…"

"OUT," he roared. "You have ten seconds."

She staggered to her feet, limbs quivering. But instead of running, she tried once more, "Thomas, I never wanted to hurt you."

"You *did* hurt me," he rasped. "You fucking tore me apart. I gave you my heart. I believed you were mine and you were never even available."

She sobbed, wanting to reassure him but at a loss for words.

"You think this is over? Oh no, baby. We're not finished."

Her heart hammered as she realized how dangerous this moment was. "Thomas…" she began.

"You're gonna suffer just like I did. Now get out before I lose my mind tonight."

She stumbled toward the door, tears and mascara staining her cheeks.

He refused to move from his spot, breathing like a wild animal, letting her pass. She yanked the door open, throwing one last panicked look over her shoulder. But he glared at her with a hatred she'd never thought was possible.

He told her to leave, but he knew deep down he would never let her go that easily. He would make her realize that betraying him was the worst mistake of her life.

# Control 18
## The Weight of Her Lies

Victoria barely registered how she made it home. Her mind was a blur of tears and confusion. She pulled into the driveway and stumbled inside, forcing herself to smile weakly at Davis. She mumbled something about feeling ill, and possibly having an allergic reaction, and apologized for not being in the mood to talk. All she wanted was to crawl into bed and disappear.

She tossed and turned for hours, chasing restless sleep that never fully arrived. Every time she closed her eyes, she saw Thomas's face twisted with rage, spitting out words of betrayal. She kept replaying the shock and fury in his eyes when he revealed he knew everything. The memory made her chest tighten as though she couldn't draw in enough air.

When morning finally came, she felt numb and exhausted. She had gotten maybe an hour or two of uneasy dozing, her body aching from tension. She had messaged Tabitha and told her that she was sick and unable to come to work. Tabitha, of course, said she would handle the office and told her to get better. Victoria breathed out a shaky sigh of relief. At least the business wouldn't crash without her, for now. But the real storm howled inside her. She had always been the woman with a plan. Now, everything had come crashing down. Hugging a pillow close, she stared at the ceiling. *Why did I let it get this far? How did I underestimate Thomas so badly?*

She dialed Thomas's number. Once… twice… six times, only to reach voicemail every time. She typed out a text, then hesitated. Should she apologize? Beg? She sent short, frantic messages: *Thomas, please call me. I'm so sorry. Please answer.* But no response came.

Every minute dragged her deeper into panic. She left one voice message, words trembling, breath ragged, promising she would do anything. When she hung up, emptiness settled. Eventually, she realized she was flooding him with calls and texts that went nowhere. She threw the phone aside, sobbing into the covers. She thought to herself that maybe she should wait and let him cool off. Thomas could be hotheaded, but in a day or two, he would calm down enough to hear her out.

Victoria began planning out how she would see Thomas again. "I'll go see him Friday," she whispered. "He can't ignore me forever. We have too much history. He needs me as much as I need him. We can fix this."

She pictured his arms around her again, his lips on hers, and it gave her a hollow comfort. In truth, she was terrified that Thomas's silence meant he was done. The mere thought made her chest tighten until she could barely breathe. She refused to entertain the idea of losing him.

# Control 17
## What's Done in the Dark

Tabitha could hardly catch her breath. This was one of the busiest weeks she had seen in a long time, maybe ever. Meetings, trainings, and the pressure of winning over new prospective clients all piled onto her shoulders. Victoria had chosen *this* week to be sick. Yet the urgency of it all fueled her in a way she hadn't felt before. It was like she had something to prove, both to herself and to everyone else who assumed she was just a sidekick.

She leaned back in her chair, inhaling slowly, but despite the chaos, Tabitha felt a fierce determination simmer in her chest. *I was built for this*, she told herself, pressing her lips together in a tight smile. *I can handle it.*

Her mind drifted to Victoria, home in bed, supposedly sick. Tabitha wasn't dumb; she suspected something bigger was going on, but at the same time, Tabitha was almost grateful for the chance to step fully into the driver's seat. After all, she had been practically running the show for the past month or two anyway.

She set her thoughts aside and flicked open her email to confirm details for her next big meeting. S&J Enterprise was due to arrive in just twenty minutes. She remembered how S&J had been a thorn in Victoria's side with negotiations that never went anywhere. But Tabitha had a feeling she could seal the deal if she played her cards right. *This is my moment,* she thought.

The CEO of S&J Enterprise, Cliff, entered the conference room. He was tall, with an easy smile that could slip into arrogance.

"Welcome, Cliff," she said, gesturing for him to take a seat. "Thank you for coming in."

He glanced around, noticing the absent boss. "I thought I'd be meeting with Victoria today. Where is she?"

"Unfortunately, Victoria isn't feeling well." She bristled internally at the idea that he might think she was just a stand-in. "But I assure you, I'm more than capable of discussing all aspects of the business."

"Really? Last time I was here, you were basically handing her documents and fetching coffee. I'm surprised to see you running the show now."

Tabitha's heart clenched, but she forced her composure. "I did start off assisting Victoria, yes, but I've grown into a larger role. You could say I'm her partner in many respects."

Cliff arched an eyebrow. "Partner, you say?"

She nodded, ignoring the flush of annoyance that threatened to creep up her neck. "Yes. I take on a range of duties from client acquisition to project oversight. Lately, I've been leading several deals that boosted our revenue significantly."

"That's impressive. I've heard Social Brilliance is doing really well these days. I couldn't ignore the buzz even if I tried."

Tabitha smiled. "We've definitely grown, which brings me to what we can do for you, specifically."

She launched into her pitch, describing Social Brilliance's track record of elevating businesses' social media presence, drawing in new customers, and expanding brand reach.

He listened intently, occasionally glancing through the data. "I'm impressed," he said. "Seems like you all have the formula for success. But I remember Victoria quoting me some sky-high prices. She never budged, which is partly why we didn't finalize anything before."

"Right, Victoria does tend to hold firm on her rates, but I'm open to negotiating, if that's what you need."

Cliff let out a satisfied chuckle. "That's what I like to hear. Because, while I see the value, I also have a budget to respect. I was hoping we could meet somewhere that feels fair to both sides."

Tabitha felt a flicker of excitement. This was her chance to prove she could close a big deal on her own. "Why don't we discuss some numbers and see what you're comfortable with? Then I'll propose a flexible structure that satisfies everyone."

They talked for nearly forty minutes, hashing out specifics. During the conversation, she had to fight off a wave of annoyance when Cliff referred to her as "the assistant." *I'm so much more than an assistant,* she reminded herself. *And soon enough, people will know.*

Finally, they reached an agreement. Cliff sat back, grinning, and extended a hand. "Well, Tabitha, I think we have ourselves a deal. Congratulations."

She shook his hand, her pulse racing with a sense of accomplishment. "I'll send you a preliminary contract by the end of the day, then we can finalize signatures tomorrow."

"You're shaping up to be quite the businesswoman, Tabitha. Keep it up."

She stayed polite, nodding, until he disappeared down the hall. The moment the door shut, she let out a long exhale, feeling a surge of pride bloom inside her. She had done it; secured a big client on her own. No Victoria, no overshadowing presence hovering to take credit.

Tabitha walked back to her office and sank into her chair, thoughts swirling in triumph. Her mind turned to the arrangement she had just made, deciding she would handle S&J's contract personally. She told Cliff that all payment details, all major decisions, would come directly through her.

It wasn't something she would typically do, as Victoria was in charge of everything. But Victoria wasn't here, and Tab knew how to handle it herself. *I'll manage it the way I see fit,* she mused. *And keep it separate, a bit private.* After all, she deserved a bigger piece of the pie. Why shouldn't she set aside a portion for herself after all the labor she had put in?

She smirked, thinking about the many late nights, stress, and responsibilities she had carried on her shoulders, all while Victoria breezed in and out. *It's time I benefit from my own skill,* she thought. Maybe it was a small step toward forging her own path. She had let Social Brilliance do the heavy lifting, but she would reap the main rewards.

A flicker of guilt tried to surface; the notion that she was essentially funneling a part of this deal outside of Victoria's direct oversight. But then she remembered how many times she had saved deals that Victoria nearly let slip, how she had practically run the company in Victoria's many absences. It felt fair.

She remembered her man's words from the sidelines, urging her to go bigger and reminding her she was too talented to remain in anyone's shadow. He told her the time had come for her to step up and become who she was meant to be. Perhaps this was that turning point when Tabitha started carving her own name into the foundation of Social Brilliance. No more sidekick. No more shadow. From here on, every move, every deal, and every client that she signed would be hers.

# Control 16
## By Sunset

Friday arrived in a flash, though for Victoria the week had dragged like years. Every hour had crawled beneath the weight of worry and what-ifs. Davis was already gone. She still heard the echo of the front door closing, the jingle of his keys, the trace of his cologne lingering in the hallway. The house felt hollow without him. The silence pressed against her like a reminder: the choice she had been postponing could not wait another moment.

In the top drawer, hidden beneath folded camisoles, the burner phone lay mute. She didn't need to check the blank screen to know that Thomas had ignored her all week. His silence was exactly why she had to go now.

In the closet, she hesitated. She needed something that said confidence, that reminded her of the woman Thomas once looked at like she had hung the moon. The scarlet wrap dress called to her. She stepped into it, tied the sash in a snug bow at her side, and it fell just above her knees. She looked at the woman in the mirror and whispered, "You're going to breathe, tell him everything, and hold your ground."

Victoria parked across from his ivy-clad brick building and sat in the silence, heart pounding as memories crowded in. She pressed her palm to her sternum, trying to steady herself. She opened the car door, adjusted her dress, and stepped out. She rang the doorbell and heard a faint chime echo inside, but no footsteps followed. She waited, then pressed again. Still nothing. The prickling at her neck spread until her skin burned. She knocked three times, hard enough for her knuckles to sting. Silence pressed back.

His vehicles were parked outside, so he was there. She tried again: bell, pause, knock. She slipped a hand into her purse and dove for her phone, thumb hovering over Thomas's contact. Just as she was about to call, a metallic click echoed inside, and the door unlocked. The handle turned slowly, as the door eased open a sliver. Faint light and the scent of warm vanilla drifted out, but no face appeared yet. She exhaled a shaky breath, bracing herself to meet Thomas's eyes.

The door inched wider, and an unfamiliar, petite silhouette leaned into the frame. Victoria's pulse stuttered; she couldn't make out details yet. The person seemed to hesitate, then stepped forward into better light.

For a full second, Victoria's mind refused to believe what she saw. A young woman, maybe late-twenties, stood before her, wearing an oversized gray T-shirt that hung off one shoulder. She had long, silky, straight hair and vivid green eyes that flicked over Victoria, assessing her. The stranger's lips tilted up in a faint, amused smile. Victoria's lungs froze; air stalled between rib and throat. She blinked hard, expecting the image to alter, but the woman remained.

"You're cute," the woman said, voice soft, almost lazy, as though waking from a dream. She rested her head against the doorjamb, green eyes glittering with casual interest. "I see he has a type. What are you doing here?"

Victoria spoke in confusion. "Excuse me? Who are y—"

She never finished as a second set of footsteps approached from inside. Thomas emerged and wrapped his arms around the woman's waist. The sight burned. She leaned into him, looked up, and smiled as her hand slid along his arm.

He flashed the woman back a smile, the kind Victoria thought belonged to her. Victoria could feel the anger boiling over inside of her.

"What are you doing here?" Thomas asked.

The words jolted her out of shock. "I… I need to talk to you," she managed. "Please, Thomas. I've been calling and texting you for days. Please, can we just talk?"

The woman rolled her eyes and chuckled. "Is she really begging? Wow, that is just—"

"I got this," Thomas interrupted, gaze still locked on Victoria.

The woman lifted her hands in mock surrender, but didn't move, staying pressed against him as though her place was unquestionable.

Thomas looked at Victoria and said, "I was, well, we were busy before you decided to show up."

The word *we* slammed into Victoria. Her pulsed spiked as the woman nuzzled closer against Thomas, laughing softly, her display twisting like a blade. Rage bubbled up and broke loose.

"Who the fuck is this woman, Thomas?" Victoria snapped.

Both heads turned toward her. The woman arched her brows, entertained. Thomas's jaw tightened, his words sharp as glass. "She's a single woman, Victoria. That's who she is. She's single and not here to play mind games with me."

He paused, letting the statement hang like a verdict. "The real question is: who is Davis? You know, your husband. The one you lay next to every night. The one you claim to love. The one you keep going home to."

The woman flashed a surprising look. "Oh, wow. Married?" She murmured.

Victoria's cheeks flushed hot, her breath shaky. "I just want to talk, Thomas. Please."

The woman looked up at him. At his subtle nod, she sighed, amused. "Well, that's my cue to leave, but first, I'm going to need to find my underwear," she said, laughing lightly. She slipped from his embrace and padded up the staircase.

Victoria's chest heaved as she whispered and pointed toward the woman's direction, "Really, Thomas? You know what, never mind, I can't really say anything."

"Damn right you can't say anything. You're married. You don't get to storm in here furious about who I have in my home."

"You're right," she admitted. "I don't."

"Fucking right you don't," he snapped.

The woman returned, dressed in shorts that hugged slim hips. She brushed her lips against Thomas's cheek, and murmured, "Call me when you need me again." Her eyes flicked toward Victoria with a mocking grin before she slipped out, leaving the air heavy and raw.

Victoria stepped inside the loft. For a heartbeat she simply stood there, pulse screaming while the familiar scent of cedar and expensive coffee pressed in from every side.

"Thomas, please," she began. "Just let me say what I need to say. I know you're angry, and you have every right to be. I lied to you. I took what you gave me and treated it like it would always be there. I'm so sorry. I never meant to hurt you."

She swallowed. He didn't move, didn't soften, so she pressed on, fighting to keep her breaths even. "You were supposed to be a fleeting moment, one reckless night for me to remember when life felt dull. But there was something about you I couldn't shake. I tried. God, I tried to forget you after that first time, but every thought circled back to you. I've never met a man who made me feel the way you do. You unlocked something inside me, something wild, something alive. You made me see how numb I'd been."

Thomas's jaw twitched, but he said nothing. Victoria felt tears gather behind her lashes. She forced herself onward, voice cracking like thin ice. "I didn't know how to tear myself out of the life I'd built and still hold on to you, so I lied. I lied because I panicked. But nothing I felt with you was fake. Every laugh, every touch, every word; it was real to me. These last two days without you have been hell. I've called and texted until my fingers cramped. I don't chase anyone, ever, but I chased you. Doesn't that show how much you mean to me?"

Thomas's eyes held hers, cold and unreadable.

"Thomas, I don't know the right way through this, but I do know I can't lose you. I want you in my life; I need you."

The silence stretched, and at last, Thomas's arms unfolded. He took a slow step forward, face drawn tight with anger. His voice was low but razor-sharp. "So, what now, Victoria? Am I supposed to sit here like some toy on a shelf until you feel like picking me up again? The side guy you slide into when playing perfect wife gets boring? You think I'm supposed to be okay with you leaving the bed you share with him and crawling into mine when it suits you? Is that how this game is supposed to be played?"

Victoria flinched but held her ground. "I don't know. I just know I'm not happy in my marriage—"

"Are you serious right now?" Thomas's eyes widened. A sharp laugh escaped him before he stormed to the hall closet. He yanked out the cardboard box and tossed the stack of glossy photos from her Savannah trip with Davis into her hands.

"This isn't a happy woman?" he demanded.

One photo showed Victoria feeding Davis a bite of dessert by the waterfront. Another showed her laughing in the glow of candlelight, as they danced under string lights.

Thomas's voice cracked as he spoke. "Poolside romance, a candlelight dinner; looks like paradise to me."

She stared at the images, shame burning. "I know what it looks like," she whispered, "but that's not reality. Those moments, they were staged, forced. They don't show the emptiness in between."

Thomas smirked. "You are something else. I thought maybe you had come here ready to face the truth, but you're spinning the same story. It's over, Victoria." The last two words fell like iron. "For good."

The room tilted. Her vision tunneled, ears filled with the roar of blood and disbelief. *Not over. Anything but over.*

Thomas turned toward the door. "If you come back, if you text, call, or show up, I'll have you arrested for harassment."

Panic exploded through her. She threw herself in front of him, blocking his path. "Thomas, please. You're all I think about. I wake up thinking of you. I think about you at work, on the drive home, in the shower, when I lie beside *him*. You visit me in my dreams. I can't picture the world without you. I love you, Thomas Carter."

The words hovered between them, raw and trembling. Thomas jerked his head back, surprise flickering.

She repeated, softer but clearer, "I love you, Thomas, with every part of me."

"How do I know that this isn't another part of your twisted fantasy? You only chase thrills, maybe this is just the next high."

"Would I be here," she countered, "risking everything, my marriage, my name, if it were a game?" She lifted his hand, laid it over her racing heart. "Does this feel like make-believe?"

"Do you really love me, Victoria?" he asked.

She stepped closer, the courage of desperation pushing her. "Yes, I do."

He pulled his hand back, then shook his head as if clearing fog. "Then *prove* it."

She blinked. "How?"

"It's him or me." His words were stone. "Right now. Right here. No more halfway."

"What do you mean?"

"If you love me, then leave Davis. Not next week, not next year. Now. You walk out of that house, and you don't go back. Then you come to me."

"But we're married, Thomas." Her mouth felt full of sand. "I can't just snap my fingers. There are papers. Accounts. Property. Assets. The business—"

"Fuck that. Do you want me or him?" He asked.

The robe at his waist slipped loose, and suddenly his bare, chiseled body pressed against her, muscles tense and warm. The power she once wielded had flipped; he now held every card. She felt small, fragile, and stripped of all control.

"So, who is it going to be, Victoria, him or me?" His voice was a low growl.

Her lips trembled. "Baby, I love you, but I need time—"

"This is the only chance I'm giving you," he said. "I want you in my bed by sunset tomorrow. If you aren't, then don't call, text, or show up. Ever again."

He cupped her cheek, tender thumb brushing away a tear even as his words gutted her. *By sunset tomorrow.*

She couldn't speak. She only nodded and stumbled past him as he opened the door and stepped aside. On the landing, Victoria braced against the wall, breath breaking in harsh bursts. *By sunset tomorrow.* Everything now balanced on the single deadline.

# Control 15
## The Crossroads

Victoria lay still, blinking at the ceiling as the sound of running water hissed from the bathroom. The steady rhythm told her Davis was showering after his Saturday run. For a moment, she let herself pretend that everything was normal, but Thomas's voice cut through the illusion and she was reminded of the ultimatum he had given her. Be *in my bed by sunset tomorrow or never come back.*

Thomas never bluffed; he had proved that many times. The idea of that door closing forever, of never feeling his hands on her skin again, sent fear and heat racing through her. She sat on the mattress' edge. "Think, Victoria, Thomas or Davis?" She tried to see the choice clearly, yet nothing looked simple. With Thomas came risks and a hunger that might devour her. Maybe she longed to be devoured. *I can keep both for now*, she argued with herself. People test-drove cars; dealers sometimes let customers take them home overnight. Shouldn't love or whatever this reckless craving was deserve the same policy?

The bathroom door opened, and Victoria turned to Davis, as she forced a smile. Davis stepped into the room with only a towel at his waist. "Morning, sleepyhead. How did you sleep?"

"Fine," she lied.

He nodded and told her that pancakes would be ready in fifteen minutes. He asked whether she wanted blueberries or chocolate chips.

"Blueberries," she said automatically. Her stomach twisted. Was she really standing here choosing pancake flavors while her life balanced on a blade? She pressed her palms together to keep from shaking.

As he dressed, he studied her face. "You look pale. Are you still feeling ill?" He asked. "No. I'm actually feeling better," she said.

"Come downstairs when you're ready." He brushed past, planting a soft kiss on her temple. Then he went toward the stairs, leaving the faint scent of aftershave.

As soon as the door closed, her body folded inward. She sat on the bed, clutching the robe tightly, as her mind began spinning. *I can juggle this. A few nights a week at the loft, claim it's work. Davis wouldn't question it, but what if Thomas grew impatient?* The scent of homemade pancakes and butter drifted up. Time was ticking.

At the dining table, Davis poured coffee and loaded her plate. While he chatted about mowing the lawn, she nodded, but inside she pictured Thomas checking the time, counting down. Davis reached across and squeezed her hand; his fingers felt warm and steady. She felt the fear of losing that steady warmth for the unknown blaze of Thomas. *I don't want to hurt Davis,* she thought, curling her thumb around his, but a harsher voice answered, *you already have.*

She peered through the window. Sunlight climbed higher. The clock ticked like a drumbeat. Sunset always came fast, especially when you were running out of time.

* * * *

Davis left to run his normal Saturday errands, which meant that Victoria had a few hours to plan her escape.

*It's time.*

She tightened her robe and climbed the stairs with quick, deliberate steps. The closet opened like a vault. Neat rows of clothes and accessories stared back at her, but today they looked like a weight. She pulled down the biggest suitcase, unzipped it, and reached for everything Thomas loved: the emerald wrap dress, the bodysuit, he fumbled to remove, the stilettos that made him lose his breath. Item by item, she packed for seduction.

Lingerie spilled across the bed. She shoved it all in, every lace scrap tied to his gaze. She stuffed the side pockets with perfume, makeup, and jewelry. Skincare and hair products got tossed into a duffle. She refused to think about how long she'd stay. Sunset was the only deadline that mattered right now. If she needed more, she would come back later or buy new things.

At the bathroom sink, her reflection in the mirror halted her. Her pupils looked wide, the whites bright with fear and excitement. She parted her lips and found them trembling. *Steady,* she told herself. *You chose this.*

She loaded all of her luggage and bags into the trunk of her car one at a time. A glance at the clock gave her a sliver of relief. Davis rarely cut his routine short; he would be gone at least another hour, which was enough time to plan her words.

She perched on the arm of the sofa and let her mind tumble. *Tell Davis you need space.* That could work, as it was vague, non-threatening, and true in its way. But she pictured Davis's soft eyes, the slight wrinkle he got between his brows when he worried. *This is going to crush him,* she thought. She brushed the idea aside with a swift shake of her head.

Time dragged as she sank into the couch, phone still in hand. Scrolling numbly through social media, she landed on Davis's feed and saw the posts that Davis posted of her and him in Savannah a few weeks ago. She began to smile as she saw the sheer joy and happiness in both of their eyes. She then noticed another post of Davis on his Saturday morning run talking about staying healthy and posting a selfie. She flashed a surprised look as she thought about how Davis almost never posted on social media. He always talked about the people that posted their lives on social media and how he hated it. She figured that maybe he was trying to keep up with the times, but something about it was strange. She brushed it off and continued to scroll to pass the time.

The garage door rumbled, and Victoria's shoulders stiffened. *Showtime,* she thought, pressing her fingertips to the pulse racing at her neck. Every speech she had rehearsed vanished the moment the car engine cut off.

Plastic bags crinkled as Davis entered sideways, arms full from a multi-store run. When he finally saw her on the couch, his smile widened. "Grocery hero finally home," he said, dropping his keys with a clink. Victoria didn't meet his eyes. She traced the pillow in her lap, her expression carefully blank. Davis wiped sweat from his brow. "You good?"

"No, I'm not." Her voice quivered as she rubbed between her eyes. "We need to talk."

Davis's frown deepened. He left the groceries and walked toward her. "Oh man. That doesn't sound good at all."

*Just start,* she told herself. *Rip the bandage.*

"I'm going to get right to it. I love you, Davis, and it's important you hear that first. We're okay in the big picture, but my head isn't. Work is all jumbled. I can't focus, and I haven't been mentally present. I need… space to clear my thoughts. Time to plot the next level for the business."

"I know you need quiet when you're digging in," he said. "And I respect that. The perfect place for some peace and quiet would be downstairs. We'll make it your creative cave; whatever you need to get whatever it is that you're trying to accomplish."

"That's generous, but the distractions would still follow me downstairs. I need time away from the house."

His eyebrows lifted. "Like a spa day or a weekend retreat?"

She shook her head. "A couple of weeks at least."

"Two weeks," he repeated. "You've never needed a getaway that long. Where's this coming from?"

Victoria's pulse pounded. *He's suspicious already. Keep calm, stay believable.*

She sat forward and gripped his hands. "I haven't been myself, and I'm sure you've noticed. My business can't afford mediocrity. My clients won't wait if I stall. I need to be somewhere quiet, free from distractions. A place where I can map out the next year and focus."

Davis searched her face for a beat, then asked, "Where will you stay?"

"The Ritz-Carlton," she said.

He let out a breath. "That's not exactly a budget stay."

"My peace of mind isn't cheap," she tried to joke, but it landed flat.

"If the Ritz is what helps, then okay. Two weeks isn't forever. I can handle lonely dinners for fourteen days. Tonight, I'll cook you something special to lift your spirits."

Victoria's stomach flipped. *He thinks there's cushion time,* she realized. *He doesn't know everything is already in the car.*

Davis returned to the counter and unpacked salmon and broccolini. "I grabbed some jasmine rice. How about salmon bowls tonight? A little send-off dinner."

"Actually… when I said two weeks, I meant starting today."

He froze. "Today?"

"My timer starts now. I packed this morning."

He leaned against the island; arms folded across his chest. "You packed already? How long have you been planning this?"

"I've battled with the decision for weeks, but I finally decided this morning to stop hesitating."

Anger flared in his eyes. "We're supposed to jump together, Vic. We're partners."

"Davis, I can't drag you into every brainstorm. Let me do this, and I'll come back sharper, and we'll be stronger."

"You've been distant. We don't see much of each other in the mornings, and you get home late most nights. You think I haven't noticed?" His voice cracked. "I miss my wife."

The raw hurt in his tone scraped her heart. She cupped his cheek, grounding herself in the stubble beneath her palm. Davis's shoulders eased a fraction. "When are you leaving?"

"Right after this conversation."

His eyes widened. "You're serious?"

"Yes, everything's packed and in the car."

He pushed off the island, the motion sharp. "Just like that? No warning? Vic, you act single sometimes, you know that?"

She flinched. "I'm not single. I'm fighting for us by taking this time to clear my head."

"I thought we'd spend tonight together. I bought wine." His voice went rough, almost pleading. "Just let me cook for you. Leave in the morning, please."

"If I stay, I'll second-guess myself. I have to go now."

Davis swallowed hard. "Will you call? At least text?"

"I need to unplug while I reset," she said. "But I'll check in when I can."

His jaw flexed. He stepped forward, hands slipping around her waist, pulling her close. His kiss was soft, then deep; mint and sorrow on his lips. Her body responded, but the clock in her head screamed louder.

"Save that," she murmured. "It'll mean more when I return."

"I love you, Victoria."

She blinked back sudden tears. "More than you know, Davis. Two weeks, and I'm back." She grabbed her purse and walked toward her car. She stepped into the garage and paused, turning back, watching him as he stood framed in the doorway.

"I love you, baby," she called.

"Talk to you soon," he murmured.

The engine rumbled, and she drove out of the garage. The moment the house disappeared around the curve, she let her breath collapse. Sunset was hours away, but she would reach Thomas long before then. Now all she needed was the sweet, dark rush of his mouth against hers, erasing every doubt in the hard language of skin on skin.

## Control 14
### No Looking Back

Victoria guided her BMW sedan into the familiar curb space across from Thomas's loft. "I can't believe this is happening. All night. Me and my man. No interruptions." Heat tightened between her thighs at the thought of his mouth between her legs.

At the top landing, she pressed the doorbell. Thomas opened the door within seconds and stood barefoot on the threshold. A plain white T-shirt clung to his chest, and gray sweatpants draped low on his hips, the loose fabric doing nothing to hide the thick line of his erection pressing forward.

"Victoria," he said.

"Thomas."

"Come in." He moved aside.

She stepped over the threshold, lightheaded. The door clicked shut and he leaned back against it, eyes tracking over her slowly.

"You actually did it." His gaze flicked past her. "But I don't see bags."

"They're in the car," she said.

"Good. I like knowing the trunk's full of your things. Means you plan to stay."

"Did you miss me?" he asked.

"Yes. I missed you, Thomas. Every second."

"Perfect." His palm slid to the back of her neck. He brought his mouth close enough for her to feel the whisper of his breath. "Because I'm starving."

"Starving? For what?" Victoria asked.

"You."

He seized her waist and lifted her onto the dining table. The polished wood was cool under her thighs. Before she could respond, he covered her mouth with his.

His hands moved with impatience. The button on her shorts popped; the zipper rasped. He dragged the denim down, forcing off her shoes. Her blouse came next, buttons slipping free. He smiled as her nipples tightened through satin and unclasped her bra.

She braced her palms on the table, chest lifting, back arching. He peeled the bra away with a rumble of satisfaction. He lowered his head, sucking a nipple into his mouth. Heat shot to her core. She gasped, threading her fingers through his hair.

His free hand slipped into her panties. One long finger traced the slick seam, then pressed between her walls. She moaned as he began a slow rhythm. He added another finger, sliding deeper. Wet sounds filled the quiet loft. He released her nipple with a soft pop and spoke against damp skin.

"Baby, you're soaked for me. I love how you stay ready. Ready to take care of your man." He sucked hard on the other nipple, his fingers pumping faster. Pleasure coiled tight in her belly. Every thrust of his hand sent sparks through her.

Her heel drummed against the table leg. He dragged her panties off and knelt between her legs, hooking her calves over his shoulders. He pressed his mouth to her, tongue delving fast, licking up every pulse of need. His fingers stayed buried, fucking her slow while his tongue circled her clit.

She bucked against his face. "Thomas—"

The words stuttered. Lightning lanced through her as climax tore free. She clutched the table's edge as she threw her head back. Wetness flooded his hand; he groaned, drinking her down until her thighs trembled.

Thomas rose, stripped his shirt, and slid on a condom. Victoria was still gasping for air when he lined himself up. He thrust into her in one powerful glide, burying himself to the hilt. He savored the tight clasp of her body around him, then he withdrew his himself almost entirely before driving back into her, hard, setting a merciless rhythm.

The table rocked under them. "Feel that?" he rasped. "Feel me hitting every spot?"

She cried out, legs locked around him, meeting his thrusts. He felt the flutter of her walls and pounded harder. Stars burst behind her eyelids as pleasure crashed again, ripping a scream from her throat.

He kept driving, chasing his own release. Thomas groaned, then thrust deep and spilled inside her. She felt the pulse of it even through latex, the entire length of him twitching inside her. For a long moment, only the sound of their breathing filled the room.

He slid out gently, tossed the condom, and stroked her thigh. "We're just getting started." She laughed weakly. "I need water, and about sixty seconds to find my lungs."

"Thirty seconds," he said, kissing her knee and hip.

"Thomas, please, I can't. You don't let up."

"Never." He ran his thumb across her swollen clit. "You'll adjust. A woman who wants her man every night needs stamina."

She felt him hardening again between her thighs. A flicker of worry sparked. *Thomas is relentless. Can I handle that? I have a company to run, a life outside this loft.* For a heartbeat she missed Davis's gentle patience, how he would pull back when she asked him to slow down. But Thomas's hand slid up her spine, and he pressed the head of his cock against her slick entrance. The first shallow thrust made her gasp. The next drove deeper, setting a punishing rhythm.

$$* * * *$$

Victoria woke to gray light and the hum of the loft's HVAC. For a moment, she thought she was home with Davis, until the ache in her thighs reminded her where she was. Every inch of her body throbbed with the soreness of a man who knew no limits.

Thomas lay behind her, his arm locked around her waist. Even in sleep he held her as if afraid she would slip away, pulling her back when she tried to stretch. He was all heat and grip, thrilling and unnerving. Davis cuddled, then drifted away. Thomas never let go. Every couple of hours he woke her again, slow at first, then with that animal hunger that left her gasping.

Now, in the gray hush of late morning, her muscles protested every shift. The sheets smelled of sweat and lavender. Affection tugged, but caution pricked. She eased his forearm up until she could slip out from under it.

Thomas stirred, eyes still closed. "Come back," he mumbled.

"You wore me out," she whispered. "Let me find my legs before you claim them again."

One corner of his mouth lifted, but he kept his eyes shut. "Five more minutes."

"It's almost eleven a.m." She stood, wincing at the tight pull in her hamstrings. "Some of us have work preparations to plan for the week."

"Cancel them."

"I need a bath," she said, rolling her shoulders. "Epsom salt, not bubbles."

"I've got you." Thomas stretched, muscles flexing as Victoria watched him with a mix of admiration and envy. "Sorry if I went overboard," he murmured. He walked behind her, arms wrapping around her waist from behind, mouth brushing her ear.

"If you start something, you'll have to finish it yourself. My legs are on strike."

"We'll negotiate later," he said as he kissed her shoulder.

Inside the bathroom, candles flickered on the vanity. The tub filled with frothy water, mineral grains glimmering beneath the surface. Victoria sank into the steaming tub, muscles loosening in bliss.

"Better?"

"A miracle." She sighed.

He chuckled as he stood and stretched. "Was it that intense? Your husband must've been a lightweight."

"No one matches you, Thomas. Trust me, I would know; I've had my fair share of fantasies," Victoria scolded.

"Well I really don't care to hear about your boring fantasies, because no one can do it like me."

Silence settled, and Victoria let the steam soften the edges of thought. Eventually her mind drifted to the woman who had answered Thomas's door days earlier.

Thomas leaned on the doorframe. "What's turning behind those eyes?"

"You." She paused. "And your life before me."

"My life's an open book, so whatever you want to know, just ask."

"Really? Because the other day, a woman in your T-shirt opened the door. It felt like a chapter I hadn't read."

"Her name is Jade," Thomas said.

"Is she past or present?" Victoria asked softly.

"Occasional. It's nothing serious between us. She likes what I do to her and I like that she leaves when I'm done."

Jealousy burned in Victoria's chest. "How long have you two been… whatever you call it?"

"A little over two years," he admitted. "It started strictly professional. She was a real-estate agent handling some of my flips. She did great numbers for me. After a few closings, we celebrated with bottles of champagne, and one thing slipped into another."

"You said she's single, right?"

"More like she floats," he replied. "Jade does her own thing and is loyal to no one and nothing. She brags about that. She bought a string of midtown bungalows, turned them into Airbnb's, then bought a rundown strip center, sliced it into salon suites, and started charging premium rent to hairstylists. She quit hustling as an agent when her cash flow outpaced commissions."

"So, when we were on pause, you found her a convenient distraction?"

"Yes," he admitted. "But that's all she ever was."

Victoria's voice trembled. "So, if we ever get into an argument, do you run back to Jade?"

Thomas's gaze sharpened. "No. I told Jade I'm unavailable for the foreseeable future. When I have my woman under my roof, I don't need rescue fantasies elsewhere. If we argue, I'm going to fix it. If I step out to cool down, it's a walk around the block, not a detour into somebody else's bed. When I commit, Victoria, I commit fully. Loyal to a fault. Death do us part."

The phrase rang like a bell, equal parts promise and warning. "Death do us part? You're skipping a few steps, aren't you?"

He gave a ghost of a grin. "Those will be our vows one day. I'm not a psycho, Victoria. I just know what I want."

"Let's slow down on marriage talk. I still have divorce paperwork to file."

"Isn't that the pot calling the kettle black?" he asked. "You're grilling me about a woman I've hooked up with a handful of times, while you have a whole husband at home."

Shame pricked her as she stayed silent.

He continued, "You're treating life like open season. Hunt, mount, and lie when it's convenient. Should I be worried you'll grow bored with me and find another man to fulfill whatever it is that you feel you need when you need it?"

"I have no intention of hurting you, Thomas. The first night we spent together, I knew you were the man who saw me, every flaw and every hunger, and didn't flinch. I can't live without that now. I love you."

His eyes softened. He crouched beside the tub, tucking damp hair behind her ear. "I love you too and I want to be everything you desire."

She saw the earnestness in his eyes and something softer, a vulnerable glint that contradicted his iron control. He kissed her, his lips wet against hers, then broke away with a soft laugh. "I want you right now, but I'll respect your bath time. I'm going downstairs to make breakfast. I know it's almost noon, but breakfast for lunch is always a vibe. Enjoy the soak."

She slid deeper into the water, while her mind replayed every nuance of their conversation. Victoria let her eyes drift shut. Maybe there was no fairy tale in this loft, but there was truth. She felt herself inching closer to it.

# Control 13
## Unspoken Shifts

Mondays were dreaded by almost everyone. However, Victoria welcomed this one. Sunlight streamed through Social Brilliance's mezzanine windows, bright enough to turn the lobby floor into a mirror. Victoria paused in the doorway, savoring the familiar hum of ringing phones, keyboards, and brainstorming. Saturday night had wrung her body, and even Sunday's gentler session with Thomas had left her sore. A full night's sleep restored her, and she was ready to reclaim her empire.

Crossing the workspace, she greeted her staff until she reached her office and froze. Tabitha sat in her leather chair, headset on, laughing at a caller and looking absurdly comfortable in the boss's seat. Tabitha's fingers drummed the desk with casual ownership that pricked Victoria's chest.

Victoria entered and cleared her throat loud enough to be heard.

Tabitha finished the call and slid the headset off. "Good morning, V! Long time no see." She spread her arms theatrically. "I was beginning to think you'd resigned and left me the keys to the kingdom." Her laugh rang a little too sharp.

"Morning, Tab. Why are you in my office?"

"My computer glitched, so I hopped on yours to keep the Manlow Tech proposal moving."

Victoria's pulse was elevated, but she forced a cordial smile. "I wasn't prepared to see someone sitting at my desk. I need that space clear so I can set the day's priorities."

"I had no intention of overstepping," Tabitha said as she edged away from the chair.

"It's been a long weekend, Tab. I shouldn't have snapped," Victoria said apologetically.

"It's okay, babes. You're not the only one dragging. My man ran me ragged all weekend too," she said as she gave a playful twerk.

Victoria laughed. "Still the same mystery guy?"

Tabitha's cheeks glowed. "Oh yes, we're locked in, honey. He couldn't get enough of me. I feel like I spent forty-eight hours bent over every piece of furniture. He was like an animal let out of the cage." She let the sentence hang, savoring Victoria's laughter.

"I've never seen you glow like this," Victoria said. "I must meet him."

"In due time." Tab tapped the desk twice. "I'll leave you to settle. Then we can sync on the week. Your absence left quite a few mountains to climb."

"I know." Victoria positioned herself in her chair, reclaiming territory. "I'll need a full debrief. Quarterlies, new-business pipeline, anything threatening the runway."

"No need to worry. I already handled the quarterlies, secured three new accounts, negotiated retention bumps, and the lease renewal: ten percent reduction for a three-year renewal. I emailed you the revised contract."

"You did this without running it by me?" Victoria said, stunned.

"I emailed you memos and tried to call you," Tabitha replied. "But you were unreachable."

A pulse of heat climbed Victoria's neck. "I don't remember seeing any memos or missing any calls from you. Lease negotiations are only to be handled by me, but I must admit, I was a bit out of reach. Also, a ten percent reduction is quite nice. But next time, make sure you reach me before signing off on something like that. Thank you, Assistant extraordinaire.”

Tabitha’s smile cooled. “Business partner is more accurate at this point.”

Victoria laughed dismissively. “Assistant, business partner, tomato, tomahto.”

Tabitha didn’t laugh.

Victoria noticed and softened her tone. “You’re right. You’ve kept this place humming, but the boss is back.” Victoria stepped behind her chair. “Email me the summaries before lunch?”

“Of course.” Tabitha’s jaw flexed as she left.

In her office, Tabitha let the mask drop. Victoria’s laugh still rang in her ears. She had poured herself into Social Brilliance while Victoria vanished on a whim, and she had the nerve to say tomato, tomahto. Tabitha had rewritten contracts, rescued ad buys, and kept payroll on schedule while Victoria disappeared in a haze of excuses.

Tabitha’s phone buzzed on the desk. The contact flashed: My man, as she answered.

“Hey, beautiful,” his voice soothed. “You at the office?”

“Yes, and I just got a reminder of my place in the hierarchy from my so-called boss.”

“Oh, she’s back?”

“Yes, and she waltzed in like she never left me to handle all the headaches on my own. But anyways, I miss you already, even though my body is still recovering from our weekend.”

He chuckled, “I didn’t mean to wear my queen out. I can’t help myself when you turn me on.”

“We have to be careful, though, so make sure you wrap it up. I don’t want to get pregnant yet.”

“You’re my future wife, so we might as well get started.”

"We have to make sure our ducks are in a row, and I'd like to be married first," Tabitha said definitively.

"Let's talk about it more over dinner tonight," he said.

She smiled and said, "Okay. I'll have dinner ready for you by 7 p.m."

They traded I-love-yous and ended the call.

Tabitha returned to work mode, as she opened the financial dashboards and saw that revenue was up, new contracts flowed, and Manlow Tech's exclusivity offer was all lined up. The company thrived under Tabitha's command. She thought to herself: *I am no one's fucking assistant. I create my own success.*

Tabitha returned to Victoria's office with a navy binder. "Summary details," Tabitha said. "Quarterly revenue grew eight percent, marketing spend held flat, new client contracts in green, retention expansions in blue, and lease renegotiations in purple."

"This is impressive," Victoria said.

"I thought so too," Tabitha replied. "One final note: Fensen & Price rescheduled the brand launch to next Monday. They refused a later date, but we're on track."

"You did all this during my… retreat."

"Yes," Tabitha said sternly.

"I appreciate your dedication," Victoria said, though the words landed more like obligation than praise. Her eyes were already on an email that pinged into her inbox. She clicked it, effectively dismissing Tabitha without a second glance.

"Your Manlow Tech negotiation is set for two o'clock. I'll have the slide deck finalized by one," Tabitha said.

"Thank you," Victoria murmured.

Tabitha left the office, closing the door more firmly than necessary. She made herself a silent vow: *Victoria would soon understand just how valuable I am, and what it will cost to take loyalty for granted.*

Victoria barely looked up from her screen as the door shut. The binder laid open, proof of Tabitha's hustle. Tabitha's margin notes were precise. She thought to herself, *maybe Tab has earned the right to be called partner.* Victoria decided she would let Tabitha lead the first five minutes of the call, partly as recognition, but more so because Tabitha knew every cent of the numbers better than she did at this point.

*But I am still the boss,* she reminded herself. *And the boss must look ahead.* She skimmed the binder's final page; an organizational flowchart Tabitha had tweaked while Victoria was gone. One line caught her eye, Proposed restructure: COO (vacant) with Tabitha's name penciled beside it. Victoria frowned. A step too far, maybe, because Victoria and Tabitha never discussed titles, especially one that gave her a significant amount of control within the company. Victoria made a mental note to bring it up to Tab, but for now, she pushed the thought aside and prepared for the noon prep meeting with Tabitha.

✶ ✶ ✶ ✶

Thomas appeared from the kitchen, apron tied low on his bare torso, a slow smile on his lips. "Long day, boss lady?"

"One of the longest," she admitted.

He crossed the floor and kissed her until her tension melted. "Hungry?" he asked.

"For food, maybe," she whispered, "but for you, always."

"Eat first," he said. "You'll need your energy." He offered his arm theatrically, and guided her to the table, plates waiting with shrimp over angel hair pasta, salad bright with strawberries and goat cheese.

Thomas poured chilled rosé, then took the seat opposite of her. "You are glowing. What brought on this spark today?" He prompted.

She described the Manlow Tech negotiation, the revenue uptick, and the binder Tabitha had prepared. As she spoke, she noticed a flicker of calculation in Thomas's eyes, as though he catalogued her allies and potential threats.

"Tabitha sounds indispensable," he said.

"She was a lifesaver," Victoria admitted. "I may raise her salary soon."

"Mmm. Just watch that her ambition doesn't outpace loyalty," he warned.

"I don't have to worry about Tab. She's like the sister I never had. She'll be there when no one else will. She's the one thing that's constant in my life."

Suspicion flickered in his eyes before he let it fade. He didn't know anything about Tabitha and hadn't met her yet, but he always had his doubts about people that always seemed too good to be true.

"Speaking of constant, I have a question that I've been curious to ask you," Thomas said.

A nervous flutter stirred in her stomach. "Shoot."

"How long have you and Davis been married?"

"Four years," she said. "Why do you ask?"

"It just made me curious. Married couples usually toss the condoms after the honeymoon, so that got me asking myself, how come you two don't have any children? Have you ever been pregnant?"

"No. I've never been pregnant."

"Why not?"

"Davis never pressed for kids. He's always been career-driven, and he wanted me to build Social Brilliance without a pause. He said we would revisit the idea after we hit certain milestones." She offered a small shrug. "A few years ago, I had an IUD placed. It simplified everything."

Thomas processed that, eyes narrowing in contemplation. "Most men I know want children," he murmured. "Especially sons."

"I didn't object," she added quickly. "I love running my business and watching it flourish, not going to apologize for that, and the timing never felt right."

"When you close the door on the Davis chapter," he said, "I want us to open a new one. I see us in a nice house, Victoria, with a wide porch, and a big Suburban SUV in the driveway stuffed with sports gear. I want kids, plural. A safe, happy place, nothing like the way I grew up. We'll give our children everything."

As he spoke, images bloomed behind her eyes: Sunday mornings filled with waffles, backpacks by the door, and children's laughter ricocheting through the hallway. She saw Thomas bent over homework at the dining table and herself slipping out of a strategy meeting early to cheer at a soccer game on a windy April afternoon. The vision tugged at a part of her she rarely let breathe.

Thomas's voice softened. "I never had a father. My mother was out of my life at an early age. I swear to you, I'll never abandon my kids or you. I love you. I want the vows, the rings, the death-do-us-part. All of it."

A tight swell rose in her throat. She hadn't even noticed the tears until they blurred her vision. "Thomas, you're—" She shook her head. "Those words are everything I've ever wanted to hear."

He kissed each tear before it could fall, then rested his forehead against hers. "So, you want it too?"

"I do," she whispered. "I want all of it with you."

"Then watch out because I'll have you barefoot and pregnant year-round."

She swatted his chest. "Excuse me, sir, I'm not some country bumpkin."

"You'll be my country bumpkin," he corrected, leaning in to kiss her smile.

"We could start practicing now."

"No objections," she breathed.

He picked her up from the table and padded towards the staircase going towards the bedroom.

"What about the food?" She laughed.

"We'll clean that up later," he joked.

The world outside their cocoon felt far away. In this narrow slice of time, the vision that was painted glowed warm and full of promise.

# Control 12
## Fractures in the Glass

The work week flew by almost without Victoria noticing. She leaned back in her chair and flexed her aching shoulders. She had spent the last two hours dissecting a draft influencer contract, line by line. Outside her glass walls, team leads drifted past with coffee refills and quiet jokes. Everything felt under control.

Her phone rang and Thomas's name flashed across the screen.

"Hello, future wifey. How's the future Mrs. Carter doing?"

"I'm busy and starving, but pushing through it. And you? Still wrangling floorboards?"

"Not anymore. The shipment of supplies I was waiting for is delayed, so I wrapped early." He lowered his voice to a conspiratorial murmur. "I figured I'd pick up your favorite salmon salad and surprise my lady."

Pleasure flickered, followed by a dart of alarm. He was bringing lunch here? The visions collided in her mind, Thomas's strong, unmistakable presence striding through Social Brilliance, her staff whispering.

"Oh, you're coming to the office?" she asked.

"Yeah, but I didn't want to pop up and cause a security alert, so I'm giving my queen a heads-up. I'm about twenty minutes out."

"That's sweet," she began, pivoting desperately, "but you really don't have to. Traffic is horrible already. Take the salad home, I'll eat it for dinner."

"Nonsense. Why divert me every time I want to see where the magic happens?" He chuckled. "Let me guess, Davis is lurking in the bullpen?"

"No, it's just, I haven't quite announced my separation to anyone yet. If my staff sees you, rumors start. I need to keep my private life off the Slack channels until everything's finalized."

The line went quiet. "Thomas? You there?"

"So, you want to put me in a corner, while you protect… optics."

"I'm not trying to put you in a corner. I just dislike messy drama. A whisper here turns into a headline there."

"People will talk no matter what," he said. "If you love me, what does it matter? And I'm not coming in to dip you over the copier. Your staff will probably think I'm just another potential client."

Her mind shuffled possibilities at breathless speed. If she flat-out refused, he would arrive anyway, stubborn as a freighter. If she agreed, at least she controlled the narrative. A fight at the loft tonight would ruin their fragile sanctuary.

"You know what, Thomas? You're right. We'll just keep it cool, calm and collected. I'm not trying to hide you, it's just that I'm still married and I have to play this delicately."

"Understood and I'll see you soon, baby."

She ended the call, pulse fluttering as she rose from her chair. The glass walls made her office a fishbowl; she closed the door and lowered the blinds by half.

Tabitha's heels were still echoing down the hallway when it struck Victoria like a slap: Thomas was coming. He was barreling toward Social Brilliance, and Tabitha, who would gladly claw his eyes out, had no warning. Victoria's heart somersaulted against her ribs. *You have fifteen minutes to stop a volcano,* she told herself. Panic skittered beneath her skin. *If Tab sees him without context, she'll detonate in the lobby.*

She picked up the phone and called over to Tab's office. "Tab, can you swing by my office?"

"Give me a sec to—"

"Now, Tab. Please." Her voice cracked.

Thirty seconds later Tabitha arrived, a concerned wrinkle burrowing between her brows. "What's the fire?"

"Close the door."

"V, you look like you've seen a ghost."

"I don't have time for preamble, so just listen and spare me the commentary."

Tabitha's eyebrows shot up at the barked order, but she said nothing.

Victoria inhaled. "I moved out of my house. Temporarily. I'm living with Thomas."

"I'm sorry, what?"

"I'm in love with him," Victoria barreled on. "I can't let him go. I haven't told Davis yet—"

"Jesus Christ," Tabitha muttered.

"—but I will, Tab. I just need time. Thomas is on his way with lunch, so he'll be in the lobby in twelve minutes."

A stunned silence stretched. "Of course he is."

Tab took two steps forward, fury erupting in her eyes. "V, are you hearing yourself? You're walking around like a damn side-street whore, shacking up with some mother-fucker who probably isn't worth the condoms you keep tossing in the trash, and now you want to parade him through this office?"

"Watch your mouth," Victoria snapped. "You don't know anything about Thomas."

"I know he's wrecking your life!" Tab jabbed a finger toward the blinds. "You built this empire, *you,* and now you're tossing it onto the tracks because you can't stop chasing dick like a love-struck groupie."

"Thomas isn't a fling. He's accomplished in his own right. He treats me like I matter."

"You already mattered!" Tab's voice rose. "You had Davis, stable, loyal, a man who worshipped the ground you walked on. And what do you do? You abandon him and that gorgeous house to play roommate somewhere with a guy you barely know."

"That 'guy' owns more properties than half our client roster," Victoria shot back. "He's not some penniless drifter."

"Oh, yes, Mr. Real Estate King, who shows up unannounced at your job like a high-school boyfriend checking your locker. That screams secure."

"You don't have to like him, but you *will* show respect. He's important to me."

"What about respecting yourself?" Tab demanded. "You're a CEO, V. But here you are, running after the next orgasm."

"That's not fair," Victoria whispered.

"Fair died the second you let him crawl between your legs before you ended your marriage."

Victoria flinched.

"Do you know how many nights I stayed up praying to have a relationship like yours and Davis's? You were my gold standard. Now I find out you traded it for a man you've known five minutes?"

"I feel alive with Thomas," Victoria said. "He sees all of me, and he doesn't flinch. I won't walk away from that."

"Fine. Gamble your marriage and reputation. But *don't* drag me into it."

"I drag you into everything, Tab. You're my best friend."

"Then treat me like one!" Tabitha snapped.

"You're right. I should've told you about Thomas and our situation sooner, but I was scared."

"Damn right you were scared, because it's reckless." Tabitha's shoulders sagged. "Where does this end, V?"

"Me being happy. Thomas is a part of that."

"I don't have to like it, but I won't trash your guest in front of the staff."

"That's all I ask. Please."

Victoria's phone rang. The receptionist's cheerful tone floated across the speaker: "Mrs. Hart, you have a visitor waiting."

"Thank you, I'll come greet him." She hung up, then turned back to Tabitha. "He's here."

"Fine. I'll walk with you."

"You don't have to."

"Yes, I do," Tabitha said quietly. "Someone needs to make sure the lobby doesn't become TMZ. And besides, I'm curious to see the dick worth throwing away your marriage for."

Victoria managed an unsteady laugh. Together they left the office, heels echoing in unison down the glass-lined corridor toward a collision that could shatter everything or fuse it into something new.

Thomas stood at the desk, chatting with the receptionist.

"Hello, Mr. Carter," Victoria greeted, voice smooth as a board-room glide. "Thank you for bringing lunch. Please follow me, let me give you a quick tour."

Thomas's answering smile flashed, but she saw his eyes flick to Tabitha. She turned slightly. "Thomas, this is Tabitha Ramsey, my best friend and…" She almost said assistant but caught herself. "Business partner."

Thomas offered a hand. "Nice to meet the legendary Tabitha I've heard so much about."

Tabitha clasped his hand for the briefest pulse of contact, then let go. "Hello, Thomas." She pivoted toward Victoria. "I'll leave you two. I have a mountain of work that won't finish itself." Without another glance she strode off.

"O-kay," he murmured. "Did I step on a land mine?"

"She's under major deadlines," Victoria said. "Let's walk."

As they moved deeper into the open workspace, she narrated each department, but her thoughts whisked backward to the office confrontation twenty minutes earlier, and Thomas seemed to sense the tension. When she opened her office door and waved him inside, she felt the nerves flare hotter. The glass walls were soundproof, but Tabitha's office sat just two doors away. Victoria could practically feel her friend's simmering disapproval through the walls.

She took the salad container with a bright "Thank you," as she sat behind her desk. Thomas remained standing for a moment, gaze trailing across the Clio trophies and acrylic innovation plaques. "Damn," he said softly, "I knew you were a boss, but I didn't know it was *this* serious."

"Vision and insomnia. I hustled day and night to make my dream a reality."

"Your partner, she always that cold?"

"Tab's protective of me. She worries I'll be hurt."

"That protection felt a lot like hostility."

"She just doesn't know you that well yet, that's all."

The calendar pinged on Victoria's monitor: meeting in fifteen minutes.

"I have a brief meeting that I have to attend," she said. "Thank you for lunch."

Thomas rose from the chair, "Well, I'll get out of your hair and see you at home tonight."

He leaned down, brushed his mouth across her ear. "Good thing you have all the window blinds closed so no one can see us."

She laughed. "Stop it. These walls have ears."

Gathering composure, she gestured to the desktop calendar blinking in the corner: *REVISION REVIEW — 5 minutes.*

"Stay for a second. I'll walk you out after the signatures. Fifteen minutes, tops."

"Okay, boss." He dropped back into the chair. "I'll wait right here."

Thomas heard the heel-click fade down the corridor, then silence. He drew a slow breath, scanning the room once more. Framed photos lined one shelf: Victoria shaking hands with brand executives, Victoria on a Cannes stage clutching a Clio, Victoria and Tabitha beaming at a ribbon-cutting.

He smiled, equal parts pride and anticipation. *Soon this will all be ours,* he thought. *A family empire.* The idea filled his chest with warmth and pride.

The doorknob twitched. Thomas didn't expect Victoria back already, but it was Tabitha who slipped inside. She closed the door without a sound, then flicked sharp eyes over him.

"Did Victoria head to her meeting?" Tabitha asked.

"She just walked out. She said she'd be back within fifteen minutes."

"Mm." Tabitha pivoted to leave.

"Hey, Tab," he called. "Can I rap with you for a second?"

"Rap with me?"

He laughed under his breath. "Sorry. May we talk for a moment?"

"I'm listening."

"I got the sense our first hello was… tense. If I offended you, I'm sorry. I've heard nothing but great things about you from Victoria. I would really like to know the woman she calls her best friend."

Tabitha's gaze flicked to his outstretched hand, but she didn't take it.

"First of all, my name is Tabitha. Friends call me Tab. You are not my friend." She took a single step closer, setting the edge of Victoria's desk between them like a barrier.

"Fair enough. I just wanted to clear the air. When we met in the hall, I felt a little coldness. I figured I might have stepped on your toes."

"Coldness?" She laughed. "Thomas, the only toes you're stepping on are Victoria's, while you trample the life she spent years building."

"That's not how I see it."

"Of course not. Because you're too busy seeing dollar signs. Or maybe just a hot CEO who strokes your ego, and your dick, when she's bored at home."

A flicker of heat lit his eyes. "Watch the way you talk about her."

"I'm not insulting her. I'm insulting *you*, motherfucker. You blow in wearing flashy Nikes and dripping cologne, and suddenly she's swapping a stable husband for a side-street fantasy."

Thomas chuckled. "You think sneakers define me? I cleared six figures off my last flip before breakfast, sweetheart."

"This isn't about money," Tabitha hissed. "It's about *integrity*. She lied to you for weeks, lied to Davis, lied to me—"

"Because she was terrified," he cut in. "Terrified of people like you crucifying her."

"She was terrified because people like *me* have been cleaning up her messes while she's off riding you into the sunset."

"Interesting. Sounds like you enjoy being her savior. Must kill you that she's found someone else to lean on."

Tabitha's nostrils flared. "Don't twist this. I don't need her leaning on me. I need her sane, safe, and not ruining her reputation over a guy who thinks great dick equals destiny."

Thomas stepped forward; only inches separated them now. "You keep bringing up my dick, Tabitha. Makes me wonder if you're curious."

"I'm curious how long before it leads you to her bank accounts."

"I've got my own money. Hell, I could buy into Social Brilliance tomorrow if I wanted to."

"Over my dead body."

"That can be arranged," he said softly, then flashed a grin that made it impossible to know if he was joking.

Tabitha's pulse hammered in her throat, but she refused to flinch. "Listen, contractor, Victoria's been my sister for seventeen years. I won't watch her torch her marriage and her name for a man who swaggered in less than a year ago."

"You don't get to decide who she loves. That terrifies you, because if she chooses me, you're no longer center stage."

"Please. I have my own spotlight. I'm the reason this company's numbers are still green while you keep her up fucking till dawn."

He leaned even closer. "Pretty sure she's the one begging for more."

"She'll get tired of you. She always does with her pet projects."

"That's where you're wrong. She's tired of *safe*. She wants everything and a family. And I'm giving that to her."

"A family?" Tab scoffed. "Where does that leave her company? Oh right, under your name, once you convince her to split assets."

"Say that again."

"You're a gold-digging dickhead with a toolbox and a fantasy. And I'm not letting you steal her crown."

"I don't need her crown. I'm building a kingdom with her, something you can't fathom because you've hitched your whole identity to being her little gatekeeper."

The words hit harder than she expected. For a second, her mask cracked; doubt flickered in her eyes. Then rage surged to fill the gap. "Better a gatekeeper than a parasite."

"Parasite? Sweetheart, I'm the best thing that ever crawled into her life."

"She has a *husband*," Tabitha said.

"Soon to be *ex*."

"That's what you think," she spit back.

"That's what I *know*. And here's something else. If you come between us, Tabitha, you'll lose."

She held his stare. "Try me."

For a heartbeat they were motionless statues of hostility, close enough for lips to brush if venom slipped and turned to something hotter.

Suddenly, they both heard the loud thunderous footsteps of Victoria heading towards the office, and they split far away from each other.

Victoria entered, cheeks pink from her brisk walk. The tension hit her in a tangible wave.

"Oh, looks like you two are getting acquainted."

Thomas straightened his shirt. "Just exchanging perspectives."

Tabitha's lips curved in a thin line. "We were discussing… boundaries."

Victoria glanced from one to the other, suspicion blooming. "Everything good?"

"Peachy," Tabitha said. "I'll be at my desk if you need me." With that, she slipped out.

Victoria sagged against the credenza. "God. What happened?"

"Your best friend doesn't think I'm worthy of you."

"She just, she cares. She'll come around."

"She called me a parasite."

Victoria's breath caught. "I'm sorry."

"No one decides our future but us, Victoria. Remember that."

"I know."

He exhaled. "It's time for me to be heading out. I'll see you tonight at home."

✳ ✳ ✳ ✳

Victoria walked Thomas out and came back into her office to wrap things up for the day. A flashback came to her of the scene she saw earlier, between Thomas and Tabitha, and her pulse hadn't slowed since. She drew one long breath and picked up the phone and dialed to Tabitha and requested that Tab come to her office.

Tabitha stepped through the doorway and Victoria gestured to the armchair opposite her desk. "Tab, I know today has been tumultuous, to say the least."

"Ha, you can say that shit again."

"I need to understand what happened while I was in the meeting. Thomas told me you called him a parasite. Did I hear that right?"

"You know, V? I'm drained. I don't have any more energy to pour into the toxicity you call your man. Honestly, I just want to shut my laptop and go home. I don't ever care to see him again."

"Tab, you don't even know him. You came at him like a battering ram, for what? To defend me? I don't need you speaking for me; I'm perfectly capable. And another thing, stop dragging Davis into every conversation. If he's so perfect, then maybe you should be with him."

The words hung between them, sharp and reckless. Tabitha's spine went arrow-straight; her stare sharpened into something steely.

"Thomas and I are going to be together for the foreseeable future. If you can't respect my relationship, then, honestly, I don't know if we can keep being friends."

Tabitha's mouth parted, shock mingling with hurt. "Are you serious right now, Victoria? You expect me to stand here cheering while you torch everything you've built for a guy you met a few months back? I'm trying to talk sensibly, show you the bigger picture. You're throwing away years of sweat and stability for a thrill that feels good this minute. You're about to bulldoze a marriage that was solid because you're high on a man who knows how to lay pipe."

Tabitha swiped at sudden moisture at the corner of one eye and powered on. "Forgive me for giving a damn about my best friend in the whole wide world. But you know the saddest part? You would toss *me* aside for him. I've been here through everything."

"Tab, I'm sorry, I shouldn't have said—"

"It's cool, *boss*. I'll finish those Q3 forecasts and go home. See you tomorrow." Her voice was final. She turned and left, heels clicking like gavels down the hall.

Victoria crossed to the window and pressed her forehead to the cool glass. *Why does loving one person have to feel like betraying another?* All she felt was the ache of a friendship splitting along an invisible seam. And beneath that ache, a ripple of dread whispered: Storms never end where they start. Today's disaster might only be the tremor before the fault line truly broke.

# Control 11
## The Quiet Trap

The clock read 3:00 a.m. and Thomas couldn't stop thinking about Victoria and Davis. He wanted to believe the neat explanation she had given him in a previous conversation he had with her, assuring him that Davis knows the marriage is ending, but something about it didn't feel honest. *What does Davis actually think?* The question beat behind his temples. Thomas opened Facebook again, scrolling through Davis's public feed, thumbs moving slowly so he didn't miss a breadcrumb. There was the selfie: Davis in running gear, sweat glowing on his forehead, captioned: *Fellas, stay fit for your ladies.* Dozens of likes already; Tabitha had dropped a flex-arm emoji in the comments. Thomas snorted. *Cute.*

Thomas pictured the route: five miles of rolling hills. He decided at last that he would be there; just another jogger lacing into the morning. A smile touched his mouth. *Keep your enemies closer.* He didn't hate Davis, but Davis stood between him and the life he wanted.

Thomas rolled out of bed at 3:35 a.m., long before the streetlamps flicked off. The expressway was nearly empty. The dashboard clock glowed 4:20 a.m. when he eased into the tree-lined park that was less than three quarters of a mile from Davis's neighborhood.

He killed the engine and let the cooling metal tick while old ghosts crept in. Not Victoria this time, but the boy he had been before the Navy, before real estate. *Thomas Quincy Carter.* Three names that never felt like they belonged to the same kid. Eighteen letters he had rehearsed in every waiting room from health checks to county-court lobbies, where his file was thicker than the phone book.

The name *Thomas* came from the mother whose addiction cost her custody when he was eight years old, the day that case workers pried him from her trembling embrace and carried him into the system. *Carter* belonged to a father whose signature was a blank space on every official line. And *Quincy*, the orphaned middle name, had been tacked on by a clerk who needed an initial to finish the intake form. But it was *Q* that followed him the longest. *Back in the queue you go, Q.*

The first case worker said it with a bright, brittle cheer. He was eight, shivering beside her desk, and she had whispered the line like a secret joke because his placement list was literally called *the "Q."* The quip caught on. Every case worker after that repeated it, back in the "Q", when a foster family called to say, *He's mouthy, come get him,* or *He wet the bed,* or *He pushed our son,* or simply *He doesn't fit.*

Back in the "Q" became a mantra. After a while, the name felt less like a nickname and more like a sentence.

He was eight the first time a minivan door slid shut behind him and the world blurred into rows of unfamiliar houses. Each mailbox they passed looked the same, yet he imagined magic behind every front door: a mother who smelled like bread, a father who lifted him to the ceiling, maybe even a dog that didn't bark in a mean way. The Millers, rosy-cheeked churchgoers, met him on the porch with a stuffed bear and promises of apple pie. For three weeks, he slept with that bear under his arm and convinced himself the word *temporary* didn't apply. On the twenty-second night, he rolled his eyes when Mrs. Miller nagged him about elbow grease on dishes. Two hours later the bear was in a trash bag, and he was buckled into the case worker's sedan. *Mouthing off,* the Millers reported. *Defiant.*

The Torres family tried next. They spoke Spanish rapid-fire around a kitchen table that smelled of cumin, and for once, Thomas's mixed, brown skin didn't make him the odd one out. He had almost believed in forever again, until he lost his temper at school when a boy called him *half-breed.* The principal phoned home and the Torres's decided they *weren't equipped for behavioral challenges.* Back in the "Q."

By age eleven, Thomas knew the pattern: honeymoon, minor infraction, quiet packing at midnight. He told himself he didn't care. Still, the ache of leaving each *almost-home* burrowed deeper than any bruise. He began testing families faster, pushing buttons sooner, because rejection stung less when you ripped the Band-Aid off yourself. His file thickened with words like *oppositional* and *volatile,* but the truth of the matter, he wouldn't hurt a fly, but reading those words on paper painted him as a scary and threatening brown kid. Foster parents read the summary and saw a storm they didn't want in their living room.

At age fourteen, the "Q" ended. The county placed him in Brookridge Youth Development Center, a polite mouthful for a concrete maze no one confused with home. Thirty bunks, one television bolted inside a metal cage, and dinner trays that tasted of bleach. Staff turnover was a revolving door. Most days the counselors looked as weary as the kids. But Brookridge taught him skills the suburbs never could—how to size up a threat without blinking—how to laugh at the right joke so the pack wouldn't smell fear—how to tuck his rage away and unleash it on a punching bag instead of another boy's jaw.

He learned something else, too—discipline. Wary of the cops who circled Brookridge like vultures, he ran laps in the cracked asphalt courtyard every dawn. First, two miles, then three. Foot-pounding rhythm calmed the noise in his skull. By sixteen, he could do six miles without breathing hard. The PE coach took notice and slipped him a pamphlet on junior enlisted programs. *The military likes kids who can run and follow orders.*

He aged out of the foster care system at eighteen with two garbage bags of clothes, a handshake from the case worker, and a bus voucher. No family showed, but the Navy did. Boot camp was brutal but simple—pushups instead of paperwork, clear consequences instead of cheerful lies. You screw up, you redo it until it's right. Nobody sent him back to any queue because there was nowhere else to send him. He thrived, rose to petty officer, stacked ribbons across his chest, and learned carpentry when ships needed refit. He carved muscle over boyish angles and discovered calm in precision work—measure twice, cut once, never leave a seam weak enough for water to seep through.

But nights on watch still cracked open old wounds. He would stare at black ocean stretching to black horizon and feel the hollow echo of every porch he had left behind. *Forever* was a myth. *Home* was a rumor. If he ever found either, he told himself, he would burn every bridge before abandoning it.

Discharge led to real estate flips and eventually to the small café where a powerhouse named Victoria Hart made small talk with him. When their eyes locked, something primal clicked, telling him the wandering was over. Victoria wasn't shelter; she was an empire, and she had chosen him. He clung to that truth the way his younger self had held his stuffed bear, fierce, certain, and terrified to lose it.

Because Victoria did what no foster parent, group home counselor, or squad mate had ever done—she *saw* him. Not the troubled note in a file, not the chip on his shoulder, or the scarlet letters of *unwanted* and *temporary* stamped across his childhood. She saw the man beneath the armor. She laughed at jokes others called rough around the edges and heard wit instead of warning signs. When his temper flickered, she didn't flinch or reach for the phone; she touched his forearm, grounded him, proved that anger could meet understanding instead of exile.

For Thomas, who had spent a lifetime yanked from one "forever" to the next, the shock of being chosen and *kept* felt like oxygen after drowning. Victoria's love gave him something the system never offered: permanence without conditions. Every time she said *I'm not going anywhere,* the eight-year-old who had watched caseworkers box up his life, felt a stitch close in an old wound.

That's why he wouldn't let her go. Losing her wouldn't be like losing a girlfriend. It would rip open every eviction, every *back in the "Q"* that had ever taught him he was disposable. Victoria was proof that he was finally more than a file number. In her eyes, he was not a liability to manage, he was a future to build, and for a boy who had learned to live under borrowed roofs, that kind of belonging was a treasure you guarded with blood and bone.

Now, sitting in the silent pickup, he reminded himself why he was there. Forever had to be protected. Davis Hart may be a good man by all accounts, but good men had first-rights in the civilized world, and Thomas Quincy Carter had never been handed first-rights to anything. He would take what he needed, gently, if possible, ruthlessly if not.

* * * *

He stepped down from the truck and began to stretch. He straightened, rolled his neck, and started toward the neighborhood entrance.

*Give it five minutes,* he thought to himself.

A silhouette emerged from the neighborhood entrance. *Target acquired.* Thomas turned on his phone's flashlight and searched the grass as though he'd lost something.

"You lose something, man?" The voice matched Davis's video posts.

"Yeah, my ring. Slipped right off somewhere in the dark… ah, there." Thomas stooped, palmed a pebble, and slipped it into his pocket. "Thank God."

Davis chuckled. "Wedding band?"

"Oh God, not yet." Thomas said grinning. "Just a ring that my fiancée likes for me to wear. Says it keeps the vultures off."

"Bro, that would've been your last day alive if it had been a real band."

They shared a quick laugh. Thomas extended a hand. "Quincy. But folks call me Q."

"Davis," the other man replied. "You run out here a lot?"

"Couple times a month," Thomas lied smoothly. "I like the hilly terrain. Mind if I tag along? Hills always go faster with company."

"Some company never hurts. My route's exactly five miles."

Thomas fell into pace beside him, matching his cadence with practiced ease. Air Force and Navy stories surfaced, stitched together with dark humor and scars. Thomas noted Davis's breathing pattern and stride, which was efficient and controlled. Davis appeared to be a man accustomed to disarming rather than attacking.

*This is the guy?* Thomas wondered. *The rival?* A pang of pity flickered. Davis was decent, too decent, maybe. No wonder Victoria had hungered for chaos and flame. Davis radiated calmness.

After they finished the five-mile loop, they slowed to a walk. Davis tipped his head back, breathing deep. "Gotta tell you, Q, it feels like I've known you ten years."

"Likewise, bro. You know, we should grab a few beers and catch a Braves game sometime."

"Sounds like a plan to me."

They traded numbers and shot the breeze for a few more minutes before ending the conversation. Relief flooded Thomas: mission phase one accomplished. But as

he walked back to the truck, guilt crept in. Davis was undeniably likable, the kind of man who would give jumper cables to strangers without expecting thanks. *This is the man
whose marriage I'm dismantling?*

Traffic had started to thicken by the time the loft came
into view. Thomas stripped off his sweat-soaked clothes,
quickly showered, and climbed into bed beside Victoria,
careful not to wake her. He pressed a soft kiss to her shoulder and settled against the pillow. Phase one complete.
Phase two in progress.

# Control 10
## The Edge of Honesty

Victoria sketched the day's hours ahead in her mind. At 1:00 p.m., she would sit down with Davis at the house they once called their forever home. She had practiced the opening lines: *We need some time apart. I have to be honest about where my heart is now.* For now, she would leave Thomas's name out. Any attorney would seize on proof of an affair and turn it into leverage for alimony, asset splits, and even a claim on Social Brilliance. First would come a calm request for separation. Later, once legal counsel laid out the safest course, she would untangle the rest.

* * * *

Victoria stepped inside of her home, feeling the weight, as the door shut behind her. Davis hurried in from the kitchen, wiping his hands on a dish towel. He looked trim in his running shorts and a clean white T-shirt, cheeks still tinted from his morning jog. "Vic, you're here." He pulled her into a hug, and she stiffened for a second, then let herself fold into the comfort.

"Lunch is ready. I made your favorite Cajun chicken salad, with fresh croissants, fruit, the works." His grin was proud.

Normally, Victoria would have devoured two croissants, but today her appetite was a knot. She smoothed her blouse, forcing a smile. "That sounds amazing."

"Come see." He guided her toward the kitchen. On the island sat a large glass bowl filled with a colorful salad, a plate of flaky croissants, and neat rows of fruit.

The sight stung. He had no idea what truth she carried inside. "It looks perfect," she said.

"Hope you haven't eaten a big breakfast, yet, but before you eat," Davis said, "I got a few things done around the house and figured you'd like to see it."

He led her into the master bedroom without another word. He stopped at the double doors of her walk-in closet. "Ta-da," he said, pushing them open.

She stepped inside and gasped. The broken shelf she had nagged him about for weeks was replaced by a polished walnut unit. Beside it, built-ins now held her handbags, each shelf lined with soft gray velvet. A row of new LED lights bathed everything in a gentle glow.

"I promised you I would fix it," he said.

"It's beautiful." She felt tears start to climb her throat, but she swallowed them back. *Why now, Davis? Why today, of all days?*

"I missed you," he murmured, slipping his arms around her waist. "This closet felt empty without you fussing over every shelf." He nuzzled her neck, breathing her in. "You smell so good."

She stiffened. "We… we should slow down. We need to talk, remember?"

"It's been two weeks since I held you, Vic. Since I kissed you. Let me love my wife." His hands slid to the button of her trousers.

Panic zinged through her. If she pushed him away outright, he would suspect something. *Think, V.* She forced a small laugh. "Look at you, acting like a horny teenager."

"Baby, I'm starving for you. Two weeks is a long time to be locked up without a conjugal visit." He unfastened her button, tugged the zipper.

"Davis—" She tried to catch his hands, but he lifted her off her feet and carried her into the bedroom. The mattress dipped as he laid her down on the duvet. He leaned over her, lips insistent.

Inside, her mind screamed warnings: *Thomas. Honesty. Separation.* But the cold fact was she was still Mrs. Davis Hart on every legal document she owned. There had been no talk yet of separation, and as far as he knew, she was still his loving, devoted wife. If she refused him now, there would be suspicion.

Davis kissed her deeper, as his hand slid up beneath her blouse, thumb brushing her bra strap. She closed her eyes, willing her body to relax even as her heart thudded. In the corner sat her teal chaise. She focused on that color and let it anchor her as Davis moved with practiced tenderness. When he whispered, "I need you," she laid still for a beat, then lifted her arms so he could pull the blouse over her head. The sight of his familiar face twisted her stomach. *I'm doing this for the exit,* she reminded herself. *I'm clearing the path for Thomas.*

She closed her eyes and allowed her husband to have his way with her. Each minute felt like a nightmare she couldn't wake up from. Finally, he rolled to his side, arm draped over her middle, eyes closed in contentment.

"God, I missed you," he murmured. "Promise me you won't stay away that long again."

Her heart thumped hard, as she stared at the ceiling, blinking against the sting in her eyes. "We'll… we'll talk about it," she whispered.

Victoria and Davis dressed and headed downstairs for lunch. Victoria followed Davis onto the covered balcony that felt warmer than it should have on a mid-September day.

"You're quiet today," he said, splitting a croissant with practiced hands. He scooped generous spoonfuls of chicken salad into the flaky bread. "I thought you'd be excited to see your closet fixed."

"I am. It looks amazing, Davis. Really."

"Good." He slid the plate toward her, making sure the arrangement was perfect. "Eat something. You look light-headed; I can tell you didn't have breakfast."

Victoria glanced at the food. The Cajun chicken salad should have tempted her, but her stomach coiled. *Just begin,* she urged herself.

"So," Davis said, "tell me about the Ritz. Was it everything you needed?"

*This is it,* that inner voice whispered. *This is your moment.*

"Davis, before we talk about, well, anything, I need us to have a real conversation."

"All right, what's on your heart?"

"These last two weeks, I've been doing a lot of thinking and some soul searching, about who I am now, who I want to become, and what that means for us. It hasn't been easy."

"We can handle anything, Vic. Just say it."

"I'm not sure how to say this gently, so I'm just going to say it. Please let me finish before you respond."

Victoria's voice wavered, yet she pressed on. "I love you, Davis. You've been everything a woman could ask for. You carried my dreams when they were heavy. You were the calm when everything around me spun too fast. But I've realized that sometimes love alone isn't enough to keep two people moving in the same direction."

She felt the sting of tears but refused to look away. "Somewhere along the line, the spark we had started to dim for me. I tried to ignore it. I buried myself in work. I told myself gratitude was the same as joy. But it isn't, and pretending hasn't made the feeling come back."

Davis's brows knit tightly, but he stayed quiet as she had asked.

"I need time," she whispered. "Real time and real space to figure out where my heart is and what my future should look like. I can't do that if I keep moving through our life on autopilot, acting as if everything is still all right when it isn't."

"What are you saying, Vic?"

"I want us to separate for a while. A true separation, time apart, not just another hotel stay."

The air between them seemed to thicken. A single raindrop hit the balcony roof with a hollow *plink*.

"Separate?" he repeated. "Are you serious?"

"I am."

Davis's pupils widened, as shock washed over his face. "Victoria, we just made love upstairs. We were laughing in Savannah a month ago. We were planning beach trips, talking about repainting the guest rooms. Where is this coming from?"

"I've been unhappy for a long time, Davis. I kept telling myself to push through, to smile and pretend. I tried so hard to force it, to be the wife you deserved. But I can't lie anymore."

"Unhappy? Not once did you say a word, Vic. Not one hint." His breath came faster, chest rising beneath his T-shirt. "I thought we were—" He stopped, unable to finish the sentence.

"I was scared," she whispered. "Scared of hurting you. Scared of admitting it out loud and watching everything fall apart."

Davis pushed his chair back; the legs scraped the stone floor with a sharp rasp. He stood, pacing a few steps before raking his hands over his head. "So, what is this? You disappear for two weeks, come home, and drop this on me over chicken salad?"

Guilt struck deep, like a fist to her stomach. She rose quickly, but her legs trembled. "I was going to tell you right away. I meant to, but then we started talking, and you... things happened—"

"Oh, you mean the sex?" He let the words hang. "Must've been torture for you, huh? Letting me touch you while you plotted to leave."

Tears slid down Victoria's cheeks. She swiped at them with the back of her hand, but more followed. "Davis, please. I'm only human. These feelings tangled me up. I got confused."

Davis turned to her, his dark eyes glistened. "Tell me straight. Are you seeing someone else?"

Her stomach lurched. A wave of heat rushed through her. "There is… a friend. Someone I've been talking to. It helped me see what I had been hiding from myself. But there's nothing more. Not the way you think."

"A friend." He shook his head, disbelief etched in every line of his face. "That's not an answer, V. It's a half-step. You vanish for two weeks, come back asking for space, and now there's a mystery friend?"

"I'm telling you the truth as best as I can without making things worse," she whispered. "I need time alone to figure out who I am and what I want."

"A friend," he repeated. The hurt spread across his features like a bruise. "So, everything we are or what I *thought* we were, crumbles because you found a shoulder to cry on?"

"It isn't like that. It's about me finally facing feelings I've pushed down."

"Do you love him?"

"It's not about love. I don't even know what it is yet. I just know I can't keep living half of a life."

He stared at her as wind carried in the rain. For a long beat, neither spoke. Then, in a low voice, he asked, "Who is he?"

She closed her eyes, tears leaking past her lashes. "I can't tell you that."

"You can't?" The word exploded from him. He slammed his fist on the railing and the wood rattled under the impact. The sudden crack of sound made her flinch. "You think I don't deserve the name of the man who stole my wife? You think I don't deserve to know the man who slid into the space I've tried our whole marriage to fill for you?"

"No one stole me. I chose to go."

He pressed a trembling hand against his chest. "So, every late-night grocery run when you were burning the midnight oil, every foot rub after you kicked off those heels, every single thing I did to make your life easier, none of that meant anything to you?"

"It mattered. Those moments kept me going when I felt like I was falling apart. You saved me for a long time."

"But not long enough, huh? You said you loved me."

"I do love you," she sobbed, tears streaking down her face. "I do, Davis… just not—"

"Don't," he snapped. "Don't finish that sentence. Don't twist the word *love* until it's something smaller. Don't cheapen it."

The sky grew restless, and a low roll of thunder rattled the glass in the French doors.

"I'm asking for time, Davis. Just a few weeks of real distance. Then we can talk about what comes next."

"*Next steps?* Like, divorce lawyers?"

"Maybe," she managed to say.

"Six years together, Vic. Four of them married. And you drop this on me like it's a line item on one of your meeting agendas?"

The accusation hit hard. Victoria pressed a trembling hand to her forehead. "I never meant to hurt you."

He stepped closer, stopping just short of touching her, eyes shining with hurt and heat. "Then tell me. If you won't give me the details, at least give me the reason. What does this… other life offer that I don't?"

"It isn't about what you lack. It's about something in me I can't quiet anymore; something that wants to feel awake."

"Awake?" he echoed. "You don't feel awake with me? With everything we've built?"

"You're the safest place I've ever known," she said. "You make life gentle. But lately… gentle feels like standing still while the rest of me is running."

He reacted as though her words had slapped him. "You want fireworks. Fine. But fireworks burn out, Victoria. After the pop and sparkle, all that's left is smoke."

"Maybe they do burn out, but I can't keep pretending I don't want to feel that spark. I've tried, Davis. I've tried for us. I just… I can't ignore my own heart anymore."

"Where will you go?" he asked. "Where do you even plan to sleep tonight?"

She could see the question behind his eyes: *Are you leaving me for him?* But she wasn't ready to hand him that pain. She forced herself to stand tall, though her knees threatened to buckle.

"I have a place," she said.

"Does he live there?"

Victoria's lips parted, but no sound came. She felt the answer hanging in the wet air, undeniable even without words.

He stared at the untouched food, eyes glassy. "So, it's all been a lie, then?" His voice was raw. "The Ritz, needing space to 'focus'… all just cover stories?"

"I'm sorry," she whispered.

Davis's shoulders slumped, as though the whole house had climbed onto his back at once. "What happens to us now?"

"We separate for a while. We give ourselves room to breathe. After that, we see where we are, then decide."

Davis dragged a hand over his face, fingers lingering at his eyes as if wiping away more than rain. The steady patter turned to a louder hiss. "Do I get a say in any of this?" he asked.

"Of course you do. But I need this, Davis. If we keep living the way we have been, something in me will fade. I feel it already."

For a long moment he simply looked at her, searching for the woman who used to laugh beside him on this very balcony, who used to find comfort in the quiet evenings they spent there. "I'd rather lose you than watch you fade."

She lifted her hand to brush the wetness from Davis's cheek, but he jerked back, an instinctive guard against more hurt. The sight cut her deeper than his words. After a breath, he seemed to wrestle with himself and reached forward anyway, guiding her hand into his. Their fingers laced, and they sat like that; two people holding a life that suddenly felt too fragile, as if the smallest tug might tear it in half.

Victoria helped Davis clean up the rain-soaked lunch before gathering her things to leave. At the door she paused, taking in the familiar scent one last time, then wrapped her fingers around the handle and stepped into the storm.

# Control 9
## Bound by Nothing, Tethered to Him

Thomas shut the loft door with his boot heel and set his toolbox beside the coat rack. He rolled his shoulders, working out the last bit of job-site stiffness, and let himself breathe in the clean lavender scent of the room. *Almost done,* he thought, picturing the new oak floors he had just inspected at one of his properties.

Normally he would have stayed longer putting in work at his property, but not today. Today mattered more. Victoria was facing the hardest conversation of her life: telling Davis they needed a real break. *She should be done soon,* he told himself, a smile tugging at his mouth. One more step toward their life together.

His phone buzzed on the counter. *1 unread message—HD.* He opened the text:

**HD:** *Yo Q. Going to the sports bar tonight. Sending you an invite if you want to tag along.*

He frowned, replaying the morning timeline. *HD—*Davis Hart. The very man Victoria was supposed to be talking to about separation. If Davis felt like grabbing beers, maybe things had gone calm; no fireworks, just a mutual decision. That would line up with Thomas's own celebratory mood. But another thought poked at him. *Maybe Davis* *never got the separation news at all.* Why else would he be so casual? Thomas tapped a reply.

**Thomas:** *Yo, what's up D. Sounds like a plan. Drop the location and time.*

Two minutes later, the response pinged.

**HD:** *Bet. 7:30 tonight @ GameDay Tavern in Smyrna.*

"Okay, then."

GameDay was a wall-to-wall TV joint with wings everyone swore by. He imagined clinking glasses with Davis and fishing for clues without showing his hand. It could be awkward or it could be the perfect chance to confirm the separation talk went as planned.

He felt excitement bubble, but it popped just as fast. What if Victoria lost her nerve? What if they were rekindling their love and somehow, he managed to get her back. What if she's not back at the loft yet because she decided to go back to her husband. The thought hit Thomas like a thousand knives. Thomas leaned against the island. Victoria had promised honesty from now on, but promises were easy until they met real heat.

He lifted his phone, thumb hovering over her contact. *Call her?* No. If she was still talking to Davis, a buzzing phone would only make things harder. He set it down again, exhaling through his nose.

I have to know what the truth is, and I need to meet up with Davis to get his side of the story about exactly what happened today at their meetup. Maybe I can take Victoria to the movies tomorrow, instead of tonight as I promised, he told himself, and tonight could be sports-bar bonding.

4:45 p.m. He paced to the window and looked out at passing cars, but no black BMW. *Relax, man.* He tried a pep talk aloud. *"She said she's done hiding. She said you're her future. Believe her."* The words sounded strong in the room, but doubt still flickered like static.

*** * * ***

Thomas rose the instant he saw Victoria come through the door, hope flaring in his eyes, until he registered the blotchy cheeks and damp lashes.

"Baby?" His voice broke. He covered the space between them in three strides. The second his arms wrapped around her, she burst into tears. Thomas scooped her up and carried her to the couch, as she buried her face in his shoulder.

"Victoria, talk to me. What's wrong?

Words tangled in her throat.

"It's okay," he whispered. "You're safe. I've got you."

Every few seconds she felt him press a kiss to her temple.

"That was the hardest thing I've ever done, Thomas."

"I know. I'm sorry you had to go through that. Just lie here. I'm not going anywhere." He kissed her forehead. "I love you, Victoria Hart."

"I love you too."

Thomas kept one arm around her while sliding his phone from his pocket with the other. Thomas quietly typed a message and hit send, shielding the light so it wouldn't disturb her.

**Thomas:** *Hey D. Sorry man, but can we take a rain check on tonight? Doesn't look like I'll be able to make it.*

He hit send. Moments later the phone buzzed.

**HD:** *All good. Just hit me up for next time.*

Thomas's shoulders relaxed. He set the phone aside and turned fully to her. "Night's ours," he said. "Nothing else matters. Let's get you upstairs so you can rest. Tomorrow is a new day, and whatever comes, we face it together."

In the hush that followed, she let her eyes drift closed, mountains of worry shifting just enough to let sleep in. Thomas laid awake a little longer, staring at the ceiling, one arm snug around her waist. His heart held two truths at once—sorrow for her pain and a bright, restless joy that she was here, truly his now. He pictured a modest house some-day, kids' laughter ricocheting off the walls, family break-fasts on the weekends. He saw Victoria in every scene, head held high, free of lies. *Nothing will stop us now,* he told himself.

* * * *

Victoria lay flat on her back, the loft was still dark except for a trim of city glow that drifted around the blinds. Thomas's collected breathing stroked the room like a steady clock. She studied the rise and fall of his chest and tried to absorb the calm he carried even in sleep. But calm refused to settle inside her.

She told herself last night had sealed everything. Her husband confronted, the divorce soon in motion, and a new life chosen. Yet a restless pulse beat under her skin. Less than twenty-four hours ago, she had been in Davis's arms, six years of quiet loyalty wrapped around her like a weighted blanket. Now she was tucked against a man who tasted like daring and danger. Guilt should have eaten her alive, but under the guilt throbbed a darker heat: the thrill of having pulled it off. Predator, not prey.

She shifted on the mattress to face Thomas, even half-lit, he looked delicious. She reached out and let her finger-tips skim his collarbone, slow enough not to wake him. Her nipples tightened under the cotton tee she had on, need prickling already. There was power in watching him sleep, power in deciding whether to keep him dreaming or pull him into the hunger unraveling inside her.

*Will he always be enough?* The jagged question swirled in her head. Davis had once felt inexhaustible too. The steady laugh, the safe arms, the nightly prayers that wrapped around her like bubble wrap. She had devoured that steadi-ness until it dulled on her tongue. What if this dizzy intensity with Thomas eventually flattened the same way? *Don't borrow trouble,* she warned herself. *Ride the wave you're on.*

215

Still, the thought nagged. She was a Taylor, Martin Taylor's daughter. Her father had never met a boundary he couldn't slip across with a grin and an apology. She had inherited his charm, his appetite, and the restless itch that flared after every conquest. Even now, half the thrill with Thomas wasn't just loving him, it was knowing she had taken him, and toppled walls to do it.

Thomas shifted and rolled onto his side. Possession zinged through her veins. *My man,* she thought, palms warming. She slid closer, pressed her knees behind his, and curved her body to his back. She brushed her lips against the nape of his neck.

"Baby?" Thomas's voice was hoarse and half asleep.

"Mmm." She let her hand drift across his stomach, then lower to the waistband of his boxers. The bulge beneath stirred against her palm. She smiled against his shoulder. Power tasted sweet.

"What time is it?" he murmured.

"Early," she whispered, grazing his earlobe with her teeth. "Still dark."

He gave a sleepy chuckle. "You trying to start trouble before sunrise?"

"Maybe."

She throbbed with need between her legs, wet and ready, driving out every regret, every doubt. At this moment, she wanted nothing but his scent, his weight, his groan breaking loose when she stripped him down.

Thomas rolled onto his back, dragging her with him so she straddled his hips. He slid his palms up her thighs. "No panties?"

"Didn't want barriers," she breathed.

"You sure you're okay?"

"Less talking, Thomas." She reached under his shirt and pinched his nipple just hard enough to make him inhale sharply. "I need you."

She rose to her knees, gripped his thick cock and guided him to the entrance of her slick and pulsating twat.

She sank down slowly, as Thomas's head thudded back against the pillow, eyes squeezed shut, breath exploding.

"Damn, Victoria—"

"Open them," she commanded. He obeyed. She rode him shallow at first, watching his face shift from sleep-soft to raw hunger. Each roll of her hips rubbed her clit along his base, sparks popping behind her eyelids. He groaned as he grabbed her ass and guided her faster. Wet sounds filled the quiet loft, obscene and perfect.

Pressure spiraled inside her. She angled her hips, grinding harder. Her body jolted; pleasure rushing out and in a shaking cry, she pressed into his mouth. She clenched around him, pulses dragging him deeper. A growl so primal came from his mouth, that it thrilled her to the bone.

For a moment, they laid in silence, bodies pressed in the aftermath. Her skin cooled beneath the ceiling fan, but the charged pulse in her blood refused to settle. Everything is perfect. Satisfied for now. She smiled into his neck, even as the tiny voice of doubt whispered that hunger always returned. *Let it,* she told the voice. She would feed it again when it woke. She always did.

# Control 8
## Salt in the Wound

Thomas slid the last plate into the dishwasher and listened to the steady wash. Across the island, Victoria sipped coffee in his oversized tee. Only hours before she had sobbed so hard, her shoulders shook; now she moved with a quiet purpose that seemed to pour light into every corner of the loft.

*I have to be the man she sees,* he told himself. No doubts, no half-steps. That meant tying off every loose end, including the text thread he still shared with Davis. His thumb hovered over the *Block* option, then stopped. There was that one last promise to meet him. He had given his word, and if Thomas Carter stood for anything, it was doing what he said he would do.

*One afternoon,* he reasoned. *Then I fade out.* He nodded to himself, the plan settled.

But Victoria needed something too. Yesterday had torn her spirit to shreds; today she was holding herself together with sheer will. A day at the spa would smooth the raw edges.

"Baby girl, how about you let me spoil you today, full spa treatment. Massage, facial, hot stones, the whole nine."

She blinked, surprised. "Really? I should be spoiling you with how hard you work around the clock."

"That's sweet baby, but you really do deserve it. I want you to forget about yesterday. Let someone rub the stress out of your shoulders while you sip champagne."

"That actually does sound perfect. Are you coming with me?"

"Nah. I've got a Falcons game to catch with some buddies. It'll give you a chance to relax without me hovering."

She considered, then nodded. "Okay, let's do it, let's book it. I'll Uber there and back so I can relax on the ride home."

Thomas pulled out his phone and opened the spa app. He chose the most expensive package on the list: hot stone massage, hydrating facial, scalp treatment, steam session, and a complimentary glass of bubbly. He selected a 12:00 p.m. slot and hit *Confirm*. A moment later, Victoria's phone buzzed with the reservation.

"Look at you, big spender," she teased, glancing at the price.

"Only the best for my girl."

"Thank you, baby."

While she headed upstairs to dress, Thomas lingered at the counter, phone in hand.

**Thomas:** *Hey D. Free today if you still want to catch the game and get some wings and brews. Same spot?*

The reply from Davis came fast.

**HD:** *Headed to church now, but count me in. What time?*

Thomas's thumbs hovered. 1:00 p.m. would give Victoria plenty of spa cushion.

**Thomas:** *1:00 p.m. work for you?*

**HD:** *1:00 p.m. it is. See you then.*

Thomas stared at the exchange a beat longer than needed. Guilt pricked under his ribs. Thomas kept thinking about how Davis still thought Q was just a running buddy, the guy he traded military stories with. The man had no idea the text thread stretched straight into his shattering marriage.

Victoria descended in stretchy black pants and a denim jacket. She looked relaxed already. "The Uber should be pulling up now," she said, tucking her phone into a cross-body bag.

Thomas walked Victoria to the curb, held the car door, and told her to enjoy the spa and soak in all the relaxation she needed. She promised she would, as she kissed him on the lips before sliding into the back seat. He watched until the car merged into traffic and vanished, then exhaled a breath he had not realized he was holding.

* * * *

The moment Thomas pushed open the heavy oak door at GameDay Tavern, noise rolled over him like a hot wave. Commentators shouted highlights, glasses clinked, and a jukebox in the corner slipped classic OutKast between commercials. Every screen glowed with Sunday football, and the air smelled of fried wings, beer foam, and the sharp burn of hot sauce vinegar. Early-season energy lived in every laugh and back slap.

He paused just inside, soaking it in. He was a Braves guy first, but the baseball grind was winding down. Football crowds carried a different charge, almost tribal. Bankers in Julio Jones jerseys leaned beside warehouse workers in old Deion Sanders throwbacks, everybody equal once the whistle blew.

Near the middle of the long mahogany bar, a tall man in a black Falcons tee and a fitted cap stood and waved an arm. Davis. Thomas fixed a friendly grin. *Target spotted,* he thought, the phrase cold but steady in his mind. The sooner this meetup ran its course, the sooner he could close the book. He masked the flicker of nerves and moved through the clusters of fans.

"What's up, Q? Glad you made it, man."

"Traffic was merciful today. How you been doing?" Thomas said, as he slid onto the open stool.

"Been better, but I'm breathing. No sense whining about life when football's on. Let me introduce you to two regulars," Davis said. "This is Remy, he bleeds Jets green and Sean, lifelong Cowboys faithful. Don't judge them too hard."

Thomas let out a low whistle. "Jets and Cowboys? Brothers, that's rough."

Sean, tall and slim in a navy-and-silver No. 88 jersey, leaned forward. "Rough? My boys own five rings, son. How many the Falcons got? I'll wait." He grinned wide, white teeth flashing against dark skin.

Thomas looked at Sean and said, "Man don't get me started on Jerry and that debacle down in Dallas. Can y'all please win a game in January or better yet, can y'all please get to an NFC championship game?"

Sean looked at Thomas and said, "We'll get there before you guys see a super bowl win."

Remy, stockier, wearing a vintage Curtis Martin jersey, laughed and then spoke with a heavy Bronx accent. "And let's not forget that twenty something point lead that the Falcons blew after halftime. Old man Blank dancing in confetti that never came, then Brady tap-danced on your graves."

The stab landed. Thomas pressed a fist to his heart with mock pain. "Salt in the wound, fellas. I try hard to forget that nightmare. But a Jets fan cracking jokes? When was your last Lombardi? '69 with Broadway Joe, right? Against the Baltimore Colts. The Baltimore Colts. Let that sink in. Y'all have been hibernating since Woodstock."

Remy raised his pint in surrender. "Okay, okay, fair." He shot back. "At least we have one. You Falcons still polishing that empty trophy case. Plus, we got a healthy Aaron Rodgers this year."

"Yeah, and he's already practicing darkness retreats for next season," Thomas laughed.

Sean slapped the bar, loving the heat. Davis grinned, soaking in the back-and-forth. He didn't look like a man tongue-tied by heartbreak, Thomas noted. Maybe church had worked some balm on him.

The bartender stopped by. "What y'all drinking?"

"Budweiser," Sean said.

"Modelo for me," Remy added.

Davis nodded toward Thomas. "Get my boy Q whatever local IPAs on draft."

Thomas took his pint and let the bitter hops anchor him. This was easy ground, men yelling at TVs, teasing one another, hiding real feelings behind stats and smack talk. They talked about first-drives, bad coaching calls, and the latest Falcons rookie receiver. Thomas tossed out stats, Remy countered with New York tabloid rumors and Sean swore Dak Prescott was different this year.

Thomas found himself laughing with them, easing into the noise, but every so often he felt Davis studying him. He brushed it off as ordinary curiosity, but something about the man's eyes made Thomas glance away first.

"You good on beer?" Davis asked after the second quarter started.

"I'm straight," Thomas said. Truth was, he wanted to stay sharp. One pint was enough.

Thomas realized an hour had slipped by without a single awkward pause. Just men, football, and beer. Almost normal. Yet in the back of his head, a steady pulse of tension beat. *After today, block the number, delete the chat, move forward.* He pictured Victoria under warm towels, mint mask on her face, not knowing he sat thirteen miles away bantering with her husband. Guilt clawed him; he shoved it down.

Remy checked his phone and elbowed Sean. "Our boys grabbed a booth. You rolling?"

Sean stood, grabbing his fresh Bud. "Yessir."

Davis pointed. "They in that back corner?"

"Yup." Sean clapped Thomas on the shoulder. "Good arguing with you, man. We'll finish the debate in February when Dallas hoists number six."

Thomas laughed. "You'll wake up by March and realize it was a dream."

Remy saluted with two greasy fingers. "Take it easy, Falcons."

The pair slid off their stools and made their way through the crowd toward a semicircle booth. Left alone with Davis for the first time since he arrived, Thomas wiped wing sauce from his hands and prepared himself. The small talk was done; whatever real conversation Davis wanted would come now.

The third quarter was about to start, but Thomas's focus tightened on the man beside him. Davis Hart, thick forearms resting on the bar top, thumb tapping his phone screen constantly. Every few minutes the glow lit Davis's face; every few minutes his mouth flattened before he locked the screen again. The muscles in Davis's jaw worked like he was chewing glass.

Thomas's gut pinched. *Is he waiting on Victoria to call or text him?*

"You expecting a big call, man?" Thomas asked.

"Huh?" He followed Thomas's gaze to the phone in his hand, then gave a short, embarrassed laugh. "Oh, nah. Nervous habit, I guess. I used to always check my phone for messages or missed calls from my wife. Four years in a marriage and I'm still stuck with the habit."

"You said 'used to.' Everything okay?"

Davis took a pull from his beer then set it down. "Used to, yeah. My wife and I... we're in a weird spot. Perfect on paper, cracked as hell in real life." Davis drummed the countertop softly. "Thought we had it figured out. House, trips, matching luggage, me cooking delicious homemade meals, cleaning and making sure she never had to break a sweat doing anything around the house." His mouth twitched. "Turns out, even a dream life can rot from the inside."

Thomas felt the words slide under his skin. *House, meals, easy life, sounds familiar.* The picture mirrored his own routine with Victoria—grocery runs, wiping countertops before she noticed a crumb, shouldering it all so she could shine. Thomas cleared his throat. "Sorry, man. Four years is a long time."

"Victoria, that's my wife's name. We've been together for six years," he added. "Four married, two crazy in love before that. I thought cooking dinner, rubbing her feet, and detailing her car meant something. Guess I misread the assignment."

Thomas sipped water to hide the hitch in his breathing. Victoria never washed a plate in his loft. He had bragged to himself about that. He swallowed hard.

Davis straightened, squaring his shoulders. "We just had this sit-down, you know. She's been off 'finding herself' at a hotel for two weeks. She came home yesterday, I'm thinking she's back for good, but a couple of hours later, she's asking for a real separation and leaving right back out the door."

"I'm sorry, brother. That's rough."

"Rough doesn't cover it. She's always been… different. Mysterious? That's the polite word." His laugh was quieter now, edged with something dark. "When we first met, she lied about everything—her name, her job, and her hometown. I caught her in those lies and threatened to leave, but she cried, begged, and finally came clean." He rested his elbows on the bar. "Should have ran then, huh?"

Beer burned Thomas's throat. The story hit him like a brick. *Exact same opening move, Victoria.* He forced a neutral hum, but his pulse thudded against his ribs.

"She spins webs, man," Davis went on. "Pulls you in, makes you forget you ever doubted her." He gave Thomas a sideways glance, as if checking whether the confession still had an audience. "It's damn near witchcraft, the way she can smile and make a man drop every red flag at her feet."

Thomas's stomach flipped and images hit him. Victoria's smile. Her tear-wet apology the night he exposed that she was married. The way she arched against him that morning as if nothing in the world could come between them. Cold sweat prickled along his shoulder blades.

"You know the part that guts me?" Davis's voice dipped. "She said she needed space to focus on work. To 'rebrand' and I believed her like a damn fool."

Thomas's tongue felt thick. Davis's words rolled on, each detail matching something Victoria had confessed or maybe *failed* to confess just hours ago. Blood pounded in his ears loud enough to drown the commentators. His vision tunneled. The beer glass felt slippery. He could hear his own heartbeat louder than the bar crowd. *She told me everything starts with truth, ASAP. She swore.*

He fought to keep his tone steady. "Maybe she's confused," Thomas said.

"Maybe. Ever dated somebody who could give you the world one minute and freeze you out the next?"

"Yeah," Thomas admitted.

He thought of Victoria's vow to bear him child after child, of how easily she had abandoned her flight-attendant cover story when cornered, how she had cried and then pivoted. He tried to push the memories away, but they kept crashing through. Davis's story mirrored his own too neatly to ignore.

Davis leaned closer. "Want some advice, Q? If a woman lies about the little stuff, she'll lie about the big stuff even more." He sat back, eyes never leaving Thomas. "Remember that."

Thomas's heart hammered so hard it hurt. He managed a short nod, but his breath was tight. The world around him faded into a dull roar. *Is Victoria feeding me the same script she fed him?* The thought shivered through him like ice water. Every instinct told him that Davis knew more than he let on. A bead of sweat slid between Thomas's shoulder blades.

Davis exhaled. "Anyway, I appreciate the listening ear. Sometimes you gotta spit the poison out before it eats your gut."

"Anytime," Thomas said, though his own stomach was rolling. He thought of Victoria at the spa, imagined her lying about steam rooms when she might be with somebody else. No, that would be insane. But Davis's narrative kept looping in his head, detail for detail. *What if Victoria never files those divorce papers? What if she's already spinning a new lie for me?* He felt the room tilt, the air thicken.

"Q, you good?" Davis asked.

"Yeah," Thomas rasped. "Just… hot in here. I need to hit the head," he muttered, sliding off the stool. The floor swam underfoot, but he found the restroom sign and pushed through the door. The cooler air inside slapped him back to himself.

He gripped the sink, breathing through his nose while cold water ran over his wrist. *Pull it together. You're here to end this, not fall apart.* But the harder he tried to steady his thoughts, the faster Davis's words replayed. After a minute, the roar in his ears dulled. He blew out a slow breath, straightened his shirt, and returned to the bar.

Davis glanced up. "Everything cool?"

"Yeah," Thomas lied. He forced his hand around the cold mug. He needed to finish this beer, say a polite goodbye, and get back to Victoria and ask hard questions, demand open phone lines, something. Anything to lance the panic ballooning in his chest.

But even as he planned his escape, Davis leaned in as though to share another piece of poison, and Thomas felt the hair on his arms rise. This friendly meet-up was no casual hangout, as it was getting more intense by the minute. A cold dread curled at the base of his spine.

Thomas didn't want to, but he knew he needed to pry and get more info from Davis. "You know," Thomas said, "maybe Victoria was trying to feel you out when she first met you, to make sure you weren't some serial killer or something. You know how women are these days. So many crazy stories about men doing crazy things. It's a pretty scary world we live in, and you can never be too cautious."

Davis's laugh rolled slow and knowing. "I thought that too, but, no. That wasn't the case with Victoria. She was always the one several steps ahead. Victoria, man, she's unlike any woman I've ever met before."

Thomas nodded. *Yeah,* he told himself, *unlike any.*

Davis saw Thomas lapse into thought and said, "Man, Q, I'm sorry. We're supposed to be here having a good time, watching the game, and here I am unloading all my personal problems on you. My bad, dawg."

"Oh no, it's okay. These women out here think they're so smart. They know exactly what they're doing—they've got us, hook, line, and sinker."

"Don't they!"

When the scoreboard slid into the fourth quarter, Falcons were up by seven, and Thomas went for the question he had rehearsed. "So, where'd you guys leave off after that sit down? Think you'll get back with your wife, salvage things?"

"That's a good question, and I wish I knew the answer. Victoria didn't really give me an answer when she left. She said she wanted to separate a while and give ourselves room to breathe. She said we'd talk again in a couple weeks and see where we are, and hopefully we get back together then. I mean, she didn't sound like she wanted a divorce or anything. With Victoria, I never really know. I think she just needs to get whatever it is she has bottled up out of her system. When she's done, she'll come back."

Thomas's pulse hammered. *No divorce discussion.* Victoria had sworn she would call a lawyer this week. The floor seemed to pitch.

"What does that mean, 'get it out of her system'? You think she's with another man?" Thomas asked.

"She mentioned she had a friend, but I don't think it's anything serious. I doubt she's having sex with him because when she was at the house yesterday, that's the first thing we did before we talked." His mouth curved in satisfaction.

"I brought her upstairs, and we made *sweet, passionate love* right there in our bed."

Thomas's vision blurred. Every sound in the tavern muffled, like cotton packed into his ears. His hand convulsed around the bottle, glass groaning.

"Not to bring sex into our hang-out," Davis went on, leaning in as if sharing locker-room gossip, "but I'm just saying, if she *is* with another man, he ain't hitting it. Because she *wanted* it. Like *needed* it." He chuckled, deep and slow. "The way her body responded to me and the way she was moving, whew, had my eyes rolling in the back of my head. So, if there is another guy, I'm not really worried."

Thomas's grip tightened until the beer bottle creaked. Images crashed through his mind. Victoria sobbing into his chest, straddling him at dawn and whispering forever. Yet less than a day earlier she had been in another man's house, in another man's bed.

White heat flooded Thomas's skull. *She came home sobbing, telling me that was the hardest thing she had ever done. She fucked him, then fed me tears. She fucked him, then promised me babies.* His stomach lurched. Sweat slid beneath his shirt, cold as river water.

Davis lifted a fry, bit it in half. "That body remembers who feeds it. You feel me?"

A black roar filled Thomas's ears. He stared at the football broadcast yet only saw Victoria bent over a mattress that wasn't his, saw Davis behind her, saw her face twist in pleasure that she claimed belonged only to him. Rage flashed so bright he nearly blacked out.

He forced breath past his teeth and released the bottle. The label was half-torn beneath his fingers. *If I swing on him, I go to jail. If I swing on him, I lose everything.*

"I think that last one took me out," Thomas rasped. "I better get home before I need to call an Uber."

Davis nodded.

"Thanks for the invite," Thomas said, already sliding off the stool.

"Yeah, man. You're a pretty cool dude. And don't worry about the tab, I'll pick it up."

"Oh no, I can't let you do that."

Davis insisted, patting Thomas's back. "Get home safely."

Thomas turned and headed toward the exit. The slam of the tavern door behind him was like a gunshot. Sunlight knifed across his eyes, but the brighter the day, the darker the thoughts clawing at his mind. *She fucked him yesterday. She lied to my face. She promised me forever with his taste still on her tongue.*

His steps faltered. He braced one palm on the brick wall outside GameDay Tavern and dragged in a breath that scalded his lungs. Around him, traffic whooshed, strangers laughed, but Thomas heard only the echo of Davis's satisfied drawl. *That body remembers who feeds it.*

Victoria's tears, vows, and moans that morning—had any of it been real? Beneath the rage bloomed something colder, the sense that Davis had *known* exactly which nerve to press. As if the man had studied him, waited for the moment, then slipped the knife between his ribs and twisted. Thomas straightened and forced his legs toward the parking lot. A single plan formed in the white-hot silence of his skull. *Confront Victoria. Tonight.*

# Control 7
## Heat of the Moment

Victoria inhaled the invigorating smell of eucalyptus and a hint of orange peel, as she waited for the massage therapist. Soft flute music played in the background. The massage table sat center, draped in ivory sheets so smooth they shone. Warm stones clinked in a copper warmer. A towel tented over a pewter bowl released curls of steam.

*Victoria, untouchable,* she thought, as she sipped the last of her champagne. Yet the word felt less like armor and more like velvet today.

There was a gentle tap at the main door. "Yes?" Victoria called, expecting Trudy, the massage therapist attendant, again.

The door swung wider, and it wasn't Trudy. The man who stepped inside could've walked off a sportswear billboard. Six-three, maybe six-four, with the smooth sway of someone who spent half his life moving heavy weight and the other half stretching it back out.

"Good afternoon, Ms. Hart. I'm Terrell, your therapist for today."

Her pulse jumped. She tried to disguise it by folding her arms, but the robe's lapels gaped, and she saw his gaze flick there for half a second, not leering, simply registering.

When his eyes returned to hers, they held a spark of curiosity she recognized too well. The exact glimmer she felt just before choosing a mark.

"Terrell," she repeated, liking the taste of it. "Nice to meet you."

"I see you're getting the deep-tissue with hot-stone enhancement. Pressure is customizable. I can start moderate and go deeper, unless you prefer intensity straight away."

*He can go as deep as he wants.* The thought flashed so hot she felt it between her thighs. "I'm new to deep tissue. I'll trust your judgment."

"Understood. Any areas you'd like me to avoid?"

"I carry tension everywhere."

"Most of us do." He gestured to the table. "When you're ready, lie face down beneath the top sheet. You may keep your undergarments on or remove them, whatever feels comfortable. I'll knock before I re-enter."

"There's no need for 'Ms. Hart' in here. Call me… Sheena."

*Sheena.* The alias slid from storage with alarming ease, her hunter's mask, the one she had worn so many times to snag men. Its consonants tasted like adrenaline in her mouth.

Terrell's eyes narrowed a fraction, unreadable. Then he nodded. "All right, Sheena. I'll give you a minute."

Victoria pressed a hand to her abdomen and exhaled. For the first time since crossing the spa's threshold, the word *relax* felt impossible. She thought of Thomas, who wanted to give her the world. She thought of the promise she had made to herself: *be the woman he believes you are.* But the predator inside her purred at the memory of Terrell's shoulders. *Ten minutes,* she told herself. *Ten minutes to enjoy how it feels to be wanted by a stranger. Then it stops.*

She walked to the table and let the robe fall from her shoulders. She laid stomach-down and listened to her own pulse drumming in the well of her ear cradle.

Terrell returned and crossed the small treatment room in that unhurried, voracious stride she had learned to read so well. He stopped beside the table where she sat in a crisp white sheet, the smell of warmed oil and eucalyptus hanging between them. "You asked about deep tissue work, specifically, how deep I can go?"

The question lingered until she tipped her chin and answered with a single steady word, "Yes."

"Let me demonstrate," he said as his fingers brushed her jaw. Then his mouth was on hers, coaxing rather than claiming, letting her feel the subtle slide of breath and the patient tease of a tongue that tasted of wintergreen lozenge and something unmistakably male. Her spine melted and her palms slid up the hard planes of his chest.

"I was hoping that you would've taken everything off for me," he said.

Pushing off the table, Victoria let the sheet drift away from her shoulders and opened a deliberate distance between them as she began to undress. The clasp of her bra snapped as she let the lace tumble to the floor. A beat later, she hooked her thumbs in the thin band of her thong and eased it past the curve of her hips.

She straightened, bare, boldly meeting his gaze. "All done."

Terrell skimmed her waist with his palms and drew her back against the linen-draped table, letting her feel the unmistakable press of his arousal through the cling of scrub pants. "I'm going to savor every inch of you," he breathed against her ear.

Victoria's gasp broke the hush as he guided her thighs over his broad shoulders. His hands framed her hips as his mouth began a slow, torturous exploration. First, the delicate skin at the inside of her thigh, then drifting higher until she trembled. When his tongue finally found the slick ache at her center, the jolt was so electric she nearly arched off the table.

He was meticulous, his mouth moving in a patient rhythm that rose and softened until she forgot every word but his name. A low chant slipped from her lips, "Yes… yes, right there, don't stop." Her begging for more seemed to please him, judging by the satisfied hum he gave in reply. Pressure grew, coiling tighter with every wet sweep of his tongue, until her vision blurred at the edges and her fingers dug into the table in mute plea.

Her release came like a breaking wave, and he drank her pleasure as if it were nectar. "You taste better than fine wine," he whispered.

She levered herself fully onto the table and parted her legs in an open invitation. "I want you all the way."

The restraint that flickered across his features lasted barely a heartbeat before he shucked his shirt and pushed his pants down just enough to free the heavy erection already straining for her. He settled between her thighs and guided himself forward, skimming the slick entrance of her body, before sliding home in a single, deliberate thrust that stole the air from her lungs, driving into her with a pleasurable force they both got lost in.

He found her mouth again, the rhythm of his kiss matching the deliberate power of each movement. His hand rose to her throat, fingers curving with quiet command, a hold that was both restraint and connection. Her nails dug into his shoulders as she whispered his name, wanting more of the pull that left her trembling.

"Is that deep enough?" he murmured.

"Deeper," she managed to say.

Dark heat flared in his eyes as he angled his hips, driving into her until she swore she felt him in her spine. Pleasure sharpened into something close to pain before breaking into rapture. Their bodies locked, her cry spilling as he groaned against her neck, before climax took them both.

For a moment neither of them moved. Their breathing slowly settled, bodies still warm against each other. The soft tick of the wall clock felt distant, as if time had paused just for them.

A soft knock fractured the haze.

"Sheena? Is it all right if I come in?" The voice of Terrell was muffled through the door.

Reality crashed over Victoria. Terrell vanished. The table beneath her was real enough, but the muscled body above hers dissolved into vapor, leaving her alone in a riot of pounding heartbeat and slick heat.

She jerked upright, cheeks flaming. "Just, just a couple more minutes!" she called, voice wobbling between shame and panic.

Her head spun as she stripped off the damp sheets in frantic handfuls from the table, balling the evidence of her soaking wet daydream fantasy into the laundry hamper. She smoothed a fresh set of linens into place with shaking fingers, then paused, noticing the damp cling of lace against her skin. No way could she keep the ruined thong on. She stepped out of it and let the scrap of silk disappear beneath the used sheets.

Wrapping the crisp drape around her torso, she leaned against the table, pulse still twisting. Victoria tightened the drape around her nakedness, forcing her breathing to calm. The daydream had rattled her, shaken something loose she wasn't sure she could tuck neatly back into place, since her body knew exactly what it wanted now.

Another gentle knock. "Ready?"

"Yes," she said.

As the doorknob turned, Victoria braced herself. The memory of his hands still warm on her skin, the promise of power he carried lingering like a scent she could taste. She wondered whether today's careful professional boundary could survive the restless whisper of her craving. Victoria laid prone across the padded table, chin propped on folded forearms, ready for Terrell to walk in.

Terrell slipped through, closing the door behind him. "Everything all right?" he asked.

"Oh, yes. I'm ready whenever you are."

He began at her shoulders, palms gliding through warmed oil. Heat pooled under his hands, sliding down the length of her spine in slow bright ribbons. By the time he inched to her lower back she was weightless.

"Deeper," she whispered when he paused to check in. He obliged without hesitation.

A hum bloomed in her blood, one part relief, one part something darker. She didn't try to stop it. The line between therapeutic release and the rush of arousal blurred, and why shouldn't it. Touch was touch. Want was want. She imagined the heat of his palms without the oil, imagined scrubs abandoned on the floor, imagined kneeling to taste her—

*Stop.* She breathed deep, corralling the images, letting them dissolve in lavender haze. *You came here to relax, not to hunt.*

Halfway through, he laid a clean sheet over her back and asked her to roll over so he could work on the front of her body—her thighs, chest, and the tight muscles in her neck. She watched him from the side. His eyebrows pulled together as he focused. Sometimes he bit his lower lip while his thumb pressed out a knot. He never looked where a pro shouldn't. That careful respect somehow made her want him even more.

Ninety minutes slipped by like a secret. When at last he smoothed the final splash of oil into her deltoids, he murmured a quiet *"All set,"* then stepped outside to fetch water and grant her privacy.

Victoria eased off the table, her legs shaky and loose.

Terrell returned with a chilled glass bottle. "Hydrate well," he reminded, handing it over. "It flushes the metabolic waste we just freed up."

"Mm-hmm." She swallowed, but barely heard the words, as her mind was somewhere else. Her body still buzzed from his touch. While he talked, she stared at his neck, noticing how the muscles moved under the skin. Her fingers tingled, remembering how she had held those strong shoulders in her daydream.

He launched into discussions about after care, but she only caught a few words out of everything he stated. All she could think was, I want you, right here and right now.

"Any questions?"

"Yes, actually." She folded her arms under her breasts, squeezing them together just enough to test whether his gaze would flicker down. It didn't. "Deep-tissue once won't fix twelve-hour desk days. I think I will probably need more sessions."

"Most clients do. We can set bi-weekly or monthly sessions, whatever fits."

"My calendar's a beast. Some weeks I barely see daylight. I'm thinking that private sessions might be easier for me. Do you offer that?"

"I travel for a few regulars. Homes, hotel suites, studio rentals. As long as there's space for the table, it works."

Her heart hammered. She gave Terrell a slow, tempting smile, the kind that closed business deals and opened bedroom doors. "Great. You're really talented, Terrell. I need those hands again." She softened her last word, making sure he caught the hint.

He returned the smile, gentle rather than hungry, and something about it snagged her attention. An indefinable softness. "Thank you. Massage is my lane, always has been. It actually took a nudge to believe I could do it full-time, though. My partner Kevin all but pushed me into school."

*Partner.* The syllables landed with unexpected weight.

She lifted her brows. "Your business partner?"

He gave a short laugh. "He's my life partner. Kevin is… he's my soulmate. We'll hit ten years together next summer." A proud smile spread across his face. "He arranged my first massage client and let me practice the strokes on him until my thumbs were ready to fall off."

The room tilted. Heat that had twined low in her belly sputtered, then guttered out like a candle in sudden draft.

She managed a polite nod, but inside gears ground to a stunned halt. *He's gay.* The revelation echoed, absurdly loud.

A strange mix of feelings rushed over her all at once. She felt relief because the urge she had been battling was no longer a real risk. But she also felt a quick, sharp let down because the fantasy she had created in the dim, sweet-smelling room had just shattered. The hunter inside her was baffled. She had never chased someone only to discover they couldn't be caught.

"I'm rambling," Terrell said, unaware of her unsteadiness. He produced a sleek black business card between two fingers. "Call or text when you're ready. I'll bring the table to you."

*I feel tiny,* she thought, smaller than an ant. She felt the heat of embarrassment, as it crept down the backs of her legs.

"Thank you," she said.

"Pleasure was all mine, Sheena. Take care of yourself."

He left on a hush of hinges. The door clicked shut. For three long beats she simply stared at the card, reading and re-reading the name as if repetition might soothe the inexplicable sting.

Why sting at all? She had made promises to Thomas and to herself that she would be truthful and present. The universe had just handed her a velvet-gloved correction: *not this time.* Still, her pride hurt. Terrell hadn't even *seen* her that way. It was silly to care, but she did.

Victoria stepped outside the spa and let the glass door swing shut behind her. A black Cadillac slid to the curb within minutes. She slipped into the back seat with her nylon tote pressed to her chest like a shield. She leaned her forehead against the window, watching reflections skate across the glass, as told herself this ride was a reset. Terrell was a near-miss, nothing more. She closed her eyes and let the hum of the engine steady her breathing as she anticipated going home to Thomas.

✳ ✳ ✳ ✳

Tabitha pressed the cool napkin to her lips and tried to will the sour taste away. The small dining set in her one-bedroom condo rocked when she shifted. She had never bothered to tighten the screws underneath. Her stomach rolled again, sharp and quick as a wave hitting pier planks. *Greasy sausage links… never again,* she scolded herself, though deep down she knew the sausage was not the real problem.

The front door unlatched. Tabitha wiped her mouth, steadied her smile, and watched it swing open. Her man entered with quiet confidence.

"Hey, honey," she said.

He noticed something was wrong the moment he saw her. "You look a little pale. Are you feeling all right?" he asked, moving closer to press a kiss to her lips.

Tabitha turned her head to the side and held up a hand to stop him. "Please, not right now. I was sick to my stomach earlier and threw up twice after breakfast. I brushed my teeth and rinsed with mouthwash, but I still feel uneasy, and would rather not kiss until the queasiness passes."

"That's why mints exist, sweetheart." He guided her to the sofa with gentle pressure at the small of her back. "Tell me what's going on," he urged. "Is the nausea still as strong as before, or has it eased at all?"

"A little better. I think the problem was the sausage I made for breakfast. There was too much grease in the pan, and my stomach just couldn't handle it."

"Or," he replied, his eyes lighting with a playful, almost secret happiness, "it might be that my little man that's growing in there already knows he doesn't like pork."

He laid his palm on her stomach, fingers moving in a slow, easy circle as if he were memorizing the shape of a future child.

A tight lump rose in Tabitha's throat. "I'm not pregnant." She wanted her words to sound strong, but worry still slipped through. She had thrown up three mornings in a row. The smell of coffee now reminded her of burnt oil. Her breasts felt sore in ways she couldn't ignore. Saying she wasn't pregnant helped her pretend it couldn't be true.

"Tabitha, we've been raw dogging it for months, so, the chances of you getting pregnant were always there, waiting. I haven't exactly been careful because I want a baby with you. I told you that from the start. I picture a little boy or girl running around with your smile and my laugh. I think about that every single time I'm with you. You know this is what I want. I thought it was what you wanted too. Maybe this happened sooner than we planned, but if it does happen, we can handle it together. You wouldn't be alone in this."

Tabitha smoothed the blanket and tried to find steady words. "I've told you the timing is wrong. My job is crazy right now. The plan we mapped out is not finished. If I got pregnant today, everything would spin out of control. I would be sick, I would miss meetings, I need to keep things going the way it's going at work in order for—"

He cut in, his tone firm but even. "We'll handle it. We'll do it the same way we handle everything else. We'll have our house, marriage, kids... All of it will land exactly when I say it will."

His palm flattened on the cushion, the muscles in his forearm tightening as if to underline each promise. "You do believe I keep my word, don't you? When I say something will happen, it happens. I've never let you down, Tab, and I'm not about to start now."

Tabitha nodded quickly. She had learned that disagreeing with him could bring out the colder part of his nature, the part that turned every word into a sharp edge.

"I believe you. You've always done what you promised. I'm not doubting that. I'm only saying I feel worn out today. My stomach is still shaky, my head is heavy, and when I'm this tired, I start to worry about every little detail."

"Then rest and stop repeating the same worry. I don't like hearing the same thing over and over."

"I'm sorry," she answered at once. Wanting to show she understood, she scooted closer and laid her head on his shoulder. It was her way of making peace, giving herself over so he could feel her trust.

"Better," he murmured. "When you lean on me, I know we're on the same page." He gave a small squeeze, neither rough nor truly gentle, more like a reminder of who sets the pace.

He lifted her chin until their eyes met. "Have you managed to eat anything since you were sick this morning?"

"I nibbled on some crackers, but if you're hungry, honey, I can cook you something to eat. Maybe beef tips and potatoes with veggies?"

"Food can wait. I think I'm in the mood for something else right now."

The intent in his eyes left no room for doubt. Without a word, he rose and offered his hand. Tabitha placed her fingers in his and felt the firm, guiding squeeze that always told her who was in charge. He pulled her up from the couch and started toward the hallway.

Inside the bedroom, moonlight leaked through half open blinds, striping the bed in silver bars. "Tonight," he said, voice thick with need, "I just want you present. No talk. No worries. Just us."

He guided her to the mattress, laying her down with gentle pressure. When it was over, he shifted to his back and rolled an arm across his face. His chest lifted and fell in heavy pulls of air, the sharp edge in his features softening with each exhale.

She turned onto her side and propped her head on one hand. A warm certainty spread through her chest. *He loves me,* she told herself. Every touch, every hungry kiss, every time he reached for her first, they all added up to the same truth. He needed her steadiness, her softness, the way she smoothed the rough edges the world carved into him. That need was a kind of vow, stronger than any ring.

He spoke without lifting his arm. "Go buy a test in the morning as soon as you wake up."

The order tightened her stomach like a fist. She tried to soften the edges, to keep some say in the matter. "If I still feel sick when I get up," she said carefully, "then I'll pick one up."

"Not *if.* Tomorrow. First thing."

She dipped her head in quick surrender. "All right. I'll do it tomorrow."

Silence settled over the room like a heavy blanket. He stayed stretched out for a moment longer, then finally, he swung his legs over the side of the bed and crossed to the bathroom for a shower.

Tabitha rolled onto her side and pressed a hand against the flat plane of her stomach. If a baby was really growing inside her, it could weld them together forever.

Ten long minutes passed before he returned, towel riding low on lean hips. He bent to pull on jeans, then straightened and reached for his wallet and keys.

"I need to run a few errands," he said. That single word, errands, always meant another step toward the outcome he never fully described, and she had learned not to pry.

"All right. Please be careful out there. I love you." The words came out small but sincere. Loving him felt as natural as breathing, even when it frightened her.

He paused at the doorway and, for once, let a smile soften his face. It was brief, but it lit something hopeful inside her. "Always," he said. A moment later she heard the dead bolt click, leaving her alone with the rhythmic thud of her own heart.

Tabitha sat on the edge of the bed for a long time after he left, listening to the quiet settle over the condo. Tomorrow she would choose a pregnancy test, and face whatever answer appeared in the window. She rested a palm over her belly and spoke in a low voice only the walls could hear. "Hold on, little one. Mommy still has work to finish." She was ready to guard the fragile future that she was working so hard to keep.

**✳ ✳ ✳ ✳**

Thomas arrived home without remembering the drive. The road had been a blur, his mind somewhere between the ache in his chest and the truth he still couldn't swallow. Breathe, he told himself. You need to cool down before she walks through that door. Accusing her the second she steps inside will solve nothing. In his head, Davis's smug line looped again: *"We made sweet, passionate love right there in our bed."*

Each replay felt like a splinter under his skin. The picture followed. Victoria, soft moans leaving her lips, perched on the edge of a mattress that didn't belong to him. A sharp curse slipped from his mouth.

The latch jiggled, then the door swung inward, and Victoria stepped over the threshold. She walked in without a word, her keys barely making it to the table before she brushed past Thomas and headed for the stairs. She could still feel the ghost of Terrell's hands on her skin, not from the massage, but from the humiliating fantasy she had let herself sink into, right before reality snapped back and reminded her that he wasn't interested in her or any woman.

Thomas followed her up the stairs, sensing the shift. "So, you're not going to talk to me at all? No 'Hey, baby, the spa was amazing;' not even a quick story about cucumbers on your eyes?"

"I planned to tell you everything after a shower. Right now, I feel like I'm wearing the whole day on my skin, and I just need it gone."

He slowed behind her, watching the distance widen even though they were only a few steps apart. Something felt off. He told himself it might just be the long day or the weight of everything they had been handling, yet the unease wouldn't sit still.

"Tell me how it went," Thomas said.

"It was beautiful. Warm stones, lavender oil, dim lights… I could've fallen asleep right there. It was exactly what I needed."

Thomas watched her face more than her words. The glow in her eyes looked real, but something behind them felt carefully measured. "Sounds like heaven."

"It was. Thank you for setting it up. I didn't realize how much I needed it."

She shifted closer and rested her head against his chest, arms circling his waist like she wanted to melt into him. He held her, but his mind didn't settle. There was a quiet space between her sentences, one that felt like she was leaving something out.

After a few seconds of silence, he asked, "Are you feeling any better today than you were last night?"

"Much better. That spa day worked wonders."

"There's something we skipped over. We never really talked about your sit down with Davis yesterday. What… happened while you were at the house?"

Her fingers fidgeted in her lap. "It was hard. A lot of emotions. We said things we'd both been holding for months. We agreed we still need space, but we're planning to meet again in a couple of weeks to talk about next steps."

"Did the discussion of divorce come up at all?"

"No," she admitted. "Not yet. It felt like too much to drop on him after everything else we had just discussed. I'd already torn his heart out. I didn't want to crush it on the same night."

"Did you mention me at all? Us?"

"I told him I had… a friend," she said carefully. "Someone who's been there for me. Someone important."

"Just that? No name, no details."

"I spared him that much. He was already hurting. Dropping the full story in that moment would've been cruel and again, Thomas, I was trying to tread lightly."

Thomas let out a slow breath through his nose. Part of him understood the mercy in that. The other part felt the familiar shift, the one where truth thinned and shadows took its place. "Okay. Thank you for telling me at all. Is there anything else that happened during the visit that I should know?"

Victoria's throat bobbed once, twice. "There is. Please let me explain before you react."

Thomas nodded, though the weight in his stomach dropped lower.

"When I got to the house, he was excited. He walked me straight to my master closet he'd repaired. I thanked him, tried to keep it short, but he was already on a different track. He took my hand and led me to the bed."

Thomas's jaw tightened, but he stayed silent.

"I pulled back a little, but I didn't stop it. I was scared he would sense something was off about us, about the separation. I told myself it was easier to keep things smooth. So, I let it happen. I didn't kiss him back, I didn't move. I just laid there and waited until it was over."

The confession hung in the quiet room, not angry, not defensive, just raw. "I left, drove around to clear my head, and came home to you," she said softly. "I made love to you that morning because you're the man I've chosen. What happened there, with Davis, will never happen again. I promise."

Images flashed through Thomas's mind. He didn't move, didn't speak, just let the burn crawl through his chest until it settled like a stone. "When I first asked if anything happened, you told me there was nothing I needed to know."

"And I'm telling you now because you asked again. I need you to believe that I'm not trying to hide anything from you, Thomas."

"It's hard. Hard not to picture it. Hard not to feel like I'm the last one to know what's really going on."

"I understand. If our places were switched, I'd feel the same. But I'm here, telling you everything. That has to count for something."

Thomas kept his eyes on the floor until he was sure he wouldn't snap. Yes, she had told the truth, but only after he pushed. That part still scraped at him.

At last, he looked up. He made his voice steady, even though the words felt jagged in his mouth. "So, you slept with him, and then a few hours later you came home and slept with me. Do you see how that messes with my head? And how I can't stop thinking about the overlap?"

"I do. I know how bad it sounds. But please believe me, it meant nothing. I went through the motions with him because I was afraid to have questions raised. Here, with you, it's real. I love you, Thomas. I'm choosing you."

Thomas let her promise soak in. He laid his palms over hers, feeling the light tremor still running through her fingers, and spoke slowly so the words would land.

"I don't want to share you, Victoria, ever. But I also know life is tangled right now. I'm choosing to believe you when you say it's over. I'm choosing to believe it'll never happen again."

"It won't. We'll push through the ugly parts. Once that's done, nothing will sit between us. Nothing."

The simple faith in her tone tugged at him. He wrapped his arms around her and let out a long breath he had been holding all day. They were trying to trust that love could be stronger than old habits, that a promise spoken in the bedroom could hold against every doubt waiting outside the door.

# Control 6
## Beginning of the End

Victoria placed her handbag in her desk drawer and drew a slow breath. She hung her blazer, woke her computer, and watched a wall of color-coded flags bloom across the screen—bids, budgets, and meetings stacked like dominoes. She skimmed the first email, fired off replies, and was halfway down the page when a soft knock broke her rhythm. The door eased open and Tabitha stepped in like she owned every tile. Her smile was so bright it almost looked painted on.

"Good morning, babes! How was your weekend?" Tabitha's voice was light and cheerful, as if no hard words had ever passed between them.

The question hit Victoria like a tap on a bruise. The weekend meant Thomas, Davis, and trying to sort her heart into boxes that never stayed shut. "It was… eventful."

Tabitha pulled a guest chair close, planted her folders on the desk and leaned in. "Okay, start talking. I want every detail."

Victoria let out a slow breath and sank into the high back chair behind her. "Saturday, I drove out to my house. Davis was there of course, and we had a deep, emotional conversation. I said I wanted a real, official separation."

"V… that sounds rough."

"Brutal is the right word. Davis tried so hard to make it normal. He set the balcony table with our best dishes, folded little napkins the way he knows I like, and he made an amazing lunch. It was sweet, and it killed me. I told him the truth straight out. The color drained from his face like someone pulled a plug. He didn't yell or argue. He just stared, as if his whole world folded in on itself."

Tabitha reached across the desk and squeezed her hand. "You did what you had to do."

"Maybe, but that doesn't get the picture out of my head."

Tabitha slid her arms around Victoria, pulling her into a full embrace. The gesture felt practiced, the way people hug when words will only bruise.

"I'm sorry, V, I know you loved him. This cannot be easy."

"I feel like I ripped out his heart. I watched him try to be brave and I still swung the axe."

"You had to speak your truth. Staying silent would have been worse. Pain now means less pain later. You taught me that with business deals—cut once, clean and quick."

"This was never clean," Victoria whispered. "Nothing about this is."

For a while they stayed like that. Two friends curved into each other, breathing in sync, the office hum replacing the words they couldn't fix. Finally, Victoria drew back enough to meet Tabitha's gaze.

"Thank you for not judging, Tab."

"Always, sis. Whatever road you pick, I'm on it with you."

The words cooled something hot and tight inside Victoria's chest. For weeks, every time she and Tabitha spoke, it felt like stepping into a boxing ring—gloves on, chin tucked, waiting for the next hit. Now there were no jabs, only an easy quiet that settled between them like a soft blanket.

"I've missed us," Victoria said, voice small but honest. She hadn't meant to sound so tender, yet the truth of it pressed on her ribs.

"Me too. We've both been living in storm zones. Sometimes you don't realize how loud the thunder is until it stops."

That simple line made Victoria's throat tighten. She thought about the last month, the raised voices, the hurtful looks, the endless need to defend her choices. All that noise had hidden what Tabitha used to be to her—calm.

"I guess I got used to shouting," Victoria said.

"Then let's practice quiet together." She reached for a tissue on the desk, dabbed at a smear of mascara under Victoria's eye. "We'll find our normal again, okay? Different maybe, but still us."

Victoria nodded. For the first time in days, she felt there might be space to breathe.

"So, after the tears with Davis, please tell me something good happened. I need a bright spot."

"Actually, yes. Yesterday Thomas booked me a day at Serenity Spa. Ninety-minute deep-tissue massage, hot-stone upgrade, facial, even one of those sugar-salt foot scrubs. The works."

"Must be nice," Tabitha said, rolling her eyes in mock envy. "But seriously, V, I'm glad Thomas is stepping up for you. You deserve to be pampered after... everything."

Tabitha's smile widened. Inside, a flutter of calculation moved like a chess piece sliding to its next square. *Keep her talking, keep her happy,* she reminded herself. Tabitha studied her friend. The circles under Victoria's eyes were still faint, but the hard tension had eased from her brow. *Good,* Tabitha thought. *A relaxed Victoria is easier to guide.*

"Did you and Thomas do anything after the spa?" Tabitha asked.

"We just relaxed at home and ordered some take-out."

"That's sweet." Tabitha's teeth showed in another approving smile, but her pulse quickened with fresh information.

"Look, I know I've pushed hard in the past. I questioned every move you made, and that wasn't fair, V. I'm here now. No judgment."

"I needed to hear that."

*Hook set*, Tabitha thought to herself.

"By the way," Tabitha added lightly, "when you're ready, invite me over. I should apologize to Thomas in person, clear the air."

Victoria brightened. "He would like that. We can plan something soon."

"Perfect." Tabitha rose, smoothing the front of her blouse. "I'm going to grab a water before the staff meeting. Need anything?"

"I'm good. Thanks, Tab."

Tabitha started toward the door, heels tapping a steady beat. Just before she stepped out, she glanced back, caught Victoria watching her with open affection, and returned a sunny wave.

The door shut softly behind her. Victoria exhaled, long and slow. Maybe, she thought, the storm clouds were finally parting. She scooped a stack of client files closer and got back to work, the echo of Tabitha's hug lingering like a promise.

Down the hall, Tabitha walked with measured steps, her own pulse drumming a steady beat. Patience, she told herself. Almost there.

✴ ✴ ✴ ✴

Victoria let herself into the loft just after four, dropping her bag on the entry bench and pausing to listen. The space felt cavern-quiet without Thomas's music drifting from his overhead speakers. Tonight, she would hand Thomas the proof he kept hoping for. No more cautious promises, no more *I'm working on it.* A signed retainer, a stamped receipt, and a complaint drafted in black-and-white language that even she could hardly believe she had approved. It was real now.

She brought out candles and the silver ice bucket and nestled a bottle of champagne in crushed cubes. By five-thirty the loft smelled of roasted garlic, warm bread, and the faint bite of champagne corks cooling in ice.

When the front door finally clicked open at 6:30 p.m., she was by the kitchen island, pretending to adjust the napkin rings. She heard the heavy thud of his keys in the ceramic bowl, the low rumble of him kicking off boots.

She watched him cross the threshold into the open living space, as he stood there, taking in the candles, the muted lighting and the table set for two.

"Baby?" he called, uncertain but amused.

She emerged fully, stepping into the glow. His gaze swept her from stilettos up the length of the slip to the loose curls framing her face. She felt heat bloom behind her collarbones.

"Sweet Jesus," he breathed, grinning. "You look beyond stunning. What's the occasion?"

"It's a celebration. Our celebration."

"Celebration of what? It's only Tuesday."

Instead of answering she stepped to the credenza where she had placed the thick envelope. "Open it."

He took the envelope, brow furrowing. With careful fingers, he slid out the paperwork. As his eyes flew over the headings, his breath hitched. She watched the moment it landed—first disbelief, then widening shock, the papers trembling in his grip.

"No way," he whispered. Then louder, "no fucking *way.* Victoria, tell me this is real."

"It's real. I met with a divorce attorney today and paid the retainer on the spot. The divorce process has officially started as we speak."

He stared another heartbeat, then let out a raw, unfiltered shout of joy. The papers fluttered to the floor as he scooped her up with both arms. "This is the best day of my life. I love you. I love you. I love you."

She laughed, dizzy and giddy, clinging to his shoulders. *This* was what she had pictured through restless nights—Thomas's disbelief melting into awe, his arms sure around her rib cage.

When he set her down, he pressed a fast, hungry kiss to her lips, then paused, noticing the fragrance of chicken and butter. "I smell heaven," he said, wiping moisture from his eyes. "But I'm covered in sweat and sawdust. Give me a few minutes to shower and get cleaned up, baby girl."

"Ok. I'll keep everything warm."

✳ ✳ ✳ ✳

Midway through the meal, Victoria broached the subject she dreaded. "I had a long, heartfelt discussion with Tab yesterday. She wants to come by. She's ready to make peace."

Thomas's fork paused. He swallowed, gaze narrowing. "Out of the blue?"

"She's realized this isn't a fling. She wants to see us together and offer her support."

"Victoria, she trashed me the last time we crossed paths. Now she wants wine and cheese? Feels fake."

"She's my best friend," Victoria pressed, even though a whisper of doubt flickered in her mind. *He's right, Tab turned on a dime.* But she pushed on. "She sees I'm serious. That I'm building a future with you. She wants to be part of my life, which means part of *our* life."

"If it matters to you, we'll do it. I'm just protective. I don't want drama."

"I appreciate that. But we can't live in a bunker forever. She needs to see we're real."

He squeezed her fingers. "Then let's invite her over."

They moved on to dessert. As they sipped the last of the champagne, Thomas grew quieter, rolling the stem between his fingers. "Can I ask something serious?"

"Anything."

"When the paperwork hits Davis… are you safe? I know you say he's not violent. But truth changes people."

"Davis values image above all. He won't lash out, especially with legal eyes on him. He'll definitely have a lot of emotions, but he would never in his life, ever hurt me." *I hope*, she added silently. Then, more firmly, she said, "if it makes you feel better, I'll stay alert. The attorney is ready if anything shifts."

"Good." He stood, walked around behind her chair, and rested his hands on her shoulders. "Because I plan to keep you, forever."

*This is what I want*, she told herself. *No more hidden phones, no more two addresses, no more waking up in the middle of the night terrified someone knows.* Here, in the gentle slide of his palm along her spine, she found peace she hadn't realized she craved.

"We're really doing this," he said.

"We're really doing this," she echoed.

# Control 5
## The Kiss of Judas

Victoria moved through the loft like a gust of warm wind. *Breathe,* she reminded herself. *It's already perfect.* The reassurance barely settled before she was smoothing the ottoman again, checking the puddle of the linen drapes, adjusting the light bulbs so their glow felt soft instead of interrogation-room bright.

Across the open floor, Thomas leaned against the island with a crooked grin, arms folded across the shirt that clung to his shoulders. "Baby, this loft stays clean, okay?" He chuckled. "You need to sit and chill."

"I know. I'm just...nervous, I guess. This is the first time we've had a guest here and I just want it to be perfect."

"Trust me, it's perfect. Tab is your friend, right?"

"Yes."

"Well then it's all good. I'm sure she's not a health inspector looking to pass or fail us, well, maybe not on cleanliness, but she's definitely up to something."

Victoria swatted lightly at his arm. "Stop. She's coming with good energy tonight."

Thomas slipped an arm around her waist. "Relax, baby. She'll be here soon. Let's just relax and wait for her."

"Okay, I'm chill."

A dozen blocks away, Tabitha idled at a red light and rehearsed her own lines. The bright screen of her phone glowed with her man's last text: *Let me know what you find. Details matter. Ensure that you ask about cameras.*

In truth, he was looking out for himself, and Tabitha was just a part of that net.

*I'm gathering intel,* she reminded herself, tightening her grip on the wheel. *Get in, get what we need, get out.* Still, unease twitched behind her ribs. Betraying Victoria didn't sit clean on her tongue, no matter how many times she told herself this was for a greater plan.

Back at the loft, the doorbell finally chimed. Victoria sprang up and crossed the floor in quick steps. Thomas stayed a few paces behind, shoulders squared.

"Hey, Tab, come on in."

Tabitha stepped across the threshold in a lavender wrap dress, a smile dialed to friendly. The two women hugged, Victoria's arms tight with real affection, Tabitha's a fraction stiff before she forced herself to soften. Over Victoria's shoulder, Tabitha caught Thomas's silent scrutiny, tall and careful, protective.

"Hey, Thomas, how are you?" Tabitha offered, voice airy.

"Hey, Tab, I'm civil, how about you?"

Victoria shot him a warning look that said *behave.*

Tabitha chuckled, raising both palms. "I'm actually good today. Not looking for any trouble, just coming in peace and trying to make amends."

"Okay."

"Come on into the living room and sit," Victoria urged, cutting the tension. "Can I get you something to drink?"

"I'll take a bottle of water."

"Gotcha," Victoria said, heading for the kitchen.

Tabitha's eyes swept the loft as she moved deeper inside. The space looked lived-in yet curated, as if someone fed on order. *That tells me something about him,* she noted. Tabitha chose the oversized chair angled toward the couch.

Thomas sat on the opposite end of the sofa, leaving space before Victoria returned with the water. She sat on the couch and tucked herself under Thomas's arm. The gesture was small, but it spoke volumes—intimacy, possession, a united front. Tab clocked it, and offered a friendly, slightly forced, compliment.

"This is a nice place you have here, Thomas. Very nicely decorated. I'm impressed."

Victoria beamed, gazing up at him. "My baby has great taste."

Tab offered a half smile, letting her gaze drift toward the high rafters. *No security cameras in sight,* she observed.

"So, Thomas. I don't think I know much about you. Where are you from?"

"Miami."

"Oh, nice. I love going to Miami. The food and the culture there is amazing." She leaned in a fraction, hoping the warmth would coax him open. "Were you born and raised there?"

"Yeah… something like that," he said. His steady gaze carried a hint of warning.

Tabitha felt the wall he was putting up and tried again. "How did you end up here in Atlanta?"

"I didn't know it was interrogate Thomas day."

"Really, baby?" Victoria whispered, pressing a palm to his chest. "Come on, please. You said you wouldn't do this."

Thomas read the worry in her eyes, worry for their peace, for how this visit could unravel. He didn't want to be the reason she hurt tonight. He exhaled, brushing a kiss across her forehead. "I'm sorry, baby, you're right. I apologize."

They shared a quick smile, a silent *we're okay.*

Tabitha fake swooned. "Wow, you two are so cute."

Thomas settled back, ready to give just enough truth to satisfy, nothing more.

"I was born in Miami, but I was raised in the trenches."

Tabitha blinked, confusion flickering.

"I was pretty much in foster care most of my life and went into the military at eighteen, traveled the world, and ended up here in Atlanta."

Tabitha's eyes widened. The story landed heavier than she had guessed, heavier than she wanted to feel. *Stick to the plan,* she warned herself. Still, genuine awe crept into her voice.

"Wow, that's heavy. You're definitely a success story. Look at what you've managed to accomplish."

"Thanks, but I wouldn't call myself a success until I accomplish the ultimate goal in life, which is, marrying you Victoria, giving you the world... and you giving me lots of babies."

Victoria's heart fluttered as he pulled her into a hug, lips brushing her temple in a tender kiss.

"You guys talking marriage?"

"Yes, as soon as the div"—then paused, the moment catching in his throat. He glanced at Victoria, a flicker of hesitation in his eyes.

"It's okay, baby. She's my best friend. I was going to tell her, but I guess now would be in order."

"Tell me what?" Her voice was smooth, friendly, but inside her chest, her heart hammered. *Is this the moment?* she wondered. *Will she finally say it?*

"I went to see a lawyer a few days ago... and I filed for divorce."

Tabitha lifted her water bottle to her lips, but as the cool liquid touched her tongue, her throat clenched. She coughed once, twice, hands coming up to her mouth.

"Tab, are you okay?" Victoria sprang to her feet, rushing around the sofa to grab a handful of paper napkins.

Tabitha patted her cheek, blinking rapidly. The napkin came to her like a lifeline. "Thank you. I'm... I'm fine," she managed. "You caught me off guard when you said you filed for divorce. Already, V?"

"I know. It does seem like we're moving fast."

Before Tabitha could respond, Thomas jumped in. "Hell, it's actually not fast enough for me!"

Victoria playfully swatted his arm. "Hush."

Tabitha forced a smile, though heat flared in her cheeks. *Smooth, Tab,* she told herself. *Don't let them see.*

"Things with Davis haven't worked for a long time, Tab. I've told you that. Thomas is my soulmate. When you know, you know. We're not getting any younger. I'm ready to settle down with him. I want children, a family… a real life together."

Tabitha pressed a hand to her own stomach, when Victoria mentioned children. That dream she knew all too well.

"I applaud you, Victoria, for living in your truth and making your dream happen. I support you both 100 percent. You're right, this is the age to start having kids. You deserve it, babes."

"Aww, thank you, Tab."

Thomas leaned forward, curiosity lighting his eyes. "So, Tab, who's the love of your life? Any wedding bells soon for you in the future?"

Tabitha gave a quick, nervous laugh. "Yes. I'm hoping to be just like you guys soon. Married and starting a family."

Victoria cocked an eyebrow. "What? Are you still with this mystery guy? Wow, y'all have been going strong for a long time. And hold on, you're talking marriage and kids and I still don't know him? I still haven't met him nor do I know anything about him. What's his name? I don't think you ever told me or I don't remember."

"Yeah, I did tell you, silly."

Victoria looked confused. "Oh, I don't remember."

"That's because you were wrapped up in your boo thang."

Victoria and Tabitha both burst into giggles, the tension melting as the room echoed with genuine laughter.

Tabitha felt a pang, guilt, maybe, but she chased it away. *Remember your mission.*

Tabitha shifted in her seat and quickly pivoted in order to change the subject. "You know what I'd love? A tour of the loft. I just can't get over how amazing this place is."

Victoria's face lit up. "Absolutely! Come on upstairs."

Victoria led the way up the open steel staircase, while Tabitha followed.

"He really outdid himself here," Tabitha murmured. She let her fingers hover over the smooth edge of the built-in desk, then traced a line on the reclaimed oak railing. *Solid construction,* she noted to herself. *No give, no gaps.*

Victoria smiled, proud. "Thomas spent months on this. Every shelf, every beam, it's all his handiwork."

They stepped toward the loft's single bedroom. Tabitha paused at the threshold, checking the latch. *Simple deadbolt. No electronic lock. No cameras in sight.*

"You know what's interesting? I didn't see a ring camera or anything when I came to the front door. Most people with a place this nice, and a contractor, no less, would have cameras everywhere."

Victoria laughed. "No cameras. Believe it or not, he isn't paranoid like that. He thinks cameras actually watch you and that people can hack them. So, he doesn't believe in them."

Tabitha tilted her head, hiding her relief. *No cameras, no recorded angles.* She offered a breezy "Oh, interesting concept," then followed Victoria back down the stairs, slipping her purse strap higher on her shoulder. *Everything's just as I need it.*

They rejoined Thomas, who was perched at the island, mixing himself a scotch on the rocks.

Tabitha sank into the armchair by the window. "So, Thomas, what do you think of Victoria's parents? Did Mr. Martin give you the talk yet?"

"I'm glad you asked. I've been asking her when will I get to meet them, and she always says, 'in due time.'"

"So, you haven't met them yet? Wow."

Victoria waved a hand, half exasperated, half amused. "Wait a minute, before you two gang up on me, this is a lot to spring on them. I've been talking to my parents a bit, but I haven't laid it all out there yet. I'm going slowly."

Thomas's eyes softened as he turned to Victoria. "Well, Victoria, you've filed for divorce, don't you think it's time to start laying it all out there? We said no more secrets, no more lies, right?"

"I'm not lying. I just… I don't know. I guess I was delaying the inevitable. But like I told you, I'm going to dinner with Mom and Dad tomorrow. That's when I'll spill everything and set up a date for you to meet them."

Thomas's face lit up. "For real? Oh my God, I'm so happy. This is getting official, baby. Meeting the parents is huge. I can't wait to show your dad who I am, to have him accept me as his son-in-law. God's really blessing me with the family I've always wanted."

"You don't even know them yet. How do you know you'll even like them or want them in your life?"

"If you came from them and I love you, then I know I'll love them." He reached across and kissed her hand.

Tabitha watched them, chest tight. For a moment, she felt a pang of real empathy. *They're so in love.* But she pressed it away, recalling why she was there. *Keep smiling, keep notes.*

Victoria cleared her throat and called softly, "Tabitha? You okay?"

"Sorry. What were you saying?"

"I was asking if you want to go out for dinner or order in."

Tabitha stood, smoothing her skirt. "I'm actually going to head out and go home. I'm running on fumes," she said with a tired laugh.

"Yeah, it's Friday and we did work almost a full day. I get it."

"Thank you so much for having me over, Thomas. It was good talking with you tonight and I appreciate the hospitality."

"Likewise."

Tabitha turned to Victoria and gave her friend a tight embrace and a *kiss* on the cheek. "I love you, babes."

"I love you too. Get home safely and see you soon."

Tabitha stepped back, her smile steady as she lifted a hand in farewell. "Thank you," she said, as she walked out into the cool night air. *Mission complete.*

In the hush of the empty loft, Tabitha walked down the concrete steps, each step echoing her next moves. The details were in her mind—no cameras, a solid lock, an open invitation to Thomas's world. *Perfect,* she thought. *Now to report back.*

Victoria pressed her body close against Thomas's side as she kissed him. "Thank you, baby."

Thomas returned her kiss with gentle curiosity. "Thank you for what?"

"For making tonight a success. I was so worried about everything being perfect, and it was. We had a great time."

He half-smiled, polite but unconvinced.

She tilted her head, concern flickering behind her smile. "What are you making that face for?"

"Nothing. I'm good." But his voice was quiet, and his eyes held a different story.

"No. I know when your wheels are turning and you're thinking. Spill it, babe."

"Victoria, I just know there's something about her that's off. Did you notice when I asked her about her love life, she didn't really talk about it much? You asked her who this 'mystery guy' is, and she just laughed and blew it off. And we never got back to that subject. I don't even remember how she changed the topic, but she sure as hell didn't mention him much." He stopped to find her eyes. "And if you two are best friends, how does she know everything about you, and you know little to nothing about her love life? Doesn't it seem like she would be excited to tell you about him, let you meet him, at least tell you his name?"

Victoria closed her eyes for a moment, thinking through Thomas's words. She did remember meeting Tabitha's other boyfriends. She had been supportive, hopeful the way an older sister might be, but those relationships never lasted. This new one, Tabitha spoke of him with a dreamy hush, but she had never brought him around. Now, hearing Thomas say it out loud, the truth felt sharper.

Her stomach fluttered, but she swallowed hard and pushed the thoughts away. She didn't want to believe there was anything untoward here. "I really do believe she's holding on to this relationship because she seems in love, and she's been with him a while. It seems like it's going somewhere, unlike her past relationships, which were… well, train-wrecks that I could spot from a mile away. I would always tell her that. So, I do think she's keeping me away from him, for the simple fact that she may not want my opinion or want me to see something she's not ready to show me. I think she's guarding this relationship, not jinxing it, so to speak."

"You're getting soft. You're letting your guard down way too much. What happened to the super-hard exterior Victoria that I first met?"

Victoria leaned in and wrapped her arms around his neck. "Well, she's gone. Now it's the new Victoria. The one focused on you, on becoming your wife, settling down, becoming a mom. I don't care about all that other stuff right now. Let Tabitha hide whatever she's doing. I'm not focused on her. She'll handle whatever life is throwing at her, and I'll be there as her best friend if and when she needs me. But she's a big girl, she can handle it. As for me, I'm focused on you right now, Mr. Carter."

"Is that right?"

She gave a mock-serious nod.

"I thought we were supposed to be getting food," he said, heat dancing in his eyes.

"We will, but right now I'm hungry for something else."

Without warning, she hopped into his lap, wrapping her legs around his waist. Holding her close, he spun her around, and their laughter filled the living room as he carried her off toward the bedroom.

They let the world slip away, embracing each other, sharing breath and heartbeat as the night deepened around them. In the hush after every tender touch, Victoria felt her world narrow to Thomas, his steady warmth and the certainty of his love. And somewhere deep in her mind, Victoria vowed to trust her heart first, even as shadows of doubt lingered at the edges, but tonight, she was exactly where she belonged.

# Control 4
## Warning Before Destruction

Thomas waited until Victoria's taillights disappeared down the street before he let out the breath he had been holding. He sat on the couch, flicked on the TV, and landed on a Miami Hurricanes game. Green jerseys blurred across the screen, the announcer's bass booming through the speakers. *Good,* he thought, *something loud enough to fill the room.*

It didn't work. Instead, a tight heat coiled low in his stomach, the same burn he had felt yesterday the second Tabitha stepped over their threshold. *Leave it alone,* he told himself. *Victoria thinks it's nothing. Trust her judgment.* He tried, but the coil only cinched tighter.

He muted the TV and let the crowd noise fade. The silence was heavy. *Maybe Tab's jealous,* he thought, but the idea fell flat. Jealousy felt too small for the jolt in Tabitha's eyes when Victoria said, *I filed for divorce.* She had gone pale, slapped a hand to her throat, nearly choked on plain water. Beneath it, he glimpsed something raw and scared.

*Stop spiraling,* he warned himself, yet the memories kept coming. Davis's Saturday jog selfie. Tabitha's immediate heart emoji response. That tiny red icon had seemed harmless until Thomas noticed it showing up on every solo photo of Davis. But on any post with Victoria and Davis together, nothing. Not even a thumbs-up.

*Maybe it's coincidence,* he thought. But the word rang hollow in the empty room. He grabbed his phone, his thumb hovering over the Facebook icon. He hesitated, but tapped anyway.

Davis's profile loaded. More selfies at the hangar, a sunset over the runway, another jogging photo near his subdivision. Under each post, Tabitha's name glowed beside a red heart.

Thomas's chest tightened as he scrolled to a photo of Davis and Victoria standing together in Savannah. No reaction from Tabitha. Not a single one.

"That's weird," he muttered. His mind jumped to their conversation about Tabitha's "mystery guy." Victoria questioning her, *What's his name? Why haven't I met him yet?* And she had dodged it like a pro boxer, laughing, deflecting, pointing out the walnut shelves instead. He remembered glancing at Victoria, waiting for her to press Tabitha harder, but she had only smiled, completely oblivious to the fact.

*Could Davis be her mystery guy?* The thought felt ludicrous, like a plot twist in a bad soap opera. Davis adored Victoria. He had bragged about her in that bar, called her "my whole heart." Still, the puzzle pieces came together in Thomas's mind. Tabitha's praise of Davis, her silence about her own boyfriend, the way she choked when divorce came up, the hearts on Davis-only photos. *If she were crushing on him, that fits. But would Davis answer?* He pictured the aircraft mechanic at the bar, eyes warm as he talked about Victoria's laugh. During that whole conversation, Davis never once mentioned another woman.

Thomas felt half stupid, half furious. Furious at Tabitha if she was pining after her best friend's husband, furious at himself for even imagining it. He needed proof or at least stronger hints before raising this with Victoria. The last thing he wanted was to sow mistrust without solid footing.

He opened Davis's last jogging post again. Three comments down, Tabitha replied, "Keep grinding, champ!" Davis had replied with a flex-arm emoji and, "Appreciate you, T."

*Maybe she's just a supportive friend,* he argued with himself. *Yeah, a friend who ignores photos of her so-called sister with the same man.* He tossed the phone onto the coffee table, harder than intended.

A plan began to form. He would watch and pay attention. If Tabitha kept reacting to Davis's posts, if her mystery boyfriend never appeared, he would talk to Victoria. He would protect the love they were building, even if it meant asking painful questions.

✳ ✳ ✳ ✳

The hostess led Victoria past the open kitchen, where the scent of smoked pecans and rosemary chicken drifted on the air, and slid a polished menu in front of her.

She drew a breath and rehearsed her opening line for the tenth time. *Dad, Mom, I'm leaving Davis. There's someone else. His name is Thomas.* Even in her head the confession sounded jagged, as if she were sawing through the wood of her own life. *Just tell the truth, well, most of it,* she coached herself, smoothing a nonexistent wrinkle from her blouse.

A flash of familiar salt-and-pepper hair appeared at the door. Her father paused at the hostess stand, scanning the room until she lifted her hand. His face lit with relief as he hurried forward. His embrace swallowed her, sturdy arms and faint cologne that always reminded her of childhood goodnight hugs. She closed her eyes for a second, grounding herself in his steady warmth.

"Hi, Daddy."

"Hey, honey." He kissed her cheek, then stepped back, brown eyes searching hers. "You look tired but happy. Been burning the candle, I bet."

"Something like that. Where's Mom?"

He sighed and slid into the booth across from her. "Your mother has an extreme headache from so much happening this week. She's been stretched so thin over the past few days with helping the neighbor, choir rehearsal, and sewing costumes for the ballet company and private customers. So, she finally had to lie down. She hates missing dinner with you, but she just didn't have any strength left."

"I know she does. I'll stop by next week, take her some lemon tea cakes, and give her an update in person."

"That'll cheer her up. You know your mother never passes up an outing unless she's really spent."

"Exactly," Victoria said, as she signaled the waiter, who approached with water and a practiced smile.

They placed drink orders and selected their entrées quickly. The waiter vanished, leaving a polite promise to return with skillet cornbread.

Victoria's hands fidgeted beneath the tablecloth, twisting her napkin. *Start light,* she told herself. She cleared her throat and managed a small smile. "How's work, Dad?

"Busy as always."

"That's good." Victoria sipped her water, letting the bubbles settle on her tongue. "You and Mom planning any trips? Maybe a quick weekend destination before the holidays roll in?"

"Not this year. We're just gearing up for Halloween decorations. You know how your mom likes to outdo the neighbors. Then it'll be Thanksgiving and Christmas right behind it. You're still coming to carve pumpkins with us like old times, right?"

"As long as you promise not to carve another lopsided grin," she teased, tension loosening. They laughed together and for the next fifteen minutes, they traded updates. The easy banter steadied her heartbeat, but she knew the longer she waited, the harder the plunge would feel. Cornbread arrived in a cast-iron skillet, steam curling upward like a beckoning hand.

Her father set his fork down between bites and fixed her with a familiar, measured gaze. "So, dear, how's Davis? How are you two doing?"

*This is it,* she thought. "Dad, I need to be honest with you. Davis and I aren't living together anymore. We're separated, and…" she drew a slow breath, feeling the words settle like stones… "we're moving toward a divorce."

A small muscle jumped along the edge of her father's jaw, but his eyes stayed level and steady. "Hmm. Okay. I see." He lifted his glass of sweet tea, held it for a moment, then took a long, slow sip.

Victoria's heartbeat thudded in her ears. No raised brows, no dropped jaw, just that quiet nod? "Is that all you're going to say? Dad, I just told you we're getting a divorce. Doesn't that surprise you at all?"

"I won't lie, when I first heard the news a little while ago, it caught me off guard and I was in complete shock. Since then I've been waiting, figuring you'd sit down with your mom and me when you were ready. But we're still in the dark, sweetheart." He paused, meeting her eyes. "Help me understand. What changed? How did things go from married bliss to talk of divorce?"

*He heard recently? From whom?* The question hammered at her while she straightened in her seat. "Dad, hold on." Her voice shook more than she meant it to. "What do you mean you *heard?* Who told you? Has Davis been calling you? Have you two been talking behind my back?"

"No, honey, I haven't talked to Davis. But I did speak with his mother, and she was the one who brought me up to speed."

The information landed like a cold drop of rain on Victoria's skin. *Of course, Ms. Evelyn would reach out,* she thought. Davis's mother never missed a chance to share news the instant she had it. She drew a calming breath and pressed the linen napkin flat against her lap, knuckles whitening at the corners.

"I'm sorry you had to learn everything from Ms. Evelyn. My plan was to sit down with you and Mom first, explain it myself, on my terms, when I felt ready. You both deserved to hear the whole story straight from me."

Martin's expression eased for half a second, then the familiar business mask slid into place. "You know Evelyn calls me from time to time. She always has questions about itemizing donations or how to properly list something on her return. She flew in earlier this week, wanted to see Davis face-to-face after he told her the news about y'all separating."

Martin shifted forward, elbows resting on the edge of the table. "She came by the office on her way back to the airport yesterday and asked if I had heard anything from you. I told her I hadn't. So, I'm asking now, Lestie, how did you and Davis reach this point? Where did it start, and why didn't you come to us first?"

"It's messy, Dad. For a long time, things at home just felt empty. Davis is kind. He fills up my gas tank, he brings me soup when I'm sick, he's loving and caring, but somewhere along the way, things just fell flat. The house got quiet even when the TV was on. I would sit across from him at dinner and feel like there was a glass wall between us."

She took a sip of water, gathering the next line. "I waited, hoping it was only a season—busy schedules, stress, something temporary—but the space kept stretching. We tried date nights, weekend trips, but nothing closed the gap. I started waking up at three in the morning with this cold feeling that my life was shrinking around me."

Victoria steadied her voice. "Then last fall I met someone—his name is Thomas. It was supposed to be once, but something clicked. I felt awake for the first time in years. I told myself it would be a single evening and then walk away, but it turned into something more. Dad, I fell in love… hard. We've been seeing each other for a year, quietly."

Her gaze dropped to her lap. "About a month ago I packed up, left the house in Smyrna, and moved in with

Thomas at his loft. Davis and I talked, cried, and agreed the marriage was over. Lawyers have the paperwork now, and the first filing is already underway."

She lifted her eyes to meet her father's. "I know it sounds fast and selfish, but it also feels right. I didn't plan to fall for anyone, but I can't go back to feeling half alive. Thomas feels like the rest of my life, and I need you to understand why I'm choosing this road."

Martin's face stayed almost blank, but Victoria saw a tiny twitch at the corner of his jaw, a quick pulse that always showed when something didn't add up. He leaned back a little and fixed her with the kind of steady stare he used on clients who left out half the story. "How did you meet him?"

Victoria felt her fork grow heavy. She traced a pattern in her mashed potatoes and kept her gaze down. "At a café."

Martin let the silence grow, knowing silence was a kind of lever. "Just a café? You sat down, ordered a latte, met his eyes, and that was it?"

"Something like that."

"You're giving me the headline, Lestie. I'm asking for the article." His voice dropped, almost a whisper. "Do you remember that talk we had back in my office when you were in college?"

The air in Victoria's lungs thinned. Images flooded back—the door to his private suite cracked open, the muffled sound of a woman's moan, her father's shirt half-buttoned while he stood behind that woman in the room he called the *relaxation room,* giving her pain and pleasure.

"I remember."

"And the rules I gave you?"

"Never let feelings in," she recited. "Never see the same fling twice."

A flicker of approval crossed his face. She could almost hear the rest of what he had said that day: *You stay the hunter, Lestie. You choose, you enjoy, you move on. Otherwise, you turn from predator to prey.*

Martin's gaze chilled, turning sharp the way a jeweler studies a flawed diamond. "Those rules are there to keep the board clean. You spot what you want, you take it, and you walk away while it's still warm. No numbers saved in the phone. No good morning texts. No brunch the next day. No threads left for someone to pull. Done means done."

He held her eyes a moment longer, letting the silence bite. "That's how you stay the hunter. You keep the teeth in *your* mouth. The moment you circle back for another taste, second date, second night, second anything, you hand the bite to them. Now the game has teeth, and they are aimed at you. And once the roles flip," he snapped his fingers, "you are no longer stalking. You are bleeding."

Victoria pulled in a slow, uneven breath and pressed her napkin flat so he wouldn't see her hands shake. "I did follow the rules, Dad, right up until I met Thomas. I left that first night telling myself it was over. For two whole months, I stuck to the plan, no calls, no follow ups, no second taste. I kept his number buried in my second phone and tried to forget his smile. I convinced myself he had already moved on, that he probably didn't even remember my name. But the harder I tried to erase him, the louder he echoed in my head. One day, I gave in and texted him." Her mouth curved in a bittersweet half smile. "Less than sixty seconds later he wrote back telling me that he remembers me and misses me. The moment I saw those words, something inside me cracked open. I felt, seen and wanted in a way that wasn't just physical. After that, I couldn't help myself. We met up and spent time together and each time felt stronger. I stopped counting nights, because each one pulled me closer. With him, I'm not hunting, Dad. I walk through the door, and it feels like I've finally come home."

Martin let out a slow breath and shook his head like a man who already saw the ending of a movie no one else had watched. "Lestie, you're opening the cage door and walking right inside. A hunter cannot stalk from behind bars. Predators don't last in cages."

Victoria felt heat push up her throat. "I'm not in any cage. I'm choosing this. I'm the one steering."

Martin's eyes narrowed.

She leaned closer before he could speak again. "Listen, Dad, I still hold all the levers. Davis is calm, signing papers because *I* said it was time. Thomas is with me because *I* decided to answer that text. And me? I'm the one driving my own life, every turn, every stop. I'm not trapped. I'm free, and I picked the road."

Martin's lips pulled into a slow, lopsided smile, more a warning than a show of warmth. "Lestie, you're my blood. I've seen that spark in you since you could walk. It's the same spark I carry. But remember, fire is light and heat only when you keep a safe hand on it. Hold it too close, and the same flame that guides you will blister your skin." He let the words hang, eyes searching for a crack.

Victoria felt the weight of his stare, but she refused to look away and met his gaze head on. "I hear you, Dad, but I won't lose myself. Not to Thomas, not to Davis, not to anyone. The flame is still mine to steer. I'll keep it bright and not let it burn me. I promise."

"Lestie, I've shown you how I live. One night. I give a woman what she's looking for—attention, thrill, release— and then I'm gone. It keeps my world neat, with no open doors for trouble to walk through. You're swinging every door in your house wide open. Divorce hearings. New lover. Emotions braided through both. That's a tangle, and tangles attract hunters of their own. Divorce is messy. Love is messier. That's not predator play, that's prey waiting to be cornered."

Heat flashed up Victoria's spine. "Maybe I want messy if messy is honest. Maybe I'm done treating people like disposable thrills. If real love means risk, then I'll carry the risk. I'm not afraid of getting scratched if the feeling on the other side is worth it."

"Messy comes with a bill," Martin said. "Lawyers on retainer, court dates that eat your calendar, headlines you cannot yank off the internet. You could lose the Smyrna house in a split, or half the business you've poured sweat into. Folks gossip, and clients start to wonder if their money is safe with someone whose personal life is on fire. And don't forget plain old safety, Lestie. Angry spouses do reckless things when they feel cornered."

He drew a slow breath and went on. "Davis was your storm shelter. Solid credit, no drama and name clean as white linen. You could've kept that shelter standing, kept the lights on, and still stepped out when you wanted to feel a spark. Scratch the itch, close the door and come home to steady footing. That was the plan."

"I'm done living like life is a spreadsheet," she said. "I won't trade truth for a roof that doesn't feel like home. I'd rather risk the storm than keep pretending the weather is perfect."

Martin's eyes narrowed, the way they always did when he weighed numbers on a balance sheet. "You know, you sound a lot like your mother when she decides something is going to be true no matter what I say. Quiet on the outside, granite on the inside." He eased back in the booth, laid one arm along the top of the seat, and went on. "All right, Lestie. Let's hear about this Thomas guy of yours."

Relief trickled through her shoulders like warm water. "Thomas works with his hands, real carpentry, not plywood shortcuts. He can read the grain on a board the way some folks read sheet music. He built floating shelves in the loft out of old walnut—the joints are tight and seamless." A smile crept in despite herself. "And he laughs at the dumbest hour, like midnight, when the city is dead quiet. He'll remember some joke from a podcast and start wheezing until I'm laughing, too."

Martin's face stayed neutral, but his eyes followed every word.

"He listens, Dad. When the panic in my chest hits, when I think the world's going to tip, he sits beside me, breathes with me until the room feels right. No rush, no fixing, just steady."

"He sounds solid. I'd like to meet him."

Relief flooded her chest, and a bright smile spread before she could stop it.

Martin shifted subjects as smoothly as turning a page. "By the way, Lestie, I've been looking over the year-to-date figures for Social Brilliance. Revenues are climbing, nice curve upward. You're running a sharp ship."

A flicker of pride warmed her chest. "Thank you, Dad—" She stopped mid-sentence, brow drawing in. "But that surprises me a little. I haven't forwarded the last quarter's numbers yet. They aren't due on your desk until next week."

"Oh, I have them. Tabitha sent the updated spreadsheets on Wednesday and answered a few follow-up questions while we were on the phone."

A thin spike of alarm slid down Victoria's spine. "Tab already sent the reports?" She tried to keep her tone neutral, but it rang a note too sharp. "I didn't realize she had closed out the quarter and pushed the data."

"She said you were buried in meetings and told her to handle the upload. Everything looked tidy, so I signed off on the review."

Victoria forced a nod, though her mind whirled. *Why move numbers without looping me in? And why didn't Tab mention it yesterday?* The new ache behind her brow told her this was one more thread she would need to tug, and soon.

"Tabitha has really come into her own these last two quarters. The balance sheets she sent were spotless. Every vendor payment matched to the penny, projections lined up with actuals, footnotes clear as daylight. Sharp girl. Quick, organized and already thinking like a senior partner."

Victoria nodded, but an uneasy flicker crossed her mind—the way Tabitha's laugh had sounded tight yesterday when she had dodged questions about her love life, and the phone screen she kept face down. A small itch crawled at the base of Victoria's neck.

"Dad… How come you and Tab are talking so often? I didn't realize the two of you were on the phone about firm business that much."

Martin's brows pulled together, confusion softening the lines at the corners of his eyes. "Lestie, she's your business partner. All we talked about were invoices, payroll dates, and tax estimates."

"It's just… yesterday I asked Tab about the man she's seeing. She ducked every question. Then she dropped your name kind of out of the blue, asking if Thomas met you yet." The words tumbled out faster than she could shape them. "Dad, are you sleeping with Tabitha?" The question hung between them like a struck bell, still ringing in her ears.

Martin's jaw clamped shut so hard she heard his teeth click. A quick flash of fire lit his eyes, as if she had just struck him across the face. His voice came out tight and rough but packed with heat.

"Lestie, why on earth would I lay a finger on my own daughter's best friend?" His hands had curled into fists on top of the table. "Are you out of your mind?"

Flames raced up Victoria's neck and filled her cheeks. The room seemed to tilt for a heartbeat. "I'm sorry, Dad. I'm stretched so thin right now. Tab's keeping secrets, and when you mentioned talking with her—"

Martin cut her off with a sharp shake of his head. "Don't ever throw a charge like that at me again." His eyes held hers, demanding she understood the line she had crossed.

"I won't. I shouldn't have said it. I'm sorry."

Martin let out a long breath through his nose, shoulders easing only a fraction. They both turned their attention back to the plates, but the bright flavors had gone flat. Between them lay a quiet too thick for small talk, yet too fragile for more argument.

They rose from the booth at the same time. They threaded through the Saturday crowd, past tables humming with other people's laughter. Outside, the autumn air felt cool and sharp against her cheeks, clearing away the heavy warmth of the dining room.

Martin stopped beneath a pool of light and turned toward her. "Remember the rules, keep your eyes open and don't forget who you are."

"I know exactly who I am."

Martin's jaw eased. He gave one short nod, then released her shoulder. Without another word, he turned toward his car. Victoria watched the taillights flash as he pulled from the curb. She drew a long breath and headed for her own car, her heart heavy but her resolve firm.

# Control 3
## The Trigger

Victoria realized that she left her cellphone at the table and went back through the double-glass doors of the restaurant with her jaw clenched so tight it hurt.

The waiter who had served them stood by her old booth, phone in his palm, scanning the entry like a lifeguard hunting for a lost child. "Ma'am, I was just about to run this to lost and found," he said, holding out the slim rectangle.

"Thank you. I can't get two steps without this thing." She slipped the phone into her purse, then turned toward the exit, ready to clear the room, clear her head—

"Victoria!" a man's voice boomed across the floor.

Victoria turned and pasted on her best networking smile. Striding toward her was Cliff Adkins, broad in the shoulders, tie knotted too tight, gold watch flashing under the lights. He waved with a thick-fingered hand, the gesture almost theatrical, as if he wanted half the restaurant to notice. *Just what I need*, she thought.

"I knew it was you. Victoria Hart. How long has it been? Six, seven months?"

"At least. You're looking well, Cliff. Business treating you right?"

He rocked back on his heels, thumbs hooking the edge of his belt. "Couldn't be better. We've got orders stacked to the ceiling and new contracts every single week."

"Happy to hear it. But you know what would move your numbers from *great* to downright *spectacular*?" She angled her head, letting the small tease of a smile bloom. "Bringing S&J over to Social Brilliance. We've got the tools to scale you nationwide in, oh, six quarters tops."

Cliff threw his head back and let out a sharp, booming laugh that turned a few neighboring diners' heads. When he looked at her again, his brows hopped toward his hairline in playful challenge. "I have to hand it to you, Victoria, Social Brilliance must be a real giant now. Big enough that the left hand doesn't always know what the right hand is signing."

"What exactly are you talking about, Cliff?"

He planted his feet a little farther apart, clearly enjoying whatever nugget he was about to drop. "I signed with you folks two months ago. Your partner, Tabitha, tracked me down herself and set up a meeting in that glass conference room. She gave me a pitch that, honestly, I couldn't walk away from."

Victoria felt her smile stiffen around the edges, the corners of her mouth aching. "Is that right?"

"Oh, absolutely. At first, I thought it was adorable, her working so hard to be the next Victoria while you were away from the office. But the girl has got teeth. She's actually quite astute and is a brilliant negotiator. She sliced my onboarding fee clean in half." He raised two fingers, chopping the air to illustrate. "Half the price you quoted me last year. Hard to argue with savings like that. Tabitha knows how to make a customer feel appreciated and satisfied. You have an amazing business partner in her. Make sure you tell her *thank you* for me, will you? I'm over the moon." He gave an exaggerated wink, then tapped at his ringing phone and lifted it to his ear, already starting to turn away, leaving Victoria with a frozen smile on her face and a storm boiling behind her eyes.

"Gotta grab this," he said, already backing away. "Good seeing you, Victoria. You look amazing. We'll talk soon."

She stared after him as he disappeared between tables. *Half price? A secret contract?* Heat rushed from her chest to her face until her vision blurred at the edges. Victoria spun on her heels, clicking like pistol shots, and pushed through the front doors.

She strode to the parking lot, anger pulsing hot in her veins. Reaching her black BMW, she yanked the door open and slid into the driver's seat. Her fingers were shaking so badly she almost missed the phone icon. She jabbed Tabitha's name.

Ring.

Ring.

Voicemail.

She ended the call and stabbed the screen again.

Ring.

Ring.

Voicemail.

A third time, straight to voicemail. Each automated, *please leave a message*, felt like another match tossed on dry leaves.

"Pick up, Tab," she growled. Her own quick breaths fogged the windshield.

*Breathe, Vic.* The engine rumbled to life, and she was just about to slam the gearshift into reverse when the phone lit up:

**INCOMING CALL: TABITHA RAMSEY**

Victoria swallowed hard and touched *Accept*, forcing her voice to stay level. "Hello."

"Hey, babes!" Tabitha sang. "I saw your name pop up a bunch. Everything okay? Sorry, I was, um, wrapped up with my man." A breathy giggle floated down the line and what sounded like sheets rustling. "He's giving me the side eye for pausing the fun, but you know you're top priority."

Victoria squeezed the steering wheel. "Everything is not okay."

The cheerful hum on Tabitha's end went silent. Then a small, shaky laugh followed. "Whoa, V. Talk to me. Do I need to swing by and pick you up? You sound tense."

"I just bumped into Cliff Adkins. He's thrilled that you signed S&J Enterprise to Social Brilliance two months ago at half the rate I quoted him last year, Tab. Half." Victoria drew a breath that trembled with fury. "Funny thing, I've never seen S&J on a single ledger, invoice, coordinator concierge list or onboarding sheet. Want to tell me how a client that size sneaks past my desk?"

The other end of the call went so quiet, Victoria thought the line had dropped. Then she caught a single, shaky inhale from Tabitha pulling air like someone who had slipped under water.

"V... you have to believe me, I would never try to cut you out. I did bring Cliff in, yes, but only because you were out and he wanted a deal that day. I figured if I could lock him down with a smaller starter fee—"

"With a *what*, Tab? A discount that'll cut our margins in half? A sweetener that makes *your* pockets look good on the side, huh."

"No, no, listen, my head was on the future. The plan was to start him at a lower rate, then upsell once he saw the results. It was temporary. I fully planned to loop you in after his first quarter. I swear I was protecting the firm."

"Monday morning, first thing," Victoria said, voice trembling with controlled rage, "we pull the covers off every single account. I want a line-by-line audit, contracts, invoices and email trails. And I want it on my desk before lunch. Is Cliff the only shadow client, or are there more that you signed behind my back that you've been profiting from?"

"V, plea—"

Victoria jabbed the red circle before Tabitha's last word could fully form. The screen went dark, cutting off the breathy excuse mid-syllable. For half a heartbeat the BMW's cabin was silent except for Victoria's own jagged breathing.

*Half price, behind my back, while I was away from the office dealing with life…* The thought tasted bitter. And the way Tabitha had stammered, every syllable dripping with lies. She pictured Tabitha on Monday morning, sitting across the conference table while she dropped a stack of surprise ledgers. *Line by line, sweetheart,* she thought, jaw clenching. *Every little side deal, every penny you sliced off my margin, on the record.* Rage flickered hotter at the idea of how many other Cliffs might be out there, thrilled with cut-rate contracts she never approved.

Another memory barged in. Martin's voice at dinner: *Once you open the cage door, Lestie, the game grows teeth.* Had Tabitha been one of those teeth all along? The possibility twisted her gut.

* * * *

Tabitha sat frozen on the edge of the mattress, the phone still warm in her grip. The screen had gone black, but she kept staring at it, as if Victoria's voice might flash back to life and scold her once more.

Beside her, the mattress shifted. The man who had been making love to her only minutes ago, pushed himself upright. "Tabitha, talk to me."

She dragged a trembling hand down her face. The words jammed in her throat. A strangled whimper escaped.

He angled closer. "What's going on?"

"Victoria. She bumped into Cliff Adkins—the owner of S&J Enterprise. He's one of the side deals that I signed a couple of months ago and hid the contract under my personal branch code so Victoria wouldn't see it. Cliff must've been bragging to her when they bumped into each other tonight, wherever they were, and told her about the deal he has with Social Brilliance, AKA, me, and Victoria put two and two together, knowing that she's never seen his company on any ledgers and in the main system."

She pressed a flat palm to her sternum, as if that could calm the pounding. "Now Victoria's furious. She said first thing Monday she's pulling a full audit, line by line. If she digs down that far, she'll find everything. Every side account. Every hidden invoice. If she combs through the numbers, she'll spot Cliff's files, and once she spots one hidden file, she'll keep digging. She'll trace every side deal I've buried. Everything."

He frowned, a deep line cutting between his brows. "Everything?" His tone stayed low, but the single word landed like a weight on the bed between them.

"Yes."

"Breathe, Tabitha. Panicking helps no one," he said sternly.

"I can't breathe. The minute she sees those files, it's theft, plain and simple. She'll kick me out, press charges, maybe drag it into court. And then… " Her hand slid to the small curve of her belly. In her mind flashed the two pink lines she had stared at only a week ago. Tears pricked her eyes. "I'm pregnant. I can't go to jail. What'll happen to my baby?"

He grabbed his jeans from the chair, yanking one leg on. "We planned for loose ends. You losing control now only hurts the baby. Slow your breathing and calm down."

Tabitha gulped air, trying to calm down, but her chest still hitched.

"Listen," he said. "We'll handle this like we said. You keep calm, follow the script, and let me shut the doors before Monday arrives."

Tabitha drew her knees to her chest, arms wrapped tight around her shins, as she rocked on the edge of the mattress. "This was never meant to snowball like this. I only planned to tuck one or two tiny accounts under my code, starter clients, nothing anyone would miss. But then Cliff showed up waving that brag book of numbers. He wanted the whole suite. And you said big accounts meant faster money. Faster freedom.”

“It still does. You landed him clean. Cliff’s only problem seems to be that he can’t keep his fat mouth shut in public.”

“You don’t understand. Victoria isn’t just my boss. She’s my sister in everything but blood. When we were younger, I crashed on her couch after disasters, and ate Sunday dinner in her parents’ kitchen.” Tears pricked harder. She pressed her palms to her eyes, but a sob still slipped out. “I love her. I love you. I love the baby. And now all of it feels like glass that could shatter at any moment.”

He crouched in front of her. Two fingers lifted her chin until their eyes locked. “You love what we’re building. A fresh start, a house that’s ours, a life for the baby where money isn’t tight. Keep looking at that picture. Hold steady a little longer. I’ll handle this.”

“Handle it how?”

“By putting our plan in motion,” he said. “Tomorrow, we move. By sunrise Monday, everything will be handled.”

A second jolt of panic shot through her ribs. “If we rush it, something could break and our plan could come crashing down right on us—”

“Our plan is airtight. We've rehearsed every path, every detail. No more stalling, Tabitha. The longer we wait, the more doors she kicks open. Now is the perfect time.” He rose and reached for his jacket on the chair.

She reached for him, fingers brushing his wrist. “Stay, please. My head is spinning. If you walk out, I’ll… ” Her voice thinned. “I can’t think straight without you here tonight.”

“Listen to me. Picture the little one. Picture that house we talked about with trees out back, no neighbors close, a quiet secluded area where nobody knows our names. Do you want that life or not?”

“Yes. More than anything in the world.”

"Then hold yourself together. I'll call you at first light." With that, he stepped into the corridor. The door eased shut, and the lock turned with a slow, final click that echoed in the condo's hush.

Tabitha sank into the mattress, as images crowded her mind one after another. She saw herself at nineteen, barefoot on a chilly dorm room floor, hunched over a hot pot while Victoria cracked the last packet of ramen. They attended different colleges, but being near one another gave them the opportunity to visit each other. Victoria had tossed her a plastic fork and said, "This is gourmet on a student budget, girl."

The scene shifted to three years ago. Tabitha slumped at a wobbly café table—late fees and eviction notices spread like playing cards. Her checking account sat at eleven dollars.

Victoria arrived in a rush, slid onto the opposite chair, and pushed a thick envelope across the Formica. "Pay me back when you can."

No lecture, no pity, just help. Tabitha had cried into her coffee while Victoria covered her hands and said everything would work out.

The memories stacked until Tabitha felt buried. Hot tears slipped down her cheeks. *I'm sorry, V. If I could roll the clock back, I would.*

She touched her stomach and felt the quiet swell beneath her palm. The baby was real, warm, and waiting. The man promising safety was real, standing somewhere beyond the condo door, already laying out the future like fresh lumber. And beyond that, shone a life without late fees, a life where her child would never sleep in a car. The glow of that promise pulled at her even as guilt clawed inside. She wiped her eyes and whispered to the dark room, "Hold on, little one. Mama is going to get us there."

$$\text{\Large ✳ ✳ ✳ ✳}$$

Victoria shoved the loft door shut so hard the frame rattled. Thomas was leaning against the kitchen counter in gray sweatpants and a loose cotton tee, finishing a mug of tea. At the sound of the door, he glanced up. One look at her flushed cheeks and fire bright eyes, and the mug nearly slipped from his fingers.

"Whoa, Victoria, are you okay? What happened?"

"How did you know?" Her voice cracked at the edges. "How were you able to see it and I couldn't? How could I be so stupid? Everything was right there and I let it slide because I trusted her."

"Baby, slow down. What are you talking about? Come sit."

Victoria turned as if to start pacing, but Thomas reached out and wrapped his hands around her wrists.

"Look at me," he said. "Breathe with me for a second."

She let out a shaky breath. He could feel the tremor run through her arms. "Okay, first things first," she said. "There was one bright spot tonight. Dinner with dad was wonderful. He kept talking about how much he wants to meet you. He's ready to meet the man that I love and adore so much. Dad invited us over next weekend, so you can finally meet my parents."

Thomas's whole face brightened. He pumped both fists like a kid whose team just scored. "Yes. I finally get to meet the Taylors." He bent and brushed a quick, grateful kiss against her forehead. "Thanks, baby. That means a lot."

The pleasant spark faded almost at once. "The good mood ended fast. On the way out, I remembered I had left my phone on the table, so I went back inside for it. And who's strutting toward me the moment I head for the door? Cliff Adkins, loud suit, louder voice. You remember the guy I told you about who always wants champagne service for tap water money?"

Thomas's head tilted, a slow nod forming while the pieces clicked. "Talks like he should be chauffeured in a Bentley but never wants to pay more than scooter money."

"Exactly. So, he stops me, all grins and showmanship, and drops this gem: he's been a Social Brilliance client for two months. Two. And guess who brought him in? My 'partner.' Not only that, but Tab also gave him my full package for half of what I had quoted him last year."

Thomas's brows climbed toward his hairline—the edges of his mouth tightened.

"He didn't hide a thing. He stood there in that restaurant telling me how 'astute' she is, how she's my 'mini-me.'" A sharp, humorless laugh slipped out. "Half price, Thomas. She runs the work through *my* servers, uses *my* staff, and then stuffs all the profits in her own pocket, secretly hiding this account."

Thomas shot off the couch arm like a spring. "I— knew—something—was—off." He stabbed the air with his finger on every word, pacing a short, angry line in front of the coffee table. "From the first day I met her. Big grin, all hugs, but her eyes were scanning the place, counting everything that wasn't nailed down. Acting like the office, your whole life already belonged to her. I saw straight through that bitch, Victoria."

"Don't call her names," Victoria barked, reflex still trying to protect the friendship. "No, fuck that. Tonight, I don't care what you call her. I'm past mad."

"She's been siphoning your company drop by drop. Think about every marketing outreach campaign you set up yourself, every penny you rolled back into new software. She took all that sweat and flipped it for lunch money."

Victoria's hands curled into hard knots. "Monday morning, I pull everything. I want a printout of every single ledger, old, new and archived. Client list A-to-Z. We match invoices against the bank feed, one line at a time." She scoffed. "Tab swears it's just S&J, but you can hear the shake in her voice. If that roster turns out longer, God help her, because paperwork will be the least of her worries.”

Thomas lowered himself until he was eye level with her, knees brushing the hardwood. “Look at me. She’s earned every bit of fire you’re ready to throw. But don’t throw it with your hands, throw it with paper, with lawyers, with the rules that protect what’s yours. You’ve built too much, Victoria. One swing, one headline, and you’re the one who pays.”

Hot tears shimmered along Victoria’s lashes. “I want to drag her ass across the floor.”

“I know. But cuffs on you? Your name splashed across the news? That only helps her. Let’s hit her where it really hurts, pink slip, every stolen dollar on a repayment sheet, and if she still mouths off, we let a judge finish it.”

“First thing tomorrow, I’m on the phone with our lawyers,” Victoria said. “I need to know exactly what we can do because those side accounts are already plugged into every service line we offer. This is going to be a contract mess, and I have to see how deep it goes. Monday was supposed to be strategy day, not damage control day.”

“Then I am in it with you,” Thomas said. “Monday, Tuesday, Wednesday, however long it takes. If I have to camp at the reception desk while you meet with lawyers, that’s where I’ll be. You won’t walk down this path by yourself.”

The words settled over her like a blanket. He shifted closer and slid his fingers through hers until their palms knit tight. “We’ll muscle through this week, baby. After that, it’s family time. Your dad, your mom, you, the whole Taylor crew.” His eyes softened. “I’ll shine my good shoes, iron my best shirt. Your dad can give me the third degree, your mom can tell me I look too thin, and we’ll make new memories that have nothing to do with audits or side deals.”

She squeezed his hand, feeling the steady beat of his pulse. “Thank you for standing in the fire with me.”

He brought her knuckles to his lips, brushed a kiss across them. "Always," he said.

# Control 2
## The Taste of Trust

Sunday crept in under a low, gray sky, the kind that made the city feel hushed. The loft still held a trace of last night's warmth, as if the anger and talk had left heat in the walls. On the counter, Thomas lined up plates and small bowls for the breakfast he'd just finished preparing.

He caught the sound of Victoria's footsteps and turned, a gentle smile curving his lips. "Morning, beautiful." He tugged a stool from under the island and set it behind her knees. Before she could sit, he brushed a soft kiss against her cheek. "I kept it simple," he said, sliding a plate in front of her.

"House rule for today," he said. "You're not going down the rabbit hole with work today and starting the auditing process. It's only going to stress you out and cause you to spiral and I want you to relax today. Tomorrow is the day the battle starts, but I want you rested and focused on something else today and not that yet. The legal team clocks in tomorrow morning, and that's when the fight starts. Today, your only job is to breathe."

"Easy for you to say. Resting is hard when the person you trusted most suddenly feels like a stranger with a knife."

"I understand the storm in your head but give yourself twenty-four hours off the battlefield. Tomorrow you'll have a whole team behind you. Today is just air in, air out."

"I'll try."

Midway through breakfast, a sharp buzz rattled the countertop. Victoria jerked at the sound, and Thomas's eyes flicked to the phone, then to her face. The preview banner glowed:

**D. Hart:** *Good morning, Vic. Can we meet today around 2:00 p.m.? I want to talk about the divorce and go over the assets, the house, bank accounts, and the next steps.*

"It's Davis," she murmured.

Thomas's jaw flexed once, but he held steady, letting her decide where the moment went.

Victoria let the air slide out of her lungs in one long, slow push. "Back on Tuesday, right after I signed the papers, I sent him a warning text," she said. "I wrote that official documents were headed his way and that we would have to sort everything soon. I couldn't bring myself to hear his voice, so I left it at the text. Now he's asking to meet today, at two o'clock, to discuss how we plan to split things."

"I'd rather you guys didn't meet in person. You both have lawyers, so I say you all should talk through them. I don't like the meet-ups."

"Davis and I have been together for some time, and after all these years, I feel like I have to give him one clean conversation. I need to sit across from him just once, say the hard words face-to-face, and close the door the right way."

"I hear you, and yes, respect does count, but pick somewhere public, somewhere with people and bright lights. Neutral turf. No going back to that Smyrna house. Too many old shadows in those rooms."

"I'm with *you*, Thomas. All in. You know that, right?"

Thomas closed his fingers around hers, a steady, comforting pressure. "I know. My worry isn't about you, it's about him, and how people act when their world tilts."

Neither of them had much left to say after that. They let the quiet settle, each lost in separate thoughts that hummed just under the surface. Thomas rested both elbows on the island, watching her face. "Well, you should answer him. Make it clear you'll meet, but not at the house."

Victoria's fingers hovered above the keyboard for a moment. She drew one steady breath, then let her thumbs move.

**Victoria:** *Yes, we can sit down today, but let's meet somewhere other than the house.*

The screen flashed *Delivered.* She watched the gray bubble fade, then turned the phone face down, sliding it a few inches toward the center of the counter as if distance alone could mute the weight of what it held.

Thomas stepped in front of her and let his palms settle on her shoulders, the weight firm enough to ground her, but gentle enough to soothe. "This talk is only step one. Nothing you agree to today is final. Paperwork and lawyers lock things in, not hallway chats, not cafés."

"Right. One clear conversation, then everything funnels through counsel. No more private meetups."

"When you're finished, send me a text, just two words: 'All done.' If anything feels off, call me ASAP. Doesn't matter where I am or what I'm doing, I'll drop it."

She managed a small smile, lifting one hand to cover his. "Deal. One text and you'll know."

"Good." He squeezed her shoulders once more, then let his hands slide away, leaving a gentle warmth where they had been. "You've got this."

"Thank you, baby," she said with love.

Victoria went upstairs to get dressed, nothing fancy, just some pants and a cashmere sweater that felt like a shield. Victoria slipped her phone into her purse, looped the strap over one shoulder, and picked up the BMW fob from the entry table. Her fingers found the little wooden puzzle piece charm Thomas had tucked on the key ring weeks ago—she rubbed its smooth edge once for luck. At the threshold she halted, turning to cast one more look across the loft.

Her eyes landed on the coffee table. The thousand-piece sunrise lay there quietly. Thomas tracked her gaze, feeling the same tug in his chest. So many mornings they had talked about hanging the finished puzzle in the hallway, proof that good things could be built one fragment at a time.

"We'll lock that sun in place tonight," she promised.

Thomas stepped closer, wanting to memorize every line of her face in the gray noon light. "Absolutely. We'll race to see who clicks the last piece."

"You'll cheat. You always stash one edge in your pocket."

"Strategic reserve," he teased, lifting both hands in sur-render. "Safe travels, sunrise thief."

Victoria laughed once, the sound bright and light, softer than it had been in days. She opened the door and paused again, as if listening to something only she could hear. Then she looked back, eyes shining with a warmth that made Thomas's chest tighten.

"Love you," she said.

He pressed his palm to his heart. "Love you more. Don't forget to text me when you're done."

She gave a decisive nod and slipped out. The door eased shut with a gentle click. The latch seat felt final some-how, though Thomas couldn't say why. He waited until her footsteps faded away before he finally exhaled, as if he was releasing a weight he hadn't realized he was holding.

✳ ✳ ✳ ✳

Victoria steered the BMW up the familiar cul-de-sac and felt a tug deep in her chest. The brick house looked exactly the same, but it no longer felt like home. Davis stood beside his SUV, sliding a wicker picnic basket into the trunk space.

She eased out of the car, smoothing her sweater. Davis's smile caught the light. He opened his arms and she stepped in, accepting a careful hug—but not the kind that pulled her close the way it once had. They separated after a beat, and she rested both palms on the strap of her purse.

"Thanks for agreeing to ride together," Davis said. "This will give us a few minutes to talk before we dive into the hard stuff."

"Where are we headed?"

"I wanted to redo the lunch that we never got to enjoy when we had our last sit down. So I figured a picnic at Weatherly Park would be nice, with open space and other people around, as you requested."

She glanced at the back of the vehicle, the wicker basket and folded blanket peeked through the rear window. "All right," she said. "I'm ready whenever you are."

Davis walked to the passenger door and opened it for Victoria. She climbed in and clicked the belt across her waist. For a heartbeat, they sat without speaking, the engine idling, a soft hum beneath their breaths. The drive to Weatherly Park took twenty minutes. Davis filled most of it with gentle chatter and Victoria answered in soft hums, saving energy for the talk ahead. Once, at a stop sign, she glanced over and caught him studying her profile. He looked away quickly, clearing his throat.

They turned beneath a moss-stained stone archway where ivy curled through the carved word, WEATHERLY. Beyond the entry, the park unfurled in broad, gentle slopes, fresh-cut grass glowing beneath an afternoon sky and maples beginning to turn toward autumn gold.

Davis parked under an oak tree and gathered the items he had prepared for the picnic. He spread the plaid blanket near a knobby tree root and began unloading food from the basket. First came the small plastic containers—Caprese salad, neat turkey spinach wraps—and a scatter of mixed berries glowing like rubies. He wanted to save the best for last, as he lifted out a clear, individual sized punch bowl covered in cling film, layers of vanilla cake, whipped cream, and bright strawberries rippling inside.

"Is that my favorite strawberry shortcake punchbowl dessert?" Victoria whispered, eyes widening the way they had the first time he had made it for her after a brutal quarter-end at work. "I cannot remember the last time I had this."

"This is the famous strawberry punchbowl shortcake." He said, as his eyes lit up with pride. "Last time we tried to eat outside, the sky opened up and washed everything away. I wanted to make up for that. I figured your favorite dessert might buy me a little goodwill while we sort through the heavy stuff."

They ate beneath shifting patches of shade. They talked about the house and agreed that selling the house was best for the both of them. The memories that they created in the home would always resurface and make it difficult to move on.

"The only thing I really want are my belongings, like my clothes of course, tools, vehicle and the kitchenware. Everything else, you can have, Vic. It's only fair because of everything you've built, especially the brokerage account."

Victoria was blown away at how cooperative Davis was. He's never been an uncooperative person, but she was prepared for them to at least disagree on some minor things, but he was calm, collected and appeared to be at peace.

She watched him spoon bright cubes of melon into his mouth. His face showed an almost peaceful relief, as if the past twelve months had been a storm and now the sky found blue again. It should have calmed her, but instead, it set nerves humming under her skin, like a wire pulled too tight.

When he uncovered the punchbowl dessert, that hum climbed an octave. Layers of cake and whipped cream glowed pink with strawberry syrup. "Dig in. I made this all for you. I figured you deserved one last sweet dessert from me, which is the least I can do for you."

She forced a grin. "Thank you." The spoon sank with a wet sigh, the cream almost velvety. The first mouthful hit her tongue and still the little voice sharpened in her head: *Everything you want, handed over. Everything tastes sweet. Why?*

Victoria set her plate down, wiped her lips with the back of her hand. The breeze shifted and the oak leaves hissed overhead. A kid squealed near the playground, high and shrill, then fell silent. For half a second the whole park seemed to pause, as if someone had drawn a curtain of quiet over the scene.

She glanced at Davis. He was looking at her, smile gentle, eyes soft, a look she once would have called love. Today it struck her as something else, something she couldn't name. The muscles in her stomach knotted.

*Ask him what he really wants,* the voice urged. *Why is he not fighting for the house, why isn't he haggling over the money.* Sweat beaded at her hairline despite the mild breeze. She said nothing as she swallowed another sweet and creamy spoonful, and told herself she was being paranoid. Maybe he simply wanted the day to stay civil. Maybe this was two grownups doing the hard thing right. Victoria exhaled and let the uneasy edge slide back beneath the surface. She picked up her fork and scraped every bit of the punchbowl cake out until there was nothing left.

"We've handled this better than I expected today," Victoria said at last. The words were a little slow leaving her mouth—a vague heaviness clung to her tongue.

"I'm glad it went this way. I'm glad everything went civilly. This way, we can at least end and close out this chapter without wreckage."

His gaze held steady on her, as though waiting to see if she felt the same.

Victoria nodded, though a faint unease rippled in her chest. The calm was welcome, yet it sat oddly on the moment, like a book closed too neatly after a stormy chapter.

Still, she chose to accept it, at least on the surface, and offered him a small, measured smile in return.

"Well," he asked, "are you good? Ready to head out, or do you want to stay a little longer?"

"I'm good. Thank you for all of this. Everything tasted amazing." She meant it. The Caprese had been perfect, and the punch-bowl cake had hit every nostalgic nerve. "Really, the dessert was wonderful."

Davis smiled. "Glad you enjoyed it."

Victoria braced a hand against the blanket to stand. The ground suddenly felt far away. She pushed up, but her legs turned to sand. Her vision blurred at the edges. She swayed.

"Whoa, whoa," Davis muttered, lunging forward. His hands caught her elbows just before her knees buckled. She felt the warmth of his grip through her sweater, strong and steady.

"Vic, are you okay?" He peered into her eyes.

"I'm… I'm good," she answered, though the word came out slurred at the edges. "Probably ate too much. I feel… heavy. Dizzy."

He held her upright, his gaze locked on her face with an intensity that made her uneasy. For a moment, the world narrowed to his irises. An old tenderness stirred there, something she hadn't seen in months, and it frightened her more than dizziness. She pulled back gently.

"Thank you, but I'm okay," she insisted. The ground steadied an inch.

Davis nodded and released her arms, though one hand hovered near her waist as if ready to catch her again. "I'll load all the things up in the back, why don't you climb in and get comfortable, and I'll be right there."

The SUV sat only a few paces away, but the short walk felt like a hallway that stretched longer with each step. Her feet seemed to sink in wet sand. She reached the passenger door and eased into the seat. The cool leather hugged her back, and she let her head tip against the headrest, her eyelids fluttering.

*Too much sugar,* she told herself. *Or maybe the sun.* But the sky was mild, the breeze was gentle, no heat to blame.

Through the windshield, she watched Davis shake out the blanket, fold it with crisp edges, and stash it in the hatch. He dusted crumbs from his hands with the precision of someone finishing a chore on a checklist. Then he rounded the vehicle, slid behind the wheel, and started the engine. "Home in twenty. We'll get you some water and maybe a nap and you'll feel better."

She tried to nod, but the weight in her head made the motion sluggish. A wave of nausea rolled through her stomach and receded, leaving cold sweat on her upper lip. She closed her eyes and focused on the hum of the tires. It felt safer than looking at the spinning trees outside.

Davis spoke now and then. "We did great today. I'm so proud of us that we were able to keep it cordial. I'll call the realtor sometime this week." His words droned like distant highway signs, slipping past her ears. She wanted to answer, to say something about closure, but her tongue felt thick, pinned to the floor of her mouth. She turned her head toward him, lips parted.

"I need to call… " The sentence broke apart, vowels dissolving on Victoria's tongue.

Davis glanced over. "What's that? Call who?" Concern etched his voice, but it sounded like it came through cotton.

Victoria blinked, trying to pull Thomas's name forward. She pictured his hands slotting puzzle pieces, the promise to finish the sunrise. She tasted strawberries again, stronger now, with a faint metallic echo underneath.

"I…" she began, then the words melted, dribbling into a quiet mumble. She wasn't sure if any sound left her throat at all.

"Hey, stay with me." Davis slowed. His hand rubbed her arm in firm strokes up and down, like reviving a chilled swimmer. "You're pale. Let's get you home. I'll take care of you."

She wanted to insist she was fine, that she only needed fresh air, maybe text Thomas a quick *running late*, but her fingers wouldn't curl around the imaginary phone. Her arms laid heavy in her lap, tingling.

*Hang on*, she ordered herself. *Stay awake. Thomas will worry.* But her pulse thudded thickly, arms turning to stone. Somewhere beneath the roar in her ears, she felt the SUV turn, easing to a stop before rolling forward again, each movement blurring into the next as if the world outside was slipping further away.

"Almost there," Davis murmured. He squeezed her wrist gently, as if confirming a pulse. "Just breathe."

The last thing she registered clearly was Davis's right hand leaving the wheel, brushing her forehead as if to check for fever. Victoria's lips shaped Thomas's name, but no sound emerged. Darkness flushed across her vision, soft and relentless, and the humming tires faded into silence.

# Control 1
## The Hour of Wolves

Thomas settled at the wide walnut coffee table, the loft's late-afternoon light sliding across his laptop screen. A subcontractor's spreadsheet glowed in pale blue cells. He clicked through an order form, calculated how many sheets of drywall he could squeeze into the box truck, then fired the purchase off to his supplier. With a swift amendment and a steady hand, he signed his name, the motion deliberate and final.

He leaned away from the screen and reached for his mug of black tea just as the doorbell rang.

Two crisp chimes.

Thomas stiffened, hand still wrapped around the mug. He ran his loft like a workshop, every knock accounted for, every face expected. Friends sent a text before heading over, neighbors rarely bothered him, and couriers left parcels neatly at his door without ever pressing the bell. Victoria was miles away meeting Davis, and he hadn't ordered dinner. Nobody should be ringing the doorbell today.

He stepped across the hardwood floor and through the peephole he expected a stranger in khakis or floral print church dress. Instead, there stood Tabitha Ramsey, hands buried in the pockets of a thin gray sweater, shoulders hunched, eyes ringing with sleepless shadows. The sight jolted him so hard he blinked twice. *You've got to be shitting me, he thought. What kind of joke was this?*

He opened the door only as wide as his body and planted one arm against the frame. "What the *fuck* are you doing here, Tabitha? You got some nerve darkening my doorstep."

Tabitha's face crumpled at the edges and grief leaked through the thin smile she attempted.

"Thomas, listen, I'm not here to stir anything up. Victoria called and asked me to meet her here. She said we all needed to talk about the mess at the office."

"You and Victoria talked? After what you pulled with Cliff?"

"I know how it looks. Cliff can be a circus, but that discount was a temporary ninety-day introductory rate. It was meant to hook him, then renew at full price. It's on my laptop, all documented."

She lifted a battered canvas tote, tapping the zipper. "I brought every file. I told Victoria I needed to see her face-to-face and clear this before Monday."

Tears brightened her eyes, but Thomas wasn't sure if they were regret or performance.

"She was there for me when nobody else was. I'd never steal from her."

Suspicion tightened in Thomas's stomach. "If Victoria really asked you to come, why didn't she loop me in first?"

Tabitha seemed confused. "Thomas, right before we hung up, she said, 'I'll message him now and give him a heads up, so he's not surprised.' I thought the text would've reached you before I even got out of my driveway."

"I've got nothing."

To be sure, he retreated a few paces, snatched his phone from the coffee table, and powered the screen awake. A single notification glowed in the dim loft light—one missed message he had somehow overlooked.

**Victoria (3:57 p.m.):** *Hey. I spoke with Tab, and she's coming over at 5 p.m. Giving you a heads up so you can let her in.*

Thomas stared at the timestamp, just over an hour ago. The tight knot in his chest eased half a notch, but distrust still pricked. A dull pulse pounded behind Thomas's eyes. The message stared up at him in bright-blue certainty, unread only because he had let supply orders swallow the last hour. He dragged a hand across his forehead, muttering a curse under his breath, then strode back to the door.

Tabitha still hovered on the landing. She shifted her weight from one foot to the other, as her thin sweater was no match for the cooling air that funneled between the buildings.

"I got the text. But it doesn't mean I trust you. You wait out here until she walks through that door."

Tabitha swallowed, nodded once, and tightened her grip on the laptop bag as another gust rattled the metal railing beside her.

"Okay, I understand." Her voice barely carried over the rising wind. She eased down onto the top concrete step and drew the canvas tote tight against her rib cage. A cool gust teased a loose strand of hair across her cheek, and she tucked it behind her ear with fingers that trembled just enough to betray her composure.

Thomas pushed the door until it settled against the latch. He walked to the sofa and brought up Victoria's contact. The first call rang through to voicemail. He pressed redial, again, no answer, only her recorded greeting. Frustration tightened his jaw.

Thumbs flying, he tapped out a brief message.

**Thomas**: *Tabitha's here at the loft. What's going on? Call me.*

His thumb hovered over SEND an instant longer, then he added a second line.

**Thomas:** *Love you.*

He hit send, watching the bubble slide up the screen, a pale blue arrow shot into silence.

Seconds later the phone pinged:

**Victoria:** *Finishing up. Driving back soon. Will explain when I get there. Let her in and wait for me.*

The reassuring ping from the phone cooled him only a little. He drifted back to the narrow pane of glass beside the door. Outside, Tabitha sat hunched on the top step, arms wrapped around her waist as if she could hide from the wind.

A flicker of sympathy tugged at Thomas. He remembered the stories Victoria told him about the nights Tabitha used to stay late with her at the office, ordering cheap take-out and cranking through slide decks until sunrise so a pitch would be perfect. In those moments, she had seemed loyal, but any warmth he felt now was smothered by heavier doubts. Whatever history they shared, mistrust sat on his shoulders like wet cement.

He let the curtain fall back into place and stepped away from the door. Until Victoria walked in and explained, Tabitha would stay exactly where she was. Another sharp gust made the doorframe tremble. Victoria's text was clear. If he ignored it, he would only complicate an already twisted day.

With visible reluctance, he opened the door. "All right. The message says you can come in." His voice was level but flinty. "Ground rules: you sit exactly where I tell you, you don't put a single fingerprint on anything else, and you wait until Victoria walks through that door. Are we clear?"

"Crystal," Tabitha murmured.

She pushed herself upright, muscles stiff from the chill, and stepped over the threshold. A wave of heated air met her, carrying the faint scent of lavender and coffee. She closed her eyes for half a second, letting warmth spread across her skin, and released a shaky breath tinged with spearmint gum.

Thomas pivoted, pointing to the same armchair she had occupied two nights earlier. "There, sit." He stayed on her left flank all the way to the chair, as though escorting a suspect.

Tabitha perched on the cushion, clutching her laptop to her chest and pressing back into the couch as he swung the door shut. The bolt drove home with a decisive clack that seemed to lock more than just wood and steel. It sealed the tension between them inside the loft's high brick walls.

✳ ✳ ✳ ✳

The driveway blurred into view as Davis turned the wheel, easing the SUV inside of the garage. The engine idled for a moment before he cut it off, the sudden quiet amplifying the hum in Victoria's ears. Her head lolled slightly toward the window, the familiarness of their home swimming in and out of focus.

"We're home," Davis said gently, placing a hand on her knee. "You okay, Vic?"

She blinked slowly. Her lips parted, but the words came out tangled, slurred. "Mmhm… yeah. Just… tired."

Davis reached over and brushed a strand of hair from her cheek, studying her face like he was memorizing it. "You ate a good bit, but it was all light food," he said with a chuckle. "Didn't think Caprese salad and a slice of cake would take you down."

Victoria tried to smile, but her face felt… slow. Not numb exactly, but like her skin had forgotten what movement was supposed to feel like. Her chest felt tight, but not in a painful way, just full, like she needed to stretch but couldn't quite lift her arms.

She turned her head toward him, her voice no louder than a whisper. "I… I feel off, Davis. I think maybe… the sun or something."

Davis nodded, but there was no urgency in his movement. No rush. Just the steady calm of a man who didn't seem surprised. "Let's get you inside. You can rest a little and drink some water."

He stepped out and circled the SUV with unhurried ease. Victoria watched the blur of his figure through the windshield, her mind trying to catch up to her body. Something in her gut whispered, too slow, but she shook it away. It had been a long and emotional day. Her body was probably just reacting to all the stress, to the lunch, and the sheer weight of everything.

She felt the door open beside her and the rush of cool air that followed.

"Come on, sweetheart. Let's get you inside so you can lie down."

She tried to lift herself, but her legs buckled halfway out. Her knees gave under her and Davis caught her just before she hit the ground.

"Whoa, gotcha." His arms wrapped around her with practiced strength. "It's okay. You just need a second. We'll go slow."

Victoria's head sprawled against his shoulder. "I... I don't know what's wrong with me," she murmured, fear just beginning to push its way through the haze. "Something... is wrong."

"Just a little overexerted," Davis whispered near her ear. "Let me take care of you."

As he helped her toward the house, each step felt like dragging through sand. Her breath caught in her throat, not out of panic, but out of sheer exhaustion, like her lungs were running on half capacity. She blinked rapidly, trying to keep the path in front of her in focus, as the doorframe seemed too far away.

*Say something*, her brain urged. *Ask him for help. Tell him you're scared.* But her mouth wouldn't form the words. Her tongue felt like it didn't belong to her. Davis opened the garage interior door with one hand, still holding her steady with the other, and guided her inside.

"Almost there. You just need to lie down for a bit."

Victoria slumped onto the couch as he eased her down. The cushions felt like clouds. She tried to sit up, but her spine felt like it had melted into the upholstery.

"Could I… get some water?" she rasped. "I think… I need—"

"Already on it." Davis was already in the kitchen. She heard the clink of glass and running water, but it all sounded farther away than it should.

Her eyes drifted across the living room, every corner steeped in familiarity, in what once felt safe. Yet unease coiled in her chest. She knew this house, the place where they had tried to build love, and where silence had spoken louder than words. Now, all of it was coming undone.

Her mind drifted to Thomas, his voice, the last kiss, the unfinished puzzle, the promise they made to finish it tonight. *Call him,* she thought. *Tell him something feels wrong.* But her bag, it was still in the SUV.

Davis returned with a tall glass of water and crouched in front of her. "Here, just sip slowly."

The water tasted like nothing, but it felt like ice sliding down her throat. She closed her eyes, letting it cool her from the inside out. She tried to lift her hand, to hold the glass herself, but even that felt impossible. Davis gently pulled the glass away and set it down on the coffee table. His eyes lingered on hers, watching her.

"You should lie back. I'll bring you a blanket. You'll feel better in no time."

She opened her mouth, but the sentence didn't come. Just three words stumbled out. "…don't feel right."

Davis's expression did not shift. Not a single twitch. Just the same soft calm. "I know, baby," he whispered, brushing a hand across her hair. "But I've got you now. Just rest. Everything is going to be okay."

He stood and walked to the hall closet. Victoria stared after him, her vision narrowing at the edges. That voice inside her was screaming now. Her body was still, but her soul was pounding at the walls of her chest. *Something is wrong.* She knew it.

"Davis… I think I need… you to call… 911."

He didn't move. Just rubbed his fingers in slow, soothing circles at her temple.

"Please… I'm scared…"

He leaned closely. "There's nothing to be scared of Vic. I'm here. I've always been here."

"Davis, please…"

His voice shifted. "It's funny, you know. How you always chased noise. Chaos. Some new thrill, some new man. You never stopped. Never slowed down long enough to just, appreciate what you had."

She tried to lift her head, but it was too much effort. A tear slid down the bridge of her nose and into her hairline.

"You had a good man," he said, brushing a knuckle along her cheek. "A man who cooked, cleaned, went to work and came home and waited for you like some damn puppy. A man who put up with every eye roll, every cold shoulder, every lie."

She gasped, a small, broken sound, but he only smiled faintly and kept stroking her hair.

"You remember that time you disappeared to Tennessee for that fake conference? I knew you were lying. I knew you weren't with Tab, but I stayed quiet because I thought maybe she'll stop. Maybe she'll realize she already has everything."

He shifted, staring down at her as her body grew more limp beneath the weight of whatever she had ingested.

"But you never did, and I stopped waiting."

Tears welled in her eyes. "Davis… please. I don't feel right… something is wrong…"

"I know," he said gently, brushing her tears away with the pad of his thumb. "You're dying, Victoria."

Her breath caught.

"But you're not dying in vain. You're dying because choices have consequences. Because you treated people like shit. Because you mistook patience for weakness. Because the people that you thought were beneath you, were actually watching, learning and waiting."

Her lips parted in disbelief. "You did this?" she rasped.

Davis leaned down and kissed her forehead like a goodbye. "You did this, Vic. I just made sure you felt it."

Victoria's chest heaved shallowly beneath the cashmere sweater she had worn to look neutral, safe, reasonable, but now it clung to her like fabric dipped in fear.

Davis was really watching her now. The mask of the husband had slipped. What remained wasn't cruel. It was colder than cruelty. It was detachment. The practiced calm of a man who had been waiting a very long time.

"You remember how I used to rub your feet when you got home late? You would toss your heels off and barely say a word. You never once looked me in the eye. You would just flop onto the couch and put your feet in my lap like I was a servant. But I did it. Every time. Because I loved you."

He let out a quiet laugh. "God, I loved you."

Victoria whimpered, her fingers twitching against the couch. She tried to roll to her side, but her muscles refused. Her body was growing heavier by the second, as if gravity had doubled in the room.

"I waited for you every single night. I made your favorite meals and kept the house spotless. Paid bills. Planned anniversaries. And what did you do? You fucked strangers in hotel rooms. You gave your body to anyone who made you feel important. Like I wasn't standing right there the whole time."

Her eyes widened, a gasp caught in her throat.

"Yes. I knew. Every trip. Every lie. You think you're sly, but you're not. You never were."

Victoria's throat burned. Her limbs trembled against her will.

Davis repositioned himself on the floor in front of the couch, watching her. "You see… this was never just about revenge. It was about clarity. I needed you to see what you really are. Because I spent years thinking I was the problem. That I wasn't sexy enough. Man enough. Dominant enough.

That maybe if I lifted heavier weights, or wore better cologne, or grew a beard, you would want me. But it was never about me. It was you. You were rotten from the start."

She cried out, the sound raw despite its weakness. "Why… why are you doing this?"

"Because you never asked that when you were betraying me. You never once paused long enough to think, 'Is this man okay?' You didn't care." He stroked her cheek again, gentler than his words. "Now you do. Now you care."

"Please… call someone…"

"I am someone. And I'm here. With you. In our house. The house that I made a home for us. The house where you used to fake orgasms and scroll your phone while I tried to kiss you. Where you cried after sex and said it was hormones. The house where I learned to hate you without even realizing I was doing it."

Victoria sobbed, searching his face for any trace of the man she'd married.

"There's no one coming, Vic. No sirens. No miracles. Just me. Just us." He kissed her knuckles as they laid limp in her lap.

"You always talked about freedom. About how I smothered you. How you couldn't breathe. Well, now you're free."

Victoria tried to lift her hand again, but it was like her muscles had been dipped in wet cement. She could feel her body slipping from under her own command. The heaviness wasn't just in her limbs now. It was in her chest. Her lungs had to fight for air, her thoughts moved in sludge, but she could hear him. Every word.

"You know what broke me? It wasn't the sex or the lying or even the nights you didn't come home. It was the way you smiled when you were lying."

"Davis…"

"That little smile," he continued, ignoring her. "That smug, polished, well-practiced smile that made me feel like

I was crazy for questioning you. Like I was insecure. Like I was not man enough to hold a woman like you."

Victoria squeezed her eyes shut. Her body was betraying her, but the real pain was the unraveling of everything she thought was hidden. Every shadow she'd kept hidden now stood in the middle of the room, named aloud.

"I watched you flirt with that guy that was momentarily at your office. The one with the slick hair. What was his name? Theo? Or was it Terrance?" He snapped his fingers as if trying to remember. "Doesn't matter. You thought I didn't notice the way you lit up when he texted. Like a schoolgirl. Like you weren't a whole wife."

"Please… you're scaring me…"

"You should be scared. Because you've spent our entire marriage disrespecting me. Making me feel invisible. Making me feel like I wasn't enough. And now you get to feel that."

He finally turned to face her again. "I did absolutely everything. I did every grocery run. I reminded you to take your vitamins. I rubbed your back when you couldn't sleep. I set the alarm for you. I rescheduled your appointments. I folded your underwear. I washed the sheets. I washed your clothes…" His voice cracked, just slightly. "Even when they smelled like cologne that didn't belong to me."

Victoria gasped, a sound halfway between guilt and heartbreak.

Davis stared down at her, jaw trembling with the effort to stay calm. "But I still stayed because I believed people could change. I thought maybe you were just confused, or lost, or trying to heal. I thought if I loved you hard enough, deep enough, patient enough, you would come home to me, but you never did."

Victoria was sobbing, barely able to catch her breath. Her body felt like it was shutting down in layers.

"I… I didn't mean to hurt you…"

"But you did. Over and over. With a smile."

His hand reached for hers again, but this time it wasn't gentle. It was firm. Like a tether. Like he needed her to stay present, to hear all of this before it was too late. Victoria gasped sharply, pain seizing her chest in a way that had nothing to do with the poison slowly spreading through her.

"You always thought you were so ingenious, but I saw straight through your bullshit. I made a vow that it was time to put your bullshit to an end, and from that moment on, I stopped being your husband. I became your lesson."

He reached over and adjusted the throw pillow beneath her head like he was tucking her in for a nap. "You still with me?" he asked softly.

Victoria swallowed, but her throat burned. Her tongue felt dry, too heavy to form words.

Davis nodded as if she had spoken. He sat back slightly, hands clasped between his knees, watching her. "You look like you have something to say. But it's too late for words now, Vic. This is the part where you listen."

"You know what broke me?" he began, his voice deceptively gentle. "It wasn't just the lies. It wasn't even the cheating. It was knowing that while I was home making your favorite cuisine, you were out in some stranger's bed, letting him fuck you like I never existed."

Victoria whimpered, barely a sound, but her face twisted with pain, not just physically. Her eyes pleaded with him, silently begging.

"Oh, don't look so surprised. You thought I didn't know? Thought you were so clever with your lies. Your little 'client meetings' and 'conferences,' Jesus, Victoria. You weren't even trying."

He leaned closer, his voice now a whisper meant to cut deeper than any scream. "You didn't just cheat on me. You humiliated me with your precious, *Thomas*. You spread your legs for him over and over again and then came home and kissed me goodnight like nothing happened. I know how he fucked you, Victoria. I know how he made you come with his dick so deep inside you, you saw stars. You couldn't get enough of it, could you?"

She gasped as tears spilled, horror spreading across her face at his words.

"I know how he shoved it in your mouth while you moaned like a slut," Davis continued, his voice laced with venom now. "I know how you begged him for more. I know everything."

Victoria let out a broken sob, trying to move, to protest, but her body was betraying her. Her legs refused to obey. The room spun, but her heart was still screaming and it shattered completely when he said the next words.

"And you know what the sickest part is?" His tone was conversational. Almost amused. "Thomas really thought he was the clever one. Thought he was in control. That smug motherfucker actually believed he played me."

Victoria's brow furrowed. The name alone, Thomas, cracked her in half. The sound of it made her body twitch, but it was what Davis said next that started to crush her from the inside out.

"That little run in on a Saturday morning?" Davis laughed. "That wasn't fate or coincidence. I orchestrated that."

Her lips parted in confusion, breath stuttering. "W-what...?"

"Yeah." He tilted his head, eyes dark and steady on her face. "You think that man just *happened* to jog past our neighborhood, early on a Saturday morning? You think that kind of luck just drops out of the sky? No, baby. I baited him. Thomas was apparently stalking my Facebook feed and accidently 'liked' one of my posts while he was scrolling and being nosy, so that was when the light bulb went off in my head and I lured him straight to me. I fed him the trail."

Victoria's eyes filled with panic.

"I started posting about the neighborhood. The five-mile area that I jog every Saturday. I left just enough bread-crumbs, that made it all seem casual. He found me, but only because I wanted him to."

Tears broke loose from Victoria's lashes, trailing slowly down her temples as her mind tried to catch up to what her body already knew. She had no idea what Davis was talking about. No idea that Davis had crossed paths with Thomas, and that she had been walking into a trap from the beginning.

"He thought he was slick. He thought it was all his plan, but he was a goddamn puppet, just like you. He thought he could take what was mine and never pay for it." He leaned in closer again, his breath brushing her cheek. "But don't worry, he's being taken care of too, right now as we speak."

The sound that escaped Victoria's throat was raw, like a wounded animal. She writhed weakly, trying to sit up, her arms trembling as they buckled beneath her. "No… no, please," she choked out. "Not Thomas…"

"Oh, now you want to fight? Now you want to cry? For him?"

She tried again, clawing at the edge of the couch cushion, dragging herself an inch forward before collapsing. "You can do… whatever you… want to me," she slurred. "But don't… don't hurt him… please…"

Her vision was fading fast now, white fuzz clouding the corners. But her body throbbed with desperate energy, her love for Thomas burning like the last candle flickering in a collapsing cathedral.

"I need… to call him," she whispered, fingers twitching as if to reach for a phone that was not there. "Please, Davis. Don't hurt him…"

Davis rose slowly to his feet, towering over her now. "You made your choices and now you'll live with them or not."

He bent down again, not with affection, but to look her in the eye, to make sure she heard every single word through the fog of death tightening around her. "I warned you, Victoria. I begged you to love me, and when you wouldn't, I promised myself that I would make you feel *everything*."

She sobbed then, real, guttural sobs that shook what little strength she had left.

"Thomas…" she croaked. "Thomas…"

Davis's face showed no joy, no triumph. Only resolve.

He turned away from her, walking calmly toward the kitchen. "I'll be right back, just going to grab something sweet. You always liked to end things on a sweet note."

And with that, he disappeared around the corner.

The loft was quiet, almost eerily so, as Thomas moved about the kitchen with his usual precision. He wasn't the type to host often, but with Victoria expected home soon, he knew he needed a drink to steady himself before dealing with the unexpected guest in his home.

He sat down on the far end of the couch, leaving distance between him and Tabitha like a warning line. His fingers curled around the glass as he took a slow sip. The tension in the room was thick as fog, clinging to every word. Tabitha, ever the actress, crossed her legs and tried to soften her posture, but Thomas wasn't buying it.

"I really want us to be good, Thomas," she said. "We have to find a way to be friends. Cordial, at least."

Thomas looked at her over the rim of his glass, unimpressed. "I ain't gotta do shit."

"Why do you talk to me like that? You think acting hard makes you look strong? You think it intimidates me? We need to show respect to one another. We owe that much to Victoria."

"What I think is, you owe Victoria more than an apology. What you owe her is every last cent you stole from her."

That wiped the polite smile right off her face. "I told you. I didn't steal anything. I'm not a thief."

Thomas barked out a short, bitter laugh. "Whatever you say, Tab. Tomorrow morning will tell us everything we need to know. So, if you've been dirty, better pray that audit doesn't blow you to pieces."

He stood and moved to the kitchen for a refill, clinking ice into the glass like it was the only thing keeping him from saying what he really wanted to say. He knew what this whole visit was, Tabitha showing up with her little rehearsed speech, pretending to be sorry, playing damage control. He had seen it coming a mile away.

As he dropped back onto the couch with his second drink, Tabitha's tone shifted. "You know, I have to say, I commend you," she said, looking at him with something like pity. "Most men find Victoria intimidating. All that power and polish. CEO, boss woman. Most guys wouldn't be able to handle that. But you? You follow her around like a good lap dog."

He turned his head slowly, setting his drink down. "I don't follow anybody."

"Oh, sure. That's not what Victoria told me. She said you have so many voids in your life that you latched onto her like she was your lifeline. She actually said she was tired of playing mommy and lover at the same time."

His jaw clenched. The glass in his hand almost cracked from the pressure.

"I think she's just a little over it, you know? A little tired of being everything to a man who couldn't be anything on his own."

Thomas stood slowly, his body taut with rage. "The only void I'll have is your name being voided from the door of that office you used to sit in."

Her smile faltered.

He stepped closer, towering over her. "Keep playing with fire, Tab, and you gon' get burned. Now stay your ass right there while I take a piss. Don't move."

He didn't wait for a response. He walked toward the bathroom, footsteps echoing off the hardwood floors. The second the door clicked shut behind him, Tabitha's hands moved like quicksilver.

She pulled a tiny bottle from her tote, clear and unlabeled—deadly. From the other side, the soft sound of water running masked the quiet unscrewing of the dropper cap. She leaned forward, her hand steady as a surgeon's, and tipped several droplets into his glass. It dissolved instantly. No scent, no color. Just a little extra kick. She sat back just as quickly, eyes darting to the bathroom.

Seconds later, Thomas came out of the bathroom drying his hands with paper napkins, his eyes narrowing slightly as he looked across the room. Tabitha was still sitting exactly where he left her, legs crossed, hands tucked beneath her thighs like some obedient schoolgirl. Too still. Too patient. Something about it didn't sit right, but he chalked it up to her being fake as hell, performing whatever role she thought might soften him up.

He tossed the paper napkin into the trash and picked up his phone from the armrest of the couch. A couple of texts from his subcontractor flashed on the screen. He scrolled through them absently, half-reading the updates on drywall delivery delays. His other hand absentmindedly reached for the glass, the one he had left on the coffee table. The drink was still ice cold, as he took a long sip.

Tabitha watched him, her mouth twitching like she wanted to speak but decided not to.

He caught her stare and sneered. "What?" he asked, setting his phone down. "You want to talk some more shit about me following behind Victoria like a lost puppy?"

"No. I think I've said enough."

He raised his glass again, tilting his head. "Damn right you have."

He took another sip, but something shifted inside him, not quite pain, not yet, but a strange flutter in his gut, like his insides had suddenly become unfamiliar. His hand paused mid-air. He blinked, once, twice. His chest felt heavy.

Tabitha leaned forward just slightly, feigning concern. "Are you okay?"

Thomas waved her off and leaned back on the couch. "Yeah, I just... I'm fine. Maybe it was something I ate earlier." His tongue felt thick, the aftertaste of the drink tasted metallic and bitter.

She tilted her head, watching him closely. "Or maybe it's something you drank."

He frowned. "What did you just say?"

But even as he asked, the room had begun to tilt, not violently, but in slow, creeping degrees. The warm buzz of the alcohol turned sour.

Tabitha stood up and took a slow step towards him. He tried to rise, but his legs didn't obey. His arm dropped to the side like it belonged to someone else.

"I said," she whispered, crouching beside him now, "maybe it's something you drank."

Thomas stared at her. A bolt of realization sliced through the fog in his mind, but it came too late.

"Y-you bitch," he slurred, struggling to lift his arm again. "You... you did something…"

He tried to stand again, gripping the armrest with shaking fingers, but his knees buckled, and his weight slumped back into the couch. His chest heaved with labored breaths and panic crept into his eyes.

Tabitha's eyes glimmered with cold satisfaction. "And just think. You thought you were going to be the one cleaning house tomorrow. Funny how fast the roles switch."

Thomas's breathing quickened. "I... I need... I need help..."

"Help's not coming, Thomas. Not for you. Not for Victoria either."

He shook his head weakly, trying to make sense of her words, trying to fight against whatever was dragging him down.

That's when she stepped back, coolly, calmly, and slipped on her gloves, like she had done it a hundred times. From a hidden pouch, she pulled out a small vial and a capped syringe.

Thomas's head rolled to the side. He groaned. "What… are you doing…"

She walked over calmly and crouched beside him. "Let me explain it to you. You're not going to make it to tomorrow's audit, Thomas. You and Victoria thought you were going to take me down? Take away everything I've built?"

He blinked slowly, mouth working but no sound coming out.

"Well," she said, tapping the needle, "Victoria was never on her way here. She's probably barely alive right now. And you? You're about to join her."

She uncapped the needle and held up the vial. "This is insulin, and you're not diabetic, are you? That's the beauty of it."

His fingers twitched weakly.

She smiled. "When a non-diabetic person gets a massive dose of insulin, their blood sugar tanks. Their organs start to shut down, and they go into a coma. It looks like a seizure or a heart attack. Very tidy."

"Stop…" he croaked.

"Too late." She rammed the needle into his arm, pressed the plunger down slowly, watching his face as his body trembled and weakened.

Thomas groaned in pain. He tried to lift a hand, but it dropped like stone.

Tabitha leaned in, lips close to his ear. "You never mattered. You were just a stepping-stone, and now, you're just a stain."

His body convulsed once. Then twice. Then stillness.

Tabitha stood, the gloves still snug on her hands. When she turned back, Thomas's chest was barely rising.

She picked up her phone. One ring. Two.

"It's done," she whispered. "I'm heading to you now."

She hung up, slipped out the door, and just like that, the loft was still again. The glass sat on the table, half-empty, glistening under soft light. And Thomas, strong, cocky, full of life, was now nothing more than a quiet echo in a room that would never hear his voice again. Across the city, two homes fell silent, and in that silence, the wolves claimed their prey.

# Control 0

## The Final Hour: Roots of Vengeance

Victoria lay curled on the couch, her body too weak to hold tension, but her mind swam in a violent current of dread. Her breathing had grown shallow, her fingertips cold and trembling against the throw pillow she had clutched to her chest. Her eyes drifted toward the archway, and even though the world kept dimming around her, she could still make out Davis's silhouette standing in the doorway of the kitchen, backlit by the amber glow of the overhead lights.

He was so calm. She hated him for how calm he was. He had been stroking her head gently moments before, whispering sweet, bitter poison into her ears, words that now clung to her skin like ice—*You're dying, Victoria.* She tried again to sit up, but her arms gave out. Her mouth opened, trying to form words, but all that came was a painful gasp.

"Shhh," Davis called softly from the kitchen. "You'll ruin the surprise if you get too worked up."

Her eyes fluttered. "Sur...prise?" Her voice was a cracked whisper.

He chuckled under his breath. It wasn't loud or theatrical. It was soft, almost nostalgic, like he was recalling an inside joke that only he was in on.

"I did say we would have company tonight. And I keep my word, even when the person I'm married to doesn't."

She felt her stomach twist. Her breathing staggered.

A knock came at the door. One sharp knock followed by another and then silence.

Victoria's body tensed as a last surge of strength rose in a single heartbeat. Her eyes flung wide open, and her heart pounded in her ears. That knock was so familiar. Something in her soul recognized the rhythm before her mind could catch up.

Davis moved methodically, like he was performing a ritual. He walked to the front door and paused. He took a moment to smooth out his shirt, checked his reflection in the mirror above the console table, and then unlocked the door with a slow, satisfying click.

Victoria's stomach dropped. When the door swung open, her heart collapsed inside her chest. Standing on the threshold, framed by the evening and dim glow of the porch light, was *Tabitha*. Her best friend. Her confidante. The woman she shared every dark secret with.

Tabitha stepped inside slowly, calmly, as if she had been here a thousand times. Her hair was pinned up neatly, her makeup light. But her eyes… her eyes were not kind.

Victoria's mouth moved but no sound came. Her lungs were too tight.

Davis closed the door gently behind her. "I thought it was time for a reunion. Wouldn't you agree, Tab?"

Tabitha gave a polite smile. She didn't look at Victoria at first. She kept her eyes trained on Davis, then scanned the room, taking in the scent of sickness, the stillness in the air. Only then did she turn toward the couch and met Victoria's eyes.

"Tab…" Victoria whispered. "What… are you… doing here…"

Tabitha walked closer. Not slowly. Not cautiously. Like a woman who belonged. "I'm here because this is where I belong, V."

Victoria flinched. "No, no…" she croaked, shaking her head. "This… isn't happening."

"Oh, but it is," Davis said from the side, leaning against the wall, watching them like it was theater. "You were so busy chasing thrills and lies, you didn't even realize the person closest to you was recording and reporting your every move."

Victoria blinked hard, trying to focus, trying to breathe, trying to survive.

Tabitha tilted her head. "You think you're so cunning. Sneaking off, making excuses, and gaslighting everyone around you like we were all too dumb to figure it out." She stepped closer. "But I knew. I've known. Every single time."

Victoria let out a broken sob, her body wracked with tremors. "I trusted you…" she choked out. "You were… my best friend…"

"You had a funny way of showing it. You treated me like an employee. A subordinate. You barked orders at me in front of the team, belittled me when I made mistakes, and made damn sure I always remembered my place."

Davis interjected, "And yet, Tab was the only one who saw me. The only one who asked if I was okay when you came home late. The only one who noticed the bags under my eyes when I stayed up cooking for you, waiting for a woman who wouldn't even kiss me goodnight."

"Davis, stop… " Victoria pleaded.

Davis stepped in, crouched next to her, smiling like a devil dressed as a savior. "Tab fed me everything. Every place you snuck off to. Every name you saved under fake contacts. Every time you lied to my face and said you had meetings downtown. She was tracking you while I was making your favorite gumbo. That's the kind of partnership we built. That's the kind of trust you could never offer."

Victoria turned her head, sobbing. "Why… why would you do this…"

Tabitha took one final step, standing over her. "Because you got so obsessed with your next thrill that you stopped seeing people. Real people. People who bled for you. People who sacrificed for you. You thought we were beneath you. And now? Now you're beneath us."

Tabitha looked at Victoria and her voice began to rise, not angrily, but emboldened, as if a dam had finally burst. "You remember that day we argued in the office, V? You said—" her voice turned mocking— "'If Davis is so great, why don't you just go be with him?'"

Tabitha took a step forward. Victoria flinched.

"You remember that don't you? That moment, V, you handed him to me on a silver fucking platter."

"No…" Victoria whispered. "No, I didn't mean that…"

"Oh, but you did," Tabitha hissed. "Because you thought you were untouchable. You thought I'd always be your little sidekick. Your assistant. Your charity case. But I'm not. Not anymore."

Victoria's head sank back against the cushions. Her mind screamed, but her body wouldn't obey.

"And you want to know the truth?" Tabitha asked. "I admired you. I wanted your life. Your house. Your car. Your career. Your man. And slowly… I got it. One piece at a time."

Davis stood behind Tabitha, silent, letting her finish the monologue like he was proud of her performance.

"You had everything," Tabitha said, "and you treated it like garbage. You were always chasing someone else."

Tabitha looked at Davis. "But not me. I would've worshipped the ground Davis walked on."

Davis smirked, almost bashfully. "Thank you, baby."

Victoria's heart twisted violently in her chest. "You said… you loved me," Victoria whimpered. "Both… of you. You said—"

"I loved the idea of you," Tabitha cut in. "But not the woman who laughed behind my back. Not the woman who turned love into a transaction."

Victoria's eyes darted to Davis. "And you… you let her? You fucked my best friend in our house?"

Davis tilted his head, then spoke with terrifying calm. "You remember that time you told Tab that you were in Louisiana with me to check on my mom? And Tabitha just happened to be in the neighborhood to supposedly drop off mail?"

Victoria blinked. "I… I…"

"That wasn't an accident," he said. "I told her to come over and to call you and make you sweat a little; to disrupt whatever you had going on with your precious Thomas."

He stepped closer. "But then… she came inside and, uh, let's just say she made me sweat a lot," he said as he licked his lips at Tabitha.

Victoria let out a broken sound, somewhere between a gasp and a cry. Her sobs were quiet but jagged, her voice lost to a grief she never saw coming.

Davis drifted to the center of the living room. He folded his hands behind his back, an executioner in business-casual ease, and let a soft whistle curl from his lips. "Oh, speaking of her precious Thomas," he said, "do you want to give Victoria a little update on him?"

Tabitha's chin lifted, but her gaze fell to Victoria with a strangely gentle focus, as if she wished she could soften what was coming and knew she couldn't. "Sure," she whispered, clearing her throat.

"You know, V, I never cared for him. I told you that before I ever met him. Something about him felt smug. A contractor who walked like every hallway was built just to show off his shoulders." Her lips twisted, part disdain, part regret. "Today proved I was right."

Victoria tried to speak, but her tongue lay heavy in her mouth.

"I went to the loft," Tabitha continued. "Thomas opened the door a crack, just enough to spit out, 'What the fuck are you doing here?' The way he said it, like I was gum on his sole." She swallowed. "He left me outside, V. Made me sit on the steps while the cold came up through the concrete. I almost called the whole thing off," she confessed. "Thought maybe our plan would fall apart right there, but then I remembered the night you laughed at me in that damn office, telling me to 'get some ambition.' I remembered how small I felt. So, I played the part. I hugged myself, shivered, forced tears to the edge of my eyes. He caved and invited me in with that arrogant warning: 'Sit and don't move.'"

Davis chuckled and reached to tuck a strand of hair behind Tabitha's ear. "I knew you'd find a way."

"He poured himself a glass of bourbon and lectured me about audits and prison time. I waited. I smiled. I agreed with every word." Her breath hitched, pride and horror mixing in her throat. "When he went to the bathroom, I tipped the drops into his glass. They sank without a ripple. He came out and swallowed half of the drink in one pull. By the time he set the glass down, it was already in his eyes, confusion first, then fear."

Victoria gasped, the sound ragged. Tears raced toward her hairline. Thomas's laughter, *That's my baby girl*, flashed behind her eyelids. The memory cut deeper than the poison in her veins.

Tabitha's next words were soft, almost a confession. "He tried to stand, but his knees folded. I steadied him, told him it would be all right. He called me a bitch, said I had dosed him, and I told him the truth, V. I told him that he never mattered." A single tear slid down Tabitha's cheek. She didn't wipe it.

"Then I gave him a huge amount of insulin. Right into the muscle for a faster effect. He tried to pull away, but his muscles were already cotton. He started to convulse and then he was still. The loft went so quiet I could hear the clock tick." Tabitha raised trembling fingers, then snapped them. The small sound cracked across the silence. "Just like that."

Victoria's cry rose, fragile as tissue in a storm. Her body shook, not from the toxin anymore, but from grief detonating in her chest. Every memory of Thomas collided at once—the night he traced the skyline with his thumb along her jaw, the farmer's market peaches he sliced for her breakfast, his giddy vow to impress her father. They flared like fireworks and then snuffed out, leaving only smoke.

Davis clapped, slow and mocking. "Damn, Tabitha. Ruthless as hell." He slid an arm around her waist, pulling her close enough to kiss her temple. "Remind me never to break your heart."

She leaned into his touch, but her eyes did not leave Victoria. Something wavered in her expression—satisfaction, sorrow, or both—before settling into a fragile calm. "You know I'd never hurt you," she murmured to Davis. "I love you." She pressed her lips to his, letting the kiss linger until Victoria sobbed aloud, the sound raw and desperate.

The kiss broke. Tabitha stayed close to Davis but addressed Victoria again. "I'm sorry you're hurting, babes. Truly. But you have to understand, he was a threat. To Davis. To me. To what we're building."

Victoria's eyes, soaked and wide, found Davis. "Why... do this? Why didn't... you just let me go?" The words shredded her throat.

Davis crouched beside her, studying her as if she were a puzzle finally solved. "Because just letting you go would have given you freedom. And freedom is more than you deserve." His voice softened, but the softness was lethal. "I wanted you to feel what I felt each night you stayed out— the fear, the rage, the emptiness. Thomas's death was the easiest way to carve that into your heart."

His gaze drifted to Tabitha, pride glowing. "And she was my scalpel."

Victoria's breath trembled. She wanted to scream, to crawl toward the door and into the streets—anywhere that might lead her to Thomas. Reason told her he was already beyond saving. Her body wouldn't move. Only her mind flailed, drowning in sorrow.

Tabitha's shoulders shook once, and she bit her lip. "He, he asked for Victoria right before the end. He kept saying her name, over and over and I almost stopped, Davis. I almost… " Her voice cracked. "I almost didn't inject the insulin."

Davis's hand tightened at her waist. "But you did it," he murmured. "Because you love me."

Tabitha nodded, tears slipping down. "Because I love you," she echoed. "And because Victoria never loved either of us the way we needed."

Victoria's gaze blurred, but she saw the tears, saw the trembling. In a flicker of terrible clarity, she realized Tabitha still sought her approval, even now. The thought speared her with a grief so sharp, she thought her heart might stop before the poison could finish its work.

Tabitha inched forward, kneeling at Victoria's feet. She took Victoria's limp hand and cradled it between her own palms. "I didn't mean for it to be like this," she whispered. "I just wanted someone to choose me for once. To say I was more than your sidekick."

Victoria's lips quivered. She tried to squeeze Tabitha's fingers, but her strength ebbed away with every heartbeat. "I… did… love… you," Victoria mouthed. "I… was… wrong."

Tabitha's face collapsed. She bowed her head, shoulders trembling, a silent apology rippling through her. But Davis cleared his throat, one sharp, commanding note. Tabitha looked up, and his cold stare froze any further confession on her tongue.

"Time's nearly up," he said. "She doesn't get absolution, Tab. Not after what she cost us." He cupped her cheek. "Not after what she cost you."

Tabitha nodded reluctantly, wiping tears with the back of her wrist. The conflict carved lines in her face, but she stepped back, letting Victoria's hand fall. The limp touch felt like a farewell.

Victoria closed her eyes. In the darkness behind her lids, Thomas smiled, reaching for her across sun-drenched grass. The warmth of that memory seared through the chill of betrayal, then dimmed, then guttered out as her pulse slowed beneath the poison's steady tide.

The taste of metal clung to the rim of the glass as Davis lifted it once more to Victoria's lips. Her eyelids fluttered, and each sip seemed to slide down her throat in fragments. Some of it dribbled at the corner of her mouth, tracing a cold path along her chin before soaking into the collar of her blouse. Davis dabbed it away with the edge of a linen napkin, as though the gesture could mask the violence of what he had done.

Tabitha paced the perimeter of the living room in tight loops. She stopped once, halfway through a turn, and stared at the framed photo on the sideboard—Victoria and Davis on their wedding day, her hand cupping his cheek, his eyes fixed on hers as if nothing else in the world existed. Tabitha's stomach twisted. She remembered polishing that very frame last Christmas while Victoria entertained friends by the fireplace, oblivious to how Tabitha lingered over every detail, secretly cataloguing what she envied.

Davis set the glass on the end table with measured care. "Just a few more minutes," he murmured, brushing a stray lock of damp hair from Victoria's forehead.

"I don't understand why you need her awake at all," Tabitha said. "You've proved your point. She's paying for everything she did. This is enough, she's fading already. Let her go." The words caught in her throat because even now a sliver of loyalty still bound her to the woman on that couch.

Davis squared his shoulders and faced her head on. "Listen, Tab, we're only halfway finished. I want her clear enough to see the final piece of payback and feel every bit of it." He fixed her with a hard stare. "If that shakes you, swallow it. Got it?"

"Yes." The single syllable tasted of iron and regret. Her eyes slipped to Victoria, whose breath came in shallow flutters. Tabitha wanted, just for a heartbeat, to press her forehead to Victoria's and beg silent forgiveness. But Davis's presence loomed behind her like a winter wind.

Davis checked his watch. He glanced at the door, as if he could sense the presence of someone just beyond it. And then, with no warning, the bell chimed, slicing the hush like a scalpel.

The sound slammed through Tabitha's pulse. "Davis, who—" She couldn't finish. The question caught in her throat. The house seemed suddenly smaller, as though the door itself exhaled the weight of everything they were about to face.

"Breathe," Davis admonished, smoothing a hand down the front of his shirt. He crossed the foyer, every movement composed and unhurried. Tabitha trailed him at a distance. Davis opened the door. The porch light spilled across a woman of dignified posture, her coat collar turned up against the misting air. Silvery hair caught the light, and her eyes took in Davis first, then Tabitha behind him. A slow smile softened her features.

"Hello, baby," she murmured.

Davis gathered her into an embrace, pressing his face to her hair. The gesture was tender, startling against the cruelty he had exhibited moments earlier, and it jolted Tabitha with a pang of jealousy so sharp it almost doubled her over. *Davis never held me like that, never radiated that warmth with me,* Tabitha thought to herself. When they parted, he kept a hand on her shoulder, guiding her across the threshold.

Tabitha edged forward, limbs stiff.

Davis gestured. "Mama, this is Tabitha."

Evelyn's attention swung to her, as though she were flipping pages in an open file. A faint smile curved her mouth, polite, but not kind. "I've heard so much," she said, each syllable brushed smooth yet carrying weight enough to bow Tabitha's head.

"Likewise, Ms. Evelyn," Tabitha managed.

"Come," Davis said, escorting his mother toward the living room.

Evelyn moved with the measured grace of someone accustomed to entering rooms where she commanded the air itself. The moment she saw Victoria sprawled on the couch, her steps slowed. Her gaze sharpened, flicking between Victoria's ashen face and Davis's tranquil expression.

"Victoria," she breathed, the name carrying equal parts surprise and inevitability, as if she had imagined this scene long ago and now found it exactly as pictured. She turned to her son, voice calm but edged. "Is she alive?"

The question hung like smoke. It settled on Tabitha's shoulders, seared across Victoria's fading pulse and echoed inside Davis's unreadable eyes. And for a breathless second, every heartbeat in the room froze, waiting for the verdict that would decide whether this night ended in death or something worse.

Evelyn glided to the couch with measured steps. Davis hovered behind her, quiet and watchful, while Tabitha stood frozen near the doorway.

Davis's voice broke the hush. "Yeah, she's still with us." He spoke as if answering a question no one else had heard. His tone carried neither pity nor malice, just fact.

At his words, Evelyn lowered herself to the rug, one knee first, then the other, moving with surprising grace for a woman her age. She leaned close, and her shadow fell over Victoria like a veil.

Victoria's eyelids fluttered, the poison turning each blink into slow exposure. She saw Evelyn's face, and a tiny gasp slipped through cracked lips.

"Please... help me," Victoria whispered.

Evelyn brushed a lock of damp hair from Victoria's forehead. For a breath, her eyes softened, grief pooling in their depths. "Oh, Victoria," she murmured, stroking the side of her face. "You never stood a chance."

The warmth vanished. Evelyn's mouth hardened, and a chill rolled down Victoria's spine. "You can thank your father for your demise." The words were low, steady and terrifyingly calm.

Evelyn leaned closer, lips nearly grazing Victoria's ear. "You don't have long, child, so listen carefully. I must give you these final words before you leave us."

Victoria's brows pulled together. Confusion mingled with fear, but her voice had shrunk to a rasp. "Why... my father...?"

Evelyn drew a breath that sounded like it scraped against old bone. "Victoria, let me tell you a story. I once had a daughter as beautiful as you. Brighter than dawn, so ambitious she believed the sky itself was too small." A soft tremor slipped into her voice, but she pressed on. "We were close, but ambition breeds friction. We argued about her future, about sense versus fantasy. She was my only child, my only daughter, and every dream I carried for her was wrapped in love. I pictured her in a white medical coat, steady hands saving lives, a future built on purpose and respect. But while I clung to that vision, she longed for something entirely different—billboards, flashing lights, a world that had no use for quiet ambitions."

Victoria's lips parted, but no words escaped. Evelyn's hand returned to Victoria's cheek, not gentle now, more like a parent keeping an unruly child's gaze.

"She left Louisiana at twenty, against my advice, and we became estranged for quite a long time," Evelyn said, eyes fixed somewhere past the wall. "Atlanta offered bright promises, a few runway gigs and headshots that cost more than rent. In the end though, she waited tables to survive. And then," Evelyn's tone dipped, resentment coiling inside each syllable, "a man came into her café."

Tabitha's breath caught. She wrapped her arms tighter, as if drawing a shawl against rain that wasn't there.

"He won her over in a single afternoon," Evelyn continued, her voice edged with bitter remembrance. "He called her a goddess, filled her head with promises of roles she had never dreamed of—a wedding beneath the Spanish moss, children who would carry her smile. For ten years, she revolved around him like a moon circling a dead planet. When she got pregnant, she was excited and cried with joy because she was giving him his first child, a piece of their love made real, and it felt like the beginning of everything she had ever wanted."

Victoria's eyes glistened with unshed tears. Even the poison seemed to still, as if the world itself was holding its breath.

"But he was married," Evelyn hissed, bitterness flashing. "A wife in a gated suburb, a mortgage and two puppy dogs. My daughter was his secret, his weekend escape from responsibility."

Evelyn's jaw clenched so hard a pulse flickered in her temple. "When she confronted him, he laughed, denied it, then called her crazy. Finally, with proof of his marriage in her hand, he confessed. He told her that if he divorced his wife, it would cost him everything, but he told her that he was willing to take that chance if she aborted the pregnancy. She believed him. She believed him because love can make a genius into a fool."

A tear slipped down Victoria's cheek. Her throat convulsed in a silent sob.

"My daughter terminated her pregnancy," Evelyn said. The sentence landed like a blunt weapon. "She handed a piece of her soul to that man, thinking it bought her forever." She paused, gathering herself. "Two weeks later, he filed a restraining order and blocked her number." Evelyn's lips shook but she refused to let them tremble. "He stole her prime years, her faith and her child. She swallowed her pride and called me after the warfare was over and I told her to come back to me. When she came home, she was hollowed out, a violin with the strings snapped."

The room's silence vibrated. Tabitha's throat clicked as she swallowed. Davis remained still by the doorframe, arms folded, eyes unblinking as he watched the story land on Victoria like a slow avalanche.

"She tried to restart," Evelyn whispered. "I cooked her favorite étouffée, read Psalms at her bedside, but her smile never reached her eyes again." Evelyn lifted her hand, examining her own palm as if it carried the memory of her daughter's heartbeat. "Two years later, a bottle of pills ended what that man started, and I found her dead in her bedroom."

Victoria's breath stuttered, a sob rolling through her chest. "I… I'm sorry," she managed, though the words scratched her throat raw.

Evelyn's head snapped back to the present, pain sharpening into purpose. She leaned down, her voice dipped in acid. "And do you know who that man was?"

Victoria tried to speak but her voice broke on emptiness.

Evelyn moved closer, so near that Victoria felt her breath. Her eyes, storm-grey and cold, bored into Victoria's soul. "Martin. Taylor." She spat each word like poison. "Your father."

Victoria's breathing rattled like paper caught in a fan. She tried, one last time, to drag air past the poison that clamped her lungs. Evelyn's words kept echoing, **Martin Taylor**, hammering against every warm memory she had of her father until they cracked. She wanted to defend him, but she couldn't lift her tongue, and the doubt permeating through her veins felt colder than the toxin.

Evelyn leaned in close, her gaze hard and steady. "Your father took my daughter away from me, Victoria. And tonight, I hand him back that same sorrow." Her voice was calm, but every syllable hit like a hammer. "After he tossed her aside, I came to Atlanta for a bit and sought Martin out. I wanted to see who the evil bastard was that killed my baby. I kept to the edges, stayed hidden—street corners near his office, coffee shops he frequented with that slick smile. I saw him shake hands, crack jokes, live his easy life as if my daughter never mattered. Then word reached me that he had named his little girl Celeste Victoria. The moment I heard your name, I knew the world had shown me the door to his heart, and how to break it wide open."

She rose and turned to Davis, eyes softening only for him. He laced his fingers with hers. A quiet pact passed between them. "I took in this boy," she said, her voice carrying through the stunned room, "and shaped him for one purpose—to make Martin's daughter love him, then take her away." She brushed Davis's cheek. "You did well, baby."

Tabitha's knees buckled, and she caught the edge of the coffee table for balance, fingers whitening against the polished wood. Her free hand sprawled over her stomach as though she could shield the life fluttering there from the words hanging in the room.

Tabitha stared at Evelyn, then Davis, and back again, her eyes glassy with disbelief.

"You… " The single syllable broke apart, thin as cracked ice. She swallowed hard and tried again. "You raised him for this? To marry Victoria, to love her, and then to end her?" Tabitha's voice quivered, climbing higher before it splintered. "All these years, you groomed him to kill her?"

The truth landed like a stone dropped in Tabitha's chest. Every memory, Davis's soft laughter, his gentle hand on her back, the first time he whispered he loved her, rearranged itself, twisting into something Tabitha no longer recognized. She felt the room tilt, her heartbeat knocking in her ears. Tears welled and spilled, tracing hot lines down her cheeks. "Tell me it's not true," Tabitha pleaded. "Tell me you didn't set this up from the start."

No one answered. The deafening silence pressed in.

Davis caught Tabitha's elbow in a hard clamp, his thumb pressing into bone until she winced. "Keep your voice steady," he warned, low and sharp. "You knew exactly how the night would end. Don't act brand new."

Tabitha's breath hitched, tears blurring her sight. "I knew she would die, yes," she whispered, shaking her head, "but I thought you were doing it for us because you were sick of Victoria's cheating, because she would find out that I was skimming, and you didn't want her ruining the only real thing we had." Tabitha's free hand covered her stomach as if the child could feel her regret. "I believed this was about making room for our life, not some old revenge story."

Davis leaned closer, his grip tightening. "It was always bigger than your little hustle," he said, eyes cold. "Victoria's death was never just a favor to you. It was the closing move in a game that started long before you showed up."

A shiver rolled through Tabitha. She tried to pull back, but his fingers dug deeper. "I thought you loved me enough to clean up the mess," Tabitha pleaded, voice cracking. "I thought killing her was about protecting us from her audit, her lawyers, her wrath."

Davis shook his head, a thin smile curling. "You were never the main reason. You were simply a piece on the board—useful because I needed you, beautiful because it made you easier to keep close, and willing because you didn't know any better. Don't ever forget that."

Tabitha's tears fell harder. She glanced at Victoria's still form, then back to Davis, horror settling in. "I helped murder an innocent woman for a story I never knew," she breathed. "What kind of family am I bringing my baby into?"

Davis bent low, his mouth almost touching her ear. "Lower your voice," he growled. His fingers dug deeper into her arm until sharp pain shot down to her wrist. "Think you can back out now? Fine. There's space on that couch, right beside Victoria. I can make room for you in a heartbeat."

A raw sob tore from Tabitha's throat. She slapped a shaking hand over her lips, trying to trap the sound. Davis kept hold of her elbow and walked her toward the kitchen like she was a misbehaving child. Each step felt colder than the last. At the counter, he forced her onto a tall stool.

"Sit. Breathe," he commanded. The word carried no warmth, only warning. His eyes stayed on her, daring her to make another sound. Tabitha drew in a shaky breath that stuttered at the edges, praying her tears would stop before they angered him further.

Evelyn stood and walked toward the kitchen entrance, one shoulder resting against the frame, eyes glinting like polished steel. The scene before her pleased her, a faint light dancing in her gaze as if every broken soul in the house were a candle lit in her honor. She crossed her arms, the fabric of her coat whispering against itself. "A grandchild was never part of the first plan with Victoria," she said, her voice smooth as syrup yet thick with intent. "But the Lord blesses us on roads we don't expect." Her focus locked on Tabitha. "You carry my son's child," she stated, each word slow and clear. "And you'll give him more. Healthy ones. Strong boys to carry his name." Evelyn's smile unfolded, thin and cold, a promise carved in stone. "We'll start a new branch. A line built clean, under my eye."

Tabitha swallowed, panic pounding in her temples. *Sons? More children?* She had wanted a family, but not inside this storm. Her hand slid to her stomach. She felt small beneath Evelyn's greedy hope, beneath Davis's possessive touch.

In the living room, Victoria's breaths shortened into wet gasps. Her vision narrowed to fragments: Davis's back, Evelyn's silver hair, Tabitha's shaking shoulder. She tried to speak, tried to warn them, forgive them, something, but no voice emerged.

Evelyn knelt again, smoothing Victoria's hair as if tucking in a child. "Hush now. Let it go," she whispered. "Your father will soon know what it feels like to have a child snatched away from him that he can never get back."

A tear slipped from Victoria's eye. She pictured her father at some late-night desk, pen in hand, teaching her to sign her name. *Rules keep hearts safe*, he'd said. *Follow them and you'll never bleed.* She wanted to scream, *Why didn't you follow them, Daddy?* But her mouth filled with a metallic taste, and the room drifted away.

Victoria's chest lifted one last time and then stayed still, as her next breath never came. The hush that followed felt too heavy for the room. Tabitha noticed first. Her eyes widened as her voice scraped out of her throat. "D-Davis…" It was no louder than a frightened whisper. He glanced back. His jaw tightened, muscles working beneath the skin. For a heartbeat a soft pain flashed in his eyes, but it vanished before it could settle. He said nothing.

Evelyn moved with quiet certainty. She laid two cool fingertips against Victoria's throat, waiting for the flutter that never came. After a counted moment, she drew her hand away and slid her thumb over Victoria's eyelids, easing them shut as though closing drapes at dusk.

"It is done," she said, her tone calm as a closing prayer. The words dropped into the silence, final and cold, and the room seemed to exhale, leaving nothing but the stillness and the weight of what could never be taken back. Silence swallowed the house, thick as cement. Outside, the wind rattled a loose gutter. Inside, the three of them stood in a triangle, each drawn toward the body on the couch, which anchored the room like a dark sun.

Tabitha's knees buckled. "We really did it." Her whisper quivered. She stared at Victoria's lifeless face, at the lips that once called her sister. "She's gone."

Davis drew Tabitha to his side, his arm settling over her shaking shoulders. "Mission finished," he murmured. His eyes slid to Evelyn, silently asking if the curtain could finally fall.

Evelyn released a slow, tremorous breath, then lifted her chin until her posture was rigid once more. "Martin will know before dawn," she replied. "And when the news reaches him, he'll understand what was taken, exactly as I planned."

Shadows clung to the corners of Evelyn's eyes, marks even triumph couldn't bleach. She rested her palm over Davis's chest, feeling the strong, steady beat beneath his ribs. A flicker of warmth softened her face, and she spoke just above a whisper, words meant for herself more than for him. "Some truths stay buried," she murmured. "And I'll keep them buried, no matter who comes digging."

Tabitha caught the hushed vow. Her spine stiffened, dread curling in her belly. *What truth does she mean?*

"We need to clean up," Davis said, guiding them toward the hall. His tone was firm, but a quiet tremor edged each word.

The trio disappeared down the corridor, leaving Victoria in moon-washed silence. Silver light spilled over her still hands and silent lips. Far across town, a phone would soon ring in Martin Taylor's study. The news of his daughter's death would strike hard, but deeper still ran the secret Evelyn guarded with iron will.

Tabitha lingered at the threshold, staring at Evelyn's back. *There's something she's hiding about Davis*, she realized, fear and resolve tangling in her chest. *Something even he doesn't know. For my child's sake, I will uncover it.*

Evelyn paused, sensing Tabitha's stare. She looked over her shoulder, eyes cold and calm, a silent warning. In the quiet, unanswered questions coiled like smoke. What was Evelyn guarding so heavily? And how deep did Martin Taylor's sins truly run?

The house held its breath. Outside, night pressed close, listening for the next crack in the story, one that would not stay buried for long.

# ACKNOWLEDGMENTS

This book would not exist without the people who stood beside me while I chased an idea that refused to let me go.

To my husband, thank you for always supporting my wild ideas and for giving me the space to be my authentic self and pursue the things I love. Your patience and belief in me made this possible.

To my daughter, thank you for pushing me forward and encouraging me when I wanted to stop. You helped me research, problem-solve, and move forward with confidence instead of doubt.

To my son, thank you for the joyful interruptions and youthful distractions that reminded me to step away, breathe, and rest when I needed it most.

To my parents and my brothers, thank you for always cheering me on and supporting my dreams.

To my sister, who found this story tucked away in a notebook and insisted I finish it — thank you for believing in me when I struggled to believe in myself. You spent countless hours reading draft after draft, through every change and revision. I truly could not have written this book without you.

To my wonderful beta readers, Mary, thank you for the excitement and joy you showed while reading and for encouraging me to continue this story beyond its first ending. Kelley, thank you for reading the manuscript in one night and for your thoughtful feedback — you truly made my day.

This journey was not easy, but I would not trade it for anything. To everyone who encouraged me, supported me, and believed in this story, I am deeply grateful.

To the readers who chose to spend their time with these characters and this story, thank you for opening this book and giving it a place in your life. I hope it stayed with you long after the final page.

Here's to many more stories.

— I.V. Monroe

# ABOUT THE AUTHOR

I.V. Monroe writes psychological suspense that explores obsession, control, and the fragile lines between love and possession. Her stories focus on complex relationships, hidden motives, and the consequences of choices made in the name of desire.

You Never Stood A Chance is her debut novel and the first installment in a continuing series.

She lives in Georgia with her family, where she spends her time writing, reading, and developing new stories that linger long after the final page.

Readers can look forward to future installments in the series.